Jennifer Lewis has been dreaming up stories for as long as she can remember and is thrilled to be able to share them with readers. She has lived on both sides of the Atlantic and worked in media and the arts before she grew bold enough to put pen to paper. She would love to hear from readers at jen@jenlewis. com. Visit her website at www.jenlewis.com.

New Zealand-born to Dutch immigrant parents, **Yvonne Lindsay** became an avid romance reader at the age of thirteen. Now married to her "blind date" and with two surprisingly amenable teenagers, she remains a firm believer in the power of romance. Yvonne feels privileged to be able to bring to her readers the stories of her heart. In her spare time, when not writing, she can be found with her nose firmly in a book, reliving the power of love in all walks of life. She can be contacted via her website, www.yvonnelindsay.com.

Brenda Jackson is a *New York Times* bestselling author of more than one hundred romance titles. Brenda lives in Jacksonville, Florida, and divides her time between family, writing and traveling.

Email Brenda at authorbrendajackson@gmail.com or visit her on her website at www.brendajackson.net.

Risking it all...

JENNIFER LEWIS
YVONNE LINDSAY
BRENDA JACKSON

MILLS & BOON

First Published in Great Britain 2018
by Mills & Boon, an imprint of HarperCollins*Publishers*
1 London Bridge Street, London, SE1 9GF

RISKING IT ALL... © 2018 Harlequin Books S. A.

A High Stakes Seduction © 2014 Jennifer Lewis
For The Sake Of The Secret Child © 2010 Dolce Vita Trust
Breaking Bailey's Rules © 2015 Brenda Streater Jackson

ISBN: 978-0-263-26712-9

05-0418

MIX
Paper from
responsible sources
FSC™ C007454

Printed and bound in Spain
by CPI, Barcelona

A HIGH STAKES SEDUCTION

JENNIFER LEWIS

For Dwnell

ACKNOWLEDGMENTS

Many thanks to my editor Charles Griemsman.

One

"**J**ust get rid of her as quickly as possible. She's dangerous."

John Fairweather scowled at his uncle. "You're crazy. Stop thinking everyone's out to get you."

John didn't want to admit it, but he too was rattled by the Bureau of Indian Affairs sending an accountant to snoop through New Dawn's books. He glanced around the grand lobby of the hotel and casino. Smiling staff, gleaming marble floors, paying customers relaxing on big leather couches. There was nothing he didn't love about this place. He knew everything was aboveboard, but still…

"John, you know as well as anyone that the U.S. government is no friend of the Indian."

"*I'm* friendly with them. They gave us tribal recognition. We ran with it and built all this, didn't we? You need to relax, Don. They're just here to do a routine audit."

"You think you're such a big man with your Harvard degree and your Fortune 500 résumé. To them you're just another Indian trying to stick his hand in Uncle Sam's pocket."

Irritation stirred in John's chest. "My hand isn't in anyone's pocket. You're as bad as the damn media. We built this business with a lot of hard work and we have just as much right to profit from it as I did from my software business. Where is she, anyway? I have a meeting with the contractor who's working on my house."

The front door opened and a young girl walked in. John glanced at his watch.

"I bet that's her." His uncle peered at the girl, who was carrying a briefcase.

"Are you kidding me? She doesn't look old enough to vote." Her eyes were hidden behind glasses. She stood in the foyer, looking disoriented.

"Flirt with her." His uncle leaned in and whispered. "Give her some of the old Fairweather charm."

"Are you out of your mind?" He watched as the woman approached the reception desk. The receptionist listened to her, then pointed at him. "Hey, maybe that is her."

"I'm serious. Look at her. She's probably never even kissed a man before," Don hissed. "Flirt with her and get her all flustered. That will scare her off."

"I wish I could scare you off. Get lost. She's coming over here."

Plastering a smile on his face, John walked toward her and extended his hand. "John Fairweather. You must be Constance Allen."

He shook her hand, which was small and soft. Weak handshake. She seemed nervous. "Good afternoon, Mr. Fairweather."

"You can call me John."

She wore a loose-fitting blue summer suit with an ivory blouse. Her hair was pinned up in a bun of some kind. Up close she still looked young and was kind of pretty. "I'm sorry I'm late. I took the wrong exit off the turnpike."

"No worries. Have you been to Massachusetts before?"

"This is my first time."

"Welcome to our state, and to the tribal lands of the Nissequot." Some people thought it was cheesy when he said that, but it always gave him a good feeling. "Would you like something to drink?"

"No! No, thank you." She glanced at the bar, looking horrified, as if he'd just thrust a glass of neat whiskey at her.

"I mean a cup of tea, or a coffee." He smiled. It would to be quite a challenge to put her at ease. "Some of our customers like to drink during the day because they're here for fun and relaxation. Those of us who work here are much more dull and predictable." He noticed with chagrin that his uncle Don was still standing behind him. "Oh, and this is my uncle, Don Fairweather."

She pushed her glasses up on her nose before shoving out her hand. "Pleased to meet you."

Don't be so sure, John wanted to tease. But this was a business meeting. "Let me take you up to the offices, Ms. Allen. Don, could you do me a favor and see if the ballroom is set up for the Shriners' conference tonight?"

His uncle glared at him, but moved off in the right direction. John heaved a sigh of relief. It wasn't always easy working with family, but in the end it was worth the hassle. "Let me take your briefcase. It looks heavy."

"Oh, no. I'm fine." She jerked away as he reached toward her. She was jumpy.

"Don't worry. We don't bite. Well, not much, anyway." Maybe he should flirt with her. She needed someone to loosen her straitjacket.

Now that he'd got a better look at her, he could see she wasn't quite as young as he'd first assumed. She was petite but had a determined expression that showed she took her job—and herself—very seriously. That gave him a perverse urge to ruffle her feathers.

He glanced at her as they headed for the elevators. "Is it okay if I call you Constance?"

She looked doubtful. "Okay."

"I do hope you'll enjoy your time at New Dawn, even though you're here to work. There's a live show in the Quinnikomuk room at seven and you're most welcome to come see it."

"I'm sure I won't have time." Mouth pursed, she stood and stared at the elevator doors as they waited.

"And your meals are on the house, of course. Our chef used to work at the Rainbow Room, so our food here is as good as any fancy restaurant in Manhattan." He loved being able to brag about that. "And you might want to reconsider about the show. Tonight's performer is Mariah Carey. Tickets have been sold out for months."

The elevator opened and she rushed in. "You're very kind, Mr. Fairweather—"

"Please call me John."

"But I'm here to do my job and it wouldn't be appropriate for me to enjoy…perks." She pushed her glasses up her nose again. The way she pursed her lips made him think how funny it would be to kiss them. They were nice lips. Plump and curvy.

"Perks? I'm not trying to bribe you, Constance. I'm just proud of what we've built here at New Dawn, and I like to share it with as many people as possible. Is that so wrong?"

"I really don't have an opinion."

When they arrived at the floor with the offices, Constance hurried out of the elevator. Something about John Fairweather made her feel *very* uncomfortable. He was a big man, broad shouldered and imposing, and even the large elevator felt oddly small when she was trapped in there with him.

She glanced around the hallway, not sure which way to go. Being late had her flustered. She'd planned to be here half an hour early but she'd taken the wrong exit ramp and gotten lost and—

"This way, Constance." He smiled and held out his hand but withdrew it after she ignored him. She wished he'd turn off the phony charm. His sculpted features and flashing dark eyes had no effect on her.

"How do you like our state so far?"

Again with the charm. He thought he was pretty hot stuff. "I really haven't seen anything but the highway medians, so I'm not too sure."

He laughed. "We'll have to fix that." He opened the door to a large open-plan office space. Four of the five cubicles she could see were empty, and doors stood open to the offices around the walls. "This is the nerve center of the operation."

"Where is everyone?"

"Down on the floor. We all spend time serving the customers. That's the heart of our business. Katy here answers the phones and does all the filing." He introduced her to a pretty brunette in a pink blouse. "You've met Don, who's in charge of promotion and publicity. Stew handles building operations, so he's probably out there fixing something. Rita is in charge of IT and she's in Boston looking at some new servers. I handle all the accounting myself." He smiled at her. "So I can show you the books."

Great. He shot her a warm glance that did something really irritating to her stomach. He was obviously used to having women eat out of his hand. Lucky thing she was immune to that kind of nonsense. "Why don't you hire someone to do the accounts? Aren't you busy being the CEO?"

"I'm CFO and CEO. I take pride in managing all the financial aspects of the business myself. Or maybe I just don't trust anyone else." He flashed even white teeth. "The buck stops here." He tapped the front of his smart suit with a broad finger.

Interesting. She felt as if he'd thrown down a gauntlet and challenged her to find something wrong with the books. She liked that he took personal responsibility.

"It's a family-run business. Many of the people in the office are tribal members. We also outsource to other local businesses—printing, web design, custodial services, that kind of thing. We like to support the whole community."

"Where is the community? I booked a room at the Cozy Suites, which seemed to be the nearest motel, but I didn't see it as I drove up here."

He smiled. "The nearest town is Barnley, but don't worry. We'll set you up in a comfortable room here. We're booked to capacity, but I'm sure the front desk can figure something out."

"I'd really rather stay elsewhere. As I said, it's important to be objective."

"I can't see how where you stay would affect your objectivity." Those dark eyes peered at her. "You don't seem like the type to be swayed by flattery and pampering. I'm sure you're far too principled for that."

"Yes, indeed," she said much too fast. "I'd never let anything affect my judgment."

"And one of the nice things about numbers is that they never lie." He held her gaze. She didn't look away, even though her heart was thudding and her breath getting shallow. Who did he think he was, to stare at her like that?

She finally looked away first, feeling as if she'd lost a skirmish. Never mind, she'd win the war. The numbers themselves might not lie, but the people reporting them certainly could. She'd seen some pretty tricky manipulations since she'd gone into forensic accounting. The BIA had hired her accounting firm, Creighton Waterman, to investigate the New Dawn's books. She was here to make sure the casino was reporting profits and income accurately and that no one had skimmed anything off the top.

She braced herself to meet his gaze again. "I specialize in looking beneath the shiny rows of numbers that companies put in their annual reports. You'd be surprised what turns up when you start digging."

Or would he? She was looking forward to getting her fingers on last year's cash-flow data and comparing it with the printed reports. She wouldn't have time to look at every single number, of course, but she'd soon get a sense of whether there was fudging going on.

"The Nissequot tribe welcomes your scrutiny." His grin did something annoying to her insides again. "I'm confident you'll be satisfied with the results."

He gestured for her to walk into one of the offices. She hurried ahead, half-afraid he was going to usher her in with one of his big hands. The office was large but utilitarian. A big leather chair sat behind the desk, and two more in front of it. A New Dawn wall calendar was the only decoration. Annual report brochures from the last three years sat on the big, polished wood desk, and filing cabinets lined one wall. A round table with four chairs sat in one corner. The realization crept over her that this was his personal office. He pulled open a drawer. "Daily cash register receipts, arranged by date. I add up all the figures myself first thing every morning."

He rested a hand on the most recent annual report, fingers pressing into the shiny cover. Such large hands weren't quite decent. He certainly didn't look like any CFO she'd encountered. All the more reason to be suspicious.

"Make yourself comfortable." He looked at the chair—his chair. She had to brush right past him to get to it, which made her skin hum and prickle with an unpleasant sensation. Worse yet, he pulled up another chair and sat down right next to her. He opened the most recent brochure, which had a picture of a spreading oak tree on the cover, and pointed at the profit data at the top of the first page. "You'll see we're not kidding around here at New Dawn."

Forty-one million in net profits was no joke, for sure. "I've seen the annual reports already. It's really the raw data I'm interested in."

He pulled out a laptop from the desk drawer and punched up a few pages. "The passwords change weekly, so I'll keep you posted, but this account information will get you right into our daily operation. You should be able to look up and analyze any data you need."

Her eyes widened as he clicked through a few screens and she saw he was letting her peek right at the daily intake and outflow.

Of course the numbers could be fudged. But she was impressed by how quickly he could click from screen to screen with those big fingers. They were large enough to hit two keys at once. Was he wearing cologne? Maybe it was just deodorant. His scent kept creeping into her nose. His dark gray suit did nothing to conceal the masculine bulk of his body, which was all the more evident now that he was sitting only inches from her.

"These documents here are monthly reports I do of all our activities. If anything unusual happened, I make a note of it."

"How do you mean, unusual?" It was a relief to distract herself from noticing the tiny dark hairs dusted across the back of his powerful hands.

"Someone winning a suspiciously large amount. Anyone who gets banned, complaints from the public or from staff. I believe in paying close attention to the small details so the big ones don't take you by surprise."

"That sounds sensible." She smiled. Why? She had no idea.

Just being professional. Or so she hoped. He'd smiled at her, flashing those dazzling white teeth, and her face had just mirrored his without her permission.

She stiffened. This man knew he was having an effect on her. "Why do you produce annual reports when you're not a public company?"

"I don't answer to investors like a public company, but I have a greater responsibility. I answer to the Nissequot people."

From what she'd read on the internet, the Nissequot tribe was mostly his immediate family, and the entire reservation was a creative interpretation of local history for the sole purpose of pursuing a very profitable business venture. "How many of you are there?"

"We've got two hundred people living here now. A few years ago, there were only four of us. In five years' time I'm hoping we'll number in the thousands." There was that smile again.

She jerked her eyes back to the screen. "It probably isn't too hard to persuade people to come when you're offering a cut of forty-one million dollars."

His silence made her look up. He was staring right at her with those penetrating eyes. "We don't give individuals any handouts. We encourage tribal members to come here to live and work. Any profits are held in trust for the entire tribe and fund community initiatives."

"I'm sorry if I offended you." She swallowed. "I didn't mean to." She felt flustered. The last thing she wanted to do was put him on the defensive.

"I'm not offended at all." He didn't smile, but looked at her pleasantly. "And maybe we could build the tribe faster if we just handed out checks, but I'd rather attract people more slowly and organically because they want to be here."

"Quite understandable." She tried to smile. She wasn't sure it was convincing. Something about John Fairweather rattled her. He was so…handsome. She wasn't used to being around men like him. The guys in her office were mostly introverted and out of shape from sitting hunched over their computers all day long. John Fairweather obviously spent a good amount of time at his desk, judging from all the material he'd showed her, but somehow—tan and sturdy as the oak tree on the cover of his annual report—he looked more like someone who spent all day outdoors.

"Are you okay?"

She jerked herself out of the train of irrelevant thoughts. "Maybe a cup of tea would be a good idea, after all."

Constance lay in her bed at the Cozy Suites Motel, staring at the outline of the still ceiling fan in the dark. Her brain wouldn't settle down enough for sleep but she knew she needed to rest so she could focus on all those numbers at the casino tomorrow. She wanted to impress her boss so she could ask for a raise and put a down payment on a house. It was time to move out from under her parents' wing.

It was one thing to move back home to save money after college. It was another entirely to still be there six years later, when she was earning a decent salary and could afford to go out on her own. Part of it was that she needed to meet a man. If she was in a normal relationship with a nice, sensible man, a practiced charmer like John Fairweather would have no effect on her, no matter how broad his shoulders were.

Her parents thought almost everyone on earth was a sinner who should be shunned. You'd think she'd told them she was planning to gamble all her savings away at the craps tables the way they'd reacted when she announced she was going to Massachusetts to look into the books of a casino. She'd tried to explain that it was a big honor to be chosen by her firm to undertake an important assignment from a government agency. They'd simply reiterated all their old cautions about consorting with evildoers and reminded her that she could have a perfectly good job at the family hardware store.

She didn't want to spend her life mixing paint. She tried to be a good daughter, but she was smart and wanted to make the most of what natural talents she had. If that meant traveling across state lines and consorting with a few sinners, then so be it.

Besides, she was here to root out wrongdoing at the casino. She was the good guy in this situation. She shifted onto her side, trying to block out the thin green light from the alarm clock on the bedside table. If only she could get her brain to switch off. Or at least quiet down.

A high-pitched alarm made her jump and sit up in bed. Something in the ceiling started to flash, almost blinding her. She groped for the switch on her bedside light but couldn't find it. The shrieking sound tore at her nerves.

What's going on? She managed to find her glasses, then climbed out of bed and groped her way to the wall light switch, only to discover that it didn't work. The digital display on the clock radio numbers had gone out.

A jet of water strafed her, making her gasp and splutter. The overhead sprinkler. A fire? She ran for the door, then she realized that she needed her briefcase with her laptop and wallet in it. She'd just managed to find it by the closet, feeling her way through the unfamiliar space illuminated only by the intermittent blasts of light from the alarm, when she smelled smoke.

Adrenaline snapping through her, Constance grabbed her briefcase and ran for the door. The chain was on and it took her a few agonizing seconds to get it free. Out on the second-floor walkway of the motel, she could see other guests emerging from their rooms into the night. Smoke billowed out of an open door two rooms away.

She'd forgotten to bring shoes. Or any clothes. She was more or less decent in her pajamas, but she could hardly go anywhere like this. Should she go back in and get some? Someone behind her coughed as the night breeze carried thick black smoke through the air. She could hear a child crying inside a room nearby.

On instinct she yelled, "Fire!" and—clutching her brief-case to her chest—ran along the corridor away from the fire, pounding on each door and telling the people to get out. Had someone called the fire department? More people were coming out of their rooms now. She helped a family with three small children get their toddlers down the stairs to the ground floor. Was everyone safe?

She heard someone calling 911. She rushed back up the stairs to help an elderly couple who were struggling to find their footing in the smoky darkness. Then she ran along the corridor and banged on any doors that were still closed. What if people were still in there? She hoped that the sirens and lights would have flushed everyone out by now, but…

A surge of relief swept over her as she saw fire engines pull into the parking lot. It wasn't long before the firemen had finished evacuating the building and moved everyone to the far end of the parking lot. They trained their hoses on the fire, but whenever the flames and smoke died down in one area, they sprang up in another.

"It's a tinderbox," muttered a man standing behind her. "All that carpet and curtains and bedspreads. Deadly toxic smoke, too."

Soon the entire motel complex—about twenty rooms—was ablaze and they had to move farther back to escape the heat and smoke. Constance and the other guests stood there in their pajamas, watching in stunned disbelief.

At some point she realized she'd put her briefcase down while helping people out, and she had no idea where it was. It had her almost-new laptop in it, her phone and all the notes she'd made in preparation for her assignment. Most of the information was backed up somewhere, but putting it all back together would be a nightmare. And her wallet with her driver's license and credit cards! She started to wander around in the darkness, scanning the wet ground for it.

"You can't go there, miss. Too dangerous."

"But my bag. It has all my important documents in it that I need for work." Her voice sounded whiny and pathetic as she scanned the tarmac of the parking lot. The fire glowed along almost the entire roof of the motel, and acrid smoke stung her nostrils. What if she didn't find her bag? Or if it got soaked through?

"Constance."

She jerked her gaze up and realized John Fairweather was standing in front of her. "What are you doing here?"

"I'm a volunteer firefighter. Are you cold? We have some blankets on the truck."

"I'm fine." She fought the urge to glance down at her pajamas. How embarrassing for him to see her in them, though it was pretty selfish and shallow of her to be thinking about how she looked at a time like this. "Is there anything I can do to help?"

"You could try to calm down the other guests. Tell them

we'll find room for everyone at the New Dawn hotel. My uncle Don's driving over here in a van to pick everyone up."

"Oh. That's great." She'd made quite a fuss about not staying there. Now apparently she would be anyway.

"Are you sure you're okay? You look kind of dazed. Maybe you should be treated for smoke inhalation." His concerned gaze raked over her face. "Come sit down over here."

"I'm fine! Really. I was one of the first ones out. I'll go talk to people." She realized she was flapping her hands around.

John hesitated for a moment, then nodded and hurried off to help someone unfurl a hose. She stood staring after him for a moment. His white T-shirt shone in the flashing lights from the fire trucks, accentuating his broad shoulders.

Constance Allen, there is something very, very wrong with you that you are noticing John Fairweather's physique at a moment like this. She picked her way barefoot over the wet and gritty tarmac to where the other guests stood in a confused straggle. One little girl was crying, and an older lady was shivering even under a blanket. She explained that a local hotel had offered them all rooms and that a bus would be coming to fetch anyone who couldn't drive there.

People realized they'd left their car keys locked in their rooms, and that started a rumbling about everything else they'd lost and only intensified Constance's own anxiety about her briefcase and all her clothes, including a nice new suit she'd just bought. She tried to soothe them with platitudes. At least no one was hurt. That was a big thing to be grateful for.

Still, she didn't have her car keys, either. If she'd flown

here and rented the car she could have just called the rental agency. But she'd decided to be adventurous and driven her own car all the way here, so now she couldn't even get into it. She was starting to feel teary and pathetic when she felt a hand on her arm.

"I found your bag. You left it at the bottom of the stairs." John Fairweather stood beside her, holding her briefcase, which dripped water onto the tarmac.

She gasped and took it from his hand, then noticed with joy that it was still sealed shut. "You shouldn't have gone back over there." The fire was now out, but the balcony and stairs were badly damaged and collapsing.

John's T-shirt was streaked with soot. "You shouldn't have brought it with you. We firefighters hate it when people retrieve stuff before escaping."

"My…my laptop." She clutched the handle tightly. Tears really threatened now that she had her bag back. "It has everything on it."

"Don't worry, I'm just teasing you. I'd have a hard time leaving my laptop behind even after all the training I've had." His warm smile soothed the panic and embarrassment that churned inside her. She felt his big hand on her back. "Let's get you back to the hotel."

Her skin heated under his unwelcome touch, but she didn't want to be ungracious after he'd found her bag and offered her a place to stay. The flashing lights from the fire trucks hurt her eyes. "My car keys are gone."

"We'll get you another set tomorrow. I'll drive you back in my car." His broad hand still on her back, he guided her through the crowd toward his vehicle. *Oh, dear.* Even amid all the chaos, her skin heated beneath his palm as if she was still too close to the flames.

And now she was going to be trapped in his glitzy hotel in nothing but her pajamas.

Two

"We were lucky the motel had a good fire alarm system." John steered his big black truck down a winding back road. "It went up fast. Everyone got out, though."

"That's a relief. I'm glad the firefighters got there quickly and had time to check all the rooms. How long have you been a volunteer?"

"Oh, I joined the first moment they let me." He turned and grinned. "More than fifteen years ago now. When I was a kid I wanted to be a firefighter."

He should have become one. Much better than a gambling impresario. On the other hand, her strict upbringing had formed her distaste for gambling, but now that she was here it didn't seem so different from any other business. She admired how John had pitched in and done anything and everything he could to help. He was thoughtful, too, talking to the other evacuees and reassuring them that the hotel staff would help them track down car keys, clothes and things like that in the morning. There was certainly no need for him to have offered everyone rooms at the hotel. He was being very generous. "What changed your mind?"

He shrugged. "I discovered I had a head for business. And at the time I was glad to leave this quiet backwater behind. I got seduced by the bright lights of the big city."

"New York?"

"Boston. I've never lived outside of the great state of Massachusetts. After a while, though, I started to miss the old homestead. And that's around the time I cooked up the whole casino idea. But when I came back I signed right on with the fire department again." His disarming grin cracked her defenses again. "They missed me. No one can unfurl or roll up a hose as fast as me."

"I'm sure they appreciate the help. But there don't seem to be too many people around here." They were driving through dark woods, not a house in sight. The area around the casino was very rural.

"Nope. That doesn't seem to stop fires breaking out, though. Last week an abandoned barn caught fire out in the middle of nowhere. We had to pump water from an old ice pond to put it out. Could have set the whole woods on fire, especially right now when everything's so dry."

It was early summer. Not that she really noticed the changing seasons much from the inside of her pale gray cubicle.

As they continued driving, she could see the pearl-white moon flashing through black tree branches. The woods were beautiful at night.

"I think it's nice that you find the time to volunteer when you're so busy with the casino." There. She'd said it. She'd been a little short with him this afternoon and now she felt bad about it.

"I enjoy it. I'd go crazy sitting behind a desk all the time. I like to have my hands on as many things as possible."

One of those hands was resting on the wheel. For one breath-quickening instant she imagined it resting on her thigh.

She crossed her legs and jerked her gaze back to the moon, only to find it had disappeared behind the trees al-

together. What was wrong with her? His hand was filthy
from fighting the fire, for one thing. And she would rather
die than let a business client touch her.

Not that he'd want to anyway. She'd seen the gossip-
column pictures of him with all those glamorous women. A
different one every week, from the looks of it. He'd hardly
be interested in a frumpy accountant from Cleveland.

She let out a sharp exhale, then realized it was audible.

"Fires are stressful, but don't worry too much. Everything you lost can be replaced. That's the thing to remember."

She turned to him, startled. She hadn't even given a
thought to all her burned-up stuff. Clearly she was losing
her mind. "You're so right. They were just things."

They drove in silence for a minute.

"It's a shame you missed Mariah Carey. She was awesome." He turned and smiled.

"I'm sure she was." She couldn't help smiling back.
Which was getting really annoying.

"What kind of music do you like?"

"I don't really listen to music." She shifted in her seat.
Why did they have to talk about her?

"None?" She felt his curious gaze on her. "There must
be some kind of music you like."

She shrugged. "My dad didn't allow most music in the
house."

"Now that's a crime. Not even gospel music?"

"No. He thought singing was a waste of time." She
frowned. Gaining maturity had given her a perspective
on her father's views that made living in the house difficult. What was wrong with a little music? He thought even
classical music was an enticement to sin and debauchery.
Sometimes her friend Lynn drove them both to lunch and

they listened to the radio on the way. She was surprised by how some tunes made her want to tap her toes.

She noticed with relief that they were pulling into the casino parking lot.

"So what did your family do for fun?"

Fun? They didn't believe in fun. "We didn't have too much time on our hands. They run a hardware store, so there's always something to do."

"I guess organizing rivets made accounting seem like an exciting escape." He grinned at her.

She bristled with irritation, then realized he was right. "I suppose it did." He pulled into a parking space in front of New Dawn, then jumped out of the car and managed to open her door before she even got her seat belt undone. There was no way to avoid taking his offered hand without being rude, and she didn't want to be obnoxious since he was going out of his way to help her. But when she did, his palm pressed hotly against hers and made all kinds of weird sensations scatter through her body.

Get a grip on yourself! Mercifully he let go of her hand as they paused at a back door to the hotel block and he unlocked it with a key. She was grateful not to have to walk through the glittering lobby in her pj's.

Then he put his arm around her shoulders.

Her skin tingled and heated through the thin fabric of her pajama top. What was he thinking? He was talking and she really couldn't hear a word. He probably thought this was a warm and encouraging gesture for someone who'd been through a traumatic experience. He couldn't have any idea that she hadn't had a man's arm around her in years and that the feeling of it was doing something very unsettling to her emotions.

His arm was big and heavy. He was so much taller than she that he simply draped it casually across her shoulders as if he was resting it. Then he squeezed her shoulders gently.

"Right?"

"What?" She had no idea what he'd just asked.

"You still seem kind of dazed, Constance. Are you sure you didn't get concussed or something?" He paused and pulled his arm from around her shoulders so he could peer into her eyes. "You look all right, but these things can sneak up on you. Maybe we should call for the nurse. We have one on staff here, to look after any guests who need attention." They were standing next to an elevator and he pressed the button.

"I'm fine, really! Just tired." She spoke a bit too loudly, then peered imploringly up at the digital display, only to find that the elevator was three floors away.

"No problem." He pulled a phone from his pocket and made a call. "Hi, Ramon. Is six seventy-five ready yet?" He nodded, then winked at her. *Winked?* It was probably just some friendly indication that the room was indeed ready. Her social skills were rather limited, since she only interacted with accountants. Still, it made her heart start racing as if she'd run a marathon.

She didn't know why, either. Yes, he was handsome. Tall, dark, all the usual stuff. But right now she was tired and stressed out and if she was anywhere near as dirty as he was she must look very unattractive, so he certainly wasn't flirting with her.

The elevator doors opened and she darted in and pressed the button for six. He strolled in after her. She focused her gaze on the numbers over the door as the elevator rose. He didn't say a word, but his very presence seemed to hum. There was something...unnerving about him, something that made her hyperaware of his presence.

When the elevator doors opened, she leaped out and

glanced about, trying to figure out which way to go. She jumped slightly when she felt his fingers in the hollow of her back.

"This way." He guided her down the hallway. She walked as fast as she could and his fingers fell away, which made her sigh with relief. He didn't mean anything by it; he probably didn't even notice he was touching her. He was one of those overly friendly types who hugged everyone—she'd noticed that after the fire. All she had to do was get into her room, shower, get some sleep and she could deal with everything else in the morning.

He pulled a key card from his pocket and unlocked the door. The spacious hotel room beckoned her like an oasis—crisp white sheets, closed ivory curtains, soothing art with images of the countryside. "This looks amazing."

"I'll need to get your clothes from you so we can wash them."

She glanced down. Her pj's were smudged with soot. "I'm going to need some real clothes for tomorrow."

"What size are you? I'll have one of the girls find something for you."

She swallowed. Telling John Fairweather her dress size seemed dangerously intimate. "I think I'm a six." And what would he tell them to buy? "Something conservative, please. And I'll pay for it, of course."

He grinned. "Did you think I'd ask them to pick out something racy?"

"No, of course not." Her cheeks heated. "You don't know me well, that's all."

"I'm getting to know you. And I'm getting to like you, too. You stayed calm during the fire and were very helpful. You'd be surprised how many people lose their heads."

She fought a burst of pride. "I'm a calm person. Very dull, in fact."

His dark eyes peered into hers. "Don't sell yourself short. I'm sure you're not dull at all."

Her mouth formed a silent *oh*. Silence—and something bigger—lingered in the air. Panic flickered in her chest. "I'd better get some sleep. I have a headache." The lie would probably give her a forked tongue, but she was on edge and John Fairweather was not helping her sanity.

"Of course. You can leave your clothes outside the door. There's a laundry bag in the closet."

"Great." She managed a polite smile, or was it a grimace? Her body sagged with relief as his big, broad-shouldered presence disappeared through the door and it closed quietly behind him.

Constance showered and washed her hair with rose-scented shampoo. The luxurious marble bathroom was well stocked with everything she needed, including a comb and a blow-dryer. She dressed in the soft terry robe with *New Dawn* embroidered in turquoise on the pocket. She'd put her dirty pajamas in a laundry bag outside the door for the hotel staff to pick up. Her briefcase had mercifully kept her laptop and important papers dry, so she'd emptied it and put it on a luggage rack to dry out. There was nothing more she could do for now. Hopefully she could relax enough to get some sleep.

But as soon as she laid her head on the cool, soft pillow, she heard a knock on the door. She sat up. "Coming." It was very late for someone to knock. Maybe the hotel staff had a question about the bag she'd left outside the door. Or maybe they'd already found her something to wear tomorrow?

She took the latch off the door and opened it a crack… to reveal the large bulk of John Fairweather blocking the light from the hallway.

"I brought you some aspirin." He held up a glass, then opened his other palm to reveal a tiny sachet of some painkiller that actually wasn't aspirin at all.

"Oh." She'd forgotten about her "headache." With considerable reluctance, she opened the door wider. "That's very kind of you." She took the pills from his hand, making sure not to touch him.

"And I brought you some clothes from the gift shop downstairs. It's lucky we're open twenty-four hours." She noticed a shiny bag under his arm.

"Thanks." She reached out for it, only to find that he'd already walked past her into the room. She shook her head and tried not to smile. He wasn't shy, that's for sure. Of course, it was his hotel.

"Did you find everything you need?" He put the bag down on the desk and turned to her with his hands on his hips. "It's not too late for room service. There's someone in the kitchen all night."

"Thanks, but I'm not hungry."

John had also showered and changed. He wore dark athletic pants and a clean white T-shirt that had creases as if it was right out of the package, except that the creases were now being stretched out by the thick muscles of his broad chest. His dark hair was wet and slicked back, emphasizing his bold features and those penetrating eyes.

She blinked and headed for the shopping bag. Before she got there, he picked up the bag and reached into it himself. He pulled out a blue wrap dress with long sleeves. It looked like something she'd wear to a cocktail party. "We don't really have office attire in the guest shop."

"It's lovely and very kind of you to bring it." *Now please leave.*

"And we found some sandals that almost match." He pulled out a pair of dark blue glittery sandals and looked at her with a wry grin. "Not exactly the right look for the office, but better than being barefoot, right?"

She had to laugh. "My boss would have a heart attack."

"We won't tell him."

"It's a her."

"We won't tell her, either." He looked at her for a moment, eyes twinkling, then frowned slightly. "You look totally different with your hair down."

Her hands flew to her hair. At least she'd blow-dried it. "I know. I don't ever wear it down."

"Why not? It's pretty. You're pretty."

She blinked. This was totally unprofessional. Of course, nothing about this situation was professional. She was standing here in her bathrobe—in his bathrobe—in his hotel that she'd explicitly said she wouldn't stay in. And now he was giving her gratuitous compliments? "Thanks."

She felt that stupid smile creeping over her mouth again. Why did this man have such an effect on her? *Think about computational volatility in Excel spreadsheets. Imagine him cheating on his taxes. Imagine him...*

Her imagination failed her as his mouth lowered hotly over hers.

Heat rushed through her, to her fingers, which were suddenly on the soft cotton of his T-shirt. She felt his hands on her back, his touch light and tender. His tongue met hers, sending a jolt of electricity to her toes. *Oh, goodness.* What was happening? Her brain wouldn't form thoughts at all, but her mouth had no trouble responding to his.

The stubble on his chin scratched her skin slightly as the kiss deepened. His arms wrapped around her, enveloping her in their embrace. As her chest bumped against his, her nipples were pressed into the rough texture of the bathrobe and sensation crashed through her. She dug her fingers into the roping muscle of his back, plucking at his T-shirt as their mouths moved together.

A humming sound startled them both and they broke the kiss. "My phone," he murmured, low. He didn't reach for it. Still frowning slightly, he raised a thumb and smoothed a strand of hair from Constance's cheek.

She blinked, wondering what had just happened. And why? "I really must…" She wasn't even sure what she really must do. Go to bed? Take a cold shower? Throw herself out the window? Heat darted through her body, and she didn't know how much longer her knees would hold her up without his strong arms around her.

"Take your aspirin. I'll see you in the morning." He hesitated, phone still vibrating in his pocket. An expression of confusion crossed his face and he shoved a hand through his wet hair. "I'll call a local dealership about replacing your car keys first thing."

"Thanks." The word was barely audible, but it was a miracle she managed to force it out at all. He walked backward a couple of steps, gaze still riveted on hers, before he nodded a goodbye and strode to the door.

As it slid quietly shut behind him, she stood there, mouth open, knees still trembling. Had he really just kissed her? It didn't seem possible. Maybe she'd imagined it. In fact, maybe she'd dreamed up this whole crazy scenario while sleeping fitfully in her lumpy bed at the Cozy Suites Motel. A fire and a kiss in one night? Impossible.

She pinched herself and it hurt. That wasn't good. Maybe she *should* throw herself out the window. A desire to gulp in cool night air made her hurry to it, but it was one of those big modern ones that didn't open.

Probably a good thing. She looked out and could see nothing but dark woods barely illuminated by a cloud-shrouded moon.

She'd grabbed him, fisting her hands into his T-shirt, and clawed at his back. Had she totally lost her mind? Her breath came in heaving gasps and blood pounded in her veins.

It had been a very long time since she'd kissed anybody. Since anyone had kissed her, or even shown the slightest interest in doing so. Her one and only boyfriend, Phil, had broken up with her right before they graduated from college. Four years together, sustained by promises of marriage and family and happily ever after, and he'd simply told her that he wasn't ready and he was moving to Seattle without her. Her parents would die—or they'd kill her, or both—if they knew she'd given Phil her virginity outside the sanctity of marriage. They'd blame her for throwing herself away and point out that of course he wouldn't want to marry a woman like that.

The pain and shame of it all was achingly fresh even after six years, so she tried not to think about it.

And now something like this? She could taste John's lips on hers, his tongue winding with hers, and the memory made her heart pulse harder. She couldn't even blame him. She couldn't swear that he'd even started the kiss. It had just happened. And it had happened all over her body, which now hummed and throbbed with all kinds of unfamiliar and disturbing sensations.

She'd lost her clothes, her car keys and now her mind. How would she ever get to sleep now?

Three

"Thanks for picking everyone up last night, Don." John leaned back in his chair in the hotel restaurant and brushed croissant crumbs from his fingers. "I know I interrupted your hot date."

"Anything for you, John. You know that." His uncle sipped his coffee. "Though why you feel the need to help a bunch of total strangers, I don't entirely know."

John shrugged. "Nowhere else for them to go. And Constance Allen was with them." His lips hummed slightly at the sense memory of their kiss. He hadn't planned it, and the chemistry between them had taken him by surprise.

Don put his cup down with a bang. "What? I didn't see her."

"I brought her in my car." He schooled his face into a neutral expression.

"So she's here, right now, in the hotel?" His uncle's eyes widened. "And you didn't even tell me?"

John sipped his coffee. "I'm telling you right now."

Don's long, narrow mouth hitched into a half smile. "Did you put a move on her?"

"Me?" He raised a brow noncommittally. He didn't want to give Don the satisfaction of knowing. And he hadn't kissed her to please anyone but himself.

Don laughed and slapped his hand on the table. "You

kill me. I bet she'll look like a startled rabbit today. Heck, she looked like one yesterday."

John frowned. "You need to stop making assumptions about people, Don. I'm sure she has a lot of dimensions you know nothing about. At the fire last night, for example, she kept her cool and was very helpful. Nothing like a startled rabbit."

Don cocked his head. "If I had half the charm you do I'd never be lonely again."

"You're not lonely all that much now, from what I can see."

"The money from this place doesn't hurt." His uncle laughed. "I was lonely a lot before. I didn't have the knack for making bank that you were born with."

"It's not a knack. It's called hard work." He kept checking the door, waiting for Constance to show up.

"All the hard work in the world doesn't help if you aren't lucky." Don took a bite of his eggs. "Luck is our bread and butter."

"You make your own luck." John scanned the dining room. Had he missed her coming down? He wanted to see her. "Statistics are our bread and butter. Anyone dumb enough to rely on luck will lose it all to the house sooner or later."

"Unless they know how to game the system."

"Impossible." John drained his coffee. "I personally make sure it's impossible. I'm going up to the office. Don't forget to send out the press release about the new lineup of shows. I want press coverage."

"I know, I know. Who booked them all?"

"You did. And Mariah Carey was amazing last night." Don grinned. "I love my job."

"Me, too." John slapped Don on the back as he headed out of the dining room. His uncle could be a pain in the ass, but underneath all the bluster he had a good heart and put a lot into making the entertainment here as much of a draw as the gaming tables.

But where was Constance? She wasn't in his office. He'd tried calling her hotel room, but no one picked up. He didn't want to knock on her door again. That hadn't gone entirely as planned last time.

He strolled across the lobby.

"You seen Constance Allen?" The staff at the front desk shook their heads. He would have to go up to her room again. He took the elevator to the sixth floor, excitement rippling in his veins. Why had she let him kiss her? In retrospect, it surprised him. She'd seemed so uptight and buttoned-down, but she'd opened like a flower and kissed him back with passion.

He couldn't wait to see what would happen this morning. Of course he probably shouldn't be entertaining lustful thoughts about the accountant investigating their books for the BIA. On the other hand he knew she wouldn't find anything wrong, so what did it really matter? No one would ever know but the two of them.

He knocked on the door. "It's John."

He heard some rustling, and cracked his knuckles while waiting. The door opened a crack and a pair of bright hazel eyes peered out at him.

"Good morning." A smile spread across his mouth. Chemistry crackled in the air again. Which was odd, really, because by any objective standards he wouldn't have thought they'd be a match. Maybe it was that opposites-attract thing.

And she was pretty.

"Um, hello." The door didn't open any farther.

"Can I come in?"

"I don't think that's a good idea." He saw her purse her pretty pink lips.

"I promise I won't try anything," he whispered. "In fact I'm not sure what happened last night, and if an apology is in order then I offer one." Not that he was sorry.

The door still didn't budge. Now she was biting that sensual lower lip. Which had an unfortunate effect on his libido.

"I called the dealership about your car. They're going to program a new key and bring it over here before noon."

"That's great. Thanks."

"Don't you want to come up to the office and look through the books?"

She blinked rapidly. "Yes. Yes, I do."

"All right then. I won't come in. You come out instead."

The door closed for a moment and he heard some rattling, then she appeared again, carrying her bag. "I just had to get my laptop." She opened the door and stepped out into the hallway, looking self-conscious—and very lovely—in the blue dress he'd found for her. He wasn't sure whether to compliment her or not, and decided not to. He didn't want to make her feel any more uncomfortable.

Her hair was fastened back up into a tight bun that showed off her pretty neck. As usual she wore no makeup, and the freshness of her clear skin was heightened this morning by an endearing flush of pink on her cheeks.

"I hope you managed to get some sleep after all the excitement of last night."

Her pace quickened as she headed down the hall toward the elevator. He'd meant the fire, but he realized she'd thought he meant the kiss. The memory of it flashed through his brain, firing all kinds of inappropriate impulses.

"I slept fine, thank you." Her words were clipped and

terse. "I'd like to look at the receipts from your first two years of operation this morning."

"Of course." The temptation to touch her was overwhelming. Normally he'd probably have done it without even realizing, but everything about her energy warned him to back off. "Have you had breakfast?"

"Perhaps I could grab a roll or something from the dining room before I head up to your office."

"No need. I'll have some food brought up." He reached for his phone. "Tea or coffee?"

"Neither, thanks. A glass of water would be fine."

He sneaked a glance at her as she pressed the elevator button. Shoulders tense and bag clutched in her hand, she looked as if she might explode. She probably didn't want to risk ingesting stimulants. He could think of a few ways to help her relax, but none of them was appropriate in the circumstances.

Maybe later, though.

As they got on the elevator, he told one of the new kids who was interning for the summer to bring some eggs and toast and fruit up to the office. And a roll. And some juice and water. But even as he concentrated on ordering the food, he noticed how the enclosed space of the elevator felt strangely tight this morning, the atmosphere abuzz with…something.

He followed her off the elevator, admiring the way she carried herself as she walked across the floor to his office. Then she stopped and frowned slightly.

He gestured for her to open the door. "Head in and make yourself comfortable."

"Is there another office I can work in? I don't want to inconvenience you."

"The only way you could inconvenience me is by making me carry all the files out of my office and into another one." He shot her a glance. "So you'll do me a favor by working in here. I have things to do anyway, so I won't be around much." He hoped that would put her at ease.

She put her bag down on the round table in the corner. "When did you say my car keys would be ready?"

"Noon. And I'll drive you over there to retrieve it."

"Again, I don't want to put you to any inconvenience. Is there someone less…important who can drive me?" She was avoiding his glance as she moved toward his desk.

"We're all important here. It's how we run the place. Every Nissequot has a crucial role to play and would be missed as much if not more than me. The cashiers will be hustling today, as we're expecting twenty buses of retirees visiting from Cape Cod this morning."

"Oh." Her brow wrinkled slightly as she reached for the pile of folders she'd pulled the day before. She bumped her elbow on a jar of pens, accidentally scattering them across the desk. He grabbed one just before it flew over the edge.

Their fingertips brushed as he handed it back to her. Her hand flinched away as though she'd been stung. Somehow that only increased the tension snapping in the air.

He shouldn't have kissed her. She was here on business and was obviously very reserved and proper. She wasn't looking to get her hands on him.

Quite the opposite.

Was that why he'd been irresistibly drawn to her? Was it the challenge of the seemingly unobtainable? There was something more, though. An energy that drew him to her. Something deep and primal. And when she'd folded into his arms and melted into the kiss…

John turned his attention to the filing cabinet with the receipts she wanted. Something had happened between them and he didn't know why. Unplanned and inappropriate, it had stirred his blood and left him wanting more.

Just get rid of her as quickly as possible. His uncle's words simmered in his brain. Sensible advice, under the circumstances. The way her movements snapped with precision and anxiety right now—fingers tapping on her keyboard and eyes darting across the rows of numbers on the papers she'd pulled from the files—she was rushing to get out of here.

So it was all good, right?

John frowned. Was he really the player the Massachusetts press made him out to be? Maybe he was. "Let me know if there's anything I can do for you." The innuendo wasn't entirely intentional, but he enjoyed her hot-under-the-collar reaction. Shifting in her chair and fussing with her bag, she seemed tense enough to burst into flames.

He'd be happy to help put out the fire. "The food should be here any minute, but maybe I'd better get you some water right now."

"Just some peace and quiet will be fine, please," she muttered, without looking up. She pushed her glasses up on her nose with a fingertip. He noticed she wasn't wearing nail polish.

A smile sneaked across his mouth. He liked that she wasn't afraid to be rude. A lot of people were intimidated by him, especially now that the millions were rolling in. It was refreshing to find someone who treated him as though he was a regular guy. "I'll make myself scarce."

"Good." She still didn't look up.

He chuckled as he removed himself from his own office. He could still taste that kiss on his lips. Constance had a surprising well of passion beneath her prim exterior, and he looked forward to tapping it again—whether or not that was a good idea.

Constance couldn't wait to get her car back. Right now, sitting in the grand lobby of the hotel, she felt like a prisoner in John's luxurious den of vice. Dressed in a silky garment she'd never have chosen, surrounded by people laughing and talking too loud and drinking before it was even lunchtime, she felt totally out of her element.

Maybe her family was right and she should have tried to refuse this job. On the other hand, building a career depended on taking assignments that would enhance her profile in the company, and a contract from a big government agency was a feather in her cap. Luckily New Dawn's files were well organized and the information straightforward, so she'd probably get her work done and be out of here within a week.

She heard her phone chime and fished it out of her bag. The display revealed that it was Nicola Moore, her contact at the Bureau of Indian Affairs.

"Hello, Nicola. I'm sitting in the lobby of the casino right now." She glanced about, hoping the woman wouldn't ask a lot of probing questions that would be embarrassing to answer right here.

"Excellent. Are they allowing you access to the books?"

"Oh yes, Mr. Fairweather—" even saying his name made her blush "—has given me carte blanche to go through all the files in his office. He has the original cash register receipts for every day since the casino opened."

"Do they seem legitimate?"

"The receipts?" She glanced around, hoping no one could overhear their conversation. "They do. So far everything looks good."

There was a pause at the other end. "They think it's a routine audit, but the reason we sent you is that we have good reason to suspect fraud. They may be giving you falsified documents."

Constance bristled. "I have considerable experience in examining retail operations. I know the warning signs, and rest assured I will closely examine anything that looks at all suspicious."

"John Fairweather has a reputation for charming everyone. Don't be fooled by his suave manner—he's a very sharp and cunning businessman."

Constance fumbled and almost dropped her phone. Could Nicola Moore somehow know that John had...seduced her last night? Impossible, surely! "I'm aware of his reputation," she whispered. Where was he? She felt as if he was going to materialize beside her at any minute. "I am completely immune to charm and focused entirely on the numbers." At least she certainly planned to boost her immunity to his charms from now on. That kiss last night had caught her completely by surprise, when she was overwrought and exhausted and emotional from the evening's turmoil.

"Excellent. I look forward to hearing an interim report. The New Dawn has attracted a lot of negative attention since it opened. You may have read some of the commentary in the press. We've been hearing plenty of whispers about their operation. No one can figure out how they managed to open without taking on massive debt, or how they're operating with such impressive profits. It doesn't match the other models we've seen. Frankly, we're assuming that something untoward is going on. Those numbers just can't be real."

Constance frowned. She didn't like that Ms. Moore already assumed a crime was in progress. She'd been surprised by the negative slant of some newspaper articles she'd read about the Nissequot and the New Dawn, too. John and the tribe seemed to attract the kind of backbiting usually reserved for successful celebrities. So far she hadn't seen any evidence of wrongdoing at all. Of course it was only her second day, but still.... John seemed to be

a concerned and thorough businessman and she was beginning to get annoyed by the relentless negativity about
his success.

Not that she had any interest at all in defending him, of
course. That would be highly unprofessional. She prided
herself on complete objectivity. But maybe everyone
should be a bit more open-minded about the New Dawn's
management.

She tensed as she saw John striding across the lobby toward her. You'd think an expensive suit would conceal the
raw masculinity of his body, but it didn't. Something about
the way he moved made her pulse quicken and her brain
start scrambling. Ridiculous! She was far above this kind
of girlish reaction. She muttered quickly into the phone
that she'd report back as soon as she found anything. Guilt
made her fingers tremble as she ended the call.

She stood and clutched her bag to her chest. "Ready?"
Her voice sounded a little too perky.

"Yup. A rep from the dealership has dropped off the
new key, so you'll be a free woman again in no time."

She smiled and carefully took the key he dangled from
his fingers, without letting her skin touch his. "Thank
goodness."

"You're welcome to stay at the hotel, of course. There
really isn't anywhere else that's convenient. The Holiday
Inn is at least twenty minutes away, and that's with no
traffic."

"That will be fine." Her words sounded clipped. Thank
goodness there was another hotel! Staying here had proven
to be an even worse idea than she'd suspected. Hopefully
they could both forget completely about that insane lapse
of judgment last night and get back to business.

His gaze hovered over her mouth for a moment, and
her lips parted. She sucked in a hasty breath. "Let's go."

"Of course." He held out his arm.

She ignored it, gripping her bag tighter.

He pulled his arm back with a rueful glance. Was he really flirting with her? He must be doing it to toy with her. She wasn't stupid enough to think that a man like John Fairweather could actually be attracted to and interested in her. It must be a game for him, to see if he could get the prim little accountant all hot under the collar.

She'd rather die than let him know how well it was working.

In the front seat of his big sedan she pressed her knees together and forced herself to focus on the road ahead. Nothing good could come of watching his big hand on the manual gearshift, or noticing the subtle shift in his powerful thigh muscles as he pressed his foot on the pedals.

"What a beautiful day. I can't believe I lived in the city for so long and didn't even think about what I was missing." His low voice rumbled inside the car.

Constance tugged her gaze from the smooth surface of the blacktop and tried to appreciate nature. Trees crowded the road on both sides, filtering the sun. "How come it's all wooded? Why aren't there farms, or, well, anything?"

"Around the turn of the last century, this was all farmland, but it wasn't close enough to the cities or fertile enough to be profitable, so it was all abandoned. So far suburbia hasn't reached out here, either. If it wasn't for the new highway exit, we'd still be in the middle of nowhere."

"But you grew up here?"

"Yup." He smiled.

She squeezed her knees tighter together. It was just a smile, for crying out loud. No need to get all excited.

"I couldn't wait to get away. I thought this was the dullest place on earth. We had fifty dairy cows and I had to help milk them every morning and evening. Makes tabulating columns of figures look really interesting, let me tell you."

"You've got to be kidding." She couldn't imagine him milking a cow. "I thought that was all done by machines these days."

"It is. But someone has to hook them up to the machines."

"Do they mind? The cows, I mean."

"On the whole they're pretty enthusiastic about it. I guess it feels good to lighten the load."

"And now you milk people foolish enough to gamble their hard-earned money." She looked straight ahead. "You help lighten their heavy wallets."

He turned and looked at her. "You think what we do is wrong, don't you?"

"I'm hardly unusual in that."

"It's entertainment. People have free will. They can come and gamble or they can go do something else."

His calm response only prodded her to goad him more. "Do you gamble?"

He didn't say anything. Silence hummed in the air until she got curious enough to turn and look at him. "No. I don't."

"See?"

"See what?"

"You're smart enough to know it's a bad idea."

"I'm smart enough to know it's not for me. Believe me, it's already a gamble opening a big casino and hotel in the backwoods of Massachusetts when it seems like the whole world wants you to fail."

"I notice that you get a lot of negative press. But I don't suppose it hurts that much, considering the money you're making."

"You're right about that." He shot her another warm

smile that made her toes tingle. She cursed them. "So far we've proved everyone wrong and I intend to make sure it stays that way."

"Why does the BIA want to investigate your accounts?" Was she allowed to ask that? She wanted to hear what he thought.

He shrugged. "Same thing, I think. If we were deeply in debt to a bank in Dubai or the mob, or asking for a government bailout, no one would be surprised. They can't accept that fact that we're successful and prospering all by ourselves. It makes people suspicious."

"Why didn't you need to borrow money?" There probably would have been no shortage of offers. Everyone wanted a piece of this juicy new pie.

"I prefer to be in charge of my own destiny. I sold my software company for eighty million dollars. I'm sure you read about that."

"Yes, but why would you risk your personal fortune?"

"It's an investment, and so far it's worked out fine." She managed not to turn and look at him, but she could see his satisfied smile in her mind. It was really annoying how likable he was. And he didn't gamble? She was having a hard time finding reasons to hate him. And if he wasn't cheating, it made her job harder, because it sounded as if her contact at the BIA wouldn't be happy until Constance found something.

She'd expected them to return to the burned-out motel, but instead he pulled into a restaurant parking lot. Her white Toyota Camry sat off to one side, sparkling clean.

"I had them wash it and bring it here. I didn't think you'd want to see the wreck of the motel. It's a mess over there."

"That was thoughtful." She sneaked a glance at him but

he was getting out of the car, not paying attention to her. "But why did they bring it here instead of the New Dawn?"

Unused to the sandals, Constance stepped out onto what felt like shaky ground. At least now that she had her car back, she could go buy some more sensible clothes and book a room somewhere else. This time she might ask some pointed questions about fire safety. She didn't know what would have happened if the motel hadn't been equipped with alarms.

"I made us a reservation for lunch here."

"What?" She glanced at the restaurant, which—with hanging baskets of lush flowers and elegant striped awnings—looked upscale and expensive. "No! I couldn't possibly. I need to go buy some…toiletries, and clothes. And I want to get more work done back at the office today."

The last thing she needed was to sit opposite John Fairweather over a delicious meal. She'd surely lose the last shreds of her sanity. And really, he had quite a nerve even suggesting it. She should report his behavior to her BIA contact.

Except maybe she'd leave out the part about the kiss.

She climbed into her car and put her bag on the seat next to her. The new key started the engine perfectly, and the brakes screeched slightly as she reversed out of her space too fast. She turned and headed for the exit. It wasn't until she saw John—in the rearview mirror—staring after her that she realized how rude she'd just been.

He was smiling slightly, as if he found the situation funny.

Which made her speed away even faster.

Safely ensconced at the desk in her new room at the Holiday Inn, Constance called her boss's office to let her know why she'd had to move, and ended up speaking to her friend Lynn, the office receptionist.

"It's a bummer that you live with your parents. I wonder if you can claim the loss on their homeowner's insurance."

"I doubt they have any. Their insurance is faith in God. Even if they did, filing a claim would raise the premium."

"If the motel doesn't offer compensation you could sue."

"I'd never do that."

"You're too much like your parents. Living in the wrong century."

"I happen to like this century."

Lynn laughed. "Okay, okay. So how is it going with John Fairweather? Is he as gorgeous as he looks on the internet?"

Constance shifted in her chair. "I don't know what you're talking about."

"I know you like to pretend you're a nun, but I'm sure you can tell whether a man is good-looking or not."

"He's okay looking, I guess." That stupid smile inched across her lips again. Thank goodness no one was here to see it.

"So, how old is he?"

"Early thirties, maybe?"

"That's not too old for you."

"Lynn! What on earth would make you think he and I have anything in common?" They didn't. Nothing. She'd thought about it on the drive over here.

"You're both human. Both single. And you're very pretty, Constance, though you do your best to hide it."

"Would you stop?" She pushed her glasses up her nose. Was she really pretty enough to attract the interest of John Fairweather? It didn't seem possible.

"I'm just excited that you're away from your parents'

overly watchful and critical gaze. You need to make the most of it."

"I've been quite busy getting burned out of my motel room and trying to go through the New Dawn's paperwork."

"All work and no play makes—"

"I'm already dull, and quite happy that way." At least she had been until last night. Suddenly her mind kept churning with odd ideas. That kiss had started something. She kept thinking about it. Feeling his lips on hers. Feeling his arms around her.

Obviously she had to make sure that didn't happen again, but she could kiss someone else, couldn't she? "Maybe I should join one of those dating services when I get back."

"What!" Lynn's stunned response showed that she'd revealed way too much. Now she couldn't even remember how she'd led up to that. "You're finally coming to your senses? It's him, isn't it? Those smoldering dark eyes. Those powerful broad shoulders. I know you're far too principled to be attracted to his money, so it must be his looks."

"Nonsense. He's very intelligent. Nice, too." She froze, realizing that she'd just proved that she liked him.

Silence greeted her on the other end. "Really?" said Lynn slowly.

"Well, I don't know. I only met him yesterday. He's probably just being polite so I won't delve too far into his books."

"I wouldn't blame him. I shouldn't be kidding around like this, though. He does have a reputation as a lothario. I want you to spread your wings, but don't fly right into a fox's den."

"One minute you're encouraging me and the next you're

telling me to back off. It's lucky I have no interest in anything except the books here."

"I can't believe I suddenly feel like I have to warn you
off having an affair with John Fairweather."

"I can't believe it, either." *And I also can't believe how
much I need warning off!* "Obviously you've forgotten
that I'm the same Constance Allen who's only ever dated
one man."

"Well, as soon as you get home I'm going to make sure
you start dating someone new. When do you get back here,
anyway?"

"It'll probably take a week or so. The BIA said I can request more time if I need it. It all depends on what I find."

"I hope you find something. That's always good for
business."

"You're actually hoping that a crime is in progress?"
Constance's gut clenched at the possibility. "I'm hoping
that everything checks out fine. Then I can get out of here
as soon as possible." And preserve what was left of her
dignity.

Four

She picked up a couple of suits and blouses and a pair of shoes at a local Macy's. It was nearly four by the time she made it back to New Dawn to go over the books. Her eyes darted about, on high alert for any signs of John Fairweather. But she didn't see his imposing form anywhere. He wasn't in the lobby or the elevator. Or leaning over someone's cubicle on the office floor.

He also wasn't in his office, where she sat at the round table, which was inconveniently at coffee table height, and resumed her journey through the files. Where was he? He might be angry that she'd blown him off at lunch. Still, he needed to realize that she was here to do a job, and they'd already spent way too much time together. It would probably be more appropriate to the situation if they weren't interacting at all. On the other hand, her BIA contact had said that often the best information came during an inadvertent slip in casual conversation, so she should spend as much time as possible with the tribal members.

She shook her head. This whole situation was far too confusing for her. Just the fact that Lynn could encourage her one minute and warn her off the next proved that nothing about it made sense. She'd rather be surrounded by quiet and predictable columns of figures.

Which, supposedly, she was right now. Unfortunately

the atmosphere vibrated with the absence of John Fairweather.

Constance stayed until seven-thirty and pored over the
files he'd shown her and plenty he hadn't. Nothing aroused
her suspicion. If anything, John's accounting methods were
somewhat redundant and labor-intensive, and could benefit
from some streamlining and a software upgrade.

Relief mingled with disappointment as she descended
to the lobby without encountering him. Apparently he'd
already forgotten about her and moved on to new pastures. He was probably out on the town right now with
some willowy model.

She strode through the lobby, challenging herself not
to look around for him. Why did she want to see him? All
he did was get her flustered. As Lynn had pointed out, he
was a notorious playboy and Constance was peering behind the curtains of his successful operation.

Still, it had been nice of him to personally bring her to
the hotel last night, and to pick up her car this morning. On
the other hand, if he had her car moved, why hadn't they
brought it right to the hotel instead of to some expensive
restaurant, where he had apparently intended to continue
his inappropriate seduction?

She made her way through the parking lot to her car,
brain spinning. Was she upset that he wasn't here to flirt
with her and harass her? She should be appalled and dis-
gusted—and suspicious—of his attempts to seduce her.
Red flags stuck out of this mess in every direction. Her
career at Creighton Waterman would be ruined, and she
could lose her accounting credentials, if anyone learned
about that kiss. Yet she'd as much as told Lynn that she
was attracted to John.

Now she was thinking about him as John?

What was happening to her?

* * *

The next morning she arrived early enough to be the first person in the offices. She'd just settled into browsing through some figures, when John's deep, melodious "Good morning" made her jump. Which was ridiculous since she sat in his office.

"Hello, Mr. Fairweather." She said it as primly as possible. She didn't want him to have any idea of what he'd been doing to her in her dreams last night.

"Mr. Fairweather? Don't you think we're a little beyond that? In fact, I was thinking I should call you Connie."

She blinked rapidly. "No one calls me Connie."

"All the more reason." He sat down on the opposite side of the round table. "What's your nickname?"

"I don't have one."

"I don't believe you." He leaned back. "What do your folks call you?"

"Constance. It's what they named me, so I guess they like it. What do yours call you?"

"John." His eyes twinkled. "So you do have a point. You look great this morning. Did you finally get some sleep?"

Constance felt heat rising to her cheeks. "I did, thank you. The Holiday Inn is very nice."

"I'm sure it is." He cocked his head. "Shame about the twenty-minute drive."

"I don't mind." Why was she getting flustered?

"I'll try not to take it personally."

Of course she was getting flustered. He was staring right at her and flirting.

She watched as he rose from the chair, bowed slightly and left the room. She stared after him, through the open door. Part of her wanted to slam the door and sag against it; another much less reliable part of her wanted to run after him and call, "But wait!"

She closed the door quietly, but resisted turning the lock. As soon as she sat down again, her phone rang and she jumped as if she'd been stung. It was Nicola Moore from the BIA, according to the display. She answered it with as much professional dignity as she could manage.

"Hello, Constance. How are things?"

"Fine. Everything's fine."

"I heard about the fire. I hope that hasn't shaken you up too much."

"It was a shock, but luckily there was no loss of life." She kept quiet about John's role in helping at the fire. There was no need for Nicola to know how much time they'd spent together.

"Have you had a chance to get to know some of the key players yet?"

She hesitated. She wanted to say, *I'm an accountant. I'm better with numbers than people,* but she knew that would be unprofessional. "Sure, I've spoken with several."

"Don't be afraid to get a feel for their personal business. That can often be the most revealing information."

"Uh, sure." Her response wasn't too professional. Still, the request seemed odd. Maybe she just wasn't familiar enough with this kind of work. She knew the BIA regularly conducted audits of various Indian ventures, so they must know what they were doing. "I'll do my best."

She frowned as she hung up. John had done a pretty good job keeping her safely sequestered in his office and away from people. Maybe it was a good idea to move around and take a look at the numbers from the casino floor. There was no reason she couldn't observe the tellers in action, taking people's hard-earned money. It might help stir up her righteous indignation, which seemed to have cooled a bit. She needed to remind herself what this whole enterprise was all about. From an early age, she'd been taught that gambling was wrong, and she still didn't like it much.

She shoved the cap on her pen and put away the latest files she'd looked at. All predictably clean and tidy and all columns adding up to the right amounts. Maybe she was taking John's operation too much at face value. Time to get out there and look under the hood. Feeling like an intrepid reporter, she lifted her bag and headed for the door. She scanned the floor quickly to make sure John wasn't around. Nope. Just two employees sitting quietly at their computers, so she headed downstairs.

She approached the area where the cashiers sat with some trepidation. They were behind a barrier, like at a train station, but it was decorated to look more like an elegant bar than a check-cashing joint. To gain entrance she'd have to go in through the back, and she wasn't sure if they'd let her.

She opened a door marked "staff only," rather surprised that it wasn't locked.

"Can I help you?" A pretty girl with long, curly black hair stood in the hallway behind the door.

"My name's Constance Allen, I'm—"

The girl thrust her hand out. "I know exactly who you are. John told us you might want to see back here. I'm Cecily Dawson. Come in." She smiled, though Constance saw a hint of suspicion in her eyes. Hardly surprising under the circumstances.

"Is it okay if I watch the cashiers for a while?"

"Sure, follow me." She led Constance into the large room, where all the cashiers sat along one wall facing out. Cecily beckoned to a dark-skinned man standing behind the row of cashiers, tapping something into his phone. "Darius, this is Constance Allen."

He pocketed his phone and walked toward her. "A pleasure to meet you, Constance. John told us all about you." His handshake was firm and authoritative. He held her gaze, and her hand, with confidence. He was almost as dangerously handsome as John.

"Is there somewhere I can sit down, out of the way?"

"No need to be out of the way." He touched her arm, and she stifled the urge to flinch. "Come stand with me and watch the whole operation."

"Darius manages the cashiers. He's always on the lookout for trouble."

"In whatever form it may arrive." He shot her a dark gaze filled with mischief.

Constance blinked. "I don't want to get in your way."

"If you're in my way, I'll move." His half smile contained a hint of suggestion. He was flirting with her, too? Maybe this was part of their shtick at the casino. Constance was beginning to regret coming down here. "Each cash register records a sale in our central system and all the records are checked four times a day against the takings. I watch the customers to see if anyone's acting suspicious. It's my job to look for cracks in the system, too, so let me know if you think we could improve upon anything."

"Do you get a lot of suspicious activity?"

"Not so far. We have a lot of controls in place to prevent employees from getting tempted to put their hand in the till. That's more of a problem than the customers at some casinos."

"Are you all members of the Nissequot tribe?"

"Cecily and I are, and Brianna at the end." He pointed to a blonde girl counting out cash at high speed. "Frank, Tessa and Marie are just hoping to marry into the tribe one day." He grinned when Marie, a middle-aged woman in a conservative suit, turned to blow him a kiss. "But we're one big happy family."

His phone beeped and he checked the screen. "Our fearless leader is heading this way," he said to the cashiers. "Look like you're working." He winked at her.

Constance pretended she hadn't seen it. And now John was coming? She braced herself. The cashiers dispensed money with warm customer service and brisk efficiency. They joked and seemed to be enjoying themselves. It wasn't like this at Creighton Waterman. Joviality was frowned upon. In fact, one junior accountant, Daniel Bono, had recently been let go for smiling too much in meetings, or at least that was the rumor.

Customers were streaming into the casino, which struck Constance as a little odd since it was a Wednesday morning. "Why are so many people here at this time of day?"

"We have tour buses pick them up in Boston, Worcester, Springfield. We're adding more routes all the time. A lot of our customers are retirees. We run a brisk trade at the nursing homes."

"Should the elderly be gambling with their life savings?" She felt her brow rise.

Darius's wicked smile reappeared. "Maybe their heirs don't think so, but it's their money, right?"

She shook her head. "I don't get why people want to do this."

"It's fun. Like buying a lottery ticket."

"Do you gamble?"

He shook his head. "John discourages us from gambling. He thinks it's better to put your money in the bank. As far as I know, Don Fairweather is the only gambler in the family. Have you met him?"

"I have. He seems like quite a character."

"I heartily agree."

John burst into the room at that moment. His piercing gaze zeroed in on her. "I was looking for you."

"Now you've found me." She tilted her chin up, proud that she managed to sound so calm. "I was just observing how the cashiers work."

"I see you've met my cousin Darius. He only graduated from college two years ago and he's turning into my right-hand man."

Darius smiled. "I've learned everything from the best."

John put his arm around Darius. "He moved here all the way from L.A. to join the tribe. We're working on the rest of his branch of the family."

"They're not quite ready to move into the backwoods." Darius shrugged. "But the way things are going, this won't be the backwoods for long."

John looked at Constance for a moment. "I'd like to show you around some more."

"I think I've seen everything there is to see. I came through the gaming rooms and passed the slot machines on my way over here."

"Not just the casino and hotel. The whole reservation."

She felt herself frown. Was he trying to shunt her away from here for some reason? She'd barely had time to observe anything. Suspicion crept over her.

On the other hand, she had a feeling Nicola Moore would want her to see as much of the place as possible. "Okay."

"Excellent. We'll start with the museum. Darius can tell you what a passion of mine that has become."

Darius nodded. "It's a labor of love, all right. And thousands of hours of expert research."

"It's not easy to uncover history that's been deliberately buried. Let's go." John gestured toward the door, and she went ahead of him, nodding and smiling to the other employees, and grateful that John hadn't tried to take her hand or put his arm around her.

They walked back through the gaming rooms to the lobby. Retirees were busy wasting their savings in the slot machines, and a surprisingly large number of other people were hunched over the tables as well.

"I didn't know you had a museum."

"There's a lot you don't know." He smiled mysteriously. "All of it good, of course."

"If you're covering up a fraud, you're doing it very well."

"I take pride in everything I do." He lifted a brow slightly, taunting her.

"Are you trying to make me suspicious?" She was conscious of matching his stride as they strolled out of the gaming room and across the lobby.

"Nothing could be further from my mind." Then he touched her. Her stomach drew in and her pulse quickened as he rested his hand at the base of her spine and ushered her though a doorway she'd never noticed before, marked "Hall of Heritage."

It led into a large, gallery-like room with polished wood floors and high walls. Glass cases held artifacts and sleek, printed text and pictures decorated the walls. "It looks like a real museum." She walked ahead of him, curious. One of the first exhibits was a glass case containing a sheaf of age-tinted pages and a quill pen. There was a blown-up photograph of the front page on the wall next to it.

"That's the original treaty between the Nissequot and the governor of Massachusetts in 1648. Two thousand acres of land was given to us then."

"Two thousand? I thought the reservation was less than two hundred."

"They chipped away at it bit by bit over the years."

"The state?"

He shook his head. "Mostly private individuals, farmers, businessmen, greedy people."

"Your ancestors must have sold it to them."

"I could say that greedy people come in all creeds and colors, but research has taught me to give my ancestors the benefit of the doubt and respect that they were just trying to survive."

"You can't really fault them for that. Apparently they managed." She smiled at him. The museum didn't have that many items, but they were carefully arranged and displayed with a good deal of written information accompanying them. A long green cloak in one case caught her eye. It didn't have feathers or beading, but an embroidered trim in black brocade.

"Not what you'd expect, is it?" He looked at her curiously.

"I don't know what I'd expect."

"People seem to want baskets and moccasins and old pots. Precontact stuff. They forget that the history of the Nissequot continues after the settlers arrived. That cloak was worn by Sachem John Fairweather, the man I was named after, when he opened the doors to the first free school in this part of Massachusetts. It remained open until 1933, when the last pupil dropped out to look for work during the Depression."

"Is the building still there?" She could see a grainy photograph of six people in Victorian-era clothing standing outside a neat white building.

"It is indeed. I'm restoring it along with my grandparents' old farmhouse."

"That's very cool. I have no idea of my own family's history before my grandparents' generation."

"Why not?"

She shrugged. "I don't suppose any of us thought it was that interesting."

"Where is your family from, originally?"

"I don't know. All over, I suppose. Maybe that's the problem. It's easy to get excited about ancestry when it's all from one place with a distinct culture. If one person's from Poland and another from Scotland and another from Italy or Norway, no one really cares."

"Well, the truth is that the Nissequot are from all over the place, at this point. I don't even know who my own father was. The Fairweathers are my mother's family. Sometimes you just have to pick a common thread and go with it, and that's what we're doing here. We did find an eighteenth-century Bible with the New Testament written out phonetically in the Nissequot language, though. That's our biggest coup so far. A scholar at Harvard is putting together a Nissequot dictionary by comparing it with a contemporary English version."

She looked up at an enlarged line drawing of a man and woman in more traditional-looking dress. "Is that how you imagine your ancestors looked?"

"Nope. That's a real drawing done by the daughter of one of the first governors of Massachusetts in her personal journal. It was found by relentless digging through old records and hoping for the best. It's time-consuming and way outside my realm of expertise, but it's all coming together piece by piece."

"Impressive."

He led her through the gallery, then disarmed the emergency exit with a key code and pushed through an exterior door out into the bright sunlight. A large black truck was parked right behind the building. "My unofficial vehicle. Get in."

"Where are we going?"

"To meet my grandparents." Curious, she climbed in. His truck wasn't quite as pristine as his sedan. He lifted a pile of papers off the passenger seat so she could sit down. There was an unopened can of soda in the cup holder, and music—the Doors—started as soon as he turned on the engine. There was also a Native American–looking thing with feathers on it hanging from the rearview mirror. "They're going to like you. I can tell."

"Why?" They were hardly likely to appreciate someone who was there for the express purpose of digging up dirt on their reservation.

"You're nice."

"Nice? I'm not nice at all."

His loud laugh echoed through the cab. "True, it was cold of you to blow me off at lunch yesterday. But they'll think you're nice."

She glanced at her reflection in the wing mirror nearest to her. She wasn't sure anyone had accused her of being nice before. Organized, efficient, polite, helpful, exacting, prim, persnickety…a range of flattering and not so flattering words sprang to mind, but nice was not among them. "I'm not sure that nice is good in my line of work."

"Maybe you're in the wrong line of work?" He shot her a challenging glance.

"Look who's talking."

"I'm nice." He glanced in the rearview mirror, then over at her. She jerked her eyes from his gaze and stared out the window, taking in how they were traveling along another featureless wooded road to nowhere. "Ask anyone."

"I'm not sure that's the first word that would spring to mind if I asked someone to describe you. I'd think *bullheaded, relentless* and *determined* would be right up there. And that's just going from the newspaper articles I read about you."

"Don't believe everything you read in the papers."

"I don't, but where there's smoke, there's usually fire." That was one of the first tenets of forensic accounting. The tricky part was finding a live ember after someone had carefully tried to put the fire out.

"They do say I'm an arrogant SOB. I'm guessing you'd agree with that." She saw the corner of his mouth lift in a smile.

"For sure." She felt her own treacherous mouth smile along. "And they say you cooked up the entire Nissequot tribe just so you could open a casino and rake in billions."

"That's pretty much true." He turned and stared right at her. "At least that's how it started, but it's snowballed into a lot more than that."

"Don't you think it's wrong to exploit your heritage for profit?"

"Nope." He looked straight ahead as they turned off one winding road onto another. "My ancestors survived war, smallpox, racism and more than four hundred years of being treated like second-class citizens. Hell, they weren't even American citizens until 1924. The powers that be did everything they could to grind us out of existence and they very nearly succeeded. I don't feel at all bad about taking advantage of the system that tried to destroy us." His voice was cool as usual, but she could hear the passion beneath his calm demeanor. "If I can do something to lift up the people who've survived, then I feel pretty damn good about it."

Constance had no idea what to say as they pulled up in front of a neat yellow neocolonial house with a front porch and a three-car garage.

John had jumped out of the car and opened her door before she managed to gather her thoughts. "What're you waiting for?"

"Uh, I don't know." She'd never felt more lost for words around anyone. "Is this the original farmhouse?" she asked, taking advantage of his offered hand as she climbed down from the cab.

"Oh, no. We just built this three years ago. The old place was kind of a wreck. No insulation, no real heat and A/C. My grandparents were ready to move into someplace shiny and new."

The front door opened and a white-haired man appeared on the front porch. "Hey, Big John."

"His name is John as well?"

"Yes." They walked up the slate front path.

"Does that make you Little John?"

He smiled. "I suppose it does. But if you call me that I won't be responsible for my actions."

She wanted to laugh. As they climbed the steps she could see that the younger John towered over his grandfather by at least eight inches and was fifty-plus pounds heavier, all of it solid muscle.

"This is Constance. She's come here all the way from Ohio to be a thorn in my side."

Big John stuck out a gnarled hand. "Pleased to meet you, Constance." He shook her hand with warmth, using both hands to embrace it. "It's not easy to be a thorn in this man's side. His hide is too tough. Come in."

She followed him into a sunlit foyer, where they were greeted by a tall, rather beautiful woman of about seventy. "This is my mom, Phyllis. She's actually my grandmother, but she raised me so I've always called her Mom."

"Hello, Constance." She also had a firm handshake. Constance could see where John got his inquisitive gaze. She thought it was cute that he called her Mom. "It's not often that John brings a young lady to visit us." Her bright eyes scanned Constance from head to toe.

"Oh, I'm actually not…" Not what? A young lady? She glanced nervously at John.

"Not what?" he said unhelpfully.

"I'm here on business." She glanced from his grandmother to his grandfather. "For the Bureau of Indian Affairs."

"Is that so," said Big John. His expression hardened. She was beginning to get the impression that the BIA was not a much-loved organization.

"I was just showing her our museum. Since she's interested in Indian affairs and all." Constance saw a smile tugging at the corner of John's mouth. "Then I thought she should meet the real reasons we're all here. My mother died when I was young," he told her, "and my grandparents brought me up to be aware of our Nissequot roots. I have to admit that when my friends played cowboys and Indians I wanted to be a cowboy so I could have the gun." He smiled mischievously. "And I wasn't all that interested in hearing stories about how the world was created on the back of a turtle."

His grandfather laughed. "He just wanted to know if the Nissequot liked to fight."

"But they stubbornly persisted in teaching me everything they knew, and it must have taken root somewhere under my thick hide, because I remembered it all."

"How did you know the legends yourselves? Are they all written down somewhere?" Constance couldn't help her curiosity.

"Some stories are. Others are recited or sung," replied Phyllis. "As long as there's one person in each generation left to pass the stories along, they don't die out. Even the family members who've come back to us from places like Chicago and L.A. knew something about their heritage—a song their grandmother used to sing, or just that they were from the Nissequot tribe, even though no one else had ever heard of it. We're so blessed to have John. He's the kind of leader needed to bring the tribe back from near extinction and make it flourish again."

"And there I thought I was just trying to make a buck." He winked at Constance.

"The spirit moves in mysterious ways," said his grandfather. "Sometimes none of us are sure what we're doing until we can look back later. We thought we were trying to run a dairy operation, but we were really keeping our claim on the land going until John was ready to take over."

"John bought us eight cows last Christmas as a present." Phyllis smiled at him.

"Beef cattle," John cut in. "Aberdeen Angus. No more milking." He shrugged. "The place didn't feel right with no cattle on it."

"He missed the sound they make."

"They're an investment. Good breeding stock."

Phyllis smiled at Constance. "He's a lot more sentimental than he'd have you believe."

John huffed. "Nonsense. We'd better get going. I wanted Constance to see that we're not just numbers on a balance sheet or names on a census."

"It was nice to meet you." Constance smiled and waved goodbye, then followed John, who was already halfway out the door. His grandparents stood looking after them, amusement glowing on their faces. He bounded down the front steps and jumped back into the car. The engine was already running by the time she maneuvered herself into her seat.

"They seem very nice."

"Like me." He winked.

"I have to admit that you do seem nicer than all the media stories make you out to be."

"I told you not to believe everything you read. Don't start thinking I'm a pushover, though. I'm as ruthless as I need to be." He tilted his stony jaw as if to prove it.

"Ruthless, huh?"

He focused his dark eyes on her as they paused at the end of the driveway. A shiver of arousal jolted her and she remembered the alarming power he had over her. "Merciless."

John Fairweather knew exactly what he was doing at every moment. Including when he'd kissed her. And she'd better not forget that.

Five

That afternoon, back in John's office, Constance focused on expenses and other outgoings. Expenses were large, as would be expected, and there were definitely some extravagances, but nothing she hadn't seen at other booming corporations.

Around six o'clock she emerged from John's office, ready to head for her hotel. She was relieved that she could be done here in a day or two. Everything was checking out and she and John would no doubt both be relieved to see the back of each other.

Speaking of John's back, there it was, barring the hallway to the elevators. Her heart rate rose just at the sight of him, which was ridiculous. He stood in conversation with a young payroll employee named Tricia.

"Good night," she muttered as she skirted carefully around them.

"Constance!" His voice boomed through her consciousness. "Come down and watch the action on the floor with me. It really picks up in the evenings. You should see the place when it's busy."

"No, thanks. I need to get back to the hotel." She kept her eyes focused on the far end of the hallway. But he moved past her and pressed the button for the elevator before she reached it.

"You're knocking off work to relax when you should be examining the details of our operations? I'm shocked, Constance."

Her gaze darted to him as an urge to defend herself rushed over her. "It's really just the paperwork that interests me."

He lifted a dark brow. "I think you're being remiss in your duties. I'd think the BIA would want to know all the gory details of how we operate. I wouldn't be surprised if they wanted a full report on everyone who works here."

"They'll need to hire a private investigator for that. I'm an accountant." The elevator opened and she dived in. Of course he came right after her.

His proximity did something really annoying to her body temperature. Suddenly she was sweating inside her conservative suit. Maybe her new blouse had too much synthetic fabric in it. She felt a frown form on her brow and attempted to smooth it away. She didn't want him to know that his presence rattled her so much.

"You've only observed the casino during the day so far. We're virtually empty then. You should really take a look at the place during the evenings, when most of our customers are here. It's the best way to see how we do business."

He did have a point. If she were her boss, she'd tell her to stay. Should she really let her inappropriate attraction to John Fairweather prevent her from doing her job properly? "I suppose you're right. There's no need for you to accompany me, though. I don't want to bother you."

Constance saw that familiar sparkle of mischief in his dark eyes. "On the contrary. It would be my pleasure."

When the elevator doors opened, she prepared for him to try to slide his arm through hers, or take her hand, but he simply gestured for her to go first. She walked ahead of him toward the game rooms. Was he looking at her behind? She felt her hips swing a little more than usual, and immediately tried to prevent it. She was probably letting her imagination run away with her, which she confirmed when she turned to find him texting on his phone.

He's not attracted to you, Constance. Why would he be? He just kissed you because he could. He's that kind of man.

"Let's get you a drink."

"No!" The protest flew from her mouth so loudly it made her glance around.

He smiled. "We have fresh-squeezed fruit juice at the bars. Leon does an amazing concoction of fresh pineapple juice with fresh coconut milk and a dash of his secret spices. Totally nonalcoholic."

"That does sound good." Coconut milk was supposed to be healthy and she'd never tried it.

He ordered two of the drinks, which arrived in large glass goblets with the casino's sunrise logo on them. He lifted his glass. "Here's to you discovering everything there is to know about us, and liking what you see."

She merely nodded. She wasn't supposed to hope that she'd like everything she saw. That would discourage her from looking for problems. She sipped her drink, though, and found it creamy and delicious. "I admit this is really good. I usually just drink soda when I'm out. I guess I'll have to branch out."

"I'm always asking them to invent new beverages. There's no reason why us nondrinkers should be left out in the cold."

"You don't drink alcohol?"

"Nope. I steer well clear of it. It killed my mom."

"What? I thought she was really young when she died."

"She was twenty. She died in a car wreck. Drove off an overpass. It would never have happened if she'd been sober."

"I'm so sorry."

"Me, too. I don't remember her at all. I was only six months old when she died. Luckily for me, she'd left me with a friend for the night. My grandparents made me swear never to touch the stuff and I've never seen a reason to defy them."

"Very sensible." Her prim reply embarrassed her. John had endured a devastating loss. It must be so odd to grow up not knowing the woman who gave birth to you. "Do you get mad at her for not being there for you?"

He paused, and looked right at her with a curious expression in his eyes. "Yes. When I was younger I was angry with her for not being more careful. Seems crazy, really. It does make me keep a close eye on the younger kids here, though. Especially the ones who've moved away from family to join us. I'm a big fan of stern lectures."

She smiled. "You sound like my parents. I grew up on a steady diet of stern lectures."

"And look how well you turned out."

"Some would say I'm far too conservative for my own good."

"And I'd be one of them." He winked. "Still, that's better than some of the alternatives. Let's go watch the roulette tables."

"You're not going to make me play, are you?"

He laughed. "I'm not going to make you do anything you don't want to."

What was it about Constance that got under his skin? John stood next to her as the wheel spun and the ball danced between black and red. She was so unlike the usual stream of glamorous women who hung around him, sniffing the scent of money or promising a steamy affair.

Constance stood with her arms crossed over her prim

suit, eyes fixed firmly on the table and not a hint of flirtation in her gestures.

But he knew she was as attracted to him as he was to her. The shine in her eyes when she looked at him, the glow in her cheeks, the way she angled her body toward him unconsciously—it all spoke of the desire that crackled between them so forcefully you could almost hear it snap in the air.

She didn't want to like him. Or to want him. But somehow that only heightened the tension building as they stood next to each other, pretending to focus on the white ball.

It dropped into a slot and the wheel slowed to a halt. One woman squealed with delight and smiled as the croupier slid a pile of chips toward her. John glanced at Constance and saw the tiny hint of a smile that hovered about her pretty mouth. "That's why they keep coming back," he said softly.

"I can see how it would be fun." She leaned into him so he could hear her but no one else could. Her scent tugged at his sense. "But I'd still rather make money the old-fashioned way."

"Me, too. I'll take hard work over chance any day of the week." He leaned still closer until he could almost feel the heat of her skin. "But everyone's different."

Did he like her because she was different? It didn't really make sense. There was no good reason to flirt with and tempt this woman. She was here on professional business and it was inappropriate for him to even have sensual thoughts about her.

Yet he couldn't seem to stop.

As he'd promised, he had no intention of making her do anything she didn't want to. But making her want to? That was a whole different story.

* * *

One time at a college mixer someone had given Constance a glass of orange juice mixed with vodka—without mentioning the vodka. She still remembered the way the world around her had grown blurry, and she'd found herself laughing at things that weren't even funny. She felt like that right now, though she was sure she'd had nothing but fruit juice all evening.

"…and then after we won every game that season, they wouldn't let me go." John leaned into her again, brushing her arm with his. Her skin sizzled inside her suit. "It was a pain in the ass. All I wanted to do was study statistics, and I had to get all this tiresome fresh air and sunshine."

She laughed. He'd been telling her about how he'd joined the college football team entirely for the scholarship money and then accidentally became their star player. Of course he had. He was one of those people who effortlessly succeeded at everything they tried. Or maybe not effortlessly. He just made it look that way.

"It must get annoying being so good at everything."

"You think I'm bragging?"

"I'm pretty sure of it." She narrowed her eyes, trying to hide her smile. He hadn't really volunteered any information she hadn't asked for. She wanted to know more about him. At first she told herself she was doing "research." Now she was too darn curious to stop. "What did your team members think of you?"

"Oh, at first they made fun of me. Teased me for being from the backwoods of Massachusetts. They stopped laughing when they saw how fast I could run, though."

"Can you still run fast?" Her hand accidentally brushed his as she raised her drink to her lips. They'd moved to a sofa near the blackjack tables, where they had a good view of the whole room. Her thigh jostled against his, too. The sofa was soft and they kept sinking into it. The crowds milled about the gaming tables, ignoring them completely.

"I don't know. I haven't tried lately. I'm still pretty quick on the squash court, though. Do you play any sports?"

"No." Maybe she should start. All this energy building up inside her needed some place to go. Right now she felt like jumping up and running around the room. "My parents thought sports were a waste of time."

"And you never did anything they didn't want you to?"

"Nothing major. I read some books they didn't approve of, and they never knew I had a boyfriend."

"You kept your lover a secret from them?" He bumped against her, teasing.

"It wasn't like that."

"No? It certainly sounds like it."

"He was at college with me in a different town, so they never met him."

"And you didn't mention him. Was he someone they wouldn't have approved of?" He raised a brow.

She chuckled. "No. That's the funny part. He was so dull they'd probably have liked him." Was she really talking about Phil? She'd tried to shove him out of her mind. Which was hard, because six years later he was still the only boyfriend she'd ever had.

At least now she could admit he wasn't exactly the man of her dreams.

"Why were you dating him if he was dull?"

"I like dull."

John peered into her eyes. The effect of his dark gaze was anything but dull. Sensations she'd never felt before trickled through every part of her. "Why?"

"Predictable. Reassuring. I don't enjoy surprises."

"Or at least you think you don't." One brow lifted slightly. "Come with me."

He took her hand gently and helped her up from the squishy sofa. "Where are we going?"

"It's a surprise."

"I already told you I don't like them." Anticipation rippled in her tummy.

"I don't believe you." He led her across the busy game room to the bank of shiny elevators. Her hand pulsed inside his. They were walking along like a couple, and while it horrified her, the realization gave her a strange thrill. She should pull her hand from his, but she didn't.

He pressed the button for the highest floor and shot her a mysterious look.

"I'm not even going to ask," she murmured, trying to keep her eyes on the door. Even while she knew he was flirting with her and leading her on, she trusted John not to pull any fast moves. They'd been talking for a while and he was clearly a man who took the concept of personal honor seriously. He saw himself as a role model for the younger members of the tribe and he'd said more than once that he never did anything he wouldn't want them to know about.

Of course, maybe he was just trying to undermine her defenses by appearing principled and thoughtful.

What a shame it was working.

The elevator opened at the top floor and she was surprised when the doors parted to reveal the night sky. "Wow, a roof terrace." A broad expanse of marble, ringed with potted plants, glowed under the stars. "How come there's no one up here?"

"It's not open to the public unless it's booked for an event and, as you can see, there's nothing happening here tonight except us."

Us. What did he mean by that? Nothing, probably. "That's a lot of stars." She felt as though she could see forever, bright galaxies twinkling all the way to infinity.

"It's nice being up here above all the lights. You can see clearly. I come up here when I need to get perspective."

"Feeling like a tiny speck in the vast universe certainly puts everything in perspective."

"Doesn't it, though? All the worries that keep us little humans awake at night are nothing in the grand scheme of things."

He still held her hand, which had grown quite hot. They walked across the terrace to a seating area and he guided her onto a large sofa and sat down next to her.

What am I doing? Up here there was no pretense that they were still working. Or that she was researching anything. She was simply sitting with John, her right thigh fully pressed against his left one as they both sank into the soft cushions. The cool night air emphasized the warmth of his body.

"What do you worry about, Constance?" His hand squeezed hers very gently.

"Sometimes I worry that I'll never move out of my parents' house." She laughed, trying to lighten the moment.

"Why haven't you? You must earn enough to rent your own place."

"I don't know, really. I keep thinking that I will, then another month or year passes and I'm still there."

"Maybe you've been waiting to meet the right man."

"Probably." The confession surprised her. "After all, I've always been told a nice girl is supposed to live at home until she gets married." She shrugged.

"Why haven't you met the right person yet?"

"I work at an accounting firm. It's not exactly a hotbed of romance." She smiled.

"Don't accountants need love, too?"

"Apparently so." Was he trying to suggest that she go back and date one of her coworkers? That would be a strange suggestion from a man still holding her hand in his. "Why haven't *you* married?" Curiosity pricked at her, even though she was pretty sure she knew the answer. Why would a man in John's position want to settle down with one woman when he could have a different one every week if he wanted?

"I have been."

His answer shocked her so much she tried to pull her hand from his. "You're divorced?" Her hand flew free, and the chill night air assaulted her hot palm.

He nodded. "A long time ago. You're shocked."

"I didn't read that when I was researching you."

"It's not common knowledge. I was married in high school, right before I went away to college. I thought it would help keep us together despite the physical distance."

"Which was only a hundred miles or so."

"Less than fifty, actually." He grinned. "Young and stupid."

"Why did you split up?"

"I was so busy with school that I didn't make enough time for her and she met someone else. It proved to me that a marriage isn't something that just happens. It takes a lot of work to keep it alive."

"And that scared you off trying it again?" She attempted to pull her thigh away from his but once again the sofa was too deep and she kept falling against him.

"Pretty much." His eyes twinkled in the darkness. "I know I've got my hands full with my business, and now with running the tribe, so I don't want to disappoint someone else."

"Oh." She felt a surprising sting of disappointment, which annoyed her. Had she really imagined somewhere in the darkest recesses of her mind that John might have real feelings for her? She was getting carried away! "So you probably won't get married again."

"I damn sure will." His conviction startled her. "Don't count me out yet."

"I can see you feel strongly about it." Her smile matched his. How did he keep doing that to her? Any sensible woman would leap to her feet and go admire the view on the far side of the patio, away from this man who freely admitted he didn't have time for a relationship.

"Oh, I do feel strongly about it. In addition to any personal considerations, I have a responsibility to the Nissequot tribe to help produce the next generation." He winked.

She couldn't help laughing. "That's a weighty responsibility. Does it mean you have to marry another Nissequot?"

"Nope." His gaze grew more serious. "We made sure there were no requirements for any particular amount of Indian blood in tribal members. I hate the idea that people have to choose who they marry carefully or abandon their heritage."

"I'd imagine those kinds of rules are in place to keep the benefits—government funds, casino profits and that kind of thing—to a limited number of people."

"And what good does that do anyone? Except the people trying to keep us small in the hope that we'll fade away eventually. I'd prefer to expand to include everyone. Growth and change are the core facts of life. If you try to keep something static, it will just die. I'm here to make sure the opposite happens." He took her hand again, and she didn't pull it back. He lifted it to his lips and kissed her palm, which sizzled with awareness under his lips.

Why did she let him do that? He wasn't serious about her. He was playing with her.

Or was he?

His dark eyes had narrowed and fixed on hers with an

expression so intense that she couldn't breathe. Heat radiated through her and her body inched closer to his without any effort on her part. She should be trying to back away, or standing up and walking back to the elevator. But her entire body seemed to be in thrall to his.

His lips touched hers very softly, just brushing them. It wasn't even a kiss. She closed her eyes as she drank in the subtle male scent of him. Her tongue itched to meet his, which it did as their mouths opened slightly and welcomed each other into a real kiss.

Her fingers crept under the jacket of his suit and into the folds of his shirt. His large hands settled one on either side of her waist, gathering her to him. She was aware of the roughness of his chin as he shifted and deepened the kiss. She leaned into him, pulling at his shirt until her fingers slid underneath it and she touched the warm skin of his back.

Heat unfurled in her core, spreading through her like smoke. John lifted her onto his lap, still kissing her, and she welcomed the closeness. Her nipples were so sensitive she could feel the fabric of his lapels even through her blouse and bra, and she pressed herself against him, unable to resist the pull of sensation.

She had no idea how long they kissed. All she knew was that she didn't want to stop. The pleasure of holding him, of touching him and kissing him, was so intense she couldn't remember anything like it. When their lips finally separated slightly, she could barely pull herself together enough to open her eyes.

"There's something very powerful between us," John murmured, his voice a rumble in her consciousness.

"Yes," she whispered. Words seemed too literal in the heady sensual atmosphere of the dark night. It was easier to say what she wanted with her body, with her mouth. She licked his lips gently, savoring the taste of him. When his hand moved higher, she guided it over her breast, enjoying the weight of his palm on her desire-thickened nipple.

When he pulled back she uttered a groan of protest. She didn't want him to stop.

"Come with me." He lifted her carefully to her feet, supporting her with his arm. She was so intoxicated with arousal that she could barely walk.

"Where are we going?" It was hard forming words.

"Somewhere more private."

"This is private." No one was watching them. Only the twinkling gaze of a hundred million stars. She didn't want to leave. She didn't want anything to break the spell binding them together.

"More comfortable, too." He squeezed her. "Don't worry. It's close." They walked slowly back to the elevator, with his arm around her waist. The effort of putting one foot in front of the other tugged her out of the sensual haze she'd slipped into. What was she doing? She'd kissed John again. Kissing him one time could be seen as an accident. Kissing him twice? That was deliberate.

She wanted to kiss him again, too. What had come over her? She must be in the grip of some kind of madness. Still, she wasn't going to pull away from the warm embrace of his arm. Instead she rested her hand on his, enjoying the closeness.

At the elevator he pressed the button. "Are we going down to the lobby?"

He looked rather disheveled from her running her hands all over him. She probably did, too. "No need to. The elevator also leads directly into my suite."

"Oh, good." Her own words made her blink. She was glad about him taking her to his private apartment?

Yes. She was. Which didn't make any sense at all. She

should insist on going straight to her car and back to her hotel for a cold shower.

They stepped into the unpleasantly bright space of the elevator and she shielded her eyes from the shining mirrors by leaning against his chest as he pressed the button. His suite was on the highest floor, right beneath the roof terrace, so in a few seconds the doors opened and they stepped out, right into his suite.

"Do strangers from the hotel ever press the wrong button and end up in your room?"

He smiled and shook his head. "You have to enter a code to go to this floor or the terrace. Don't worry. No one will disturb us."

They stepped out into his suite. A wide foyer led into a spacious living room with a wall of windows. Comfortable sofas faced what must have been an impressive view in daylight. Shelves held a collection of photographs and objects. She was curious about the things he had gathered in his home, but he led her past them and through another door into his bedroom. Decorated in a simple, masculine style, the room held nothing but a low platform bed and a dresser. Three wooden masks hung on the wall opposite. She stared at them for a moment. "Don't you feel weird with these faces watching you?"

He laughed. "They're hundreds of years old. I'm sure they've seen it all before."

No doubt they'd seen a lot right here in John's bedroom. She glanced warily at the bed. How many women had writhed in his arms there? Was she really going to be the next in a long procession of girls who succumbed to his seemingly irresistible charms? What was she doing? She knew she shouldn't be here, but she didn't want to be anywhere else.

John turned to her, slid his arms around her waist and

held her close. He was several inches taller, so he had to incline his head to kiss her. Her mouth rose effortlessly to meet his and the kiss drew her back into that private realm where nothing else really mattered.

Six

John sensed her doubts even as he kissed her. Constance could hardly believe she was here in his bedroom. He could hardly believe it either. Still, his disbelief mingled with a sense of wonder as he held her close and kissed her with feeling.

She didn't have much experience. He could tell that by her sense of surprise and her awkward reaction to his simple advances. Somehow that only stoked his passion. This beautiful woman had been quietly living her life, free from desire and its complications, peering into corporate records and keeping her heart safe.

Constance was like a safe with a long and complicated combination, and his fingers itched to turn the dial until she clicked open for him. The image appealed to him. He wanted to unlock the door to her heart and let himself in.

He helped her carefully out of her suit jacket and laid it on the chair. Her blouse had a silky texture and he could feel the warmth of her body through it, so he let himself enjoy the sensation of her skin through the fabric while he kissed her.

Then he started to unbutton it. First just one button. Then another kiss. Then the second button. More kissing. Her eyes opened slightly as he went for the third button, and the sparkle of excitement in them fired his arousal.

Her hands roamed under his shirt, feeling the muscle along his back. When they dipped into the waistband of his pants, the sudden rush of sensation made him gasp. He was so hard it was difficult to be patient and careful with her, but that was the only way to unlock her closely guarded safe and enjoy the intimacy he craved. He knew he'd blow everything if he tried to rush. He wanted this to be as enjoyable for her as he knew it would be for him.

He guided her to the edge of the bed and sat her gently down, then knelt in front of her and pulled her shirt back to reveal her bra. She watched him curiously, eyes shining, as he lowered his mouth over her breast and dampened the fabric of her bra with his tongue. Already firm, her nipple thickened under his caress, and she let out a small murmur of pleasure.

She ran her fingers through his hair, encouraging him as he licked and sucked first one breast and then the other. Then he lowered his head to trace a line down toward her belly button. She inhaled sharply as he reached the waistband of her skirt.

"Lie back," he murmured, stroking her cheek with his thumb.

She blinked, not questioning anything, then eased herself down onto the soft bedcover. Her thighs clenched together as he unbuttoned the top of her skirt—which opened at the side—and started to slide it down her shapely legs.

He wanted to tell her to relax, but had a feeling that words might have the opposite effect. Sometimes it was better to touch than talk.

The removal of her skirt revealed pretty lace-trimmed panties that rather surprised him. He'd expected utilitarian cotton. And she must have bought them since the fire. Had she known he'd see and enjoy them? Had she bought them for him? It was hard to imagine, but the thought made him smile.

He didn't part her legs, which she still pressed together tightly, although he longed to taste her through the lacy fabric. Instead he kissed her thighs, her knees and her legs right down to her toes. She softened and relaxed as he traveled along her smooth skin.

He ventured tentatively toward her female center, wanting to explore every delicious inch of her. The soft silk of her panties didn't conceal the heat radiating from her core. She flinched slightly as he flicked his tongue over her, then whimpered softly as he sucked her through the delicate fabric.

Once she was thoroughly relaxed and pulsing with heat and pleasure, all resistance kneaded away, he slid off her shirt. She eagerly reached for his shirt buttons, tugging at them, as a smile spread across her face. Her hungry energy surprised him. She wanted to see him naked almost as much as he wanted to be naked with her. Together they undid his belt and shed his pants, and pulled off his shirt. Then she hesitated, frowning slightly, staring at his briefs.

He was aroused almost to the point of madness, and it showed. He wondered for a second if she'd freeze up and try to backtrack—something that just might kill him at this moment. Instead he almost died anyway when she slid her fingers inside the waistband of his underwear and took hold of him.

Constance couldn't remember being this aroused *ever*. Part of her couldn't believe she had her fingers wrapped gently but firmly around John's impressive erection. The rest of her really wanted to feel him inside her right now.

She heard his sharp intake of breath as she stroked him. It gave her a thrill that he was so excited, too.

"Hold on," he rasped. "Before we get carried away and forget."

He reached into a nearby dresser and brought out a condom packet. She hadn't even thought about contraception. She wasn't on the pill, either. Why would she be? Obviously common sense had deserted her.

Sheathed, he came close and she wrapped her hand around him again. Her body was almost trembling with anticipation as she guided him into her, not that he needed any help, and he lowered his chest over hers. He kissed her very softly right as he entered her—so slow and careful—and she felt her hips lift to greet his.

The powerful sensation of him inside her quickened her breath. She could feel her fingers clawing at his back, traveling into his hair, but she didn't seem to have any control over them. Luckily that didn't matter because he took control, moving with gentle intensity, driving her further and further into an intense world of pleasure and passion.

"I'm crazy about you," he whispered in her ear, as her breath quickened to the point of gasping. The sensation of his hot breath on her ear only heightened her pleasure.

"Me, too." Did that even make any sense? Nothing made sense, except kissing him more and reveling in the sensation of him deep inside her. His big body moved over hers with ease, shifting position to send her closer yet to the brink of...something.

Sensation was building inside her and she became more aware of it as John sucked her earlobe gently while filling her over and over again. Something was creeping through her, a wave of pleasure, or a whole tide of it, starting in the clenched tips of her toes and rising up her legs and sweeping over her belly until she felt as though she was drowning in it. Distant moaning and shrieking sounds might have come from her mouth, but she couldn't be sure. John uttered a low groan and gathered her so tightly in his arms she thought she might disappear into him completely. She wanted to say something but she couldn't make a sound, just little gasps that burst from her lips onto the hot skin of his shoulder as he clung to her.

"Am I crushing you?" John eased himself off her slightly by propping himself on his elbows.

"No." His powerful physique felt no heavier than a down comforter, enveloping her in its warmth. "You feel fantastic."

"You, too." He kissed her so softly she almost wanted to cry.

Cry? Strange emotions suddenly welled up inside her. She didn't even really know what had happened. Was that an orgasm? She'd read about them but had never come close to experiencing one before. Her body still pulsed and tingled with the aftereffects. Her heart squeezed and she held John close. She felt incredibly intimate with him right now. Which wasn't surprising, considering that they were both naked in his bed.

On his bed. With the lights on.

Her eyes cracked open as she managed to regain some grip on her consciousness. They hadn't even taken the time to climb under the covers. In fact, they weren't even at the right end of the bed.

She swallowed, trying to make sense of what had just happened. John stroked a tendril of damp hair from her forehead. "You're very passionate, Constance."

Coming from his mouth, her dull and prim name seemed sensual and evocative. "So are you, John." His name was even duller than hers, and he was the most exciting and intriguing man she'd ever met. Apparently names didn't have too much to do with anything.

"Let's get under the covers." A smile shone in his eyes.

"Okay." She let him lift her, her body feeling almost weightless in his strong embrace, and slide her under the soft white covers. Then he settled next to her and wrapped his arms around her. A soft kiss on her cheek felt so romantic she thought for a second that she must be dreaming.

She wasn't, though. There was no way she could conjure the intoxicating scent of his skin in a dream. Or the slightly rough feel of his cheek against hers, or the sparkle of amusement—and passion—in his eyes. This was real, and it was happening to her, Constance Allen, right here, right now.

"I really don't know how I ended up here." She felt like being honest.

"It's the most natural thing in the world. Two people being attracted to each other and wanting to be together."

"I don't get why you're attracted to me, though." No doubt any dating manual would issue stern warnings against such a blatant display of insecurity. But she couldn't help wondering what John Fairweather saw in her.

He wanted her, there was no doubt about that. She could feel it in the way he looked at her, in the way he made love to her, in the way he held her close, his breath on her cheek.

"I don't know where you've gotten the idea that you're not desirable. You're a beautiful woman." He stroked her cheek with his thumb.

"I am not! I'm quite ordinary looking."

"Who told you that? You have the prettiest hazel eyes I've ever seen. So curious and a little wary. When you look at me I get a jolt of something I can't explain."

Her eyes? "But I wear glasses. Where are they, anyway?"

"On the chest over there. I made sure to put them somewhere safe."

"I don't even remember taking them off." She reached

automatically for her nose, where she usually pushed them up.

"You didn't. I did." His smile made her smile—as usual. "Apparently you can see pretty well without them."

"I just need them for reading. They're a mild prescription." She could see John clearly enough right now, his dark eyes peering into hers.

"So how come you wear them all the time?"

She shrugged, or attempted to, in his arms. "I feel more comfortable with them on. Then I don't have to worry about taking them on and off to read. I do spend a lot of time reading, even if it's mostly numbers."

"Something to hide behind. I don't think you're comfortable with your own beauty."

She laughed. "I don't think I'm comfortable with much of anything, except doing my job to the best of my ability. And right now I'm not doing so well with that, either."

"Because you're sleeping with the subject of your investigation?"

"Who's sleeping?"

He chuckled. "Do you feel guilty?"

"Of course. Don't you?"

"For seducing you? No, I don't feel at all guilty. Like I said, it's the most natural thing in the world for two people who are drawn to each other to enjoy each other's company."

Of course it was, to him. That's why he had so many girlfriends. He probably never said no when he saw something, or someone, he wanted. "My boss would kill me if she knew I was in bed with you right now."

"She won't find out." He lowered his lips to hers in a soft kiss.

No. She wouldn't. This little…affair—because there

was no better word for it—had to be kept under wraps. Which meant it was wrong.

If Constance had any sense she'd push John off her right now and run screaming back to her hotel.

But she didn't want to. She wanted to lie here in his arms, to feel his rough cheek against hers. To enjoy the warm, protective embrace of his strong arms and his satisfied sigh in her ear. In fact she couldn't remember the last time she felt so completely relaxed and content.

She'd spent too many lonely nights in her bedroom. Too many solitary hours dreaming of moments like this. Everyone, including her own parents, thought she had no feelings at all. That she lived to work. That her brain was filled with numbers and spreadsheets and she spent all her spare time doing elaborate computations. But she was just like everyone else, though she hid it well. She craved companionship, romance, love.

Love? Well, she wasn't going to find that with John Fairweather. A tiny stab of regret poked at her heart. She could probably fall in love with him quite easily on the briefest acquaintance. Despite his reputation as a callous, money-orientated playboy, she'd learned he was a man of principle who put those principles into practice every day. The media was so wrong about him. Or maybe they were jealous. She could now grow quite angry thinking about the callous things she'd read about him and the tribe.

"Your heart's beating faster." His gruff voice tickled something deep inside her.

"I was just thinking about how wrong everyone is about you."

He laughed. "Are they, though? I don't lose a single moment of sleep worrying what other people think. I don't care about them at all. Maybe that's what they hate the most."

"I admire your independent spirit."

"Do you?" He sounded surprised. "I thought you were convinced that everything I stand for is wrong."

"That's when I thought you stood for gambling and drinking and cheating people out of their hard-earned money. Now I know those things are means to an end. You wouldn't be in the gambling business at all if it weren't for you trying to build the tribe, would you?"

He watched her for a moment. "I admit, the software business was a lot less complicated." A smile tugged at his mouth. "In fact, I'm planning to get back into it. We've been working on some database software to improve our business operations here and I plan to release a beta version in the next three months or so."

"Maybe it will be more successful than the casino."

"That's hard to imagine, but you never know."

"Most people would be resting on their laurels and enjoying the fruits of their hard work, but you're always trying something new."

"Maybe I'm just restless." He shifted, bumping against her and stirring desire.

"I'm not like that at all." She let out a sigh. "I'm very dull, really. I don't have any desire to set the world on fire. I'm just trying to save enough to buy my own house and move out."

"The world would be a crazy place if everyone was like me. Can you imagine? A blend of different types of people is much more peaceful and productive." He kissed her cheek.

Her skin stirred under his lips. "I suppose you're right." Was that why he liked her—she provided a pleasantly dull contrast to his high-octane self?

"Opposites attract." He squeezed her, and she reveled in the sensation of his big body pressed against hers.

"Apparently so." She caressed the thick muscle of his back. It was hard to believe she lay here in his arms, completely naked. It felt oddly natural. As had their lovemaking. Much more so than the hurried fumblings with the college boyfriend she'd planned to spend the rest of her life with.

Right now she could easily imagine herself and John having an actual relationship. Surely they were already, to a certain extent? Except that she was here to investigate his company for improprieties and she'd probably be fired if anyone found out about this.

"What's the matter?" He must have heard her breathing quicken.

"I can't believe we're in bed together."

He paused, and stroked her shoulder. "Nothing happens by accident."

"No? I didn't plan this and I don't think you did, either."

His chest rumbled with a chuckle. "You're right. But we can both be discreet."

She wasn't sure if it was a question or a command. Either way it hurt. Which it shouldn't have, because she certainly didn't want him telling anyone. "Of course."

No promises. No expectations.

No future.

She'd fallen into his arms knowing this was crazy, but she hadn't been able to help herself. Too many nights in her lonely bedroom, wondering if a man would ever hold her again. Too many dreams that hadn't come true. The last few years of loneliness had apparently left her in a desperate and dangerous condition and brought her here into John Fairweather's bed.

"We're not entirely opposites, you know." John kissed her cheek softly.

"No? How are we similar?"

"We're both stubborn and determined."

"I think I'm going to take that as an insult. I was raised to be obedient and compliant." She raised a brow.

"Well, something went wrong." He winked, and the sparkle of humor in his eyes did something strange to her belly. "Because I can tell you make up your own mind about everything."

"What makes you say that?"

"You're here, aren't you? In my arms." He squeezed her gently, and her heart tripped a little.

"I'm not sure my mind was involved in this at all. I suspect other, less intellectual parts of my body were involved."

His chest rocked with laughter. "To a certain extent, yes, but you're here and thinking right now and I don't notice you running for the door."

"Trust me, I'm thinking about running for the door." She glanced at it, as if to make sure the way was clear.

"Guess I'll have to keep a tight hold on you, then." His arms circled her completely, which felt fabulous. She didn't want to move from their embrace. "Because I don't want you to go."

"I'm sure you'd have no trouble finding someone to take my place here." She regretted the jealous-sounding words the moment they came out.

"I'm not at all interested in anyone else. I bet you'd be surprised by how long it's been since I slept with a woman."

"Really?" Her own curiosity embarrassed her.

"I won't lie. I sowed some wild oats when I was younger, especially after my marriage fell apart. I'd been a true romantic up until then and I couldn't believe that the forever she'd promised me had turned out to be less than a year. I probably got revenge on myself more than anyone else. I was mad at myself for trusting her."

"I was mad at myself for trusting in my ex. And he didn't even cheat on me. At least not that I know of."

"It's hard to put your faith in other people once you've been let down. Is that why you haven't been serious with anyone else?"

She paused, not wanting to tell the truth. But she wasn't really cut out for fibbing. "No one's even asked me out since then."

"In five or six years?" His incredulity made her bite her lip.

"Nope. Not once." Maybe that explained why she'd leaped so willingly into John's entirely unsuitable arms.

"That's insane. You are kind of intimidating, though. It probably takes someone as obnoxious as me to be arrogant enough to try."

"Intimidating? I think of myself as being humble and unassuming."

His deep belly laugh rocked her. "You can think of yourself that way all you want. The truth is you're a demanding and rather judgmental woman who probably scares the pants off most men."

"Oh." She frowned. "That doesn't sound good."

"I like it." His grin warmed her. "If you have high expectations of yourself, you should have them of others, too. I know I do."

"Hmm. Now that you put it like that, it doesn't seem so bad." Her head rested on his bicep, which was more comfortable than the softest pillow. "I suppose you're right that a lot of people find me unapproachable. I turn down so many lunch invitations and weekend plans from coworkers that people rarely invite me anywhere anymore."

"Why do you turn them down?"

"I think they're silly. I go to the office to work, not socialize."

"See? You are unapproachable." His grin revealed those even white teeth. "They're right to be afraid. What about your church? You said your family is religious. Didn't you meet anyone there?"

"Not anyone I was interested in."

"So you're also picky." He stroked a tendril of hair off her cheek.

"Shouldn't I be? What's the point of pretending you like someone when you don't?"

"None whatsoever." He grinned. "I guess that means you like me."

"I wouldn't say that," she teased. Why was he so easy to talk to? "But apparently I am attracted to you."

"And I'm attracted to you." His gentle kiss made her lips tingle. "There's some serious chemistry between us."

There was. It snapped in the air and sensitized her skin where their bodies touched. Pheromones. Mysterious substances that science barely understood, which coaxed humans into situations any sane person would avoid. Like lying cheek to cheek with the man whose business you were investigating.

"It's a shame chemistry doesn't last and that after a while you have to actually be compatible and get along." She wanted to let him know she didn't expect this crazy fling to go anywhere. Or maybe she just wanted to reject him before he could reject her.

"You have to start somewhere." He kissed her again. She wished he'd stop doing that! It stirred all kinds of sensations deep in her belly. Sensations that made her wish he were inside her again. What kind of woman had he turned her into? "How do you know we're not perfectly compatible?"

"Us? That's funny." She didn't want him to think his words had any effect on her, but they did. They were both good with numbers. Both hardworking and determined. She would have once said that he was a notorious playboy and she was the exact opposite, but her current position here in his arms proved that she wasn't so entirely different from him when the opportunity for romance presented itself.

Romance? Where had that word come from? There wasn't anything terribly romantic about their relationship so far. Romance was flirtation and candlelit dinners and hopeful conversations. They'd gone straight from zero to sixty with very little preamble.

She'd better not let herself start thinking that this was a romance, or she was likely to end up with a broken heart.

"I don't think it's so funny at all. My grandparents are very different and they've been together for almost fifty years. He was wild and considered himself a beatnik. He wrote terrible poetry and played the trumpet, and he was getting ready to run away to New York and become a jazz musician when he met my grandmother while delivering milk to a local depot. She'd just moved here with her family from Minnesota and had never dated or kissed a boy in her life. She was training to become a schoolteacher and spent her evenings reading and knitting. He charmed her and she tamed him and they've been together ever since."

"Oh." A dangerous charmer and a good girl. Sounded familiar.

"He was very good-looking. She always said that she never stood a chance against him."

"Have they been happy?" She was genuinely curious. People always talked about those opposites-attract relationships, but she didn't know how often they really worked out.

"Very. They've had their ups and downs, of course. My mom—the one who gave birth to me—was even wilder than my grandfather when he was young, and it ended up killing her. Her death put a strain on their relationship, as a child's death often does. My grandmother blamed my grandfather for not being stricter with her, and he blamed her for not being more accepting. He felt that if my mom had still lived at home maybe she wouldn't have gone out drinking and driving on the night she died."

"If things were different, maybe you wouldn't have been born." She stroked the wrinkle that had formed between his brows. "So much of life depends on chance."

She'd never had that thought before. She was a planner, and unapologetic about it. She'd had her whole life mapped out from about age eleven: she'd intended to meet and marry a nice, appropriate spouse during college, then work for several years to build their finances and buy a house before they started a family. She'd planned her career in accounting and made sure to keep abreast of all developments in the field so she'd always have in-demand skills. When her marriage plans had derailed, she'd continued full speed ahead with the other elements of her life blueprint, assuming that everything would slot into place eventually, even if not on her anticipated schedule. She hadn't spent a single moment thinking about the rather scary mechanics of chance.

"You're right. All the hard work in the world won't get you anywhere without at least a dash of luck, too. I can't tell you how many times the fate of this casino, even the whole tribe, rested on a decision made by strangers who didn't have any real stake in the outcome. There were certainly enough people hoping that it wouldn't happen. And plenty that would like to shut us down right now."

"Do you think that's what they would do if I found

that you were actually cooking your books?" Her stomach clenched. She could probably wreak havoc on John's entire existence.

"I don't doubt that they'd try. Believe me, it makes it easy to stay honest."

"Why are so many people opposed to the casino?"

"Well, there are the people who are against it for the same reasons as you." He touched her lips with a finger. "You know, gambling, drinking, people wasting time having fun. But I suspect even more of them are just jealous. They think we're getting away with something. Enjoying some benefit that they can't have because they're not Indian. No one likes to feel excluded."

"I suppose you're right, but isn't it supposed to be a reparation of sorts for past injustices?"

"I think some people see it that way, especially people who are trying to justify their gambling losses as a charitable donation." He winked. "But really it's just a recognition of past treaties, allowing us sovereignty over our own lands and people. So many of these agreements were ignored or broken over the centuries, and now things are changing. There's no element of payback in it. If anything you'd think Americans would be glad that we're finally getting with the program and embracing the complicated laws and unbridled capitalism that have made this country so powerful and influential."

John was so charming it was hard to imagine anyone disagreeing with him once they'd talked to him face-to-face. "So basically, you're just trying to fit in."

"Exactly." His wicked grin made her smile in response. And kiss him. She couldn't help herself. Something about him had totally undermined her defenses. He kissed her back. It was warm and invigorating, and soon he had to reach for another condom.

Bliss filled her as John entered her again, banishing the years of loneliness and wanting. Her body blossomed under his affectionate caresses, and her inhibitions faded away as their intimacy deepened. Was it really this easy to find happiness with another person?

She drifted off to sleep in his calm embrace, feeling utterly at peace with the world. Right now she could easily imagine herself and John as a couple, sharing their days and nights, their thoughts, their dreams.

Could this taste of paradise turn into her real life?

Seven

Constance awoke with a jolt. Sunlight streamed through a crack in the curtains, announcing that the day was well under way.

John was gone, his side of the bed rumpled and empty.

She blinked, trying to read her watch. Ten-fifteen? She'd slept half the morning away. Why hadn't John woken her? She clutched the covers around her, trying to cover her nakedness, even though she seemed to be alone in here. Where were her clothes? She barely remembered taking them off. They were probably on the floor somewhere.

She spotted them neatly draped over a chair on the far side of the room. John must have picked them up this morning. How embarrassing! She lay here sleeping while he was up and about. Right now he was probably in a meeting or doing his daily perusal of the previous night's takings, and she was just waking up from a sensual dream.

She sprang out of bed and hurried across the room, then tried to tug her clothes on so fast it was more difficult than if she'd taken her time. She kept glancing about the room as if someone was watching. She checked her phone and saw several messages, mostly from work. There was no way she could even listen to them, never mind return the calls, while standing in John Fairweather's bedroom!

Her suit was wrinkled, probably from lying in a heap

all night. She couldn't manage to get her hair to cooperate either. She certainly hoped she could get out of here without running into anyone. And she had to drive all the way to her hotel and back before she could even get to work.

She tried to use the elevator that opened right into the suite, but she couldn't get the door to open. It required some kind of code she didn't know. Cringing with embarrassment, she cracked open the door that led into a hotel hallway. A cleaner's cart sat two doors down. She'd better get out of here before they wandered in with the vacuum. Glancing around and scurrying like a cartoon character, she darted for the public elevators at the far end of the hall.

Constance pressed the button and gritted her teeth with impatience. She couldn't remember a single occasion in her life before now that she'd needed to skulk about and conceal her shockingly inappropriate activities.

Naturally the elevator opened right into the elegant main lobby, which was unusually well populated for a weekday morning. Worse yet, she could see John giving a television interview in front of the decorative mural on the far side of the room. The cameraman with his bulky mike and the aggressively tanned male reporter almost blocked her way to the main exit, and she hesitated for a minute to plan her escape.

John hadn't seen her yet and she wanted to make sure he didn't. She didn't want him to smile and wave or otherwise draw attention to her.

"…investigated by the Bureau of Indian Affairs on suspicion of fraud…" The reporter's words assaulted her ears as she got closer. Little did they know the BIA's official investigator was trying to sneak past them wearing yesterday's underwear, with John Fairweather's DNA licked into its fabric.

John was talking now, looking directly at the reporter.

She seized her chance to break for the door, avoiding his gaze as she strode across the lobby, heels clicking. Luckily the camera was facing the other way so she wouldn't be caught on tape making her escape.

She burst out into blinding sunlight with her adrenaline pounding and fumbled for her car keys, desperate to escape before anyone saw her or tried to talk to her.

Back in her hotel room, after showering and washing away John's passionate touch, Constance called the office. "Nicola Moore of the BIA called about six times for you," Lynn whispered into the phone. "She's getting hysterical. Where have you been? There's been some kind of exposé article published about the New Dawn casino and she wants to know if it's true."

That would explain the TV reporter in the lobby. "What does it say?"

"The usual stuff, how they've grown too big too fast and it can't be legit."

"That's hardly a news story."

"There's some stuff about his uncle. I forget the guy's name but apparently he has a colorful past. Money laundering or something similar."

Constance frowned. John's uncle Don? She didn't like the guy much. He gave off a sleazebag vibe. "Everything's still checking out fine. They're very profitable because there are people here throwing their money away twenty-four hours a day."

"Are you sure you're not blinded to iniquity by John Fairweather's dazzling smile?"

"Of course I'm sure," she retorted. "Sorry. Didn't mean to sound so snappy." What a shame she couldn't explain why she hadn't gotten too much sleep last night. "I'm starting to get annoyed with all the negative opinions that keep cropping up, when I can't find any justification for them. I can't help but think people are just jealous and resent the tribe's success. Why shouldn't they have some prosperity for a change? They've been kicked around since the 1600s. It's about time they got to enjoy life a bit. I don't know why people get so upset that they're making money."

"Maybe because they don't pay taxes on it?"

"Actually, they do pay some taxes. It was built into their agreements with the state. And they provide employment in an otherwise depressed area. I've totally revised my opinion of the place and I wish everyone else would do the same."

"You sound very passionate."

Passionate? What an odd choice of word. She'd certainly experienced passion last night. It dwarfed her most ambitious daydreams. "Nonsense. I'm entirely practical. I can't see why it's okay for corporations to make money hand over fist and interpret laws to meet their needs, but not tribes. This is America. We love money and profits. You and I wouldn't have a job without them!"

Lynn laughed. "So true. Anyway, you'd better call Ms. Moore. She's getting on my nerves."

"Will do. Hopefully I'll be home in a day or two." A twinge of sadness shot through her. Once she left she probably wouldn't ever see John again. Which would make last night's tryst a one-night stand. Shame swept over her in a hot tide. She'd fallen so easily into his arms. Worse yet, she craved the feel of his arms around her right now. Of his hot kisses claiming her mouth, the powerful sensation of him moving inside her.

"Are you still there?" Lynn asked.

"Yes. Yes. Just going over some notes." Now she was lying. What next? If anyone found out that she'd had an affair with the man whose business she was supposed to be investigating, she'd be fired. She'd probably lose her accreditation and would never be able to find another job in the field.

"They must be pretty interesting notes. And you're missing some exciting happenings here at Creighton Waterman. Someone walked in on Lacey, the new trainee, getting up close and personal with Aaron Whitlow."

"What?" Mr. Whitlow was the straitlaced senior executive who gave them their annual reviews. "He must be twice her age. Maybe even three times!"

"I know. Everyone is freaking out. Worse yet, the person who saw them was Leah, the head of personnel."

"Did Lacey get fired?"

"She did. It makes me mad. Why does she have to leave? Why not him?"

"He's in a position of power."

"That's hardly fair. She should file a sexual harassment lawsuit. But she didn't want to. She said it was consensual. She was so upset, crying and red faced. I think she really cared about him."

Constance swallowed. "It is odd that relationships at work are so taboo. That is where most of us spend our time, after all."

"It's because we're supposed to behave like robots who only care about doing our jobs. Not actual people with feelings. Whitlow's acting more robotic than ever, of course. Muttering orders under his breath, looking down his snooty nose at people. It does make me laugh to picture him fooling around with a much younger woman. Apparently she was sitting on his desk with her skirt up around her waist!"

"Yikes." Constance wanted to cringe. Desire. The same thing that had lured her irresistibly into John's encouraging arms. When examined in the cold light of day, it was embarrassing and inappropriate. What would Lynn—or anyone—say if they could have seen her last night, writhing with pleasure in John's bed?

"The scandal has certainly livened things up around here, let me tell you. You're missing all the fun."

"You know I hate gossip." She tried to stay out of the petty squabbles around the watercooler.

"I'll certainly never see Whitlow in the same light again, that's for sure."

"Isn't he a widower? Maybe he was lonely." Great. Now she was defending a man who'd fooled around with a much younger employee. Of course as a transgressor herself, she could sympathize with him in a way she'd never have been able to imagine even a week ago.

Maybe this whole experience was part of her journey toward greater compassion and understanding. It was pretty humbling, all right. "I have another call coming in."

"All right. Call Nicola Moore at the BIA before she comes down there looking for you."

"Will do." She hung up and grabbed the other call, adrenaline firing because she could see it was John.

"Good morning, gorgeous."

Heat rose up from her chest. "Good morning yourself. I can't believe you let me sleep in like that. I'm so embarrassed."

"You looked so peaceful that I didn't want to disturb you. I had to get up for a media interview."

"I saw you doing it." She didn't want to say what she'd heard about the accusations against his uncle. It didn't seem appropriate given their professional relationship. Still, she wanted to hear how he'd describe it. "What were they asking you about?"

He paused for a moment. "Nothing very interesting. The usual stuff."

So he was going to hide it from her. Surely he'd know she could see it on the news or read it on the internet? "I suppose they're often hoping to stir up a story. Speaking of which, there's a sex scandal going on at my office right now. If they had any idea what I was up to I'd be out on my ear."

"I won't tell them. It's none of their business."

"I suppose not. You're not sleeping with me to cloud my judgment, are you?" She said it in jest, but once the words were out she realized she wasn't entirely kidding.

He laughed. "If I was, would it be working?"

"Of course not. I have tremendous integrity." She was trying to convince herself as much as him.

"Tremendous, huh? That is impressive. And I'd expect nothing less of you. Seriously, though, you should probably know that the media has got a wild hair about my uncle Don. I'm sure it will blow over soon, but they're trying to find him guilty of something, so you may as well hear it from me and not from the BIA."

"What do they think he's done?"

"I don't know. I don't think they care. Anything they can cook up will do. Want to get together for lunch? It's almost noon."

"Noon?" She gulped. "I can't. I'm not even at the casino. I'm still at my hotel getting changed. I need to focus completely on work for the rest of the day."

"And the night?"

"And the night." She blinked. No sense giving him a chance to make plans that were going to rope her even deeper into this impossible affair. One night with him had been intoxicating enough. Another and she might never regain her sanity. "I really need to concentrate on my work. Last night was…"

"Wonderful."

"Yes, it was." She had to admit it. "But I'm here to do a job." *And we both know this is going nowhere.*

"That's true, but I want to make sure you don't work too fast. I don't want to lose you any sooner than I have to."

So he could easily admit that their affair had a built-in end. The little pang of sorrow surprised her. "I do have other projects I need to get back to."

"It's a shame your office isn't local. Why would they hire someone from Ohio to investigate a casino in Massachusetts?"

"I think they do that to encourage impartiality. Since I'm not local, I have no stake in building or maintaining a relationship with the New Dawn casino."

"Just with its owner." His voice was silky and seductive.

"That was an accident."

"A very happy one."

"As long as no one finds out about it." And really, how happy could it be when she'd be home alone in a few days, lonely as ever?

"Concealment does not come naturally to me." She heard frustration in his voice. "In fact, I'm hating this need for secrecy. I much prefer to be frank and up front in my dealings with everyone."

"But you do understand that my job and my reputation depend on keeping this secret?" Panic gripped her quietly.

"Believe me. I do. And I hold myself entirely responsible for the delicate predicament we find ourselves in." He paused, and the silence hummed for a moment. "Can I come over to your hotel?"

She sucked in a breath as visions of John's large form in her tiny hotel room crowded her imagination. "No. I really have to work."

"Bummer." He sounded so disappointed that she had to smile.

"I have more calls to return. I'll see you at the office."

"I'll make sure of it." She could hear the smile in his voice, and it made her chest ache a little. She was really going to miss John. Which was ridiculous. She'd only known him a few days and in many ways he was the most infuriating man she'd ever met.

Yet she still liked him so much. And she liked that he'd told her about the suspicions regarding his uncle. As she dialed the number for Nicola Moore at the BIA, she was pretty sure she'd be hearing Don's name again.

She was right. Nicola immediately launched into a tirade against him.

"Don Fairweather has been previously investigated for money laundering."

"Was he convicted?" Constance glanced around her room to see if there was anything else she needed to bring to the office. It crossed her mind that she could bring a change of underwear. She told her mind to get back to business.

"No. It went to trial but the jury apparently didn't find the prosecutor's evidence convincing enough."

"Oh. So he was found innocent."

"Or they just didn't look hard enough. I want you to make sure to look in places where no one would expect. There was a case recently at another casino where three of the workers managed to pocket hundreds of thousands of dollars by creating fraudulent receipts from the slot machines to bring to the cashiers. One of them created the receipts, one was the runner between the slot machines and the tills, and the other was the cashier. As you can imagine, it was a neat little racket for a while."

"How did the casino figure out what was going on?"

"Keen observation."

"You do realize that I'm a forensic accountant and not

a private detective?" She had been told she was doing a routine audit of their books. Now that she was here, it appeared that her contact had definite suspicions, or at least was trying to plant some in her mind. That didn't sit too well with Constance when she needed to stay objective.

"Indeed, Ms. Allen, we're well aware of that. We simply expect you to find whether the paperwork is truly reflective of the casino's activities."

"I understand. I'll look into every avenue I can think of."

She hung up and found herself glancing at her underwear drawer again. What if she packed a bag with extra panties and a whole new outfit so she didn't have to come back to the hotel at all?

The blunt thought shocked her. What would her parents think if they knew what she was doing? They'd issued stern warnings about stepping foot inside such a den of iniquity, and now she was having a sexual affair with a man she wasn't even in a relationship with.

She'd never have slept with her ex-boyfriend if she hadn't been utterly convinced that one day—soon—they'd be man and wife. But Phil did not have the looks or the charm of John Fairweather.

No. She couldn't bring a change of clothes. That would be admitting that she planned to do something inappropriate. If something happened spontaneously, that was different. Going into the New Dawn casino with a deliberate intention to have sex with the man she was investigating seemed far more dangerous and inappropriate. Premeditation, after all, was often the difference between manslaughter and murder.

An unplanned crime—or night—of passion was a little different.

She jumped when the phone rang, as if the person calling could read her thoughts.

And maybe they could. "Hi, Mom."

"Hello, sweetheart, are you busy?"

"Yes, very, I'm afraid." She didn't want to get into a conversation that might involve little white lies.

"How long are they going to keep you out there in Massachusetts? It's the church picnic this weekend and I promised you'd run the till. Sally is baking two hundred cupcakes to raise money for the mission in Kenya."

It was Thursday. The thought that in two days she could be back in Ohio, miles away from John, chilled her. "I don't know if I'll be back. I thought I would be, but it keeps getting more complicated. I'm sure you can run the till." She felt a bit guilty. She usually enjoyed helping out at these events. It was fun to see people coming together for a good cause. Now all she could seem to think about was herself and the affair she shouldn't be having.

"I already promised to run the lemonade stand. I suppose Sally's daughter can manage, though. I do wish you were back home. I worry about you being so far away and with the wrong sort of people."

"There's nothing to worry about. They're all quite normal, really. It's a business like any other." She glanced at her face in the mirror, wondering if her nose was getting longer. There was nothing normal about John Fairweather. He was larger than life in every possible way.

"I know people visit casinos of their own free will, but profits from gambling just seem like the wages of sin."

"They're wages like any others when you look at the account books, and that's all I'm here to do. How's Dad doing? Is he taking that new medication the doctor gave him?" Her father's cholesterol had tested high recently. She was so used to taking care of them. If anything, they'd grown even more dependent on her since she moved back home from college, and she wondered how they'd manage without her if she did move out. Especially if she moved away to a different state.

Not that she should even be thinking along those lines since it was very unlikely to happen.

"Your dad is taking his medicine, but he won't stop putting mayonnaise on everything. You'll have to talk some sense into him when you come home. It's odd here without you. The house feels empty and there's no one to do the dishes after dinner."

She had to smile. "I miss you, too. I'm still not sure when I'll be home, but hopefully by next week."

They wished each other goodbye and Constance hung up, then sighed, thinking about the endless nights of putting dishes into the machine and watching alarmist news shows that stretched ahead of her like a lonely highway. Then she shoved her phone in her pocket and headed out the door.

Without a change of underwear.

Constance spent the afternoon stalking the cashiers and wandering around the game rooms. Luckily for her, the New Dawn did not have any kind of middlemen between the customers and the cashiers. Everyone had to bring their own chips to the cashier to turn them into money.

Nothing untoward seemed to be happening at the tables, either. John had told her that the dealers were all experienced professionals, mostly from Atlantic City or Vegas, though he was hoping to train some local people soon.

She walked among the tables watching the customers gamble. People won money. Others lost money. Some won it then lost it. There was nothing that looked fishy. She paused at a roulette table, and watched the croupier spin the wheel.

"Hello, gorgeous." That deep, rich voice in her ear sent a shiver of warm lust to her core.

She resisted the urge to spin around and instead turned very slowly to face John. A smile was already creeping across her face and she worked hard not to let it get too goofy. "Good afternoon, Mr. Fairweather."

"I see you're examining our operations again with that eagle eye of yours. Do you like what you see?"

"Like it? Not so much. I'm still not a fan of gambling." She smiled primly. His own easy expression didn't budge. "And I really should keep my findings confidential at this point, don't you think?"

Now she did see a flicker of surprise in his eyes. "What findings?"

"Any findings I should happen to make." She attempted an air of sphinxlike calm. "I'm not saying I've found anything unusual."

"But you're not saying you haven't." He frowned. "You will tell me if you find anything, won't you? I'd be damn surprised, but I'd want to know right up front."

She hesitated. "My first responsibility is to my client."

"The BIA."

"I'd consider it a personal favor if you'd tell me about anything you find first." His face was now deadly serious.

"I don't think I'm in a position to offer personal favors. I'm here to do a job." This was getting awkward. He obviously thought she'd found something unexpected in the books that she didn't want him to know about it. Still, if she did, she should keep it secret while she investigated, so the casino wouldn't have a chance to cover it all up before she reported back to her client.

She glanced up and saw his uncle Don throw down some chips at a distant roulette table.

"I have no desire to interfere with your performance on the job you've been hired to do. You know that. But honestly, if you find anything amiss, I'd be as keen to know about it as anyone else." His earnest expression preyed on her emotions.

"I'll tell you if I find anything," she whispered. "I really do believe you want everything to be aboveboard. But so far, so good." She smiled. "Though I shouldn't be telling you that."

In the distance, Don swiped up a fistful of chips from the table with a smile and shoved them in his pocket. Darius, who managed the cashiers, had told her that Don gambled. She supposed there was nothing illegal in it. Or was there? This was a perfect instance of where she needed to do her own research rather than asking John about it.

Don Fairweather was now heading toward them, a confident smile on his rather wrinkled face. Constance braced herself. She'd better be on alert to see if she could pick up any information to substantiate or debunk the rumors about him.

"Consorting with the enemy, eh, John?" Don turned to her and winked. "You know I'm just kidding. We welcome the scrutiny of the BIA and all their friends in the media. Life would be dull if everyone just let us go about our business."

"My contact mentioned money-laundering charges against you." She looked at Don and came right out with it. She wanted to hear if his answer would be any less evasive and uninformative than John's. And something about Don's nonchalant attitude pushed her buttons and she wanted to see how he reacted under pressure.

"Load of bull. I used to own a chain of dry cleaners.

We were laundering shirts, not money." His grin challenged her to argue. "As you probably know, they didn't find enough evidence to convict me of anything."

"Don was found not guilty," John cut in. "By a jury of his peers."

"Not that I have any true peers, of course."

"Don is by far the most arrogant of the Fairweathers." John shot a wry glance at Constance.

"Which is saying quite a bit with you around," Don retorted with a crinkly smile. "We keep each other on our toes."

"That we do. One of my favorite things about the New Dawn is that I get to work with family every day." John wrapped his arm around Don. "Sometimes it's a challenge, but maybe that's why I enjoy it so much."

"You'd be bored if life was too easy. And neither of us knew there were so many of us. Some of them barely even knew they had Indian ancestry until John got them excited about this place. Now the kids are begging him to dig up some old songs and dances so they can compete in the big powwows."

John shook his head. "Easier said than done. I vote that they just make up their own. Why does our culture have to be old and historic? Why can't it be fresh and new?"

"Won't win any prizes with that. The judges are traditional. We already have strikes against us because we don't look like most people's idea of an Indian."

"Then people need to change their perceptions, don't they, Constance."

"I suppose they do." How did he always charm her into agreeing with him? She really didn't have an opinion of any kind on the matter. She did think it was sweet how John obviously worked hard to create a sense of community, and was paying a fortune to academics to dig up the

Nissequot tribe's shared history. "And if anyone can do that, it's you."

She blushed, realizing that she'd just praised him in front of his uncle. Don's eyebrows rose a tad. Did he suspect anything between her and John? That would be disastrous. Don Fairweather was something of a loose cannon, aside from his dubious reputation. "I really must get back to the offices."

"I'll ride up with you." John's low voice gave the innocent offer a suggestive tone.

"Actually, I need to get something from my car first." She didn't want Don to see them disappearing together.

John wouldn't tell Don about their liaison, would he? She really didn't know. Don was his uncle and they were obviously close. She reminded herself that she barely knew John at all. She nodded to them primly and hustled toward the lobby. She didn't actually need anything from her car but she'd fiddle around in there for a minute or so. Anything to get away from John's dark, seductive gaze.

She futzed around with her bag on the passenger seat for a moment, then pulled it out and closed the car door. She turned toward the casino and gasped when she found John right in front of her.

"I'm not letting you sneak off."

"I wasn't trying to sneak off." She lifted her chin. "I was getting my phone charger."

"Oh." His smile suggested that he knew it was a ruse. "You looked like you were running away from something."

"Your uncle Don doesn't know about...us, does he?"

John shrugged. "I haven't told him anything. Even if he figured it out, he'd be discreet. He's got enough skeletons in his own closet that he's not going to throw open the door to anyone else's."

Why was that not at all reassuring? "I don't think we should walk back in together."

"Why not?" He looked a little put out. "I'm the CEO of the place. I hardly think it's inappropriate of me to escort the forensic accountant up to the offices." He leaned in and whispered in her ear, "Even if I do know how she looks without her clothes on."

Constance sucked in a breath. Heat flushed her entire body and she wasn't sure if it was embarrassment or lust. It didn't really matter. Neither was at all helpful right now.

"You're incorrigible." Luckily there was no one else around.

"I know. It's an affliction. Do you think you can cure me?"

"I doubt it. I also have no intention of trying." She shifted her bag higher on her shoulder. "And I have work to do."

"Let's go." He led the way, then waited for her to catch up so they could enter the lobby together. She held her chin high, self-conscious as she walked with him through the public space. The staff all knew who she was by now. Did they suspect anything? She felt so different than she had even yesterday, it was hard to imagine that she could still look the same from the outside.

When they reached the office, John ushered her in, then followed her and closed the door. She heard the lock click and felt his arm reach around her waist and her backside crushed up against his hard form.

"Constance, you're making me crazy."

She tried to hide her smile. "Maybe you were crazy already."

"I don't know what you've done to me."

"I can't imagine that I've done anything." His big

hand splayed over her belly, where all kinds of sensations churned. "I'm just trying to do my job."

"And I keep distracting you." His lips brushed her neck and heat flickered low inside her.

"Yes. Very much so."

"I think you needed some distraction." His low voice sent a rumble of desire to her toes.

"So I'll be unable to properly investigate your books? You'll make me think you're trying to hide something."

"Maybe there is something I'm trying to hide." His voice contained more than a hint of suggestion, and she felt his erection jostle against her. She was slightly appalled by how arousing that was. What had happened to her since she met John Fairweather? It was as though a switch had turned on inside her. Now energy coursed through her veins whenever she was around him. Her mind strayed in previously forbidden directions and her body ached to do all kinds of things that she knew were wrong.

"What are we doing?" she asked in a half whisper.

His mouth played below her ear, heating her skin. "I think I'm kissing your neck."

"This is foolish."

"I won't argue with you." He went back to kissing her neck. Her nipples were starting to tingle.

"So shouldn't we stop?"

His mouth worked its way up to her ear and he nibbled softly on her earlobe, which sent a surprising surge of sensation to her core. "Definitely not."

He spun her around and kissed her full on the mouth. Her lips parted to welcome him and she felt her arms wrap enthusiastically around him without her permission. They kissed for a solid ten minutes, until she was in a thoroughly befuddled state. Then he excused himself with a polite nod and left her all alone, in a state of agonizing arousal, with nothing but ledger books for company.

She stared at the door. What a nerve! Now he had her all worked up and he'd waltzed off? He hadn't even said where he was going or when he'd be back. How could she work now that he'd left her with blood pounding in every part of her body other than her brain?

She glanced at her watch and saw that it was nearly seven o'clock. She'd wasted most of the afternoon seeing nothing downstairs. Except for Don Fairweather swiping those chips off the table.

Of course she'd seen him put chips down to bet, so nothing truly suspicious had happened, but wasn't it rather a conflict of interest for him to gamble in the tribe's own casino? He wasn't involved in the day-to-day operations on the floor. He did publicity and booked the bands, but he was obviously fairly intimate with all the other workers. She'd noticed his jovial exchanges with at least half a dozen employees on the floor. Which was hardly proof of wrongdoing.

She heaved a sigh of relief to find that thinking about Don helped dissipate the fog of passion that John had left her in. She turned to the computer and had a look through the entries from a year ago. There was no point in looking at new data, since everyone knew she was here so any would-be crooks would be on their best behavior. As usual everything seemed to add up.

Often with forensic accounting she wasn't looking for overt proof of wrongdoing. White-collar criminals were usually smart and knew how to cover their tracks. She had to look closely to find tiny holes or data that was just a little different from the norm. Then she at least had a clue for somewhere to stick in her shovel and start digging. So far she'd had no luck. Every time she'd thought she found an interesting anomaly, it had turned out to be a dead end.

On instinct she decided to look for internal records of tribal members gambling. They were easy enough to find in the casino databases, which were very well organized and clearly labeled, probably by John himself. Don wasn't the only member who gambled, but he was by far the heaviest gambler. Someone called Mona Lester had some losses, and an Anna Martin had some small winnings, but Don had won more than fifty thousand dollars last year. Could he be up to something, or was he just lucky?

The door clicked open and John appeared again. She closed the spreadsheet window with a flash of guilt. Which was ridiculous. He knew she was here to dig into the files, so she was hardly going behind his back. Still, it felt wrong to kiss a man then go looking for fraud in his own computer system.

One more reason why this whole affair was a big mistake.

He closed the door behind him and leaned against it. His sleek dark suit did nothing to conceal the raw masculinity of his body. Especially not now that she'd seen it naked. "You're coming to my house for dinner."

"You mean your suite." Her response seemed easier than choosing to accept or decline his invitation. Not an invitation, really. More of a command.

"No, I mean my house. I'm just living in the suite while I renovate the old farmhouse. The kitchen's finished, so I have everything I need to make dinner for you."

"You can cook?"

"Absolutely."

She blinked, not sure what to believe. Was there anything he couldn't do? "I can't really say no, then, can I?"

"Of course not." He offered a hand to help her from her seat behind the desk.

She must be out of her mind. But, he could cook? That was pretty irresistible. And she could go back to her hotel right after dinner. "I'll drive in my car." Then she could take off any time she wanted.

"Sure. You can follow me."

The road to his house was long and winding, an old farm road that led past his grandparents' new house and through fields dotted with grazing cattle. Gnarled apple trees lined the drive and framed the austere form of John's white farmhouse. A new cedar-shake roof gleamed gold in the lowering sun and stickers still ornamented the shiny new windows. A Dumpster filled with construction debris and a cement mixer were among the signs that a major renovation was still in progress.

"We stripped it right back to the old post-and-beam framing, and added stud walls and insulation. There's almost nothing left of the original house, but it's starting to look like it used to in its heyday. All the major work is done. Now they're reinstalling the original woodwork. I should be back living here in a month or so."

"It looks lovely." She was surprised that a notorious bachelor like John would even want a big old house when he could be catered to by staff at his own luxury hotel.

"It's coming together really well. I can't wait to move in. I'm going to get a dog."

"What kind?"

"I don't know yet. Something big. And cute. I'll adopt it from a shelter."

"That's a great idea. I've always wanted a dog."

"Why don't you get one?"

"I need to move out of my parents' house first. My mom doesn't like them."

He nodded. He must think it pathetic that she still lived at home with her parents at age twenty-seven. She needed to put moving out at the top of her goals for the coming year.

They walked up solid stone steps to the front door, which was still stripped bare of paint. John opened it and ushered her in. She glanced around his inner sanctum, taking in all the authentic details he'd had lovingly preserved.

"This house was built in 1837 by one of my ancestors. He and his sons handcrafted a lot of the woodwork themselves."

She stroked a turned cherry bannister. "This must have been quite a labor of love before power tools became common."

"All the more reason to restore it to its original beauty." He led her into a bright kitchen with ivory cabinets and big center island. "Do you like shrimp?"

"Love it."

"Good, because I've had it marinating since this morning."

"You knew you were going to ask me over?"

"Of course."

His arrogance should have been annoying. "What if I said I didn't like shrimp? Or I was allergic."

He shot her a cheeky smile. "I've got some chicken prepared as well."

"You're ready for anything, aren't you?"

"I try to be."

He grilled the shrimp and some corn on the cob outdoors, and they ate it with an elaborate salad they made together of feta cheese and pear tossed with spring greens. The million-dollar view from his bluestone patio looked over pastures and rolling wooded hills. Constance couldn't remember a time she'd been anywhere so beautiful. Her own drab environs in an unprepossessing part of Cleveland were depressing by comparison. Yet soon she'd be back there, looking off the back porch over the weedy garden, remembering this delicious dinner and her dangerously charming host.

Dark clouds were gathering along the horizon as the sun disappeared behind the trees. Raindrops spotted the patio as they brought the plates back inside, and by the time they loaded them in the dishwasher, rain was pounding on the darkened windows.

While John brewed the fresh-ground coffee, thunderclaps boomed overhead. "You'd better wait until this stops." Anticipation shimmered in his gaze.

She reached into her bag. "Let me check the satellite images on my phone to see how big the storm looks."

"I already did. It's going to continue all night."

Eight

Had John somehow planned this storm along with everything else about this evening? He seemed so vastly in control of his life and nearly everyone else's that it might just be possible. She wasn't a pawn here. She had free will. "I'm sure I can drive in it."

"I won't allow it." He towered over her in the dimly lit kitchen.

"What makes you think you can allow it or not allow it? You're not my boss."

"But I am concerned about your safety. These back roads can wash out in this kind of storm. Some of the worst messes I see as a volunteer firefighter are one-car accidents where someone tried to drive at night in the wrong weather. It's too hard to see the road when you're out in the woods in rainy darkness."

"I suppose you do have a point," she muttered. "But I can't sleep with you."

"I believe we've passed that milestone already."

"I know, but that was a one-time, spur-of-the-moment thing. If I stay over again…"

"It'll mean you actually like me." His teeth flashed in a wicked grin.

She had no idea how to respond to that. Especially since

it was true. "I don't know why I like you. You're insufferably arrogant."

"You find that refreshing because you're used to dealing with wimps."

"That's not true at all." *I'm not used to dealing with anyone.* She couldn't believe she'd actually admitted to John that she hadn't even been on a single date since she broke up with her college boyfriend.

"Then maybe I'm just likable." He crossed the kitchen in two strides and placed his hands on her hips. Heat flared between them. His gentle but insistent kiss left her speechless, and she noticed how her treacherous fingers were already sliding lower to the curve of his backside. How did he do this to her?

She didn't want to tell him she liked him. He might take it the wrong way and think she wanted some kind of real relationship with him. That was impossible, of course. She knew that. Which was why she shouldn't be here kissing a man who had no honorable intentions toward her.

Nevertheless, she found herself kissing him back with passion that that flowed from somewhere deep inside her. This was the kind of thing they'd warned her about in Sunday school. That her parents tut-tutted over when other girls from her neighborhood had affairs that quickly fizzled out, sometimes leaving them pregnant. They thought you shouldn't even kiss someone until there was a ring or a promise in the picture.

Constance had neither, and yet her fingers now tugged at John's tie and the buttons on his shirt.

"Let's go upstairs." He didn't wait for an answer but swept her along with his powerful arm around her waist. He kissed her neck with each step, caressed her backside as she walked ahead of him. Under his admiring gaze and tender touch she felt unbelievably desirable. She even had a swing in her step she'd never felt before. Being with John Fairweather was doing something very strange to her mind and body.

"This is my room." She walked into an impressive chamber with a beamed cathedral ceiling. A big hand-hewn bed gave the room a masculine air. Framed maps decorated the walls, and she peered at one as they went past. "Those are the historical survey maps of our land and the town around it." They were all different. She could see the territory marked out for the Nissequot shrinking as the maps leaped over the decades. By the early part of the twentieth century, the word *Nissequot* wasn't even there and it was marked as Fairweather Farm.

"They were trying to squeeze you out of existence."

"Almost worked, too."

He wrapped his arms around her from behind as she stood in front of the most recent map. It was from the previous year and showed the Nissequot territory proudly marked in green, expanded and with the casino buildings at its center.

"What's the blue area?"

"That's what we're planning to buy next. Even that won't take us all the way back to our colonial-era hunting grounds, but it'll give us room to grow."

Her heart filled with pride at all he'd accomplished. Which didn't really make sense, since she had nothing to do with it and he wasn't hers to begin with.

"Now, where were we?" He spun her slowly around, sliding his hands along the curve of her waist. The thunder still rumbled outside and rain hammered against the glass of the windows, but it all faded to nothing when his lips touched hers. Her eyes slid closed and she leaned into him, enjoying the closeness she hadn't even known she craved. Lost deep in the kiss, it wasn't until she opened her eyes to undo his belt buckle that she realized all the lights had gone out.

"Have we lost power?"

"Looks that way." He kissed her forehead. "We're generating plenty of our own electricity, so I don't think we need it."

She laughed. "Shouldn't we at least call the electric company?"

"Nah. They can tell when we lose power. The casino and hotel have backup generators, so they won't miss a beat."

He'd taken off her jacket and undone her blouse, and now he unzipped her skirt so it fell to the floor. The black velvet darkness felt very intimate. She managed to get his belt unhooked and his pants and shirt off, which involved some giggling and fumbling. Then they made their way to the soft surface of the bed.

He held her tight as they rolled together, pressing their bodies into the mattress and each other. She loved the heaviness of him, how big he was. When she was on top she kissed his face all over, then eased down to his shoulders and neck, leaving a trail of kisses. She wanted to explore his body, and the total darkness made her bold.

She liked the roughness of the hair on his chest. There wasn't much of it, just enough to create an interesting and masculine texture. She traced it lower, to where she could feel his hardness waiting for her. She let her tongue explore his erection, turning off any whispers in her mind of how this was indulgent and sinful. She loved the way he moved in response to everything she did, aroused to the point where he couldn't keep still. John groaned softly as she took him into her mouth and sucked, then let her tongue play about the tip of his penis.

She'd never done this before. Never even thought about

it! She enjoyed the control she had over him. She could feel the desire, the passion that racked his strong body.

"Oh, Constance. We need to find a condom."

She laughed, so aroused she could hardly think. Thank goodness he was more sensible than she. "I love how you're so responsible."

"It goes with being a leader of the tribe. I don't want to create any new members except on purpose." He chuckled and she heard him groping around in the darkness, opening a door in the nightstand. It reminded her that she was not the first woman to come to his bed. She wouldn't be the last, either.

But as he rolled the condom on in the dark, she didn't seem to care. Constance was so aroused that she took him inside her effortlessly, welcoming him into her body. Still on top, she moved slowly, experimenting with the sensations she created in herself and in him. As pressure built inside her she moved faster, letting the feelings wash over her and surprise her as her body did what it wanted.

John pulled her toward him and rolled them over again so he was on top, then he kissed her softly and started a different rhythm that soon had her gasping aloud and moaning his name.

She'd never done that before, either.

He took her almost to the brink, then pulled back, slowing down and kissing and caressing her until she felt she might burst. She tried to urge him with her hips, but he was too heavy, and only chuckled at her attempts to drive the motion. "Impatient!" he scolded her. "Everything in due time." He moved very slowly and quietly, layering kisses over her ears and neck, heightening the already intense reactions taking place inside her.

She was so aroused that she could barely breathe by the time he finally brought them both to a blistering climax that lit up the darkness with an explosion of inner electricity she'd never even dreamed was possible.

"I saw fireworks," she gasped when she could finally speak again.

"Good," was all he replied, so obnoxiously confident that she wanted to slap him—or hug him. She chose the latter.

John buried his face in her hair. They lay side by side, wrapped in each other. This seduction had taken him by surprise and it just kept gathering steam.

He hadn't realized that looking past her glasses into those hazel eyes would put him under her quiet spell. Now he didn't want Constance to leave at all. The power was back on and a soft light illuminated the room.

"Did you put your glasses somewhere safe?"

"They're on the bedside table." Her soft voice was a balm to his spirit.

"Good. I didn't remember you taking them off and I don't want them to get broken."

"That's sweet of you."

Yeah. She was bringing out the sweet in him. He wanted to cherish her and take care of her. He loved to feel her relaxing in his arms. Letting go of the prickly armor she'd used to hold him at bay. It was magic to feel her opening up and exploring her own sensuality—and driving him half-insane in the bargain.

He kissed her cheek. "You're something else, Constance Allen."

"I'm certainly something else from who I thought I was. There have been a lot of surprises for me here in Massachusetts."

"You're surprised that I'm not the greedy crook the media make me out to be."

"I had no preconceptions about you. I strive to be entirely open-minded. It's essential in my work. If you go in with opinions, it will skew how you perceive the data."

"You had no idea you'd succumb to my famous charms."

"Now that is true." Her eyes sparkled with humor. "I'm still not sure what the heck I'm doing in your arms."

"Relaxing."

"It's not very relaxing knowing that if my boss—or anyone else—found out I'd be fired and probably lose my accounting credentials."

"That's why you're not thinking about that part." He didn't want her to go back to her job and Ohio. He wanted her to stay here.

The thought struck him like a bolt of lightning. The thunder rolling outside echoed a storm that raged quietly in his heart. He was falling for Constance Allen. "Where are you hoping to go next in your career?"

"I'd like to achieve partner eventually. At least, I suppose I would. That's the logical peak of my career. If I manage not to destroy it between now and then."

"Have you ever wanted to do anything else?" Possibilities blossomed in his imagination. She could manage the casino's accounts. After a reasonable cooling-off period from her assignment, of course. Their personal relationship would seem to develop naturally out of her employment at the casino.

Uh-oh. His feelings for Constance were making him creative.

"Not really. When I was younger I wanted to be a teacher, but I grew out of that. I'm better with numbers than people."

He cocked his head. "I can see you being a teacher. And I think you're just fine with people."

"I don't know. What if the kids didn't listen to me?"

Every now and then, when she was bored out of her mind with a particular project, she wondered if she'd made the wrong choice.

"Numbers don't talk back."

"Not often, anyway." Soft and warm, she lay still against his chest. She no longer seemed ready to run away. "Though I'm always hoping that they'll yell at me. Especially in a forensic investigation."

"Like the one you're doing now." He stroked her hair.

"Exactly. I can't believe I'm lying in your arms when I'm going to be combing through your books looking for fraud tomorrow."

"Surely you've seen all you need to see by now. It's hard to prove there's absolutely no wrongdoing, but at what point do you call it quits?"

She stiffened slightly. "When the BIA tells me to."

"They still aren't satisfied?"

"They just want me to be thorough. I'm sure they're as anxious as you are to have everything check out so they can forget about the whole thing."

"I hope so. They could put us right out of business if they had a mind to. Believe me, I have no interest in doing anything that isn't entirely aboveboard. I know we're under scrutiny and that our work can stand up to it."

"Then you have nothing to worry about. I'm sure they'll get bored with paying my hourly rate soon."

"I hope not." He held her tight. "Or I might have to convince you to quit and move here." There, he'd said it. He was clearly losing his sanity, but it was a relief to get it off his chest.

She stilled. "Very funny."

"You think I'm kidding?"

"I know you're kidding."

"Don't be so sure. I like you." He kissed her on the nose. "And you like me, too."

She laughed. "I do. But not enough to throw away my life and career to prolong a steamy affair with you." He heard an odd note in her voice. Sadness. She was already mourning the end of their relationship, even as they lay nestled in each other's arms.

"It doesn't have to end." His voice emerged a little gruffer than he'd intended.

"I suppose you could always move to Ohio." She raised one of her slim brows.

"That wouldn't be ideal."

"See? It's impossible. We have our separate lives already planned out and this is just a big mistake that we couldn't seem to avoid." She said it so seriously that he laughed.

"Speak for yourself. I don't consider this to be a mistake at all. This is the best evening I can remember having. Followed closely by last night."

"You must have a short memory, that's all." She closed her eyes for a second, as if enjoying a thought, then opened them. "You'll have forgotten all about me in a month. In six months you won't even remember my name."

"How could I forget a name like Constance? I can't believe you won't let me call you Connie."

"Knowing you, I can't believe you haven't started doing it anyway, regardless of what I think."

"I'm more sensitive than you take me for." He caressed her soft cheek. "In fact, I can be quite soft hearted."

It was the honest truth. Which he usually kept to himself. He'd prided himself on keeping his emotions in check for a long time. Something about Constance made him want to let his guard down. He knew she wasn't interested in his money, or his notoriety, or even his dashing

good looks. To appeal to her he'd have to be honest and
prove to her that he wasn't the hard-hearted lothario she
believed him to be.

Was he really trying to convince her to stay here? His
logical mind argued against it but something deep in his
gut told him that if he let her go he'd regret it, possibly for
the rest of his life.

"I didn't bring a change of underwear."

"We sell some nice panties in the shop." He grinned. "I
can pick some up for you."

"No! That'll just get the staff wondering who they're for.
I'll go back to my hotel first thing in the morning. Don't
let me sleep in, okay?"

"I'll wake you. Though it will cause me pain to tug you
from your dreams." He sounded pretty sappy. For some
reason around Constance that felt okay. He could tell she
liked it. She had a tiny smile across her mouth and her
eyes were closed. She looked utterly relaxed and at peace.
Which, considering the circumstances and her personality, was quite something.

He could easily imagine her lying here in his bed, in his
arms, for a long time to come. Getting to that point, however, was going to take some careful management of what
could be a very explosive situation. He regretted joking
around with Don about flirting with her. Though maybe
that would help throw him off the scent. He didn't want
Don to know about any of this until the time was right,
which would likely be months from now, as his uncle could
have a big mouth.

Constance Fairweather. The name had an old-fashioned
sound that was strangely appealing to him.

Her breathing slowed as she slipped into sleep. All her
resistance had evaporated and she was totally comfortable
and relaxed here, with him. Of course her family probably

wouldn't be too thrilled about him taking her several states away, but they could easily move here and he could build them a nice house like the one his grandparents lived in. He'd learned from experience that all obstacles could be overcome with the right planning and some patience. She liked him, he could tell. There was no way she would be here if she didn't. And he liked her.

So what could go wrong?

Constance was awakened by John's gentle kiss on her cheek. She blinked and took in the sight of his handsome face, wondering if she was still dreaming.

"Good morning, gorgeous. I made us breakfast. You've got plenty of time to eat before hitting the road to your hotel."

"Okay." She must be dreaming. And why wake up?

They ate a feast of fresh fruit and scrambled eggs with toast, drank freshly brewed coffee and juice and chatted about their childhoods, which had both been somewhat outside the mainstream in their own way. As the hands on the vintage wall clock headed toward eight o'clock, she found herself reluctant to leave.

Sitting here chatting with him felt utterly natural. He was just so easy to talk to, and so warm and such a good host. He was spoiling her for all other men. Not that any other men were knocking on her door, but it was going to be hard to find someone whose company she enjoyed as much as John's.

Of course, there was plenty wrong with him. He was far too good-looking. She didn't value looks at all. In fact, they tended to make her assume someone was arrogant and conceited—which in John's case was entirely correct. Yet since his cocky attitude was justified by his impressive competence, somehow it seemed appropriate.

She knew he was a notorious playboy. She was just another notch on his hand-hewn bedpost. One in a long line of women, and probably less enticing than most. Once she went back to Ohio, she'd never see him again and very soon there would be another woman in his bed and sitting here at his kitchen table.

The thoughts made her gut clench with sadness. Which was exactly why she shouldn't have let herself fall into this…liaison in the first place. He could easily add it to his list of pleasurable experiences and move on. She didn't have a list of pleasurable experiences and this was going to stand out as one of the most amazing, unexpected and wonderful events of her life.

Fantastic.

John's phone kept making noises, and eventually he picked it up and looked at his messages. "Sounds like the media's still making noise about Don today."

"Do you think he's done anything wrong?" she couldn't help asking.

"No." He answered quickly. "He's made some…ill-advised choices in the past, but I know he wouldn't do anything to jeopardize what we've built here. He likes people to think he's a bad boy. He thinks it's a cool image. Doesn't bother me. All publicity is good publicity to a certain extent. We're still new enough that a lot of people haven't been here yet and you never know what will get them off the couch."

"Don sounds like quite a character."

"Oh, he is. Sometimes he drives me nuts, but he was the first person to jump on board when I came up with the idea for this place. My grandparents thought it was impossible."

"Why?"

"Too big. Too bold. How can you take a tired dairy farm in the middle of nowhere and turn it into a thriving attraction? But we're not the first, and we won't be the last. Don had faith in my ability to pull it off and he's worked hard to make it happen."

"I can tell you have a lot of affection for him."

"I do. He's my uncle. And under his flashy exterior he's a big softy." John smiled.

Oh, dear. He was being adorable again. Couldn't he be a jerk just to make it easier for her to go back home? "I'd better get going."

"I'll lead the way."

John watched Constance head for the highway to her hotel, then returned to the offices. Don was in the lobby, chatting with one of the desk clerks. He brightened at the sight of John. "Ready for breakfast?"

"I grabbed something at home."

"What'd you do that for?"

"No reason." Don would die laughing if he knew. "Just hungry, that's all." The truth. His night had been rather more athletic than usual. And he still had a distinct spring in his step. Constance was full of intriguing surprises.

"Come have coffee with me then. We can glare at any reporters and scare them off."

"It's usually better to just answer their questions with a smile." Why were reporters still sniffing around? Nothing had happened lately to arouse their suspicion. "Have you seen any today?"

"I had a phone call this morning asking questions about your lady friend."

John stiffened. "Constance?" He realized he might have revealed too much. "Ms. Allen from the BIA?"

Don nodded. "Somehow word got out that they're looking into our books. I suppose they're going on the theory that where there's smoke there's probably a fire."

"But there isn't."

"You know that, and I know that, and we just have to wait for them to realize that."

"Hmm." The press couldn't possibly suspect anything between him and Constance, could they? That would be bad, for her and for him and for the casino. Don didn't seem to suspect anything.

"She good in bed?"

John froze. "Who?"

Don nudged him. "You can't fool me. I've known you since you were two feet high. I can see the way you look at her."

"I have no idea what you're talking about." John maintained a calm demeanor but inside he was starting to sweat. Was his newfound passion for Constance really so obvious? It was essential to keep it a secret until her investigation was over and the results had been announced—for her sake, if not his own.

"Miss Constance Allen, forensic accountant. I bet she's a freak under that conservative suit."

"You're disgusting. Who do we have booked to perform in September?"

"I just booked Jimmy Cliff. I'm working on Celine Dion."

"You keep working. I'm heading up to the office." John headed toward the elevators, blood pumping.

Right now he was ready for Constance to leave.

Not because he didn't want to see her again. Because he wanted to be done with all the secrecy and subterfuge, and that couldn't end until she was no longer investigating him. He needed her to go back to Ohio, wrap up her assignment, and then they could start over again.

And that couldn't happen soon enough.

* * *

Back at her hotel, Constance showered and returned some phone calls. It was Friday and the perfect day to pack up and leave, but for some reason she had a feeling she'd no longer be irritated by a request to stay for a few more days. She wasn't ready to say goodbye to John. In fact she was secretly hoping they'd get to spend at least one more night together.

She knew such thoughts were possibly signs of appalling moral degeneration, but she couldn't remember ever having this much fun with anyone before, and she wasn't ready to go back to her humdrum existence yet.

She called the BIA with considerable trepidation. She was starting to feel like a total fraud as far as they were concerned. If they knew what she was up to with John, they'd fire her firm on the spot and probably sue her for damaging their reputation. She decided to mention the closest thing to a discovery that she'd come across. "Don Fairweather gambles in the casino. He had substantial winnings last year. More than fifty thousand."

"Did he pay taxes on his winnings?"

"I'm not sure. I haven't looked at the individual tribal members' tax returns."

"Request them, and take a look."

"Which members?" Was she going to have to look into the returns of every low-level staffer? She felt like rubbing her hands together. That would take several days.

She didn't want to look into John's, though. That seemed far too personal.

"Anyone who's been gambling," Nicola replied. "You'll quickly find out who's honest. And request returns for the key players, including John Fairweather. Take a look at income, expenses, deductions. Poke around a bit. Look into at least five people in total."

"Aren't tax returns confidential? What if they won't allow me access?"

"Then I'll secure a subpoena."

Constance felt jumpy and anxious as she pulled back into the casino parking lot. Personal income tax records? Many people didn't even like sharing the information with their spouse. She took the elevator up to the offices, hoping John wasn't there. It was awkward seeing him in the professional context of the office after what had gone on between them. She always felt her blood heat at the first glimpse of him, then that embarrassing slow smile wanting to creep across her face. And she'd rather request his tax records in a polite text or email than have to look into his eyes while she asked to pry into his personal business.

Of course he was there. Larger than life and twice as handsome. He was talking to a man she recognized from the cashier's office as she approached, but he dismissed him with a nod. The twinkle in his eyes warred with his cool and professional demeanor.

"Hi, Constance."

She straightened her shoulders and tried to affect a disinterested expression. "Good morning." As if she was saying it for the first time.

"Good morning. I trust you slept well." His low voice caused awareness to ripple through her. They walked toward his office together.

"Very well, thank you." He should know. He'd had to wake her up from her blissful slumber. She kept her voice clipped. "Can I speak to you in private?"

"Of course." They took the elevator up to his office. She could feel his curiosity heating the atmosphere as they rode up in silence. She did her best to avoid his glance, afraid of the effect it might have on her.

She took a deep breath. "My contact at the BIA has

requested that I look into the personal tax returns of several key people."

His expression darkened. "Who?"

"You." She spat it right out. She'd chosen people from different departments and in different stages of life so there would be some variety, and she'd included the three gamblers. "Your uncle Don, Paul McGee, Mona Lester, Susan Cummings, Anna Martin and Darius Carter."

"Darius? He's just a kid. He barely even pays taxes."

She shrugged. She'd picked him because he held a key role in the day-to-day running of the casino. "Shall I speak to each person individually?"

"Why these people?"

"They were chosen more or less at random." She didn't want to go into detail. It really wasn't his business. He must have read her reluctance because he paused for a moment, but didn't ask more questions.

"I'll talk to them." His brow had furrowed.

"Do you think any of them will object?"

"I'll make sure they don't. Besides, we all filed the taxes already, so what is there to hide?"

"Exactly."

"I'll have them all for you by the end of the day."

"Much appreciated." Phew. That was easy. As long as none of the individuals objected, of course.

"I want to kiss you." His voice was ripe with suggestion.

"I don't think that's a good idea." Her own voice was barely a whisper. Her lips twitched to do exactly what he'd suggested. "I have work to do."

"So do I. But that doesn't stop me wanting you."

"You're trouble."

"I can't argue with you. I certainly seem to be trouble where you're concerned." They'd reached his office. "Though I don't have any regrets."

He closed the door. They kissed for a solid five minutes, tongues tangling and biting each other's lips until their breath came in ragged gasps.

"I used to be a dignified professional, I'll have you know," she stammered when their lips finally parted.

"I used to be a sane man. Since you showed up here everything has gone out the window." Cool and calm as always, in his dark gray suit and pale blue shirt he looked the picture of sanity. Of course he was probably just pretending to be besotted with her. Or maybe even allowing himself to be as a temporary condition. He'd be over her before she even drove across the Ohio state line. "I hope it will take a while to go through all our returns."

"I hope not. It's embarrassing and totally unprofessional, but I really don't want to find anything wrong here." She couldn't believe she'd confessed that to him.

"Uh-oh. I hope I'm not compromising your professional integrity." His wicked grin warmed her as his big hands squeezed her hips gently.

"Nothing could compromise my professional integrity. Believe me, if I found something, I'd report it."

"I love that about you, Constance. I bet everyone always knows where they stand with you."

"I used to think so. I'm sure my employer would be rather surprised if they knew you were squeezing my butt right now."

He slid his hand back up to her waist with a rueful expression. "True. But since our intimacy doesn't affect your professional integrity, they really shouldn't mind at all."

"Perhaps not, but I'm sure they would." She straightened his pale yellow tie, which had gotten crooked. "Now you and I should at least pretend to do some work. Preferably in separate rooms, as we don't seem to be too professional anymore when we're in the same space."

"All right, Constance. I'll see you later, and I'll have everyone go home at lunch and pick up their tax returns."

"Perfect." Could it really be that easy? "And I might need to speak to each of them individually after I've had a chance to look over the paperwork. I might even need to look at their personal banking records to make sure everything adds up." She held her breath. No one wanted a total stranger looking into their personal finances. On the other hand, it was one of her favorite things to request, since the person's reaction told you a lot about how honest they were.

"I'll warn them. And I consider myself warned." He winked. He didn't look at all worried, which was quite a relief.

She had one more question for him. One she already knew the answer to. "Do any of the tribal members gamble in the casino?"

"I don't do it myself and I prefer that other employees don't. Besides, they know better than anyone that over time the house always wins. Don likes to play a little, but no one else gambles regularly. Believe me, I keep close tabs on all our employees, especially the younger ones."

"Does Don win?"

"He says he does." John winked. "Whether he's telling the truth is a whole different story. We do keep files on employee gambling, though."

"Could I take a look at those?" No need to mention that she'd already seen them and knew Don had big winnings. It would be interesting to see from Don's tax return whether he was claiming them. She felt a little guilty pretending to be totally in the dark, but at least now she felt as though she was actually doing her job.

"Of course." He leaned over the laptop on the desk and tapped a few keys. The file she'd found by herself popped up. "You won't find my name in there."

"I'm glad that you don't gamble."

"Me, too. It's much safer being the house than trying to beat it."

He didn't even glance at the file, so confident that the records were all aboveboard and would speak for themselves. She loved how honorable John was. Another kiss on the lips and a warm hug left her dizzy. Her heart ached as the door closed behind him. If parting from him now hurt her even a little, how was she going to feel when he was gone for good?

Nine

John didn't invite her over that night. She didn't know whether to be relieved or disappointed as she drove back to her hotel, the employees' tax returns sitting on her passenger seat. He probably had some kind of meeting. Or something important to do. Or bigger plans. It was Friday night, after all.

If she had a life she'd drive back to Ohio for the weekend. But it made more sense to stay here, save the gas money and bill more hours.

For dinner, she ate a Chinese chicken salad and drank a Diet Coke at her hotel room desk while she watched the news. The pile of tax returns now stared at her from the end of her bed. She was literally afraid to look at them. Normally the prospect of delving into freshly unearthed personal papers filled her with unreasonable glee. Now it just made her nervous about confronting her own principles.

What if she found something in John's tax return? Excessive write-offs or under-reporting of taxes owed, maybe. She'd be duty bound to report her findings, or even any suspicions. Should she tell him first, so he'd have a chance to explain? She'd told him she would, but that would go in the face of everything she'd learned about forensic accounting. Never give people a chance to cover their tracks.

He hadn't said anything at all about whether it was easy or hard to convince the employees to hand over their returns. Maybe they respected him so much they'd do anything he asked. She'd expected at least someone to put up a fight. So far it was all going too smoothly. For reasons she couldn't put her finger on, that made her nervous.

She picked his tax return off the pile first with trembling fingers. His income was exorbitant, of course, but most of it was from personal investments that had nothing whatsoever to do with New Dawn. He'd only paid himself a salary of one hundred thousand from the casino and hotel. That impressed her. He'd taken plenty of personal deductions and travel expenses, but nothing out of the ordinary. His return looked similar to many she'd seen belonging to successful company owners and high-level executives. He'd paid a great deal in taxes, mostly capital-gains tax, so the government should be quite happy to have John Fairweather as a taxpayer. After several hours combing through the schedules, she heaved a sigh of relief and moved on.

Darius's and Anna's returns reflected their modest incomes and were totally uncomplicated, and they'd both received a small amount of money back when they filed. Anna had reported her small gambling winnings, so there was no problem there. Mona had gotten divorced in the middle of the year, so her return was more elaborate, but still nothing to arouse suspicion.

She left Don's for last. It was almost as thick as John's and she soon discovered that he actually earned more than John from New Dawn. No doubt it was John's way of keeping a senior family member happy. Still, the salary was far from outrageous for a senior executive at such a profitable enterprise, and Don had paid taxes at a high rate and taken fairly reasonable deductions.

But as she combed through the schedules, she saw nothing at all about proceeds from personal gambling. Her Spidey-sense tingled with alarm. Normally this was a good feeling that she was about to earn her keep and justify her employment at a top accounting firm. But right now it came with an uncomfortable sense of foreboding. She went through the return again. Still no sign of any winnings or losses. Since the casino workers openly admitted to him gambling, and she'd seen him do it with her own eyes, it was clearly an omission. Even though table games like roulette and blackjack didn't require that the casino submit Form W2-G to the IRS, the gambler was certainly required to declare winnings and she'd seen the records detailing Don's fifty thousand dollars in profits.

Her phone rang and she almost jumped out of her skin. It was Lynn from work. What was she doing calling on a Friday night? "Hi." Constance hoped she could get her off the phone quickly.

"I hope you're back in Cleveland because you're the only person I know who will go see the new Disney movie with me."

Constance couldn't help laughing. "I would love to see it, but I'm still in Massachusetts."

"Why didn't you drive home for the weekend? I guess you can't bring yourself to leave the sexy casino boss."

"What? You're crazy. I barely even see him." She realized she'd spoken too fast and too loud.

"Oh, boy. I did hit a nerve. I always knew you'd be interested if the right man came along."

"You're talking nonsense. I could care less about John Fairweather."

Lynn laughed. "Don't you mean *couldn't* care less? If you could care less then it means you care quite a bit."

"You know what I mean." Constance leaped to her feet and paced in her small hotel room. "I'm only interested in his financial data." Now she was lying to her closest friend. "Which is checking out fine."

"What a bummer. I was hoping for a dramatic exposé and scandal that would lead to a big bonus for you next spring."

"I'm just doing my job. I have no expectations of any kind when I look into a company's books."

"I know, I know. It's just so much more interesting when you find information that someone was trying to hide."

Now would be the perfect time to mention the telling absence of gambling data on Don Fairweather's tax return. Yet she kept quiet. She'd promised to tell John about anything she found. It chilled her to realize that she felt more loyalty to John than to her own firm. Still, she wouldn't lie or cover anything up. As soon as she'd told John, she'd report back to her firm, and to the BIA.

Hopefully since it was just a personal matter, and not to do with the casino itself, it would be a storm in a teacup and blow over quickly.

"You're very quiet. Are you okay?" She'd almost forgotten Lynn was still on the phone.

"I'm fine. Just a bit preoccupied. These last few days have been a blur of numbers and figures. Casino books make corporate records look refreshingly dreary by comparison. I can't wait to settle back into my peacefully dull routine."

"Nothing's dull around here. Whitlow gave his resignation. It turned out Lacey wasn't the first young employee who's been under his desk. There's a class action suit in the works. It's all anyone's talking about."

"Wow." That could mean a partnership spot opening up. Not that she'd be eligible. She'd likely be considered too young. Still…

"Old goat. It's amazing what men will risk for a little nooky. Makes you glad to be a woman."

She laughed. "Hardly. The men who get themselves into trouble are usually doing something with a woman." Someone like her, for example, who would apparently risk her career for a few brief moments of bliss.

It didn't make any sense at all, yet she'd done it.

"True. Humans are irrational creatures. That's what makes us so interesting."

"Yes, indeed." She'd turned out to be far more dangerously human than she'd ever expected.

"Do you need anything?" Lynn's question took her by surprise.

"Not that I can think of. I'm sure I'll be back next week."

"And you've found nothing at all?"

She hesitated. "I'll tell you everything when I get back."

"So you did find something?" Lynn's voice was a breathy whisper.

"Don't twist my words. I'm still investigating." The last thing she needed was the office administrator sparking rumors.

"My lips are sealed."

"Good. Keep them that way and have a good weekend. I've got to go."

Constance hung up the phone, breathing a little faster than usual. She really wished she hadn't given Lynn the idea that something was up. On the other hand, it would have been weird to say she'd found nothing, then reveal in a day or two that in fact she had uncovered tax fraud. This whole situation was getting far too complicated.

And now she had to tell John. She wanted to email him

or text him, but somehow putting words in print felt wrong. They could be saved and used in some kind of legal situation. She didn't want to call him in case the phones were monitored. He might even record incoming and outgoing calls himself as some kind of protection. And she knew it was inappropriate to tell him before reporting back to the people who had hired her.

There was nothing for it but to hunt him down in person and figure out what to do from there.

When Constance arrived at the casino the next morning, John was in the lobby talking to Don. Since it was the weekend they had on more casual clothing: John wore a fitted shirt and faded jeans that hugged his powerful thighs and Don was dressed all in black like a movie mobster. She tugged her gaze away and headed for the bank of elevators. She didn't want to have to make polite conversation with a man she was about to report for tax fraud. Who knew how many years he'd been doing it? He could be in for a hefty fine or even a prison term.

She had no choice but to pass quite close to the two men, but she skirted around an electronic display that showed a list of the day's events so they couldn't see her.

"It's a good thing she's sweet on you." As she passed by, Don's words made her ears prick. "I don't like her snooping through our tax records. Make sure you wine and dine her tonight. We don't want her getting creative." Constance froze, despite knowing she was in a crowded lobby where others could see her, even if John and his uncle couldn't. Did Don know they were having an affair?

"My tax records are entirely accurate and I assume yours are, too." John's voice sounded dismissive. And why didn't he say something about her not being bribable? She was offended that he didn't defend her honor. On the other hand, maybe that would have been too much. He was being subtle.

Don laughed. Which sounded very false under the circumstances. "Don't you worry about me. She won't find anything in my taxes. And I'm the one who told you seducing her was a good idea. You should listen to me more often."

Constance's mouth dropped open and her heart hammered. She glanced at the bank of elevators, which now seemed about a mile away across the shiny marble floor. Had they planned this together? Was she a victim of a plot between them?

She blinked, hardly able to believe it.

"Don't be too smart for your own good, Don." John's voice made her jump. Wasn't he going to deny that they had planned her seduction? Her breathing became audible and she looked around, hoping no one was watching. She couldn't believe they were having this conversation right in the lobby where anyone could hear it.

John was now asking about a band due to perform that night. He'd simply changed the subject without contradicting Don? A sense of betrayal crept over her and chilled her blood. Suddenly she was glad she'd found the discrepancy in Don's taxes. John deserved the media's ugly attention and anything that came from it if he was the kind of person who'd deliberately set out to charm and cajole her into bed for his own purposes.

She lifted her chin and marched for the elevators as fast as she could, praying that no one would talk to her. She counted the seconds while she waited for an elevator to take her up to the office floor. What a disaster.

"Hey, Constance, where are you going?" John's voice boomed across the marble space. "It's Saturday."

She spun around.

"Up to the office floors. They are open on the weekends, I hope." She responded as primly as she could. How could he talk to her so casually in full view of the other employees and guests? Did he want them all to know they'd been intimate? Probably he did. Maybe he thought it was funny.

"Weren't you even going to say hello?"

"I could see you were in conference."

"In conference?" He laughed. "Don was just telling me about the new Maserati he ordered. Crazy. I told him I hope I won't get to practice using the Jaws of Life on it."

No mention of Don's thanking him for seducing her. And his own complicit silence. "Can we meet in your office?" She needed to talk to him. They'd gone too far for her to just go back home, report her findings and pretend they'd never slept together. The situation could blow up in her face if he decided to retaliate. Her hands were shaking and she hoped she wouldn't cry.

"But of course." His voice contained more than a hint of suggestion. "I'd be delighted to get you behind closed doors."

She glanced up at the security cameras. She hadn't even noticed them before. Hopefully no one ever listened to the tapes. "It's something serious."

All humor vanished from his expression. "About the returns?" And his voice was hushed.

"Let me tell you upstairs."

John closed the door behind them, and for once this did not lead to a passionate kiss. Which was good, because she would have had to slap him. "Is there something wrong?"

Her heart beat so fast she could barely think. "It's Don's return. He didn't declare any gambling winnings."

He frowned. "He certainly should have."

She swallowed. "The company records detail substantial winnings. You can see them for yourself in your own files."

"I'm sure there's some explanation."

She drew in an unsteady breath. "I'm telling you first because I promised I would." Though now she was having second thoughts about it. Did he really deserve it if he'd only flirted with her for his own protection? "But I have to tell my boss at Creighton Waterman, and I have to tell the BIA."

"Give me some time to figure out what's going on. I'll talk to Don."

"I can't. I'm paid to do a job here. I have to report what I found and I've already done something wrong by telling you first." *On top of all the other things I've done wrong in your bed.*

"He must have forgotten to report the winnings. Don has more money than he knows what to do with. I told you about the Maserati."

"There may well be a reasonable explanation, but I'm here to look for discrepancies and I found one. You admitted yourself that he gambles, and I've heard the same from other employees." She lifted her chin and defied him to argue with her.

"He makes no secret of it."

"Yet he didn't mention it on his tax return."

John drew in a long breath, swelling his broad chest. For a split second she ached to hug him, but instead she held herself stiffly at bay. He frowned. "Don's a key employee here. Something like this could really damage the casino's reputation. You know the kind of scrutiny we're under. I can't afford the bad publicity."

"If you don't want bad publicity perhaps you should be more careful about how you conduct yourself. Seducing the accountant who's sent to inspect your accounts probably isn't too smart, for a start." She braced for his response, glad she'd been bold enough to say it.

"That took me by surprise as much as you."

"Oh, really. That's not what I overheard downstairs."

He frowned. "You overheard Don? He was just kidding around."

"And you didn't contradict him."

His expression softened. "I didn't want to dignify his innuendo with a response. He really has no idea what happened between us."

She swallowed. "Good. As you can imagine I would appreciate it if you didn't discuss our indiscretions with anyone."

"Of course not. I never would." He held out his hand, but she stayed rigid.

"Everything that happened between us was a mistake and I regret it. Now I have a responsibility to report my findings to the people who hired me."

He took in a long slow breath, his expression grim. "The BIA is going to come down on us all like a ton of bricks."

"I have to do my job."

"I can see that." His jaw was set. She wondered for a tense moment if he'd attempt to flirt and cajole her out of making her report. He didn't. He watched her silently for what felt like an eternity.

She realized at last how utterly vulnerable she was. Her future, her career lay in this man's hands. He could end it, and ruin her reputation, in a single phone call if he chose.

"I understand." His words were cool, controlled. His eyes didn't plead with her, but the emotion she saw in them reminded her of the tender moments they'd shared.

At least she'd thought at the time they were tender moments.

"I'm going to call my contact now." She picked up her bag, burning with the desire to get out of here as fast as possible and never come back. He opened the door and stepped aside. Heat and tension flashed between them as she passed him.

Or maybe that was only in her imagination.

She heard the door click shut behind her after she passed through it, and her heart almost broke as she realized this would be the very last time she'd ever see John.

John pressed his body against the door, partly to stop himself from jerking it back open and striding after Constance. It was no use trying to argue with her. Her mind was made up and she was going to report what she found.

Could Don really have been stupid enough to fail to report his gambling activities?

He already knew the answer in his gut. He also knew how enthusiastically the circling media vultures would eat up the story.

And he couldn't even call Don, or a lawyer, because in doing so he'd have to reveal that Constance gave him privileged information. He wouldn't betray her confidence. She'd done him a big favor by telling him what she'd found. More so when she now suspected that he'd seduced her as a means to an end. He'd wanted to argue with her and try to convince her that his feelings for her came from the heart but there was no way she'd believe him now. She'd assume he was trying to butter her up and convince her to conceal her findings, which would only make her more suspicious and angry.

He cursed and banged his fist on the door. Why did life have to get so complicated? Everything was going smoothly until Constance Allen came along. His once-wild uncle had seemed to be settling into the life of a pros-

perous and trustworthy executive. Everyone in the tribe
was getting along well, which was no easy feat when you
brought people from all over the country to a small town
in the sticks. And business was booming.

Now the harsh spotlight would fall on them once again.
John knew as well as anyone that if someone was looking
for a reason to make the Nissequot disappear, they could
try to use this as a starting point and keep the tribe tied up
in legal wrangling until the moon turned blue. That was
much the same strategy that had been used by the powers
that be to whittle away the tribe's land and population in
the first place.

His number-one priority was to make sure that didn't
happen. His second priority would be to forget all about
Constance Allen. Her findings threatened to tear the fabric of the tribe. If anyone found out he'd been intimate
with her while she was looking for dirt on them, it would
undermine their trust in him. Don already suspected that
they'd had an affair. John certainly hadn't confirmed his
uncle's suspicions, but maybe by simply ignoring Don's
snide comments, he'd tacitly admitted something. He'd
have to manage Don carefully—never an easy feat—to
make sure he didn't decide to throw hints to the press and
make this ugly situation into a hot scandalous mess that
could bring them all down.

He growled in frustration. Just this morning life had
looked so rosy and promising. He'd missed having Constance in his bed last night due to preexisting plans with
an old friend, but he'd consoled himself with the prospect
of having her there for many years to come.

Not anymore. It had literally never crossed his mind
that she would find something amiss. He knew the books
of this casino way better than he knew the backs of his
hands, and he'd vouch for them with his life. The financial

affairs of the tribal members were also his concern, and he'd been pretty confident about them, too.

But Don? Apparently the smoke the media was fanning had come from a fire somewhere, and who knew what else that slippery old devil might be up to. His hand itched to pick up his phone and call his uncle, but he held the urge in check. He owed Constance that much.

But no more.

Tears blurred Constance's eyes by the time she hurried across the parking lot to her car. She climbed in and slammed the door, started the ignition with trembling fingers, and pulled out of the parking lot as fast as she could. She felt like a traitor here, which was ridiculous since she had no personal allegiance to the New Dawn casino. She shouldn't have any personal feelings for its founder, either.

The problem was that she did. Hearing that he'd discussed seducing her with his uncle should kill them stone dead. Was she a fool to believe John's denial? She wanted to believe him. And she remembered only too well how wonderful she'd felt with John's arms around her. How she'd come alive in his bed, letting herself explore a sensual and passionate side she'd never dared admit to before.

It would be very hard to just bury all those feelings again, even if the relationship had been in the wrong place, at the wrong time, with the wrong man.

She needed to call the BIA as soon as possible, just in case John did succumb to the temptation to warn his uncle. She couldn't afford to have word get out that she'd spoken to him about her findings. Nicola Moore had told her to get in touch at any time of the day or night if she had something important to report. She pulled into the parking lot of a fast-food restaurant and dialed Nicola Moore's cell number.

When Nicola answered, Constance got right to the point. "I'm sorry to call you on the weekend, but I've found a discrepancy." She kept her voice as calm as she could. "It might be nothing—" she swallowed "—but I've done all the research I can reasonably do into the situation from my end."

She told Moore about Don's reported gambling and its absence from his tax return. She'd only looked at one year, but she knew that this probably wasn't an isolated issue. From here on out it would be a matter for the IRS to investigate further. Her work was done, and she should feel a sense of pride and accomplishment in it, yet somehow she felt just the opposite.

"Good work. This will give us a foothold for further investigation."

"I didn't find any irregularities in the financials for the casino itself, just for this one executive." She wanted to limit the damage she'd cause to the New Dawn's reputation. Not that it should be any of her business.

"We've had our eye on Don Fairweather for some time. It's hard to understand why John Fairweather lets him play a substantial role in the company when he has a shady past."

"He's not directly involved in the financial operations at all. He books the bands and handles PR." Constance heard herself speaking quickly, defending John's choice to employ his uncle, and cursed herself for standing up for him. Obviously, she still cared about him. She'd let herself believe that he had real feelings for her, and now she felt foolish for being so gullible. She couldn't get away fast enough. She knew that John felt strongly about including all members of the family—and by extension the Nissequot tribe—and managing them appropriately. She also knew he couldn't control their personal choices.

"So I'm done here, right? It would be really awkward for me to hang around after making these accusations." She realized that didn't sound professional. In reality it had been awkward all along to have people know she was there looking for trouble. But she truly couldn't stand it if she had to see John again now that she knew the truth about his involvement with her.

"Yes, we'll have our legal team take it from here. Just forward all the relevant paperwork to me and I'll be in touch if I need anything further. Good work."

Heart heavy, Constance gathered her belongings from her hotel room and immediately began the long, lonely drive back to Ohio. Back to her former life of quiet work in her gray office and quiet evenings at home with her parents.

No kisses waited for her. No strong arms. No fiery passion to bring her body to life.

The worst part was that somehow her mind—or her body—couldn't accept that it was all over. She kept waiting for the phone to ring. For John to say that he'd known all along she was there for a reason, that it didn't make any difference that she'd done her job, even if it meant his family member would get in trouble.

Part of her still believed that what they'd shared was real. They'd had such great conversations, and experienced so much intimacy. Surely even if he'd started out to soften her up for business reasons, it had developed into something more. Or was it all in her head?

They hadn't even said goodbye. The last thing he'd said to her was, "I understand." But did he?

Would he have preferred for her to lie to her boss? To lie to the BIA? Then his little plan would have really paid off. She would have proved that she'd really loved him. Lucky thing she was not the kind of person who would ever do that. If she had nothing else left, at least she had her integrity, and of that she was fiercely proud.

At the office that Monday, her boss, Lucinda Waldron, was all smiles. "Well done, Constance. This was a tough assignment and once again you've proven yourself to be one of our rising stars. And it's a real bonus that you don't have a family to worry about. It's hard to find an employee who doesn't mind spending some time away from home. I have an interesting assignment coming up in Omaha that I think you'd be perfect for. I should know more details in a day or two."

"Great." She managed a smile. Omaha? And why not? As her boss pointed out, she had no life and no obligations. Not even a pet to worry about. They could ship her all over the country to ferret through companies' books and no one would even care except her parents, who would have to do their own dishes after dinner.

In her office she looked through her in-box with a heavy heart. All the employee expense reports for the last three months were in there. She was chosen to go through them, as she was considered the most trustworthy and least indulgent employee. Lynn had told her that just the idea that Constance Allen would be checking their expenses kept people from putting frivolous items on there.

Great.

"I've found the perfect man for you." Lynn peeped around her door.

"Shh! Someone will hear you." She didn't want to chat about men and dating. The whole thing seemed like a really bad idea. Obviously her judgment was questionable at best and who knew what might happen if she started putting herself in the way of available men so soon after John.

"It's not a crime to date, you know. Do you remember Lance from corporate?"

"I'd never date a coworker." And mostly she remembered Lance's receding chin. Which wasn't fair, really, as he had always been perfectly nice to her.

"You won't have to. He offered his resignation. He's going to KPMG."

"Which likely means he'll be moving to a different city. Long distance would never work."

"Why not? Better than not dating at all. Besides, you could always move."

"Leave Cleveland? What would my parents do?"

"I'm sure they'd survive."

"I'm not attracted to him."

"You barely know him. You have to give someone a chance. You might have amazing chemistry."

She looked right at Lynn. "Are you attracted to him?"

Lynn bit her lip and thought for a moment. "No. But I figured you'd want someone stable and quiet and…"

"Boring? What if I want someone wild and dangerous and exciting?" She leaned back in her chair. "What if I want someone totally different from me, who can help shake me out of my dull and rigid existence and make me look at the world with fresh eyes?"

Lynn stared at her. "Do you?"

She adjusted her glasses. "I don't want to date anyone." There was no way she could even consider looking at another man while John's handsome face hovered in her consciousness. And while his betrayal echoed in her heart. She still could hardly believe their whole affair had been planned from the start. "I have too many other things going on."

"Like reorganizing your bookshelf?"

"There's a church fund-raiser to plan."

"There's always a church fund-raiser to plan. I'm not going to let you waste your life anymore. It's time you burst out of your shell." Lynn winked and walked away.

Constance sank back in her chair. If only Lynn knew that she'd already left her shell and would never be happy in it again.

Ten

John walked into Don's rather lavish office and threw the newspapers down on his desk. "See what you've done?" Stories about the tax evasion had leaked to the press—or been planted.

"It's a load of bull."

"So you didn't gamble and win that money?" He crossed his arms and waited for a response.

"I don't remember."

"That won't cut it."

"It's worked for some American presidents I could name."

"Well, you aren't one, and you aren't senile either, so you'd better hire a lawyer and figure out what the two of you are going to say. The New Dawn is not going under the bus with you, Don. You know how I feel about following the rules. We're under way more scrutiny than the average business and I don't condone any activity that could even be seen as bending the rules."

"Sometimes you need to redefine a rule."

"Now is not one of those times. Since you aren't denying that you've gambled and failed to declare it, I have no choice but to terminate your position."

Don rose to his feet, frowning. "Are you kicking me out of the tribe, too?"

"This is business, Don, purely business. You'll always be family, but I can't have you working at the New Dawn while you're under investigation for breaking the law."

"Is it a paid leave of absence?"

John clenched his hand into a fist. "Is this my hand or is it a deadly weapon?"

"All right, all right. I can't believe you're just kicking me out. Whatever happened to innocent until proven guilty?"

"If you were declaring your innocence, I might feel differently, but you're not. I trusted you, Don. You've been my confidant and right-hand man at almost every phase of this project. I can't believe you'd risk it all to save yourself a few pennies you can well afford to part with."

"I'll pay whatever I owe."

"You know it won't be as easy as that. They're going to dig into your papers going back years."

His uncle's face darkened. "That won't be good. I told you I didn't want you to give her my returns."

"You didn't tell me it's because they were fraudulent."

"I didn't write any lies on them. I may have just not told the whole truth."

John suppressed a curse. "All this could have been easily avoided if you just did what you were supposed to do." Despite his anger, John felt a twinge of sorrow for Don. Why were some people constitutionally unable to play by the rules? "If you think a law is wrong then you can work to change it. You can't just ignore it."

Don shoved some items from his drawer—expensive Cross pens, technological gadgets—into his leather briefcase. "Everything's easy for you. You've always been the golden boy."

"I've worked my ass off for everything I've achieved and I'm not going to let you throw it all away." John wanted to take Don by the scruff of the neck and hurl him down the hallway, but he restrained himself. He also wanted to cuss his uncle out for ruining all his elaborate plans to keep Constance in his life, but he knew better than to clue Don in to that secret.

Don looked up from his desk and peered at him. "Shame you didn't use your charm to run Constance Allen off the property as I suggested."

"Charm usually has the opposite effect."

"Not on a sexless automaton like that one. A calculator in a suit."

John's hands were forming fists again without his permission. "You keep your thoughts on Ms. Allen to yourself."

"Oh, did I touch a nerve? I suppose you've seen more of what's under that suit than I gave you credit for. What if I tell the press about that, huh?"

"You wouldn't."

"Wouldn't I?"

"There's nothing to tell," he growled. "Just get out of here before I throw you out." Fury churned in his gut. Now that Constance had overturned Don's applecart, there was basically no way he could invite her into the family without it causing a major rift. Not that she'd want to come, anyway. He'd promised her all would be aboveboard, only to be proved wrong by his own flesh and blood. And now she thought he'd seduced her in a deliberate ploy to interfere with her investigation.

"I can see you have feelings for her." Don hoisted his bag onto his shoulder.

"I don't. Except that I'm mad she wouldn't let me deal with this myself. I could have made you declare all your back taxes without dragging the law into this."

A knock on the door made them both turn. "Mr. Fairweather." Angie, one of the desk clerks, appeared. "The police are here."

"I knew they'd turn up sooner or later." John shoved a hand through his hair. "Why not just send them up?"

"I'm so glad you're back home, dear." Constance peeled carrots while her mom chopped chicken breast for a pie. She'd been home for three days and they'd all settled back into their dull, familiar routine as if she'd never left. "Maybe you can talk some sense into your father about eating better. His cholesterol still isn't down where it should be and he keeps insisting on eggs and sausage for breakfast in the morning. He's even making it himself when I refuse."

"I'll bake some healthy muffins tomorrow morning. I think the best strategy is to tempt him away from the bad things he loves rather than just making him eat stuff he hates."

"You're so right, dear. I hadn't really thought of that. I've been trying to convince him to eat oatmeal and he won't even touch it. I knew you'd come up with something. I hope your job isn't going to send you away again."

"Actually my boss was talking about an assignment in Omaha. They seem to like the fact that I'm single and have no obligations."

"But you have an obligation to me and your father. You should tell them that."

"You should get used to me being gone, Mom. What if I get married?"

Her mom laughed. "You? You're married to your job. I can't even imagine you with a man. And honestly, sometimes I think they're more trouble than they're worth."

Constance's grip tightened on the peeler. Did her own mother seriously not think that she'd want to get married and have a family? Then again, why should she? Constance hadn't dated anyone at all the entire time she'd been living at home and she'd rebuffed several efforts to set her up with people she had no interest in or attraction to.

The truth was, she hadn't been interested in anyone until she met John. Why did she have to finally fall for someone so unsuitable and impossible? It could never have worked out, even if their affair hadn't been a shocking breach of professional conduct. He was a seasoned playboy who had apparently seduced her for his own purposes—at least initially—and if they hadn't been torn apart by circumstance he would have grown bored with her and cast her aside eventually.

"Why are your hands shaking?" Constance saw her mom's penetrating gray gaze fall on her fingers and she tried to peel faster. "I knew you never should have gone to that den of vice. You've looked like a ghost ever since you got back. Sally told me she read on the internet there's a big investigation going on there now. Tax evasion. I told her it was you that found out about it." She clucked her tongue. "Hardly a surprise, of course. It's always the people with the most money who are least willing to part with it. Still, I'm sure it was exhausting having to interact with people like that."

"I'm just tired." No need to mention all the stray emotion racking her and keeping her awake at night. "It was a challenging job. A lot of papers and computer files to go through. I worked really long hours." *And then played even longer hours.*

The memory of John's strong arms around her haunted her in the dead of night. Her body still tingled with awareness whenever she thought of him. Which was unfair, because she knew that right now he must hate her.

She'd seen the stories online. Don had been arrested

and charged with tax evasion and John had bailed him out with five hundred thousand dollars of his own money. He certainly wouldn't be lying around in bed thinking about how much he missed the woman who'd given the IRS probable cause for a full investigation of New Dawn. There was even talk of the casino being closed down while it was under investigation, and she knew from her examination of the books that would mean millions in losses for John and the tribe.

When he thought of her it must be with resentment and anger. Still, if she had to do it over, she wouldn't do anything differently. She'd bent her rules by leaking the information about John's uncle to him, but in the end, she'd stuck to her principles and done the job she was paid to do.

The affair with John was a whole different story. Would she let that happen again? She wasn't entirely sure she'd let it happen in the first place. It had just happened. What evolved between them had crept over her like a thunderstorm and she suspected there was nothing she could have done to control or stop the thunder and lightning flashing in her body—and her heart—when John was around.

Lucky thing she wouldn't see him again. The IRS had taken over the investigation and her firm had sent their final bill to the BIA. She could wash her hands of the whole sticky mess.

Except that she couldn't get John Fairweather out of her mind.

She'd just scraped the carrot peelings into the bin and was removing the full bag when the door to the kitchen flung open and her dad peered in. "Son of a gun, Constance, you're not going to believe what that fellow on the news just said."

"What, Dad?" Probably something to do with the upcoming local election he was up in arms about.

"That Native American from the casino who was arrested for tax evasion just claimed that the leader of the tribe engaged in personal relations with the accountant who came to investigate them. Isn't that you?"

Constance fumbled and the bin liner and its contents spilled onto the floor. "What?" Her voice was a shaky whisper. Blood roared in her ears. Or maybe it was the sound of her whole world crashing down around her.

"Said he wasn't the only one bending a few rules and he thought people should know the truth about the BIA's investigator who pointed the finger at him." Her dad's voice trailed off as he surveyed the mess on the floor. "It's not true, is it, sweet?"

She scrambled to pick up the slimy carrot peelings, plastic cheese wrappers and crumpled damp paper towels from the tile floor and shove them back in the bag. Could she really lie to her own parents?

"Constance Allen." Her mother's voice rang out. "You heard your father. Tell us this minute that these evil accusations are entirely false."

She rose shakily to her feet and held her hands under the tap, trying to rinse off the garbage. "They're not false." She couldn't even look at them as she said it. She picked up the sponge and knelt back down to try to wipe up the mess.

"You had an affair with the man you were sent to dig up dirt on?" Her mother moved closer.

"I was sent to look at the company's books. I did my job." She rinsed the sponge and wrung it out. Then she looked up at her parents standing there, so close to her, in the small kitchen where she'd made dinner with her mother for so many years. "I didn't mean to do anything else, but…" How did she explain what happened? "He was very handsome and kind, and I was very foolish."

"I have no doubt that man deliberately set out to seduce

you in order to pervert the course of your investigation." Her mother's mouth pinched into a tight knot.

"Maybe he did." She put the sponge down, hands still trembling. "But I never altered anything about the way I conducted my work. As you've already heard, I uncovered tax evasion by one of his relatives."

"Did you sleep with this man?" Her mother's hissed question made her shrink inside her clothes.

"Sarah! How can you ask such a question?" Her dad's shocked expression only deepened Constance's sense of humiliation and sadness.

"I did, Mom. I'm sorry, Dad. It's just the truth. I'm not proud of it. To this day I really don't know what came over me. He was quite a man." She let out a sigh and wished she could release the tension that heated the air in the kitchen almost to the boiling point. "Apparently I'm only human after all."

"I knew you should never have gone to that gambling establishment. A place like that isn't safe for a nice young girl."

"It's not the place, Mom. It's me. I've been living under a rock too long. I didn't realize how lonely I was. How much intimacy and affection could appeal to me."

"This man must have no sense of honor at all if he'd tell the media about your…interaction with him." Her father's usually placid brow had furrowed. "Then again, it was the other man on the news. The one you accused of tax evasion." He cleared his throat. "I suppose the dust will settle sooner or later."

"Oh, dear." Her mother's hand was now pressed to her mouth. "You'll be fired, won't you?"

"Probably." Her voice was hollow. She had no appetite whatsoever for carrots and chicken potpie. "In fact, I suppose I should offer my resignation."

"There's always a spot for you behind our counter. Our customers do love you," her dad tried to reassure her.

Constance cringed at the thought of serving people who'd heard about her transgressions.

"Are you trying to set our daughter up as a carnival sideshow, Brian? She can't be seen in public with scandal like this flying around. Though I suppose she could reorganize the shelves in the stockroom. Goodness, what will the pastor think?"

Constance hit breaking point and watched herself throw the sponge down in the sink and run from the room, leaving them staring after her. She'd known it was wrong to sleep with John and she'd done it anyway. He had been too much for her to resist. Now she'd lose her career over him and she probably deserved it. At least stupidity wasn't a crime and she wouldn't end up with a criminal record for her mistake.

She hurled herself down on the bed, tears hovering just behind her eyes. How was John coping with all of this? Was he embarrassed by the news of their liaison becoming public, or did he think it was funny? She'd loved the way that nothing rattled him and he went about his business with such good humor.

Maybe she could learn to do the same. She'd need all the sense of humor she could muster to get through the coming days and weeks.

John pounded along the trail, past the grazing cows and towards the shady woods. It wasn't his style to run away from problems, but right now he needed to let off steam. A twig snapped behind him and he spun around, expecting to see another nosy reporter.

Worse, he saw Don, sweating and panting, trying to catch up with him.

"Get lost."

"Wait! I want to apologize."

"It's way, way too late for that." Anger rushed him—again—and he turned and kept running, faster. At least his uncle Don was one problem he really could outrun.

But the footsteps got closer. "You forgot I was a sprinter in high school," rasped Don.

"Sprinting will only get you but so far. Like cheating, and lying." John kept running, though the urge to turn around and knock Don to the ground tightened his biceps.

"I promise I'll never lie or cheat again." Don gasped the words as he ran. "I'll never gamble again."

"How about if you never speak again?" John yelled. Don kept getting closer, his wiry frame must be fitter than it looked.

"That I can't promise. See? I'm not lying." Don was almost level with him.

John spun around and shoved out his hand, which caught Don in the chest with the satisfying force of a punch. Don doubled over as the air rushed out of his lungs. "I should knock you senseless."

"But that would be a crime and you're well above that."

"Exactly." John looked down on Don, who panted, hands on his knees. "And I'm trying to build the Nissequot tribe, not kill off its members with my bare hands."

"I really am sorry."

"For what? There's so much for you to regret that I can't keep track. You're being investigated for fraud along with the business I've staked everything on. You could go to prison. And on top of that you decided to announce to the local news that I had an affair with the BIA's investigator."

"I was mad at you. I didn't think they they'd really believe me. I didn't even believe it myself. You should have told me it was true and I would have kept my mouth shut. It is true, isn't it?"

"As if I would ever confide in you. I wouldn't trust

you with my grocery list at this point." He should have rebuffed Don's innuendo, instead of ignoring it. Denied his suspicions.

Except that they were true.

Even now he couldn't get Constance out of his mind for a solid minute. He'd hoped that the vision of her soft hazel eyes would fade. It had been three days and now he was seeing her face everywhere he looked.

"I know you think I'm stupid, and in all honesty, sometimes I am," Don panted, sweat dripping from his tanned forehead. His black T-shirt was soaked through. "But I know there was something between you and Miss Constance Allen. And not just sex, either. If you ask me, you're going to pieces without her."

John jerked to his feet. "Going to pieces? You're the one losing your mind. I've never been calmer. I'm just trying to think of how to prevent the enterprise we spent years building, and the tribe we've poured our lifeblood into, from being destroyed by a few strokes of a pen. I'm not even thinking about…her."

Don rose to his feet and wiped sweat from his brow. "You can't fool me, boy. I've known you too long. You need to go after her and win her back."

He certainly wasn't going to tell Don that he'd been thinking about it. "I'm sure the media would just love that."

"I'm serious. It's not a crime to fall in love. She still did her job and ratted me out."

"She has principles, unlike a certain scumbag relative of mine."

Don crossed his arms. "I'm serious. I don't want you blaming me for you losing the love of your life as well as creating an embarrassing mess in the press."

John blew out hard. "I don't need your advice to run my life, thanks. I think I can do a much better job of that by myself."

Don persisted. "So go get her."

John drew in a breath. The breeze cooled his face and a bird chirped in a nearby tree. "Although right now I hate you more than any man alive, for once you might be right about something."

John ordered a ring from Tiffany's in Manhattan and arranged to have it couriered to meet him at the airport in Cleveland. He chose a simple ring, since he knew Constance wouldn't like anything ostentatious. He had to guess the size, but they assured him it would be easy to fix if necessary. He chartered a plane at the local airport and boarded it with anticipation snapping through his muscles.

Was he jumping the gun by planning a proposal rather than simply inviting her back into his life? Possibly. But getting her to move from Ohio to Massachusetts would take a huge leap of faith on her part and he wanted her to know that he meant to offer her everything—including marriage.

The word echoed in his brain. Marriage was permanent. For life. Usually that would scare him right out the door, but now it had a reassuring, solid ring to it that steadied his hand on the wheel. His grandmother always said that when you met the right person, you just knew. You didn't have to date the woman for years or know every single thing about her to know that you were meant for each other. And his grandparents had been together long enough to test his grandmother's theory.

John trusted his gut. It had steered him right many times in the past, even when everyone else and basic common sense suggested otherwise. His gut told him that Constance was the woman he'd been waiting for all these years. He needed her in his life, in his arms, in his bed.

Now all he had to do was convince her. And that meant

convincing her that his intentions had been honorable from the start of their affair.

He arrived at the Cleveland airport and met the courier with the ring in the arrivals terminal. The diamond solitaire was as simple and lovely as he'd hoped, and his nerves sizzled as he tucked it into his pants pocket. Then he rented a car and programmed the GPS to take him to the address he'd found on the internet.

Blood thundered in his veins as he pulled into the driveway of her parents' modest house in a sleepy Cleveland neighborhood. She'd probably be freaked out that he'd stalked her online to find her address. If she wasn't sufficiently alarmed just to see him here at all. Her car was already in the driveway, so she was here. And the large white van with a hardware store decal on the side must belong to her parents, who were probably home, too. He parked behind it.

He never got nervous going into all-or-nothing business meetings or negotiating million-dollar deals. Climbing the Allen family's scuffed doorstep, however, he felt his nerves tingling. He pushed the bell and heard a chime sound on the other side of the door.

"Oh, goodness. Who can that be?" He could hear a woman's stressed-sounding voice in the distance and could make out a person's fast-approaching silhouette through the patterned glass oval in the door. He steadied himself as the door swung open and plastered on an encouraging smile. A small woman with a neat brown bob appeared in the doorway.

"Hello, you must be Mrs. Allen." He extended his hand.

"Leave us alone," the woman said, and then slammed the door in his face. Maybe she thought he was a reporter.

He rang the doorbell again. "I'm not a journalist," he called. "Or a salesman." He saw her blurry silhouette halt. "I'm a friend of Constance's."

He watched the woman turn and walk back through the glass. The door cracked open and a pair of very suspicious gray eyes peered at him. "Constance has been taken ill."

"What?" He stepped forward, one hand on the door. "What's wrong with her?"

"Who are you?" Constance's mom was a little shorter than her daughter, and dressed in a plaid blouse and navy slacks.

"My name is John Fairweather." He extended his hand again. "I'm pleased to meet you." He quietly put one knee in front of the door in case she tried to slam it again. Not a moment too soon, because he soon felt the force of the door against his arm and leg.

"Get out of my doorway, you…you scum!"

John drew in a deep breath. "I think there's a misunderstanding. Constance investigated my company, but it was my uncle's records that she found wanting, not mine."

The small woman stopped pushing on the door and came alarmingly close, her face crinkling with rage. "You seduced an innocent young girl," she hissed. "You should be ashamed of yourself."

He decided not to protest that Constance wasn't that young or that innocent. "Your daughter is a very unique and special person, and I'm sure that much of the credit for that goes to you, Mrs. Allen. I admire her integrity and am proud to know her."

"Well, she doesn't want anything to do with you, that's for sure. She'll probably get fired now that ugly rumors are flying around." At least she wasn't trying to slam the door on him anymore. "What have you got to say for yourself about that?"

"Constance has nothing to hide. She did her job with thoroughness and even ruthlessness. I'm sure her employer will find no fault with her. May I see her, please?"

Was she really sick? She must be under a lot of stress.

As John mulled it over, a timid-looking man with a receding hairline appeared at the end of the hallway. "What's going on, dear?"

"This is John Fairweather, Brian." She spoke very deliberately, without taking her eyes off him. John watched her husband put two and two together.

"You're not welcome here, I'm afraid." He glanced nervously at his wife. "You'd best go back to where you came from."

"I'm in love with your daughter." Desperation made him cut right to the point. He knew Constance must be in there somewhere. "Please, let me see her."

He smiled, to hopefully seem less threatening, but he was serious about what he said next. "I'm not going to leave until I talk to her. I'll camp out on your front lawn if necessary." Since their front lawn was about as big as a king-size bed and had a fake fountain on it, he hoped it wouldn't come to that.

Mrs. Allen glanced up and down the street. The sun was setting and so far the only people watching them were two kids on bikes. She narrowed her eyes and shot him a chilling look. "Perhaps you'd better come in."

He tried not to beam with too much excitement as he stepped over the threshold into their narrow hallway.

"Constance, dear," her father called up the stairs. "Could you come down, sweetheart?"

All eyes turned anxiously to the gloomy stairs. But no door opened. Listening hard, John could hear music playing up there. Impatience and excitement fired through him. "I think she's got the radio on and can't hear you. Would it be okay with you if I go knock on her door?"

Normally he'd have marched straight up, but since he intended for these people to be his future mother- and father-in-law, more delicate handling was called for.

The Allens looked at each other. Sarah had closed the

door behind John to block out the prying eyes of neighbors. "I suppose so," she muttered. "You can hardly make things worse than they already are."

He bounded up the stairs, feeling his pants pocket on the way to check the ring was still there, and knocked on the door. A song by Adele was playing.

"I need some time alone, Mom."

"It's me. John."

The music snapped off.

"What?"

The sweet sound of her voice made his heart swell, and his fingers reached for the door handle. But he hesitated. What if she wasn't decent? He didn't want to blow it.

"John Fairweather. I drove here to see you."

The door flung open so fast he felt his hair shift in the breeze. She was dressed in striped pajama pants and a white T-shirt and looked as though she'd been crying. She also looked unbearably beautiful and fragile, and he wanted to take her in his arms.

"You've got quite a nerve." She said it softly, as if she wasn't really listening to herself. She studied his face, then he felt her take in the rest of his body before looking back into his eyes with a confused expression.

"That's hardly news." He felt a grin spreading across his face. "I missed you."

"Did you tell Don about our affair?" Her gaze hardened. Pain hovered in her eyes.

"Never. He made it all up, in fact. I never told him anything about us. He was just mad—mostly at me because I fired him from his position."

"But you didn't deny it."

"I can't deny it. It's the truth." A smile tugged at the corner of his mouth, but he struggled to suppress it.

She frowned. "It's a shame you didn't get what you wanted, isn't it?"

"What do you mean?"

"It's a pity your plot to seduce me didn't throw me off the course and make me leave. Or convince me to cover up the truth. I overheard your conversation with Don in the lobby."

"There was never any kind of plot. Don suggested it, but I never had the slightest intention of following through."

"You just kissed me on the first night you met me because I'm so unbelievably irresistible?" She cocked her head.

"Exactly." The smile struggled over his mouth again.

"I'm not that dumb, John."

"You're not dumb at all. You're sharp as a tack and that's one of the many reasons I'm crazy about you."

She frowned and looked confused. "Why are you here? I'm not going to deny the affair if that's what you're hoping. I'd rather lose my career than tell a lie that big."

"I feel the same way." He reached for the ring in his pocket. No use beating about the bush. When she saw it she'd know he was serious. "I realize we've only known each other a short time." He pulled out the box and watched her brow furrow. "But there's something between us, something different." For once, he struggled for words. "I love you, Constance. I love you and I need you in my life. I've never met anyone like you before and I want to spend the rest of my days with you. Will you marry me?"

Eleven

Constance stared at John. It was hard enough to comprehend that he was here in her bedroom. She certainly didn't believe that he'd just asked her to marry him.

"Aren't you mad at me?" She'd pictured him cursing her and wishing she'd never been born. She knew the kind of scrutiny his casino and his whole tribe were under right now.

"For being honest and trustworthy? No way. I love you all the more for it."

She blinked. He looked ridiculously handsome, with that wary expression on his face and the pale blue box open in his hand. And that sure was a beautiful ring.

"You can't be serious. About marrying me, I mean."

"Constance, you know me well enough to know that I wouldn't joke about something like this. I love you, and I want you to be my wife." Humor twinkled in his eyes, as usual. He was always so confident. He was sure she'd say yes.

Constance stared from his face to the ring and back. This was beyond anything she could imagine. She'd never thought for a minute that John would want to turn their affair into something permanent. She hadn't allowed herself a dream that crazy. "You can't be serious."

"Are you okay in there, Constance?" She heard her father's voice on the other side of the door, which John had closed behind him.

"Yes, Dad. I'm fine." *At least I think I am. I'm not sure. I might be dreaming.*

"You're killing me, Constance. I'm in love with you." John sank to one knee on the pale green carpet. "Please say you'll marry me."

Tears sprang to her eyes. She could hear the sincerity in his voice, feel it in the air between them. "Yes." The word sounded so strange coming from her mouth. The whole situation was so surreal. But it was the only answer she could give.

He rose to his feet, dark eyes shining. "May I kiss you?"

She bit her lip, and glanced at the door. Both of her parents were probably standing outside. She looked back at John and his loving gaze melted her. "Okay."

His lips covered hers and she lost herself in the kiss, holding him tight. Kissing him again was such a sweet relief after the lonely nights and anxious days since she'd left him. He wrapped his strong arms around her, holding her up as her already shaky knees threatened to give way.

"God, I missed you so much," he breathed, pressing her against him when they finally broke for air. "I hate being without you. Will you come back with me right now?"

She bit her lip. "What about my job? They're being really supportive. They don't believe the allegations that I had an affair with you and I couldn't bring myself to admit it. Now they'll have good cause to fire me when they find out it's true and I didn't confess."

He ran his thumb over her lip as his face creased into a grin. "I do like the way you take your responsibilities so seriously. It's one of the many sexy things about you. They're going to know for sure that we had an affair when you tell them you're marrying me."

"Yes, but I need to reassure them that it didn't interfere with me fulfilling my professional responsibilities. What if they think you're back here to curry favor in the hope that I can get the IRS off your back?" She was only half kidding.

"I don't live my life worrying about what other people think." Undeterred, he kissed her mouth softly. "I know that if I choose to do what's right, I can hold my head high in front of anyone. Including your parents." He glanced in the direction of the door with a wink. "Do you think we should go tell them?"

She nodded, apprehension zinging inside her. "I suppose there's no way around that."

He opened the door to find both of them standing in the hallway outside her bedroom.

"We overheard," said her mother, with a dazed expression.

"Mom!"

"And we appreciate this young man having the honor and decency to make an honest woman of you." Her mother looked right at John.

"You do?" John looked astonished.

Her father cleared his throat. "Under the circumstances I'm truly convinced that you love our daughter. I won't say we approve of the business you're in, but we have no intention but to wish you both the best."

"You do?" It was Constance's turn to express her shock and disbelief. "I'll have to move to Massachusetts." She figured she might as well lay it all out.

"And we hope that you'll both move to Massachusetts with us," John cut in. "You'll find it's a lovely place to live."

"We do have a business to run here," Sarah explained. "But I'm sure we'd be happy to come visit."

Constance stared from one of her parents to the other,

then back to John. Did he have magical powers of persuasion? The media had as much as accused him of that when he'd created a tribe out of a few family members and a multimillion-dollar company on a few weedy acres in the backwoods.

"I look forward to getting to know you both." John shook their hands heartily. "Will you allow me to take you all out to dinner to celebrate?"

Her father still looked a bit stunned, but in a happy way. "We'd be delighted."

After a congenial dinner at her parents' favorite Italian restaurant, John and Constance drove to a nearby hotel. Once inside the room, with the door closed, they stopped and stared at each other. "Am I dreaming?" She stood about one foot from him, beside the bed, in the dimly lit room. "Because I have had strange and vivid dreams lately."

"If you're dreaming then I guess it means I'm in your dream." He held her gaze. "Which is fine with me. As long as neither of us wakes up." His lips curved into a mischievous half smile.

She felt her own now-familiar smile creep to her mouth in response. "I don't think either of us is the type to sleepwalk through life, so I suspect we're wide awake right now."

He lifted a brow. "I think you'll have to pinch me to find out."

She inhaled slowly, then reached around for his backside. It wasn't easy to pinch that much hard muscle, but she managed, at the cost of heating her blood a few more degrees.

"Yep. I'm awake." His eyes had darkened with desire. "Now for you." He slid his hands around her hips until he was cupping her rear. Then he squeezed and lifted her up so fast that she gasped as adrenaline rushed through her. "Uh-huh. You are, too." Still holding her off the ground, he let her rest against his big body and slowly slide down. She felt the hard jut of his erection through his dark pants, and it made her breath catch. "Awake, and if I'm not mistaken, every bit as aroused as I am."

She bit her lip and nodded. Heat pooled deep inside her and clouded her thinking. When her toes touched the floor, her fingers reached for the buttons on his shirt. She could hear her breathing quicken as she pulled each button from its hole and exposed his broad, muscled chest. His big fingers struggled with the tiny buttons on her blouse, and his expression of intense concentration made her chuckle.

She kissed his chest and inhaled the rich, masculine scent of him, then let her mouth trail down to where his pants sat low on his hips. It excited her to see how aroused he was. She heard his breath hitch and saw his stomach contract as she kissed his hard flesh through the expensive fabric of his pants. Then she undid the catch and the zipper with trembling fingers and slid the pants down over his powerful thighs.

It drove her crazy that this man was so intensely excited by her, ordinary little Constance Allen, who spent her days surrounded by file cabinets and calculators. But his passion-filled gaze and fierce erection left no doubt.

He slid her skirt and stockings off and pulled her onto the bed. For a moment they lay side by side, enjoying the vision of each other naked.

Seeing their surroundings made her remember that they were in a busy hotel with paper-thin walls and middle managers making phone calls in the rooms around them. "Maybe we should put the radio on."

He winked. "You're so practical. I love that about you.

And you're right. We don't need everyone in the Inn and Suites to hear your cries of passion." He reached for the radio next to the bed and turned the dial until he found a slow song. "And speaking of practical, I still have enough sense left to remember to use a condom." He fished in his bag and pulled out the packet, then opened it and settled back on the bed with her.

The soft sounds of sexy music filled the room as he rested his broad hand on her hip and slid it slowly up her waist to her breast. She watched his chest rise as he ran his fingers over her breast, stimulating her nipple. She was already so aroused that she let out a gasp. "I want you inside me," she pleaded, hardly able to believe it was her talking. She'd had no idea until she met John that she was capable of this kind of desire.

"With no foreplay?" He looked surprised.

"I don't need foreplay right now." She pressed her mouth to his for one breathless instant. "And I can see you don't either."

"True." He groaned as she wrapped her hand around him, then took the condom from him and rolled it on. With confidence and conviction that surprised her, she slid underneath him and guided him inside her. Her hips rose as he entered her and the sense of relief and exhilaration took her breath away. It felt so right. She lifted her hips to meet his and they moved together, both already on the brink of explosion, so much pent-up need and desire ready to burst over them.

"I love you." Her confession sprang from her lips—she couldn't hold back the words. Her feelings for him had been growing inside her from the first moment they kissed—maybe even the first moment they met—and she could now acknowledge what they meant. As she came to this realization, she felt the first waves of her orgasm spread through her like a tornado unwinding.

"I love you, too, sweetheart." He moved over her with a slow intensity that unraveled her completely. "I love you so, so…" His words were lost as he climaxed and she gripped him as hard as she could, fingers pressing into the hard muscle of his back.

She felt him pulsing inside her, and her heart filled until she thought it would burst. She didn't care if everyone at work knew she'd had an affair with the man she was sent to investigate. She didn't care if they fired her from her job. She didn't care if she never worked in accounting again. She didn't care about anything except being here, with John, right now.

And for the rest of her life.

His big body rested so comfortably on hers. "…So much."

She wanted to laugh, but couldn't find the energy. All the anxiety and worry and tension of the last few days had been wrung out of her by their lovemaking. The aftershocks of her orgasm trickled through her, sending a silly giggle to her chest. "What have you done to me? I feel like a completely different person when I'm with you."

"With me you're exactly the person you're supposed to be. Me, too. I was so caught up in trying to make money and avoid any romantic entanglements that I was running every minute. You were so caught up in trying to be Little Miss Perfect that you needed someone to trip you right up and stop you in your tracks."

"And catch me as I fell."

She felt his chuckle vibrate through both of them. Then he rolled gently off her until they were side by side, hugging each other. "To catch you and hold you tight so you couldn't slip away." His soft kiss sent yet another smile spreading across her lips.

She remembered the ring on her finger and pulled her hand up to stare at it. One stunning diamond in a minimalist platinum setting.

"I wanted something classic and perfect, with no unnecessary embellishment. Like you."

"It's so gorgeous. It must have cost a fortune." The diamond itself was set so that it didn't stick out or look ostentatious, but on close inspection she could see it was very large.

"What's the point of having a fortune if you can't spend it on the really important things? And you're the most important thing that has ever happened to me." His voice had a raw, honest edge to it that made tears spring to her eyes.

"I feel like I should give you something, too." What did you give the man who had everything? And if he didn't have it yet, he could buy it tomorrow.

"You are. You." He pulled her fingers gently to his lips and kissed them.

The truth of his words shocked her little. In agreeing to marry him she had given herself to him, which, she knew, meant giving up her life in Ohio and moving to Massachusetts, away from all her friends and family. She'd have to quit her job even if they didn't fire her.

"What's the matter?" He stroked her cheek.

"I'm thinking about all the changes ahead. Where will I work?"

"Well, the New Dawn has been accused of nepotism, and with good reason." He winked. "We do like to employ family members."

She frowned. "What would I do there?"

He pulled back and looked at her with a serious expression. "Whatever you think is important and interesting.

Your financial expertise could certainly be put to good use. You could even take over that part of the daily operations from me so I can focus on booking celebrities and hustling some good PR. I suspect I'll be better at that than Uncle Don was."

She inhaled sharply. "I still can't believe that he went to the press about us."

"He can be a real ass sometimes. Especially since he didn't even know we actually were involved." He ran his thumb over her lips. "I'm providing him with the best legal counsel so hopefully he won't spend the next few decades in jail, but he might wish he was safely behind bars by the time I'm done letting him know what I think about his behavior."

"You'd be surprised by how many people don't pay taxes." She ran her fingers through his hair. "They think that they earned the money, and it should be theirs to keep. Even people who have millions just think they can keep silent about it on their returns and nothing will happen. Yet they're still driving on roads and sending their kids to schools paid for by our taxes."

"Human nature. It's a constant battle for some of us to pretend to be civilized." He winked. "And trust me, I don't pay any more taxes than I have to myself. It'd probably be part of your job to finesse that, as well."

"I've been doing that for much bigger corporations for years. Maybe I'd like to do something else."

"Like what?"

She bit her lip and thought for a minute. The idea was outrageous, but then so was everything else about being here. "I always wanted to teach. My parents told me that the schools are full of unteachable, rowdy hoodlums and that I'd be miserable, which is why I pursued a career with numbers, but sometimes I wonder if I made the wrong choice."

"Interesting." He peered at her. "Now that we are gathering tribal members from far and wide, we have a lot to teach them about the business. Maybe you could start there, then get your teaching credentials and branch out to teaching in the schools."

"I like that idea." Her mind was racing, which was funny since her body still hummed with the aftereffects of their lovemaking. "It would be nice to work with people instead of numbers for a change."

"I think you'll be great at it." He kissed her softly on her mouth.

"I'll resign tomorrow. I wonder if they'll make me work for a final two weeks, or if they'll escort me out the door with my possessions in a cardboard box."

His eyes twinkled. "Once they know you're marrying me, probably the latter."

She felt a grin spread across her face. "I guess that's a good thing, under the circumstances."

"It most certainly is."

Epilogue

Thanksgiving

"Some people say that Native Americans shouldn't celebrate Thanksgiving." John stood at the head of the crowded table in the dining room of their meticulously renovated farmhouse. The fine cherry table was laden with fresh local turkey, roasted corn, chestnuts, maple-glazed squash with walnuts and glistening cranberry sauce. "They say that it was a foolish mistake of our ancestors to show the Pilgrims how to eat and survive in our land. They think it would have been better to let them starve to death."

He paused and looked around at the gathered guests. His grandparents beamed proudly and Constance wondered if they'd heard this speech before. "I disagree. Every choice we make in life shapes who we become and I'm proud to be a descendant of those who chose to offer the hand of friendship. I prefer to hope for the best and that's how I live my life. Our people have certainly been through many trials and tribulations since then, but we're still here and we're looking forward to a vibrant future."

He raised his champagne flute, and Constance lifted hers. She still couldn't believe this tall, handsome man was her husband. "And that future has just grown a little bit brighter…" He glanced at her and she smiled back. They'd talked about when to make their announcement and decided this was the perfect time. She felt butterflies in her stomach, fluttering around the tiny baby growing there.

"Because we're expecting a new member of the Nissequot tribe, who should be joining us sometime in June."

His grandmother gasped and turned to her husband. "A baby? Oh, John, did you hear that?"

"I heard it." He beamed and patted her hand. "That's wonderful."

The round of congratulations made Constance blush, and a sudden rush of emotion propelled her to her feet. A hush fell over the room as she looked around, feeling such a strong connection to the people gathered there. "These last few months have been a whirlwind. In May I was still living quietly in my childhood bedroom in Ohio, in June I got the assignment that would bring me here for the first time and now, in November, I'm an expectant mother, married to an amazing man, living in a lovely farmhouse in Massachusetts and pursuing a teaching license. I'm still a bit shell-shocked by it all, but I'm so grateful for the way you've all welcomed me into your midst and made my transition to my new life so easy and enjoyable."

Even her parents were smiling. They'd driven up here for the wedding, and now for Thanksgiving, and John's relentlessly charming grandfather had taken over the task of winning their hearts for the Nissequot tribe and casino. Although he still had a way to go, he'd made impressive progress.

John raised his glass. "I already find it hard to remember what life was like before you came here. Every day I'm grateful for the BIA investigation that brought you into our lives." A chuckle rumbled around the room. "Even Don says he's glad Constance caught up with him before he dug himself into an even deeper hole. He's lucky to have got off with only a six-week sentence."

The casino had shrugged off the scandal and the publicity from it brought in more people than ever, so New

Dawn was growing from strength to strength. "Next year we should be able to complete the purchase of seven hundred acres along our eastern border and break ground on the water park." Amusement twinkled in his eyes as he looked at Constance. The water park had been her idea. She liked the idea of expanding in a family-friendly direction and offering summer camps there for kids from all over the region. "Every day around here is a new adventure and I'm glad to be sharing them with my soul mate."

"I love you," she said softly.

"I love you, too, sweetheart." He spoke the words just to her, and emotion flowed directly between them despite all the people gathered around them. "And I'm thankful that I get to spend the rest of my life with you."

She felt tears well in her eyes and was about to blame the pregnancy hormones when she noticed that she wasn't the only one having that reaction. "Sometimes there's so much to be thankful for that it's hard to know where to start, so I suggest we all enjoy this delicious meal before it gets cold," she said.

John's grandfather chimed in. "I like the way you think. We give thanks to the Creator for this fine meal and the pleasure of sharing it together. Let's eat!"

* * * * *

FOR THE SAKE OF
THE SECRET CHILD

YVONNE LINDSAY

This book is dedicated to Kate Gordon with grateful
thanks for all her patience and help regarding so
many questions relating to Queenstown.

One

Waiting on her private dock at the edge of Lake Wakatipu, Mia Parker smoothed her uniform for the umpteenth time. She was as curious to meet the new guest for Parker's Retreat as she was nervous. The prickle of unease that had started around 3:00 a.m. this morning was now a deep-seated knot of tension situated between her shoulder blades.

"What do you think he'll be like?" her mother asked from her side.

"I don't know, but he's paying us well enough not to wonder too much," Mia answered with a tight smile.

She told herself, not for the first time, that her sudden anxiety was completely unfounded. From what her friend, Rina Woodville, had explained to her, Mia knew that Benedict del Castillo came from a wealthy family and was looking for a quiet and private respite while he recovered from a car accident. Despite that, she couldn't help wondering what type of man had the kind of money to book out her entire boutique hotel and health spa for a whole month *and* pay her a considerable bonus at the same time.

With that much wealth, why come all the way to her private oasis in one of New Zealand's busiest tourist spots? The fabulous spas and resorts of Europe would have been much closer to his Mediterranean island home. And they were more accustomed to providing the type of luxurious anonymity Mr. del Castillo seemed to require. What had happened to make the man want to travel so far?

"With any luck he'll be tall, dark and handsome and in the market for a wife," her mother persisted.

"Mom, I didn't know you were in the market for a new husband," Mia teased, knowing full well her mother was still grieving over Reuben Parker's death three years ago.

To her surprise her mother blushed, but then quickly resumed her not-so-subtle assault. "You know full well I'm talking about you, young lady. Don't think you can change the subject. It's about time you got back with the real world and stopped hiding yourself away here."

"I'm not hiding, I'm building a business. And this guy, well, he's our ticket to some much-needed financial security. That's more important to me right now than romance."

Mia closed her eyes for a moment, reliving the rush of relief and excitement that had swamped her when his first half payment had been confirmed in her bank account. Knowing she'd be able to cover her staff's wages for the duration of his stay and for a good month beyond that had brought a peace of mind she hadn't known in a very long time. The sensation was addictive, making it easy for her to justify not investigating the background of her guest further—telling herself she was merely respecting his request for privacy.

A sound on the water caught her attention, making her

open her eyes. The boat was coming and, with it, the man who would be the sole focus of the retreat's staff for the next thirty days. She could see the sleek lines of the luxury thirty-eight footer as it cut through the slight chop on the surface of the lake. She was glad she'd ignored the bank manager's advice to sell the boat after her father's death and the true state of their family's affairs had been revealed.

At times like this, the boat was a vital, and impressive, link to the outside world. A statement that, despite Reuben Parker's choice to take his own life rather than face his debtors, the Parkers would survive.

The vessel was closer now and she could see three figures standing on the flying bridge—one she easily identified as Don, her boat captain and all-round handyman at Parker's Retreat. The others must be her guest and his personal trainer, because she could already see Don's seventy-one-year-old father—and self-proclaimed boat boy—standing on the main deck, ready to cast the mooring lines.

Again that knot in between her shoulder blades tightened. Everything about her reclusive guest's visit was integral to the survival of her business. Everything.

"Everything's perfect, isn't it?" She turned and asked her mother, suddenly stricken with an irrational fear that she'd forgotten something.

"Mia, relax. You know we've done everything. Mr. del Castillo is in the Summit Suite, his trainer's accommodation is sorted, the kitchen has Mr. del Castillo's food and beverage preferences, the car and driver in Queenstown are on constant standby and you yourself have his spa visit schedule organized like a military exercise. Stop worrying so much. Besides, in the unlikely event we've overlooked anything, we can fix it without it causing any problems, I'm sure."

"Right. We'll be fine," Mia said, more for her own peace of mind than in agreement with her mother's calming words.

She stepped forward and grabbed the bow line being thrown from the boat and tied it off on the dock as Don's father nimbly sprang to do the same to secure the rear.

As soon as the boat was secured and the gangway bridged the short distance between the vessel and the dock, she painted on a smile. First to disembark was a whipcord-lean blond man, dressed casually in jeans and a lightweight ski jacket to ward off the chill winter air. The personal trainer, she guessed. She'd assumed that the trainer might be a woman, when told that her guest would be arriving with one other person, and had suspected the moniker to be one of convenience only. But the suppressed energy in the blond man's gait said otherwise. Mr. del Castillo must be taking his recuperation seriously if this was the man he'd hired for the task.

"Hi," he said, taking her hand and pumping it enthusiastically. "I'm Andre Silvain, pleased to meet you."

French, she noted, judging by his accent. "Welcome to Parker's Retreat, Mr. Silvain. I think you'll find we have all the equipment you said you would need for the duration of your stay. This is my mother, Elsa Parker. She acts as chatelaine here."

"Call me Andre." He smiled back charmingly and looked around. "This place is amazing. I'm sure Ben and I will accomplish great things together here."

His enthusiasm was almost overwhelming and Mia felt her cheeks start to ache as she turned to watch the tall, dark-haired man now limping down the gangway. Dressed all in black and clearly suffering from the contrast in temperature between his native Isla Sagrado and a southern New Zealand winter, he guided himself slowly, one hand resting on the hand rail.

Though she couldn't yet see his face, there was something familiar about him, she thought as she watched the wind tug at the silk paisley scarf he wore looped around his collar and lower jaw. The finely woven fabric slid down, exposing a shadow of a beard and a pallor to his skin at odds with the Mediterranean summer weather she knew he'd come from. The wind tousled his slightly overlong black hair, lifting it from the smooth wide plane of his forehead. The sense of familiarity increased as he lifted his head and dark chocolate-brown eyes caught with hers.

The knot in her spine intensified and sent a spear of shock straight to her heart as her worst judgment call, ever, walked back into her life.

Benedict del Castillo shivered under the heavy black wool of his knee-length coat, his hand tightening on the gangway rail as he made eye contact with the young woman standing on the dock. Instant recognition and something unexpected—something hot and feral—fired through his veins.

Just over three and a half years ago, at the weekend-long, high-society party where they'd met, he'd only known her as "M." But despite that virtual anonymity, his body knew hers with a depth of intimacy he'd shared with very few. What were the odds, he wondered, that she would be here?

Ben's eyes raked her from head to toe and he noted her not quite form-fitting uniform with distaste. The jacket and trousers were designed to conceal, rather than reveal and—if his memory served him correctly—her attributes were well worth revealing.

"Welcome to Parker's Retreat, Mr. del Castillo. I'm Mia Parker. I hope you will be comfortable here."

"So formal, M?"

He saw the fear that clouded her eyes straight away. The reaction intrigued him. Obviously, she hadn't planned to acknowledge the fact that the last time they'd been together they'd done just about every single physical thing a couple could do in the pursuit of mutual sexual satisfaction. He could understand the coolness, he supposed; given the circumstances. They had a business arrangement in place for the next month—it was not surprising that she would wish to be professional. But fear? What on earth did she have to be afraid of?

He took her hand and lifted it to his lips, pressing them to her cold knuckles. He sensed the tremor that rocked through her at his touch and he allowed his mouth to curl into a smile as he released her hand. To his amusement, she snatched it away, rubbing her knuckles against those god-awful trousers and stiffening her posture.

"I believe you'll find everything here to your satisfaction. My staff has worked hard to ensure that all your specific requirements are met."

"And you, *querida?* Do you plan to meet my—" he paused for effect, unable to resist baiting her "—specific requirements also?"

A bright flush of color stained her cheeks and her voice shook a little when she replied.

"Obviously, I'll be working closely with your trainer to ensure your recovery is as swift as it can possibly be."

His recovery. Self-disgust gouged through him, cooling his amusement as effectively as the glacier that had long ago formed the lake behind him. The memory of the car crash infuriated him, especially since it came with the knowledge that it was his stupidity and reckless taunt at fate that had come back and bitten him painfully hard. That was still a bitter pill to swallow. He tamped down the feelings that had riddled him since his accident and shifted his focus to M's obvious discomfort. A man had to find his amusements where he could and right now Mia Parker was looking very good indeed.

"Obviously," he finally responded. "And who is this charming lady here with you?"

"Oh, I am sorry." Mia flushed with embarrassment. "This is my mother, Elsa Parker. Together, we run Parker's Retreat."

"Pleased to meet you, Mr. del Castillo, although you'll have to forgive my daughter for underselling herself. She's responsible for just about everything around here."

"Is that so?" Ben replied, taking Elsa's hand and offering her the same "olde worlde" courtesy he'd just shown her daughter.

To her credit, the older woman carried herself with a great deal more aplomb than Mia but then again, she had no idea of just how well he knew her daughter.

Mia gestured to one of two golf carts parked by the dock.

"If you'd like to take a seat, Don will take you and Andre up to the main guest house. Mother and I will follow with your luggage."

She wasn't about to be rid of him that easily.

"Actually, it's only a short distance, isn't it? After all that flying, I think I'd rather walk. You go on up, Andre," he said to his trainer. "Ms. Parker can accompany me to the hotel building."

"What about your crutches, Ben? I think you left them on the boat," Andre said, his meaning clear.

"They can stay there. The sooner I learn to live without them the better, as far as I'm concerned."

"Your call, *mon ami*. I believe you would be more comfortable with them for now, but given that it's only been a couple of weeks since you came out of hospital I insist you at least use a walking stick. I have a collapsible cane here near the top of my case for exactly this purpose."

Ben grimaced as Andre handed him the cane. He'd had enough of taking it easy, and enough of being poked, prodded and mollycoddled. Coming here was his chance to build himself back up to peak strength in privacy and without prying eyes or media conjecture as to any long-term damage to his body. His family was too wealthy, too famous for him to hide his recovery from the public eye if he had stayed in the Mediterranean, but here on the other side of the world, he could finally have the seclusion he needed. The seclusion his contract with Parker's Retreat had guaranteed.

It was past time his recalcitrant body returned to the level of fitness he was used to, so he could return to his usual activities—*all* of his usual activities. He cast a sideways glance at his reluctant escort and felt a ribbon of anticipation thread through him. And he knew just where he was going to start.

He'd changed, Mia thought as she adjusted her pace to walk slowly toward the main hotel building. Gone was the affable and self-assured man who'd swept her off her feet and into his bed the summer before her world turned upside down. Oh, he was still most definitely self-assured, but there was an edge to him now. Something else lay beneath the surface of his charm that hadn't been there before and she remembered "before" in all its Technicolor glory.

Her hand still tingled where he'd kissed her. Why couldn't he have simply settled for a handshake like everyone else? But then he wouldn't be Benedict del Castillo, her alter ego replied silently. He wouldn't be the man whom she'd met at a New Year's Eve gathering at one of the Gibbston Valley vineyards. The man who'd instantly caught her attention and then held it for every split second of the hours they'd spent together during one whole glorious day and two even more glorious nights, until his departure back overseas.

A man who, even now, sent her blood thrumming through her veins. She couldn't afford to let him affect her this way. He was a guest at the retreat and she had to see him in that light and that light only.

Oh Lord. A thought suddenly occurred to her. How on earth would she cope when it came time for his sessions at the spa? She'd given her other massage therapists a vacation for the duration of the del Castillo party's stay, intending to handle the sessions herself. She was a certified massage therapist, and had thought that personally undertaking Mr. del Castillo's treatment would show her commitment to maintaining his privacy and comfort. But now she couldn't help but wonder what she'd gotten herself into.

Touching him, stroking him. Letting her hands reacquaint themselves with his body. And what a body. Even now she had no difficulty recalling the smooth tanned texture of his chest, the way his dark brown nipples would tighten beneath her tongue. The taste of him.

She clamped down on her wayward thoughts. This was most definitely not the way for her to be thinking.

She wasn't the same girl she'd been when she'd shared his bed. She had a new life now, and new responsibilities. In the past three years, she'd lost her wealth, lost her father... and gained a son. Jasper, she had to think of Jasper. To remind herself why she was working so hard to make the retreat a success. Why it was so important to her to provide some form of security for her son and her mother, as well as for herself.

But even as she did so, the memories of that long-ago tryst

still kept on filtering through her mind. She'd only had to see him to feel that sense of excitement and anticipation again.

Don't even go there, she argued with herself. What they had shared was in the past. Very firmly in the past. She wasn't that woman anymore. She was a mother, a daughter, an employer—not the wild party girl who'd always had more money to throw around than sense to realize how lucky she'd been.

Mia started to silently recite a number in her head. The exact amount of money she owed the bank. It would be years before she could honestly say she was easily holding her head above water but for as long as she could paddle and break even, she would. Benedict del Castillo's financial arrangement for the privacy he so craved, paying full occupancy rates for the hotel for a month, plus a thirty percent premium provided his needs were met, would go a long way toward her immediate security. She couldn't afford to do anything that would breach that arrangement.

But what if he wanted to resume where they'd left off? The thought came and blindsided her. She simply could not afford to upset or reject him in any way, and she could hardly be surprised if he craved a repeat of the passion and intensity they'd shared during their last encounter. Even she had to admit she found the idea arousing. It had been so long since she'd let herself indulge in an affair.

No, she shook her head slightly, ridding herself of the notion before it could bloom and take hold in her mind. As tempting as it might be, it was certainly not a part of the professional persona she now maintained.

And there was far more at stake than her professional persona now.

Jasper.

Just thinking about her little boy, nearly three months shy of his third birthday, made her know that the choices and the sacrifices she'd made were for a darn good purpose. Taking care of him—and protecting his future by focusing on growing and stabilizing her business—had to take priority. He was something she'd done all on her own and something she'd done right, for the first time in her life. She'd do anything to protect him. Anything.

She fixed her eyes firmly on the building ahead, trying to ignore the man who walked slowly beside her. The man who could undoubtedly make or break her future security.

The man who had no idea that he was the father of her child.

Two

Two

"The spa bath is right through there and, if you prefer a shower, you'll find it has multiple adjustable jets and a bench built into the stall."

A bench.

Benedict closed his eyes briefly and bit back the sharp retort that had become his standard response when faced with the assumption he was infirm. That he'd need to sit down in the shower.

She was merely extolling the features of her facility, he reminded himself. She wasn't one of the long parade of ex-girlfriends who'd turned up at his house wanting to "care" for him straight out of hospital—and sell their stories to the highest tabloid bidder.

He'd eventually sought sanctuary in the castillo where his family had lived for three hundred years. He'd been warmly welcomed by his grandfather and oldest brother—and gently cared for by his brother's wife—but even there the concern of his family and their retainers had become suffocating.

He was a survivor, dammit. For all those hours he'd been trapped in the wreckage of his car, he'd fought against the inky blackness of unconsciousness with that thought. No matter how much pain he'd been in, he knew he'd survive—he had to. No deals with the devil for him. Instead, the experience had given him a new perspective on things. A knowledge that life was indeed precious and not to be taken for granted—that time was not something to be wasted, because no one knew when that time could be cut short. In the deep dark of that night he'd also grasped the importance of family, and that promises to family were, above all other things, to be honored. His life, as he'd known it, had ended there and then—exposed for the shallow and somewhat hedonistic behavior it had been. He would no longer take his carefree and privileged lifestyle for granted.

He opened his eyes and looked out the massive picture window that framed the retreat's gardens, showing the path that led to the shore of the lake. A long, low, gray cloud snaked a line between the mountains that ringed Wakatipu. A blemish on an otherwise perfect scene. A perfect example of his life.

Blemished. Flawed.

Resentment—his constant friend since doctors had delivered the news that, despite the best microsurgery available, his injuries had left him infertile—tasted bitter on his tongue.

He turned from the vista, from the reminder that despite all outward appearances, he was no longer like other men. That he could never provide a child for his family and, with it, the assurance that the ancient governess's curse could be broken once and for all.

The old myth had haunted his family for years, but neither Ben nor his brothers had taken it seriously—until their grandfather grew ill. If *Abuelo* believed that some old curse required the three brothers to marry and have children, then that was precisely what they would do. Or rather, that was what the *others* had done.

His eldest brother, Alex, was happily married and would no doubt be announcing an impending heir sometime soon. Even Reynard, his second eldest brother, was engaged and surprisingly besotted with his fiancée. Their grandfather, the whole reason they'd embarked on the pact that had seen both his brothers race into relationships to placate the old man's fears, was beginning to relax.

However, he hadn't relaxed sufficiently. The words *Abuelo* had spoken to Ben before he'd left Isla Sagrado still rang in his ears.

"It's up to you now, Benedict. You're the last one. Without you, the curse will not be broken and the del Castillo family will be wiped from existence."

No pressure there. Thanks, *Abuelo,* Ben thought cynically as he let Mia's voice wash over him as she showed him how to operate the entertainment center, discreetly hidden behind painted silk screens that slid aside at the touch of a button. It wasn't as if he even believed in the blasted curse anyway. What relevance did a jumble of words thrown out by his ancestor's scorned lover have in today's world?

But no matter what his feelings on the subject were, he had made a pact with his brothers to do whatever it took to make *Abuelo*'s last years as happy as they could be. And it was his inability to live up to his part of the pact that now weighed heavy on his heart. The old man had stepped in when their parents had died in a skiing accident and had raised them through their turbulent teens to adulthood. They owed him. Big time. And no matter what Ben thought, *Abuelo* believed in the curse with every cell in his body.

And Ben's promise, made only four months ago, was now something upon which he could never deliver.

An all too familiar lash of anger flicked through his veins. Anger tempered with a fair serving of frustration at his own stupidity in having brought himself to this situation in the first place. He'd known as he drove his car along the coast road that he was taking a risk but, as with everything in his life, he'd wanted to push it to the absolute limits. Unfortunately for him, and the tangled pile of metal that was all that was left of a couple of hundred thousand dollars worth of car, he'd well exceeded them.

He looked at Mia, still without really listening to a word she said. The afternoon sun slanted in through the massive window and bathed her in its light, glancing off the spun gold of her hair neatly tied back from her heart-shaped face. His fingers itched to loosen her hair from its bonds—to run his fingers through it and discover whether it still felt as silky soft, to bury his face in it and find out if it still smelled the same. Then, to lose himself and his failings in the exquisite beauty of her welcoming body.

"So, if that's everything, I'll leave you to settle in. Please don't hesitate to contact reception if there's anything at all that you need."

Mia stood by the door to his suite. Clearly she was finished explaining everything, and he'd missed most of it. He fixed his gaze upon her again. Remembering anew the passion they'd shared. The passion he now craved again.

"Anything?" he answered, raising a brow.

He couldn't help it. He loved to see that cool professional facade she presented suddenly flush with heat. Heat and knowing. Remembering. If she thought that hiding her body in those shapeless rags—not to mention concealing the vibrant personality he remembered, behind a businesslike mask—would keep him from seeing her as a woman, she was vastly mistaken. It just made it more enticing to tease out a reaction in the face of her reluctance.

"We work hard to cater to our clients' specific needs, Mr. del Castillo—"

"Call me Ben," he interrupted. "After all, we're hardly on a formal footing, are we?"

He crossed the short distance between them and raised his hand to her face, one knuckle softly stroking the elegant line of her jaw. She jerked her head away, breaking the contact, but not before he felt the sizzle of electricity tingle up his arm. Oh yes—Mia Parker was exactly what he needed to aid in his recovery.

"That wouldn't be appropriate, Mr. del Castillo. Should you require company, however, I'm sure you will be able to accommodate your needs in town."

Her tone was glacial and to add insult to injury, she took a step back from him. He was not the kind of man who pushed himself on any woman—had never needed to. But they hadn't parted on bad terms. Was it so far out of the realms of possibility to want to revisit what they had shared—especially when he'd had so much taken from him already?

"*Querida,* I do not recall you ever worrying whether your behavior could be considered *appropriate* before," he drawled.

He heard the sharp intake of her breath. Saw the battle for composure flit across her features. Noted the flare of green fire in her eyes before she responded.

"That was then. I've changed."

"People don't change that much, Mia. Not if they're honest with themselves." He let his words linger on the air between them before continuing. "What we had was special—unique. Can you honestly tell me you have no wish to revisit that bond again?"

"No, I do not."

Her voice was emphatic, but he didn't miss the telltale flick of the pulse at her neck, or the sudden dilation of her pupils.

"Now, if you'll excuse me, I have work to do."

She spun away from him and let herself out of his suite, closing the door behind her with a careful "click" that spoke volumes as to the control she exhibited. As appealing as the new Mia was, with her buttoned down exterior, he wished he could see a glimpse of the old Mia who'd so absorbed him. She couldn't be too far beneath the surface, he was sure of it. Finding her—now, there was the challenge.

With every nerve in her body on full stinging alert, Mia forced herself to walk, not run, from Benedict's rooms. She'd hoped against hope that he'd be gentleman enough not to bring up their previous liaison—she should have known that such a wish was impossible. She couldn't deny that he'd spoken the truth. What they'd shared *had* been unique. But no matter how spectacular it had been, she wasn't about to throw everything she'd worked so hard for down the drain purely for the chance to rediscover the heights of pleasure she'd found in his arms. The old Mia would have jumped at the chance to renew their fling—but she wasn't that girl anymore. Couldn't be. Never would be again.

Mud had a habit of sticking, especially the kind of mud associated with her old behaviors, not to mention her father's financial misdemeanors. It had only been in the past eighteen months or so that she'd felt as if she could raise her head in a professional sphere and be recognized for her achievements here at Parker's Retreat, rather than her exploits in the latest women's magazines. She wasn't going to risk that hard-won respect for anything or any man—no matter how tempting he was.

By the time she reached the sanctuary of her office, at the end of the accommodation wing, she almost had the trembling under control. She shut the door behind her and leaned back against the paneled wooden surface.

Not for anything would she jeopardize the life she'd fought so hard to rebuild for her family. What her father had done had been the biggest abuse of trust and love he could ever have committed. It had taken all of her energy to pull her mother back from the brink of abject despair. Mia wouldn't let Elsa—or Jasper—down now. Not after all she'd accomplished.

When disaster first struck, keeping their family home had been paramount. She'd succeeded in making that happen, albeit in an entirely different manner from what they had enjoyed before. They now lived in what had once been their guest house. Guests now enjoyed the trappings Mia and Elsa had taken for granted would always be theirs, but at least she and her mother—and Jasper—still had a roof over their heads and she sure as heck planned to ensure it stayed that way.

She raised a now steady hand to her jaw. Retraced the line of skin he'd touched so very gently. It was tempting, so very tempting, to give in to the past. To take some relief from the constant daily pressures of balancing the tasks of running the hotel and spa and being a good mother and daughter.

She'd taken so much for granted during her first twenty-three years. Had lived with a silver spoon in her mouth with never a care or a thought as to what was around the next corner of her adult life. She hadn't even taken seriously the training she'd undergone as a massage therapist—at least, not until it looked as though it was the only way she was going to be able to make any money. Even then she'd had to spend vital funds on retraining before she could pick up the reins again.

Well, she'd certainly learned to grow up in a hurry. First, with the news that she was pregnant with the child of a man she hadn't—to her eternal shame—even known the name of and then second, with her father's admission of gross financial failure, followed shortly by him taking his own life.

Those had been dark days—seemingly endless with sorrow, accusations and confusion. Days when her lifestyle choices became fair game for the media—when people pointed the finger at her and apportioned their own blame on her for her father's downfall. But she'd pulled them through it. She—Mia Parker, party girl—had done what it took to hold on to what she could. And she would keep hold of what was hers.

Benedict del Castillo was only here a short time. He need never know that their blazing passion had resulted in a child. Jasper was *her* son. She wasn't about to lose another member of her family.

Besides, who knew what kind of man Benedict really was? He'd been as flip and casual as she had that summer. Had been just as happy to play along with the ridiculous game of anonymity she'd suggested. Was he capable of handling the responsibility of fatherhood? Sure, he seemed more intense now, his mood darker, but he hadn't hesitated to suggest they take up where they left off. A leopard didn't change its spots—he said as much himself. Did she really want a man like that in Jasper's life?

There had been a brief time when she'd contemplated trying to track him down. To tell him he had a fiscal responsibility to his unborn child, if not an emotional one. But the reality that such a request could backfire on her—could even have seen her declared an unfit parent and lose Jasper, given her less-than-circumspect behavior in the past and her difficulty in supporting him—had been overwhelming. She'd already lost so very much. She couldn't stand to lose her son as well. So she'd made do with less herself. Had poured her energy into supporting her mother and fighting to keep their home—a home where they could feel safe and, finally, proud of what they'd achieved together.

Her son had stability here—the love of his grandmother, his friends at day care, and all the care and love and guidance he would ever need from his mother. Ensuring Jasper didn't run across his father wouldn't be so difficult. Elsa took care of him while he wasn't at day care and during the business hours that occupied Mia's attention. She could easily keep him away from Ben. And she'd keep her distance from Benedict, as well.

Mia was not about to do a single thing that would cast a ripple on the smooth waters of their new life. Not a single thing. The terms of her arrangement with Benedict were simple. Exclusivity, privacy and therapy—for all of which she was being paid extremely well. He'd get what he paid for, and that was it.

A knock on the door behind her made her start, setting her heart to race in her chest. She took a deep breath and turned around, her hand on the doorknob before she could change her mind and pretend she wasn't in her office. She'd trained herself to face her fears, and if her current fear, Ben del Castillo, stood on the other side of that door, she'd face him, too.

"I hope I'm not disturbing you," Andre Silvain said through a charming smile. "It seems the gym is locked and I was wondering if you could show me through the facilities."

"Of course," she answered, willing her heartbeat back to some semblance of normality. "Usually we provide our guests with their own swipe key to access the pool and gym. Why don't we go to reception? I'll get that sorted out for you right now."

In a matter of minutes, Mia had organized a key for both Andre and Benedict and was leading Andre through the glass corridor that connected the accommodation wing of the hotel and the purpose-built gym she'd added to the already existing indoor swimming pool. The pool had been another of her father's extravagances—an extravagance she'd been grateful he'd indulged in as she'd never have been able to afford to have a pool installed with her current financial position.

Andre made several noises of appreciation as she showed him the facilities together with her treatment rooms.

"Since it will only be yourself and Mr. del Castillo here for the month, my usual gym and spa staff have been given a leave of absence. I will be attending to Mr. del Castillo's treatments myself."

It was a decision that had seemed like a good idea at the time, and the staff involved had accepted the offer of a month's leave, at what was usually their busiest time, with alacrity. However, now she'd learned exactly who her guest was, Mia was ruing her decision to provide the therapy herself.

"That's fine. As his trainer, I won't need anyone else in the gym. I've worked up a mixed bag of programs for him, starting tomorrow with swimming in the morning and then a gentle hike later in the afternoon, if he's up to it," Andre said. "After the hike he'll probably need some work on those muscles of his. I understand he was pretty fit before his accident, and despite his injuries I don't think it'll take too long before he's almost back to normal again."

Mia's stomach pitched on the thought of the type of injuries Benedict had sustained.

"Were they severe?" she couldn't help asking.

"Yes—mostly internal and tissue damage. His knee was also dislocated."

"Dislocated? That's unusual in a car accident, isn't it?"

"From what I've learned, it's a minor miracle he didn't break any bones. The driver's side of his car bore the full impact of the accident. It was only due to the safety features of the car that he survived at all. That and the fact that emergency services got to him in time. If they hadn't found him when they did, he could have lost his leg. A dislocation like that can do untold damage to nerves and cause blood supply to the foot to be interrupted. And that's not taking into account the internal bleeding from his injuries."

A chill ran through Mia's body. Ben could have died. She'd never really stopped to consider that before. While she'd never expected to see Jasper's father again, she had also never considered how she'd feel if she knew he didn't walk the face of the earth anymore, either. It didn't bear thinking about, she told herself sternly.

"He seems to have made a remarkable recovery. It's been, what, six or seven weeks since the accident?"

"Probably closer to five, and yes, he's one stubborn piece of work. We started his recovery program shortly before he was released from hospital. Of course, he was still getting over abdominal surgery at that stage and his knee was still splinted. He's a proud man, though, which makes it hard work. He doesn't like anyone to see him struggle or witness his pain."

Mia nodded. That made perfect sense. Even when she'd first met him, Ben had carried himself with an air of pride and entitlement that had been instantly appealing to her. After all, she'd borne herself in much the same way.

She knew what a struggle it was emotionally to come to terms with a massive change in circumstances, and felt a begrudging respect for how far Ben had come with his physical recovery from the accident. Perhaps his victory over death had given him that dark edge she now sensed hung around him like an invisible cloak.

"Well, this all looks really good," Andre continued. "I didn't expect your facilities to be as comprehensive as this but I'm impressed."

"We aim to please," Mia said, smiling. "And I like to believe that most of the time, we succeed. A lot of our business is now by referral or from returning clientele. Mr. del Castillo's booking certainly threw a bit of a spanner in the works but fortunately we were able to accommodate everything and everyone. I have to say I was surprised he was prepared to come all this way, though. Surely he could have completed his recovery at home, or at least nearer to home."

"The media wouldn't leave him alone long enough, and like I said before, he's a proud man. He didn't want pictures of himself plastered through the European papers looking anything less than his old self. Plus, he's made it quite clear to me that when he returns to Sagradan society he wants to do so in peak fitness."

Just privately, she didn't blame Ben one bit for seeking anonymity. In the aftermath of her father's death, his shame had been broadcast the length and breadth of the country. Her mother had retreated from the public eye, refusing to work on the charities that had once been a part of her life and slowly but surely severing all ties with her old friends. It had been up to Mia to hold her head high and to meet the public gaze upon their lives. She hadn't liked it one bit, but one of them at least had had to hold it all together.

She wondered whether Ben had a special someone

waiting in the wings for him when he went back home.
Someone who'd appreciate that peak fitness. Someone he
was perhaps too proud to allow to see him less than perfect.
Somehow the thought of another woman waiting for him
rankled her on a level she really didn't want to acknowledge,
because doing so would mean she had feelings for him,
wouldn't it? And she couldn't afford that. Not under any
circumstances.

Three

Mia moved around her treatment room, dimming the lights and ensuring the room temperature was comfortable. Once she was satisfied, she lit a candle in the oil diffuser she used to permeate the air with relaxing scents. Whether that relaxation was more for her benefit or for Ben's she couldn't honestly answer. The prospect of having his prone form beneath her hands while she gave him a massage was something she'd been working to keep from her mind all day.

She'd seen the two men return from their hike about an hour ago. Ben was limping more than he had when she'd caught a glimpse of him earlier today. When she'd mentioned it to Andre, he'd merely rolled his eyes and said that his client had been unimpressed with the gentle workout Andre'd mapped out for him and had insisted they take a more arduous trek. Nothing he'd been able to say had swayed Benedict's insistence and rather than leave him to go off and potentially hurt himself again, Andre had gone along with him in an attempt to at least temper the hike with enough rest stops and stretches to ensure he didn't undo any of the work they'd achieved to date.

Clearly Ben was driven to get well again as fast as he could. She carefully blended the cold-pressed carrier oil she preferred to use for massage with a few drops of pure essential oil that would aid his muscle recovery. As she did so, she wondered what drove him so hard. Was it just typical male stubbornness, or was it the prospect of returning home and getting back to his old life, and whoever was a part of that life?

Either way, it was none of her business. All she was here for today was to ensure that his workouts didn't leave him with painfully tight muscles that would keep him from his program for the next few days. Although she doubted that anything would sway him from his task. She'd seen the determination in his eyes as he'd gone through to the pool this morning and then later as he and Andre had set out for their hike. But despite the fact it wasn't her business, she couldn't deny that this new, more serious Benedict del Castillo was infinitely more appealing than the fun-loving guy she'd met the first time around.

If he'd been any other kind of man she would have thought he was pushing himself too hard. Risking further damage to an already traumatized body. But she had a feeling he knew his boundaries and that he was merely determined to extend those boundaries as far as possible.

"Where do you want me?"

Mia whirled around at Ben's voice, startled he'd managed to sneak up behind her and surprise her like that. She composed her features into what she hoped was a serene expression. He looked tired, she thought as she made eye contact with him for the first time since yesterday, and there were fine lines of strain about his eyes and mouth.

By all appearances, he was not in the mood to make small talk.

"Please, remove your clothes and then lie facedown on the table with the covers up to your waist. You can leave your briefs on. I'll leave you to get comfortable and I'll be back in a few minutes."

Without giving him a chance to respond she slipped out of her treatment room and closed the door behind her. The instant there was a solid barrier between them, Mia put a hand to her throat and took a deep breath. She could do this. She absolutely could do this—and without allowing it to affect her equilibrium. She'd remain professional at all times.

After waiting what she felt should be long enough for him to disrobe and position himself on the table, she knocked gently on the treatment room door and let herself back in. Her gaze flicked over the exposed expanse of skin of his shoulders and back and down to the tapered narrow width of his waist. He'd yanked the covers up unevenly so she took a moment to straighten them before facing the moment of truth where she would have to touch him.

"Have you had an aromatherapy massage before?" she asked, keeping her voice low as she cupped her left hand firmly over the base of his skull, while pressing her right hand flat against his upper back. She repeated the movement and pressure in segments down his back to his lumbar region. His skin was smooth and hot to touch. Achingly familiar, yet foreign at the same time.

"Not the kind you're thinking of," Ben said, his voice muffled in the purpose-built cavity for his face.

Mia fought a smile. She got that kind of comment a lot from guests using the spa. Some serious, some definitely not so.

"Then just let yourself relax. I think you'll find you'll enjoy it."

"You're touching me, aren't you? Of course I'll enjoy it."

There was a note to his voice, something unspoken, and just like that her mind filled with images of them enjoying one another. Mia shook her head slightly, and willed the images away. It was just mind over matter.

She released the gentle pressure she'd applied to his neck and used her fingertips to press individual points leading up to his skull. Beneath her touch she felt the tension in the corded muscles of his neck slowly release. Silently nodding to herself, she slid her fingers along his skull up to the tip of his head, her fingers dragging through the dark silk of his hair, before withdrawing her touch completely.

"Is that it?" he groused from on the table.

"That's just the beginning. Relax, Mr. del Castillo. Try and focus on your breathing and let your mind go."

"Ben. I told you to call me Ben."

"Fine," she breathed out a soft sigh of capitulation. "Ben, it is."

She turned from the table briefly to pour a measure of the blended massage oil into her palm, and then warmed it in her hands before applying her hands to his back. Immediately, she began the movements that now came to her as instinctively as breathing. Bit by bit, as she worked first in long sliding strokes, she could feel him respond to the soothing touch.

His muscle tissue became more malleable, his breathing deepened—and her fingers felt as if a warm buzz was building up beneath them. A warm buzz that tingled and crackled up her arms and charged her entire body. It had been so long since she'd touched him, and yet the sensations it evoked came pouring back from deep within her.

She shook her head slightly, determined to rid herself of her pitiful lack of personal control, but she couldn't deny the heated heaviness that now built inside her, or the glowing ember of need that smoldered at her core.

Mia worked her hands up from his lower back and to his shoulders, remembering the first time she'd felt his strength beneath her hands. Despite the injuries he'd sustained in the car wreck he still had pretty good muscle definition, she noted in the dim lighting of the room. His shoulders were still broad and strong—the muscles leading from his neck to the tops of his shoulders defined yet not overpowering. She let her hand slide down one arm, her fingers stimulating pressure points inside his elbow and wrist as she worked before mirroring her actions on his other side.

In fact, she was surprised not to have seen any scar tissue on his body. So far, she'd only seen the starburst tattoo he bore on the back of his right shoulder—the same tattoo she'd traced intimately with the tip of her tongue the last time he'd lain prone before her.

Her inner muscles clenched tight and an almost all-consuming flood of heat washed over her body. She always kept her treatment rooms warm but the temperature that radiated off her now had nothing to do with central heating. A demanding tremor of need shot through her, making her hands tremble ever so slightly in their ministrations.

Focus on the work, she all but shouted in her mind. The work and not the man, and most definitely not the past.

But her focus became blurred as she completed her work on his upper body and she shifted the covers to expose his legs. She worked for longer than usual on his feet and calves, avoiding the moment when she'd run her hands up along the backs of his thighs and higher, almost to his buttocks. Somehow she managed to hold it together—to regulate her breathing and to keep herself from combusting internally.

She was temporarily distracted by his knee, and took special care around the site of the damage—some residual swelling and bruising reminding her of the severity of the injury. To think he may have lost his lower leg completely if his circulation had been cut off completely to his foot. She couldn't imagine how devastating that would have been for him. A constant physical reminder of the crash.

Despite what Andre had told her of his injuries, Ben did seem to have gotten off very lightly, she thought—until she bade him to roll over while she held the covers a circumspect distance from his body. As she settled the covers in a fold down below his waist she fought to hold back a gasp at the livid lines of scarring that bisected his abdomen and crept, in lightning bolts of knotted tissue, to his hip on one side and lower, beneath the blanket, on the other.

"What happened to you?" she asked, before she could stop the words ejecting from her mouth.

Ben opened his eyes and their darkness glittered in the soft lighting of the room. His hands grasped the edge of the covers and eased them over his scars, hiding them from view.

"It's in the past. I do not wish to discuss it," he said, the words clipped and leaving her in no doubt he meant every one of them.

"I'm sorry, I didn't mean to pry. Are you comfortable with me continuing the massage or are you still abdominally tender?"

"Stay above the blanket. I'll let you know if I want you to stop."

He closed his eyes again and she studied him for a moment before adding another measure of oil to her hands and positioning herself at the head of the table. She took a deep steadying breath and began anew, trying not to think about the damage that had been wrought on his body. While some of his scars were clearly surgical, others looked as if he'd been torn into by a wild beast.

She fought back a shudder as she imagined what it must have been like to be trapped in a jumble of metal—in pain and alone, wondering when, or even if, rescue would come. The mental toughness required to survive such a thing was monumental.

As would be the mental toughness she'd need to get through the next month. Already, touching him was proving to be a torture all of its own. The long, slow strokes reminded her of another time—a time when all their attention had been solely for one another. When those strokes had led to other kinds of intimacies that had brought each of them immeasurable pleasure. Again she felt that tautening deep in her belly, that undeniable pull that ached with emptiness—ached for him. And not just for the intimate memories they had shared, but for what she wanted *now*. The very thought saw Mia nearly halt in her movements but she forced herself to continue, and forced her mind away from the treacherous thoughts that could lead only to more trouble than she could deal with right now.

By the time she neared the end of his massage, she was a mass of knotted nerves herself. Normally a full body massage left her wrung out, both physically and mentally. But for some reason, touching Benedict today, working out the knots under his skin, had energized her. Instead of her usual reviving cup of herbal tea, she wanted to do nothing more than swim off all this vitality now coursing through her veins.

Mia concentrated on the circular movements of her

fingers around his ankles and then up across the tops of his legs, finally bringing the session to an end by placing her hands flat on the soles of Ben's feet.

"We're all done for today," she said softly. "If you'd like a few minutes to gather your thoughts before heading back to your suite, feel free to take your time. I'll go and get you a glass of water to have before you go. Keep drinking plenty of water through the rest of today—it'll help you flush away the toxins that were released by the massage. Now, is there anything else you'd like from me?"

Ben pushed himself upright and swung his legs over the side of the table, the covers sliding down past his waist and revealing the hollow lines of definition that started at the top of each side of his hips. Mia rapidly averted her gaze.

"Before you go, there is just one more thing," he said.

Before she could ask what that was, Ben caught one of her hands in his and tugged her toward him, nestling her between his legs. His free hand caught the back of her neck, his fingers curling gently into the knot of hair at her nape and pulling free the clip that secured it.

He moved so swiftly she barely had a moment to realize what was happening, until he leaned forward, his mouth slanting across her lips, capturing her gasp of shock.

Ben couldn't say what had driven him to kiss her, but he knew the second his lips touched hers that he'd done the right thing. Lying prone on the table while she'd massaged his aching body, draining away what had felt like a lifetime's worth of tension, had been the kind of pleasure-pain he'd never thought he'd actively welcome into his life.

But under her long delicate fingers he'd felt the stirrings of desire—desire that demanded to be acknowledged and acted upon. Since discovering his infertility—and adding that on to the knowledge that due to his recklessness, he was directly responsible for that state—he'd wondered if he'd ever even want to make love again. Goodness only knew the pain of rehabilitation had driven all thoughts of sex from his mind.

Here, now, though, it was all different. While he might never father the son or daughter he'd always dreamed of having, he could at the very least reclaim his manhood, and with who better than the woman who'd remained on the periphery of his memory for more than three years? A woman who'd made all others since pale in comparison.

Beneath his touch he felt her resistance, the rigidity with which she held her body, her reluctance to part her lips. He teased the seam of her mouth with the tip of his tongue then gently caught her lower lip between his teeth and, ever so softly, tugged. Her capitulation was audible in the moan that rippled from her throat—tangible in the way her body relaxed into his. Ben felt a celebration of triumph as her mouth opened for him, gaining him access to her special sweet flavor and the passion she'd been hiding from him since his arrival.

Beneath his fingers her pulse bumped in a rapid beat at her wrist. He recognized its rhythm—it matched his own. Ben deepened their kiss, savoring her taste, the texture of her tongue as it danced with his.

Yes, this was what he'd needed. The unabashed, passionate response of a woman who was as attuned to his needs as he was to hers. He slid both his hands to her waist, pulling her more firmly against him, before easing his hands under the fitted T-shirt she wore, up across the satin smoothness of her belly, over her ribcage and finally over the cotton-covered mounds of her breasts.

Her nipples pebbled against the fabric of her bra and she

shuddered as he cupped her in his palms. But he wanted no barriers between them now. He wanted to feel her—all of her. He slipped one hand to her back and released the catch. The material of her T-shirt was too snug, so he eased it up over her body, pushing her bra up along with it and exposing her full rose-tipped breasts. He cupped them briefly before tearing his lips from hers and placing them around one puckered nub and laving it with his tongue, drawing it deeper into his mouth.

Mia pressed her lower body deeper into the cradle of his hips, her hands gripping his shoulders, her head dropping back and arching her breasts toward him in supplication, wordlessly begging for more. He did not plan to disappoint her. His body continued to quicken, to respond to her unabashed desire. His hands dropped to the waistband of her trousers, sliding the button from its keeper before easing the zipper open—and then everything changed.

She stiffened in his arms—one hand fluttering down from where her nails had only seconds ago been digging into his skin to halt him and to push his hand from her.

"N-no," she breathed.

He kissed her again, sweeping his tongue across her lip. "Yes."

"We can't," she said, pulling away from him. "*I* can't."

He let his hands drop from her, watching as she struggled to do up her bra and pull her T-shirt back down. In the dim lighting of the room her eyes were shadowed, but he could see the moisture that gathered at their corners and threatened to spill over.

"Mia—" He reached for her again.

"No! Don't touch me. Please, just go." Her voice broke on the last word.

"I didn't force you, Mia. There's no need to act like

an outraged virgin when we both know nothing could be further from the truth."

Frustration clawed at his insides. Frustration tempered with unaccustomed shame at the harshness of his words. He hadn't meant to lash out like that. He certainly hadn't wanted to make her cry.

One solitary tear spilled over the rim of her lower eyelid and tracked a line of silver down her cheek. She dashed it away with a shaking hand.

"I should never have let it go that far. I apologize. It was most unprofessional of me." She turned and grabbed a robe from behind the door and thrust it at him. "Please, use this. I'll see to it that your clothing is laundered and returned to your room by the morning."

He accepted the robe and wrapped it around his body. He wasn't about to let her pretend that nothing had happened. Not when that all-too-brief embrace had made him feel more alive than anything else had since his accident.

"This isn't over between us," he growled as he pulled open the door and stepped out into the foyer of the spa.

"Over? It never began. I'm not the person you think I am."

"I know this much," he said, "you ache for me just about as much as I do for you right now and we *will* see this to its natural conclusion."

He yanked the belt into a knot at his waist and stalked off, his body vibrating with a tension which warred with the cold hard truth that the nascent desire which had begun to blossom within him, was now dormant again.

He fought back the irritation he felt and instead brought forth a new resolve. He would break down the barriers of Mia's resistance, piece by piece. And he would delight in every minute of it.

Four

Mia collapsed against the table the instant he walked out the door. So much for being strong and in control. If he hadn't listened to her, hadn't stopped when she'd asked, she had no doubt he'd be making love to her right now.

God, she was so *weak!* He'd been here one day. One! And still, just a touch, a kiss from him, was all it had taken to turn her into a scrambled mess of seething need. He had her on every level and she was apparently helpless against his sensual onslaught.

Even now, after he was gone, her entire body continued to hum with desire for his touch, her nipples still contracted and abrading the soft cotton of her bra. The taste of him still on her tongue. She clenched her hands in the covers on the massage table and dragged in a deep, steadying breath.

She had to harden up. Rebuild that control she'd forged in the past three years. Remember what was most important.

Slipping into automatic mode, Mia stripped the table and remade it to be ready for the next day. Ready for Ben. She quelled the shiver of apprehension that rippled down her spine. Each day she would have to go through this again. Well, she'd just have to pull on her big-girl panties and get on with it, she told herself sternly. And find something particularly nasty to think about while she did it so that there was no fear he'd ambush her again like he had today.

She reached for the jumble of clothes Ben had left on the chair in the corner of the room and gathered them up. The crisp, citrusy scent of his aftershave wafted up to her in a wave that hit her with the subtlety of a sledgehammer. Somehow she didn't quite think that big-girl panties were going to cut it this time. Something in cast iron, perhaps, she thought with a cynical laugh out loud.

Mia bagged his clothes and set them aside to be attended to by the laundry staff overnight and finished tidying the room. It was getting late and if she didn't hurry, she'd miss Jasper's bath time and story before bed. It was precious time they spent together—just mother and son. Right now she couldn't wait to wrap her arms around his sturdy little body and ground herself again.

Later that night, after Jasper had gone to bed and Mia's mother, Elsa, had returned to her own private apartment at the back of what had been the guest house, Mia fired up her personal computer and did an Internet search on Benedict del Castillo. Many of the results that popped up in a list on her screen were in Spanish—a language she'd always loved to hear but didn't understand a single word of.

She quickly scanned through them, searching for anything with an English translation, and fortunately, there were plenty of them. Mostly tabloid links to pictures of Ben with an ever-changing bevy of beautiful women hanging off his arm at one celebrity-studded function after another. Then she found what she'd been looking for. The details of his accident.

It made for chilling reading. Apparently, he'd been speeding on the coast road toward his home when for some reason his car had gone into a skid. There was conjecture that he'd swerved to miss something on the road and that when his rear tires had hit some loose gravel, he hadn't been able to regain control. Either way, it had been early the next morning when one of his vineyard workers had noticed the marks on the bitumen and investigated the trail of rubber to the edge.

Rescue workers called his survival nothing short of a miracle. A stand of trees clinging to the steep hillside had prevented his car from tumbling to the rocks and sea below. However, those trees had exacted their own damage when a branch had penetrated the vehicle and quite literally pinned him in the wreckage.

Mia leaned back in her chair. No wonder the scarring to his lower abdomen had been so ragged. And no wonder, if he'd survived all of that, that his demeanor should be so different to that of the laugh-a-minute sex god who'd swept her off her feet when they'd first met. An experience like that changed a person—irrevocably. She knew that herself. While the damage to her life hadn't been physical, the emotional toll had been huge. The fight to survive both monumental and ongoing.

She could understand the complexities that made up Benedict del Castillo a little better now, she thought. But as she shut down her computer and got ready for bed she forced herself to acknowledge that understanding him would not make it any easier to resist him. She could only hope against hope that she would remain strong.

She slept surprisingly deeply and dreamlessly and was

woken only by a sharp cry from Jasper's bedroom. She flung off her sheets and ran to his room.

The nightlight in the corner cast a warm glow over his bed. She felt a pang of regret that her baby boy was growing up so fast. He'd transferred from his crib and into a "big boy's bed" about six months ago after she'd lost patience with the number of times he'd climbed from the crib and she'd found him pattering around the apartment. Since he'd been in the bed, however, he'd been an angel. Never once rising through the night unless he needed the potty or had a bad dream.

Checking her tearful son now, though, gave her cause for concern. His forehead was hot and his voice croaky as he tried to talk. She scooped him into her arms and took him through to the bathroom. After soaking a face cloth with cool water and squeezing out the excess, she wiped his little red face. Once he'd settled somewhat, she gave him a drink of water but swallowing just had him crying all over again. She scoured her medicine cabinet for the infant pain reliever she knew should be there somewhere and used a tiny dropper to encourage him to take the liquid.

At times like this she felt so incredibly alone. What would it be like, she wondered, to be able to share these kinds of concerns with a broad pair of shoulders at her side? Mia tried to settle Jasper back in his bed but he was having none of it.

"Mommy's bed," he cried and the big fat tears rolling from his dark brown eyes, eyes so like his father's, were her total undoing.

"Just for tonight, then," she whispered. "But don't tell Grandma, okay?"

Her mother was a stickler for children sleeping in their own beds but sometimes rules were meant to be stretched.

"Okay," Jasper croaked with a conspiratorial wee smile.

Mia was relieved to see he was feeling better with the pain reliever but she had no doubts that once it wore off he'd be miserable again. She put the bottle and dropper next to her side of the bed. At least this way, if he woke again within the prescribed time, she could administer more without disturbing either of them unduly.

The morning brought her a very unhappy little boy and a weariness in herself that had come from calming him several times over the past few hours. It was at times like this that Mia sorely missed the convenience of living in town, as she had when she'd been footloose and fancy-free. In Queenstown, she could have taken Jasper to an emergency doctor during the night and he could already have been receiving medical care. Now, she'd have to rely on her mother to take Jasper, who was becoming clingier by the minute, to their family doctor.

In an ideal world she'd be able to take him herself, but she had a staff meeting this morning and a telephone conference scheduled with her bank manager just before midday. She was no different from any other working mother, she reminded herself. Women the world over faced tough decisions about their children's care every day. But the reminder was no consolation when her mother came to share breakfast with them and the time approached when Mia would have to turn her sick baby over to someone else's care.

Elsa readily agreed to take Jasper to the doctor that morning, and made the necessary calls to the surgery and let Don know what time they'd need the boat, while Mia dressed for work.

"There, it's all sorted. It's probably just a bit of a cold coming on. You know, in my day we didn't race off to the doctor at the hint of a snuffle like you young mothers do today," Elsa said, but her smile belied the censure in her words.

"I know, Mom, but he had a fever through the night. I'd just like him checked over," Mia responded firmly.

"Of course you would. And you're going to be right as rain in no time, aren't you, Jasper?" Elsa ruffled her grandson's hair with a loving hand and pulled him into her lap for a cuddle. "How's it going with the new guest? Did he settle in all right?"

"Seems to have. I haven't had a great deal to do with him so far."

Mia felt her cheeks burn at the lie she told her mother. Under no extreme of imagination could their kiss ever be described as "not a great deal."

"What's he like?" her mother pressed. "I got the impression you two had met before."

"Just once, years ago. Besides, you saw what he's like. Tall, dark, handsome."

"Single?"

"*Mom!*"

"Well, it doesn't hurt to ask. I take it you're not interested in him, then?" Elsa arched one perfectly plucked brow in her daughter's direction. "It's about time you started dating again. You've worn your hair shirt for quite long enough."

The hair-shirt comment stung. Mia had done her best to atone for what she'd realized were her shortcomings. If she'd been a better daughter she might have seen her father's business concerns before they'd overwhelmed him. She could most certainly have cut back on her own extravagant lifestyle if she'd had any idea of the toll it was taking on their financial position.

Since Reuben Parker's death, she'd done everything in her power to restore some semblance of normality into their lives. Now that she was almost there, she didn't want to do a single thing that would rock the fragile balance of this particular boat.

"If and when I feel ready to date again, I will," she replied stiffly.

"No need to get all huffy on me, Mia." Elsa put one hand on Mia's across the table. "I know how hard you've worked and I appreciate it. None of it was your fault, you know."

"Mom—"

"No, you need to listen to me. You've been an absolute rock since your father died and it's past time I stepped up and helped out a bit more. You've had far more responsibility on your shoulders than you deserved. I know you call me your chatelaine, but I'm not so stupid or selfish that I haven't noticed that I haven't been much help to you. Honey, I'm ready now. You gave me my time to grieve and I appreciate that, even when I know it must have been so hard for you on your own. Now I want to do my bit."

Tears pricked at Mia's eyes at her mother's words. She knew firsthand how devastated and betrayed Elsa had been when all the bad stuff had hit the proverbial fan. It had been a hard lesson for them all. Her mother still rocked Jasper absently in her arms, the little boy already starting to doze again, his cheeks still flushed with a trace of fever. Having her grandson to focus upon had been an anchor for Elsa, one that had helped both mother and daughter immeasurably.

"Mom, you already help me more than you know by being here for Jasper."

"Yes, but he isn't going to need me forever. Before you know it, he'll be five and in new entrants at school. I need to get back in the saddle, so to speak. It's time I reengaged my mind on matters other than what we've lost."

Mia squeezed her mother's hand. This was the strongest she'd seen, or heard, Elsa be in years. Before everything had fallen apart, Elsa Parker had been a force to be reckoned with, leading the charitable organizations where she volunteered with her organizational skills and efficiency. It had been a double blow for Mia that after her father's death, she'd also lost sight of the strong, confident, capable woman her mother had always been. It would be an enormous relief to have her back. To be able to begin to share some of the responsibility for the hotel and spa would be monumental, even if she knew that realistically it would take some time for her mother to get up to speed with how things were run.

"Thanks, Mom. Let's take it in small steps first—see if you even like what we do here."

Elsa laughed. "Like it or not, it's our livelihood. I'll learn to love it—just you wait and see."

Mia's cell phone chirped in her trouser pocket. "That's my reminder. I'd better get into the office."

She bent and kissed Jasper, who promptly woke and broke into tears. He insisted on a very long cuddle before he'd go to his grandmother again. It was with a worried frown that Mia left the house and headed for the hotel. She hoped he'd settle and be good for her mother, and she hoped like mad that all would be okay at the doctor. With Benedict del Castillo here at the hotel she couldn't afford for her concentration to be off, not by as much as a single thought.

From his window, Ben looked out straight across the lake. The water was an inky gray, a reflection of the dark clouds gathering in the skies above and completely at odds with his memory of it during the New Zealand summer he was here. A movement on the path caught his attention and he quickly identified Mia as she walked across from her accommodation to the hotel. He hoped her night had been as fractured as his had. Far from relaxing him, her massage had left him restless and with his blood pounding through his veins.

Massage, hell, it had been much more than that. She'd aroused his body from a slumber from which he'd wondered if it would ever awake. He was keen to see if she could do it again, except this time there'd be no going back. He smiled. It was good to actually *feel* alive again—to have a new purpose. He turned from the window and headed out of his suite, determined to intercept her before she could hide in her office or elsewhere on the property.

The single-story sprawl of the hotel suited his purposes beautifully. Mia was just about at the main entrance when he caught up with her. There were dark shadows under her eyes, and the sharp icy wind had brought spots of rosy color to her cheeks.

"Mr. del Castillo," she said as soon as she saw him in her path. "Good morning."

She didn't betray her nerves with as much as a flicker of an eyelid. He had to hand it to her. She could be one cool customer. But he knew he had the power to change that, and it was a power he relished.

"We agreed you would call me Ben," he reminded her with a slow smile.

To his delight, the color in her cheeks heightened and her slender hands, hands that had stroked all over his body yesterday, tightened into small fists.

"What can I do for you, Ben?" she asked, planting her feet a small distance apart as if she was bracing herself for a blow.

"Dinner, tonight."

"I don't usually dine with our guests," she hedged.

"Don't tell me you're going to relegate Andre and me to solitary splendor in the hotel dining room every night of our stay."

"You did request exclusivity," she reminded him coolly. "I can arrange for you to dine in a smaller room if you'd prefer."

"That won't be necessary if you join us every now and then to break the monotony."

Her eyes brightened with a hint of humor. "Are you tired of Andre's company already? I'm sure he'd be crushed to hear that."

Ben allowed himself a small smile. "Not exactly, but we'd both appreciate your company at dinner tonight. Say, eight o'clock?"

He could see the idea turning around in the back of her mind.

"I'm sorry, tonight's really not a good night for me." She paused and looked at her watch. "You'll need to excuse me, I'm on my way to a meeting."

She went to pass him but he shot out a hand and caught her arm. The instant he touched her, she went rigid. She stared at his hand then cast him a look that spoke volumes. He didn't let go.

"You can tell me you've changed your mind when I come for my massage today," he said, locking his gaze with hers.

He released her, his fingers uncurling slowly, and took a step away.

"About the massage…" she started.

"Daily, as per our agreement, remember?"

She shot him a look, a flash of fear suddenly visible in her eyes. "Yes, I remember. I'll see you at four, then."

"So you will," he replied and watched her walk away.

Her reluctance to rekindle their earlier affair challenged him. He'd seen no evidence of any ring on her finger to say she was otherwise spoken for, so in his opinion that left the field well and truly open. Any man fool enough to let her out of his sight for longer than a day deserved to lose her to a worthier man, and that included him. He should have prolonged his last stay here in New Zealand until he and Mia could have worked one another out of their systems. If he had, maybe he wouldn't be so hungry for her today. Ah, but then he wouldn't have the delight of looking forward to cracking that shell of resistance she wore like some flimsy armor now.

Ben turned back to his room to gear up for the day's activities. After a supervised gym workout today, he and Andre were heading into Queenstown to go tandem paragliding—his trainer having vehemently vetoed the idea of bungee jumping at Skipper's Canyon, citing Ben's barely healed knee. Between the paragliding and his appointment with Mia this afternoon, he wasn't sure which he looked forward to more.

Five

Mia applied long, steady strokes along Benedict's back and forced her mind to divorce itself from the man and think only about him as a prone form in need of massage therapy. It worked. Up to a point. Unfortunately, while she could separate her *mind* from the action, her *body* seemed to have a mind of its own.

She tried to simply relax into the movements and let her thoughts wander to other things. Things like the staff meeting this morning where some of the staff had expressed a certain amount of boredom in their day-to-day activity now that the hotel only catered to two guests. Mia shook her head. You'd have thought they'd have been glad for the respite. Things would certainly hot up again when Benedict and his trainer were gone.

Twenty-seven more days. It seemed like a lifetime.

In an attempt to ease some of the staff's frustration, she'd worked with them to alter their rosters, giving them more time off and shorter shifts at Parker's Retreat. Of course, all of that only reminded Mia that, even though she'd have a skeleton staff here at all times, there would be less buffers between herself and Ben for the rest of the time he was here.

She sighed inwardly, concentrating her energy on working out a bunch of knots Ben had in his upper back and shoulders and tried to ignore the nagging pains that built up in her own.

Managing the hotel, as small and select as it was, was a great deal more difficult than she'd ever anticipated. Some days just topped the "too hard" list and today was very definitely shaping up to be one of those. Even the discussion with her bank manager hadn't been promising. He'd wanted to warn her that the fixed-term loan she'd originally negotiated was coming up for renewal. She had the choice of fixing it again or allowing the interest rates to float with the market. It was at times like this that Mia most missed having a partner to share the major decisions with. So much rode on her every choice.

And then, over everything, were her responsibilities to Jasper. How on earth could she be a good mother when nearly her every waking thought was consumed by work? Today she'd been torn in two leaving him with her mother. He'd been tearful and feverish and even her mother's call, once they'd returned from the doctor, to say it was a mild throat infection, hadn't allowed her to settle.

It should have been her that took Jasper to the doctor. She owed it to her little boy. She'd popped home after her discussion with the bank manager and checked on him, but he'd been asleep, her mother catching up on tidying Mia's apartment and putting away washing that had accumulated on the sofa.

She'd stood in Jasper's bedroom doorway and watched

as her son slept off his illness, his multicolored stuffed tuatara clutched in his small hands, the traces of tears dried on his cheeks. Her own tears had been easy to hide but the pain in her chest had stayed with her all afternoon.

She shifted her attention to Benedict's legs before asking him to roll over onto his back.

"Is everything okay?" he asked.

She started a little. "Of course it is. Why do you ask?"

"You keep sighing all the time," he answered.

"I'm fine. Just a lot on my mind."

"Want to share some of it? I hear it helps."

Mia shook her head. There was no way she was spilling the beans about her problems to Ben. She didn't trust him not to use the knowledge against her somehow, although even as she had the thought she wondered just where it had come from. He'd never struck her as manipulative before so why should she feel that way about him now?

Perhaps it was his dogged determination to get her to agree to his request to join him for dinner tonight.

She forced herself to smile. "No, I'll be fine. Now, let's get back to work here, hmmm?"

To her relief Ben closed his eyes again and she felt his body relax into the table as she recommenced his massage. She was on the verge of finishing up when the sound of a child's miserable wail penetrated the walls of the treatment room.

Instantly she stiffened. Oh, no. Please no. Don't let it be Jasper at the spa, she thought frantically. She couldn't deal with that on top of everything else. She should have told her mother to keep Jasper well away from the hotel, but she hadn't thought that necessary. In his usual day-to-day care, when he was well and happy, the problem never arose. But with him sick? He was hardly ever ill, so it was no surprise that he'd become difficult and clingy.

"I want my mommy!"

The distressed cry shot straight to her heart and splintered it in two. She flattened her hands on the soles of Ben's feet, as she had yesterday, to signal the end of the session.

"I'll go and get your water," she said, "and I'll be back in a minute."

She slipped from the room before he could answer. Before he could ask about the commotion outside in the spa foyer.

"I'm so sorry, Mia," Elsa said, looking far more flustered than her usual aplomb would allow, "but he was just so upset. Nothing would calm him until I said I'd bring him to you."

Elsa had tears in her eyes and Mia could see by the lines of strain on her face that Jasper had no doubt been a demanding handful. She held her arms out to her little boy and enveloped him in her hold.

"It's okay, Mom," she whispered over the top of Jasper's dark head. "I know you wouldn't have come here unless absolutely necessary."

Jasper's hand crept up her neck and started to play with the ponytail she'd pulled her hair into today. Whenever he was fractious it seemed to soothe him to play with her hair. Before long, his hiccoughing sobs had settled into regular breathing, but the instant she tried to give him back to his grandmother, he wailed again.

Mia shot a nervous look to the door to her treatment room. "Mom, I have Mr. del Castillo in there. I've finished his massage, but I still need to give him a glass of water and we really need to get Jasper away from here."

"Surely the man would understand. You are a mother, after all," Elsa countered. "Here, I'll get the water for him."

"It's not that," Mia started, suddenly wishing she'd shared the truth of Jasper's parentage with her mother earlier. "Please, Mom, take him. I know he'll be upset, but I'll try to make it up to him later. I'll be home again in about twenty minutes. Just give me some time to see Ben off and then tidy up."

"Ben, is it?" Her mother arched a brow at Mia and reached again for Jasper, who shook his head and burrowed more deeply against Mia's shoulder.

"It's not like that—he insisted on the informality. Now, please, take Jasper."

But Jasper wasn't in the mood to cooperate and set up an almighty howl as Elsa tried to pluck him from Mia's arms. Mia was almost in tears herself when a sound from behind her sent a chill of dread down her spine.

"Is everything all right?" Ben asked.

Oh no, it was her worst nightmare come true. She wheeled around, holding Jasper close to her, her hand on the back of his head and keeping it turned away from his father's curious gaze. Ben stood framed in the doorway. He'd dressed during the time she'd been out of the room and she felt at a complete disadvantage as he fixed her with a dark-eyed look.

"I'm sorry. My son, he isn't well."

"And he wants his mother. Understandable."

At the sound of Ben's voice, Jasper lifted his head and fought free of his mother's gentle hold. And in that moment all of Mia's worst fears over the past two days coalesced into a solid lump of lead in the middle of her chest. She tried to reposition the little boy, but he was determined to see who the newcomer was.

"Who's dat?" Jasper asked, letting go of Mia's hair to point at Ben.

"It's rude to point, Jasper," Mia said, grabbing his little hand and pulling it back down against his side.

Ben took a step toward them and smiled at Jasper. "I'm Ben," he said gently.

Jasper's curiosity morphed into instant shyness when the object of his attention answered him and he turned his head back into Mia's shoulder. Mia fought back her surprise at the tone in Ben's voice, but all his gentleness was apparently only for the wee person in her arms, because the look Ben gave her in the next minute was anything but.

Sensing something was very definitely amiss, Elsa stepped forward.

"Mr. del Castillo, I hope you're enjoying your stay at Parker's Retreat. I'm so sorry we had to disturb you today."

"It is nothing," he said smoothly, but Mia noted he didn't shift his gaze from Jasper for a moment.

Every nerve in Mia's body stretched until they were so taut she thought she'd snap in two. Her tension must have transferred to Jasper, because he started to wriggle in her arms, reaching for Elsa.

"Want Grandma now," he demanded.

With a sigh of relief Mia handed him over to her mother.

"It was nice to see you again, Mr. del Castillo," Elsa said. "Perhaps you can share a meal or two with us while you're here. I'm sure you don't want to be on your own all the time."

Mia groaned inwardly and cursed herself anew for not apprising her mother of the situation between her and Ben earlier.

"I'd like that, but please, call me Ben."

"Only if you'll call me Elsa," her mother replied coquettishly.

Oh, my God, was her mother flirting with him? Mia couldn't believe her eyes, and all the while her stomach was churning. She hadn't missed the sharp perusal Ben had given Jasper, nor the very pointed question in the look he'd given her earlier. She'd never been a good liar, but somehow she was going to have to put on a performance worthy of Meryl Streep to field what was most definitely coming her way.

"Mom, I think Jasper needs to head back home now."

"Oh, of course." Elsa smiled. "We'll see you later on, then. Say bye to Mommy."

"Bye, Mommy."

Jasper leaned away from his grandmother long enough to plant a wet kiss smack on Mia's cheek and she gave him a kiss and smile in return.

"See you at bath time, munchkin."

After Elsa and Jasper had gone, Mia bustled over to a cabinet set against the wall and extracted a glass before filling it from the water cooler she had in the corner by the reception desk.

"Here, you'll need this."

Ben's fingers grazed hers as she handed him the glass.

"Actually, I think I might need something stronger."

"I wouldn't, if I were you. You need to concentrate on flushing toxins from your body right now," she said, deliberately misconstruing his meaning.

Ben followed her back into the treatment room, where she fluttered about—stripping the table and remaking it, tipping out the balance of the oil and washing the container. His mind whirled with the details of what he'd just witnessed and there was a deep ache in his chest he couldn't quite define.

A son. Mia Parker had a son. One who was probably somewhere near three years old, if he could hazard a guess, given the child's size and vocabulary—not that he was any expert on children. But if he was right, and he firmly believed he was, it would make young Jasper's date of conception around the time he and Mia had enjoyed their all-too-brief affair.

Shock that she could have had his child and not made any attempt to find him, or even tell him the truth when he arrived here at Parker's Retreat, hit him with the subtlety of a wrecking ball, along with the big question—why would she deliberately try to *hide* his son from him? But then a new realization slowly dawned that, despite his injuries, he might actually be able to meet the terms of the agreement he and his brothers had come to.

But first he had to know for sure if Jasper was his. He could almost have been persuaded on appearances alone. Jasper was nothing like his mother in build or coloring.

The boy's body was sturdy, his hair dark, his eyes a rich deep brown—just like Ben's own. He fought the urge to grab Mia by the arms and shake the truth from her, to force her to state the words that would both turn his world upside down and at the same time make everything right. But appearances aside, he knew on a gut level that went far, far deeper than a simple need to be Jasper's father that the boy was of his making.

He would get to the truth, one way or another.

He drained the last of the water from his glass and set it down on the bench top with a loud "crack" of sound. Mia flinched, very clearly on edge.

"You never mentioned you had a son," he said evenly.

"It has no bearing on my ability to do my job or on your booking here. Why should I have mentioned it?"

"Oh, I don't know." He stepped to one side, blocking her attempt to walk out of the room. "Maybe because I could be his father?"

"That's ridiculous."

She tried to walk around him, but it took little effort to shift his weight and prevent her from getting past.

"Ridiculous? I would have thought it far more ridiculous to try and hide the truth."

Despite his desire to remain fully in control, he couldn't help the edge of anger that permeated his words.

"He's my son. I carried him, I bore him and I'm raising him to the best of my ability. That's the truth."

"The truth? Then who is Jasper's father, if not me?"

Ben caught her chin between his strong fingers and forced her to meet his gaze.

"Mia, tell me Jasper is my son."

She jerked herself free.

"I will tell you no such thing. Now, please let me pass. I have work to complete and a sick child to attend to. Since you're so worried about his welfare, perhaps you'd do well to remember it's you who is holding me up from being with him right now."

"We have not finished discussing this," he warned.

"I beg to differ. We have totally exhausted the subject."

She pushed past him and went to stand at the door to the entrance of the spa, holding it open for him—her foot none too subtly tapping on the floor.

"I understand you need to be with Jasper tonight, but we will talk about this further tomorrow."

"There is nothing to talk about. I told you that already."

"So you say. However, your eyes betray you, Mia."

"There is nothing to betray," she insisted, but behind her words he heard a note of anxiety.

And it was that very note that gave him purpose.

"Then meet me for dinner tonight as I suggested this

morning. Tell me about Jasper's father. Prove to me that I'm not him."

"I don't need to have dinner with you to prove you have no claim on my son."

Every muscle in her body was rigid and her face had paled, making her eyes shine with the brilliance of unflawed emeralds against her white cheeks.

"Then you have nothing to fear, do you?"

"Mr. del Castillo, my son is ill and needs his mother. Tell me, why on earth would I choose to spend time with you rather than comforting him?"

"You will call me Ben, and I am certain Jasper will fall asleep at some stage this evening. When he does, you can come to my rooms. I will wait for you. It is no matter to me—I'm used to dining late anyway."

"And if he doesn't settle and I don't come?"

"Well, then, I will have to come to you instead."

"I'll see what I can do," she eventually replied through lips thinned with anger.

He watched her as she locked the door of the spa behind them and stalked off toward the doors leading outside. He took a moment to indulge in the sheer masculine pleasure of watching the sway of her hips and the sharply straight set of her shoulders.

She would not dodge his need to know precisely who Jasper's father was and, if she tried to prevent him, she'd learn exactly what it was like to nay-say a del Castillo.

Six

Ben waited until nine-thirty before calling reception and asking to speak with Mia. Irritation at her delaying tactics danced along his spine as he paced the confines of his sitting room, the cordless phone glued to his ear, and stared out the window at the black velvet blanket of night beyond.

"I'm sorry, sir, but Ms. Parker is off duty until tomorrow morning. Could someone else help you?"

Not unless someone else could tell him every single thing that Mia had done since he'd left Queenstown after the New Year's celebrations that had surpassed all New Year's celebrations in his memory.

"Ms. Parker is expecting my call. Please put me through to her quarters."

He sensed the night receptionist's hesitation before she continued.

"Let me check with Ms. Parker first."

Her staff's loyalty and attention to observing privacy was commendable. However, he could barely stop himself from grinding his teeth in frustration.

"I'm putting you through," the receptionist breezed a moment later.

"Muchas gracias," Ben replied, forcing himself to continue to inject civility into his voice.

There was a short delay on the line before he heard a woman's voice on the other end.

"Mr. del Castillo?"

"Elsa, how are you this evening? I thought we'd agreed you'd call me Ben." He injected as much warmth as he could into his voice. If he was to get to Mia, he wasn't averse to using whatever powers he had to work through the people she had around her. "Would it be possible to speak with Mia?"

"I'm sorry but Mia is sleeping. She had a very troubled night with Jasper last night and she fell asleep shortly after his bath time this evening. I'm staying here tonight to help out in case he has another bad one. Perhaps I can take a message for you."

Ben considered Elsa's words. Was Mia truly asleep, or had she coached her mother to screen her calls?

"No, no message. I will speak with her tomorrow. I hope you all rest well and that Jasper is much improved by morning."

The words stuck on his tongue as it suddenly struck him that if he was truly Jasper's father it should be him helping Mia through the night with their son—*would* have been him, if she had done him the courtesy of informing him of her pregnancy at the time. The thought cut him to his core. He'd never stopped to consider what it meant to be a father before. Certainly hadn't given it a thought when he and Reynard had agreed to Alex's harebrained scheme to marry and start families to prove their grandfather's fears about the curse as unfounded.

In fact, truth be told, he had no idea how he would have reacted had Mia tracked him down and told him about her pregnancy from the start. Fatherhood was something he'd always assumed would happen when he was older, ready to settle down by choice rather than by some ancient dictate. But now he knew, deep in his soul, that he wanted this responsibility in his life more than anything he'd ever wanted before.

He ended the call and let the phone drop from his hands onto the sofa beside him. More than anything he wanted to know the truth about Jasper. But how was he to go about it when Mia kept stonewalling him every step of the way?

Maybe he was going at this all wrong, he thought. There was more than one way to reel in a fish, but to hook them you needed the right bait. And the question was, what was Mia's bait?

The next afternoon, when Ben turned up for his massage, he was surprised to find a different woman waiting for him at the spa.

"You must be Mr. del Castillo," the brunette said as she stepped forward to welcome him. "I'm Cassie Edwards. Mia asked me to stand in for her today as she's not well."

"Not well?"

His distrust of her statement must have been obvious, because she hastened to add, "Apparently she's come down with the same illness as her son."

Has she, now? Ben thought to himself. It was something that would be quite simple to check out and he resolved to do that the moment his session with Cassie was over.

Cassie was good, he acknowledged later, once the massage was over, but she wasn't Mia. He missed the gentle strength of her fingers as they glided over his body, even missed the way she worked out the knots in his shoulders and lower, down his back. But most of all, he missed her touch. Knowing it was her and her alone who soothed his tortured muscles.

After he was finished, he went to his suite to shower and change and decided to pay Mia and Jasper a visit. A quick call to room service soon saw a basket delivered to his door laden with fresh bread, chicken soup in a generous thermos and a selection of fresh fruit.

It was only a short walk to the building where he knew Mia stayed. He deduced the building, built around the turn of the last century, had probably been the original station house when the property was a working farm station. Literature in the hotel had told him that about three years ago most of the grazing acreage of the station had been sold and the property converted into the boutique hotel and spa it was now.

Reading between the lines, Benedict began to wonder what exactly had prompted the sudden and massive change in such a short period of time. He made a mental note to do a little more investigating. Tomorrow would be soon enough, as he planned to spend some time in Queenstown catching up with the friends he'd stayed with during his last visit to the area. A few careful questions here and there should give him the information he needed.

For now, though, his most immediate concern was finding out whether or not Mia was indeed unwell, or simply avoiding him.

When he reached the building he followed the first path that led him to a paneled green door. He rapped his knuckles against the surface and waited. After a few minutes he heard the sound of footsteps inside and eventually the door swung open.

Mia stood in front of him, her blond hair loose rather than in the ponytail or twist she usually wore. The rings under her eyes were even more prominent than the day before and her eyes shone, as if she had a mild fever.

Suddenly feeling ridiculous for his suspicions, Ben lifted the basket he'd brought.

"I heard you weren't feeling well and I thought you might like this. Can I come in?"

"Aren't you worried you'll catch whatever we have?" she rasped.

"I think if I were to get it, I would have already caught whatever it is from you," Ben answered, giving her a pointed look.

The slight flush on her cheeks deepened as he alluded to the kiss they'd shared two days ago.

"Your choice," she said, ducking her head and standing to one side to let him through. "Frankly, I'm too tired to argue with you."

"That makes a pleasant change," he quipped, brushing past her and stepping into a large open-plan sitting-cum-dining area.

Toys were scattered across the floor and the couch had been made up into a bed.

"I'm sorry for the mess. Just didn't have the energy to pick up after Jas today."

"Understandable, if you're not well. Here, sit down, before you fall down."

He took her by the elbow, guided her onto the couch and lifted her feet up before pulling the blanket over her. The fact that she didn't so much as raise a single objection spoke volumes as to how unwell she was.

"Is Elsa not here today?"

Mia shook her head. "She's staying in town for an early

appointment with her cardiologist tomorrow. He only visits Queenstown every so often so I wouldn't let her cancel."

"How has Jasper been today?"

She gave a weak smile. "Oh, he's been much better today. The antibiotics are working a treat and he's full of beans. Too many beans, actually. He's asleep now." She gestured to the chaos of the sitting room. "I probably should have tried to keep him up to closer to his usual bedtime, because now he's going to be up far too late tonight, but when he just dropped, I had to tuck him into bed."

"Have you eaten anything today?"

She shook her head. "Not much. Hurts to eat."

"I brought soup. I think you should try some. Your chef assures me it's his grandmother's secret recipe and bound to have you feeling better in no time."

"Why?"

"Why what?"

"Why are you doing this for me?"

Ben hesitated. To be honest, he didn't really know. Sure, at first he'd just wanted to prove to himself that she wasn't just avoiding him—and more to the point, avoiding his questions about Jasper. But since he'd seen her at the door he'd been filled with a disquieting need to make sure she was okay. He reached in his mind for something to say, settling on the first thing that came.

"Oh, it's nothing philanthropic, I can assure you. It's all about me. I want my usual massage therapist back as soon as possible. Cassie's good, but she's not as good as you."

She made a strangled sound, halfway between a laugh and a groan of pain.

He flung her a glance. "Is that so hard to believe?"

"No, no it's not, not when you put it like that," she said with a weak smile before struggling to get off the couch again.

"Where do you think you're going?"

"To the kitchen to get some bowls for the soup."

"Tell me where to find everything. You can stay right where you are."

Ben readjusted the blanket across her jean-clad legs, noting with approval that her jeans were a far better fit than the uniform she usually wore day-to-day around the hotel. Her spa attire was a little more revealing but nowhere near as good as his memory. And that memory became more and more distinct with every day he spent time with her again.

Under her directions, he went into her compact kitchen and found the necessary utensils and a tray. He retrieved the basket from the sitting room and set the tray for one. A fact she protested about when he brought the bowl of soup and a slice of buttered bread through to her.

"Aren't you eating, too?"

"No, I brought this for you. My mother didn't have much to do in our kitchens when we were growing up but I always remember her bringing me her chicken soup when I was sick."

Mia eyed him over the tray he'd propped onto her lap. This Benedict del Castillo was a different man from the one who'd all but threatened her over Jasper yesterday afternoon. What had brought about the change? Surely it wasn't just because she was unwell. Deep down she knew he must have an ulterior motive of some description but she felt so utterly rotten she couldn't fight through the fugue of her mind to pin it down.

She scooped her spoon into the soup and brought it to her lips. The subtle flavors of chicken, celery and some other vegetable that she couldn't quite place immediately, slid over her tongue and down her raw throat like a balm.

"This is really good—you should have some," she said, her voice not quite as raspy as before.

"Maybe. See how much you feel like, first."

Under his watchful gaze she dipped a corner of the bread into the soup and brought it to her mouth. She felt a drop of soup linger on the edge of her lip and she swept it with her tongue, her gaze flitting to Ben's when he roughly cleared his throat and looked away. A hot flush raced through her that had nothing whatsoever to do with the fever she'd been running most of the day.

Crazy. Her reactions to him were totally off the scale of reasonable behavior. Here she was, sick, and still she wanted him. Mia focused on her soup and trying to get it all down her sore throat.

No wonder Jasper had been so fractious yesterday if this was how he'd felt. She'd weighed up going to the doctor herself today but decided against it. Bed rest and plenty of fluids were all she needed, she was sure of it. If she didn't show an improvement in the next day or two she'd go to the doctor, but for now she was sure she could beat this on her own. Besides, being unwell had given her an excuse to call in Cassie, one of the therapists she usually had working at the spa during full capacity of the hotel, to take on her responsibilities with Ben.

So much for her attempts to avoid him, though, she thought as she stole another glance at him. He'd risen from his chair and was now picking up Jasper's scatter of toys and putting them in the big toy barrel she kept in the room. Usually she made Jasper tidy after himself, but today everything was just too much.

Actually, now she thought about it, even keeping her eyes open defied every ounce of willpower she had. Her head dropped back against the pillow behind her and her eyelids slid shut. She'd close them for only a minute, that was all, and then she'd be all right again.

She could tell it was much later when she next opened her eyes. The gray light of the winter afternoon had darkened to night and the tray that had still been on her lap when she'd drifted off was now gone. She felt a little better for the food and rest, though her mouth felt fuzzy and her eyes burned as if they had a week's worth of household dust behind her lids. Still weak, she pushed the blanket off and forced herself to her feet. She had to check on Jasper, and take a much-needed bathroom break, she realized.

The room spun a little and she took a moment to check her bearings. The sitting room was a heck of a lot tidier than it had been when she'd fallen asleep. Not only had her tray been cleared away, but the coffee table tidied, and from the overhead light still on in the kitchen she could see that someone had cleared up in there also.

Had Ben done all of that? The almost overwhelming sense of relief at having someone who could share the load with her was short-lived as a flush of shame and embarrassment swept through her. No doubt that would give him even more ammunition to use against her when he questioned her parenting skills. And she had no doubt that he'd use every weapon available to him when it came time to fight. It struck her that she now accepted that the fight for Jasper was only a matter of time away. The realization struck dread into her heart.

She took a look at the wall clock above the kitchen bench. It was past midnight. Good grief. She really had to check on Jasper. He'd been due another dose of the liquid antibiotic his doctor had prescribed at around seven. But first, the bathroom.

After she'd taken care of her needs and washed her

hands and face, she moved as quickly and carefully as she could across the hall to Jasper's room. She gently pushed open his door and froze in the doorway. There on Jasper's "big boy's bed," curled up with their son in his arms, lay Benedict del Castillo. Her heart lurched as she saw the two dark heads so close together.

They each had the same bone structure. A strong, broad forehead with heavy dark brows sweeping in a slight arch over their thick, dark lash-tipped eyes. Eyes that were closed in slumber, but that she knew to be the same rich, dark hue. Ben's long, straight nose was different from Jasper's, the little boy's still holding some of the lack of definition of infanthood. But their lips showed every sign of bearing the same haughty line even if Ben's were outlined with the shadow of a day's growth of beard. They even had the same indentation in their chins.

Stupid tears burned at the back of her eyes and she backed out of the room. Somehow, she must have made a noise though, because Ben's eyes flicked open. He pursed his lips in a silent "shhh" and carefully moved, tucking Jasper under his covers and joining her at the bedroom door.

He took her by the hand, his long, warm fingers clasping hers as if the action was totally normal and everyday between them. Once they were back in the sitting room he put his free hand against her forehead.

"You feel cooler than before."

"What were you doing?" she asked. "Have you been here all this time?"

"You needed the rest and I didn't see the point in disturbing you. Jasper woke shortly after you dozed off. We made it a game to see how quiet he could be. He's a very good boy for his age."

"But your dinner, his dinner—"

"I scrambled Jasper some eggs and made toast with some of the bread I brought over earlier. He wolfed it down and then reminded me he was supposed to take his medicine."

Mia was overwhelmed. This international jet-setting playboy had settled into her son's evening routine and taken care of him and she'd been totally oblivious. Her legs became too unsteady to hold her up any longer and she sat down heavily on a chair, her eyes still locked on Ben.

"I don't know how to thank you. Really, I don't. You should have woken me so you could get back to the hotel."

"It's not like I had anything more pressing to do," he said as he sat down opposite her. "Besides, you looked like you were spiking quite a fever there for a while. It was easier to let you sleep it off and take care of Jasper for you."

"What time did he go back to bed?"

"He fell asleep about nine, after insisting on several stories."

She smiled. "He's like that."

"I told him about my home country and what it was like growing up there in my family's castillo. He was fascinated. I promised him I'd take him there one day."

Mia's spine snapped straight and an icy fist closed around her heart.

"You what? You had no right to do that," she cried.

"I have every right. He *is* my son, after all, isn't he?"

Mia struggled to deny his words. So far she had managed not to lie outright to Ben—it shouldn't be all that difficult to do, should it? But right now the words of denial froze on her lips as Ben sat back in his chair and stretched out his legs.

"He told me when his birthday is—showed me on the

calendar on his bedroom wall. He was conceived when we were together, wasn't he, Mia?"

She swallowed against the sudden painful dryness of her throat and tried to draw a breath into lungs that were suddenly too constricted to fill.

"I'm not proud of my behavior back then but, honestly, any man I slept with that summer could be his father," she finally managed in a strained voice.

Ben's eyes narrowed and she saw the flare of anger reflected in their depths making them look black rather than brown. Instantly she wished her words back. It was true she wasn't proud of her behavior from that period in her life, but when it came to physical intimacy, she had little to be ashamed of. Benedict del Castillo had been the *only* man she'd shared her body with that summer.

"Why won't you just tell me the truth?" he asked, his voice as cold and steady as a surgeon's blade.

"Because I owe you nothing. Even if you were Jasper's father, why on earth would I tell you? You're hardly the kind of man I'd want in his life. Sure, I used to behave fast and loose, but all that changed when I had Jas. You, however, well—the Internet is full of your exploits and your conquests all over Europe. You change your women as frequently as you change your suits.

"You go from adventure to adventure—whether it's street racing in Monaco, rock climbing in Switzerland or anything else that catches your fancy for a moment, and then is quickly discarded again. None of that makes you father material in my book, and as far as I'm concerned you're certainly not the kind of man Jasper deserves in his life. Right now, to you, he's merely something to possess. You know nothing about him and yet because of a vague physical resemblance you expect me to give you rights you probably don't even really want."

"You know nothing about what I really want, but you will find out. Trust me on this."

"Trust you?" She forced a broken laugh. "I wouldn't trust you as far as I could kick you, and right now that wouldn't be any distance at all. Look, I appreciate what you did for me tonight but, please, leave now. You will not hear what you want to from me. Not now. Not ever."

"You're making a bad mistake, Mia."

"Oh, believe me, I'm not. If I wasn't bound to you by that stupid contract you'd be leaving here right now."

"You're bound to me by more than a contract, Mia, and don't you forget it."

As Mia watched him leave the room and let himself out she sagged back in her seat and wondered just what she was letting herself in for. It was clear he wasn't going to give up on this quest of his and, in the end, where would that leave her and her son?

Seven

Ben looked back at Queenstown as the boat motored away from the public dock of the bustling town center. A wonderfully relaxing day in the Gibbston Valley with his friends, Jim and Cathy Samson, had taken the edge off of his fury over Mia's stubbornness last night, but it had done nothing to soften his determination. Although he had no conclusive proof, he knew to the depths of his soul that Jasper was his son. Even now he felt a bond with the little boy he'd never have imagined possible.

Her words had spun in his head all night. So she didn't think he was father material, did she? At first the words had incensed him…but as he'd tossed and turned during the sleepless night, he'd been forced to admit to himself that he could understand some of her fears. Nothing from their brief, anonymous interlude would have given her the impression that he had any immediate intention of becoming a husband, much less a father. It hadn't been on his radar then at all.

But on the other side of the coin, he knew that motherhood hadn't been in her plans, either. And yet she had risen to the challenge, capably loving and caring for their child in the years since. Did she think he was unable to achieve the same growth and maturity? Was that why she'd been so determined to keep him at a distance ever since his arrival in New Zealand? Did she truly believe he was incapable of treating anyone—woman or child—as more than a temporary diversion? The thought stung, and made him all the more unwavering in his resolve to stay the course on this challenge. He *would* gain rights to his son, even if it meant fighting it all out in court.

He hunched into his wool coat and pushed his hands deeper into his pockets. It didn't have to be like this. All she'd had to do was acknowledge him as Jasper's father and they'd have been able to find a common ground on which to base their parenthood. But no. She had to fight him. Deny him his rights.

In the distance now, he could see the driver and car that had been assigned to him for today pull away from the no-stopping area on the dock. It seemed that Mia had managed to follow all his stipulations on his contract to the letter so far. For some reason, that rankled rather than satisfied him. Now he understood how important the financial side of their agreement was for her, it would have been interesting to play her a little and see just how far she was prepared to go to protect her livelihood. But he'd been unable to fault anything so far.

This morning when he'd arrived in Queenstown, he'd been whisked away from the dock in leather-seated, climate-controlled comfort, and headed out to the Gibbston Highway where his friends' vineyard and winery were situated. The scenery en route to the Gibbston Valley was at a complete contrast to his last visit but he'd found the cool white and gray beauty of the landscape equally as striking as the summer heat and colors.

His lips curled in a bitter smile. The difference in climate between this visit and last was a perfect mirror for his reception from Mia. The first time, full of heat and intensity, the second, the complete antithesis.

Except for when he'd kissed her. That had been incendiary. Yet that memory, too, was tainted by the realization that even as she'd responded to his kiss, she'd been hiding the truth from him about their son.

Well, incendiary or not, she'd soon learn that he didn't back down from what was important in his life, and his son was the most important thing to him right now. Today he'd begun to gather information about Mia with the intention of proving he was the better option to be Jasper's parent. While his objective had been clear in his own mind, he hadn't anticipated discovering how far off the mark he'd been about her. The information he'd gleaned from the conversation with his friends during the day had been eye-opening and had shown a side of Mia he hadn't expected. A side that demonstrated her grit and determination. He supposed he had to allow for some admiration of how hard she'd worked to keep her family home in the face of her father's financial failures and the fallout after his death. It couldn't have been easy for her.

Jim and Cathy had been full of praise for her—how strong she'd been for her mother, how she'd adapted to their straitened circumstances, how she'd built the hotel/spa business out of nothing, even how she'd slid into mother-hood as if it was as natural to her as breathing.

A kernel of guilt unfurled deep inside. She'd gone through hell and was holding on to her life by the tips of her fingers. It wasn't his intention to rip it all away from her. But she, in turn, had to understand that there was more at stake than merely her balking at admitting his paternity of Jasper. His entire family was counting on him now. Even if he couldn't fulfill both terms of his agreement with his brothers—to marry and start a family—at least he could produce a son to prove to his grandfather that the del Castillos would continue for at least another generation, despite *Abuelo*'s fears to the contrary.

For centuries the prosperity of the people of Isla Sagrado had been tied into the success of the del Castillo family. They had all seen some difficult times and had fought against adversity to be where they were today. While he may not officially carry the name, Jasper was a del Castillo. He deserved the chance to know his father's family, see his father's home. And Ben deserved the chance to know Jasper, too.

Ben had spent only a few hours with the boy the night before, but that brief time had been infinitely precious. To see his son smile, to hear him laugh, to have the opportunity to care for him and get to know him—it was a gift Ben had never thought he'd be able to have after he'd learned the results of the car crash. Mia had no right to take that away from him. Especially not if she was motivated by some misguided belief that he was not able to love and care for his son.

She would learn, though, that when the chips were down, the del Castillos didn't give up. Ben was not about to give up on his son. Not under any circumstances.

While Mia waited in the spa for Benedict to arrive for his massage, she filled her time with a mini inventory of supplies. Anything to take her mind off their impending time together. She'd been tempted to take another sick day.

She still felt wrung out and her throat was still a little sore but she'd realized this morning that hiding from him wasn't going to solve anything. He'd struck her as the kind of man who approached things head-on. At least if she spent whatever time necessary with him, he was less likely to be able to ambush her.

Jasper was almost a hundred percent well again today, although she'd carefully instructed Elsa on when his antibiotics were due through the day. With any luck he'd be fit for day care again soon. As far as she was concerned, right now, the less time Jasper spent in Ben's vicinity, the better.

A sound at the doorway made her stop what she was doing. She forced herself to calmly turn around and place the clipboard and pen she'd been using onto the reception desk in front of her.

"I didn't expect to see you here today," Ben said.

"I was feeling a bit better so thought I'd let Cassie off the hook." She stepped out from behind the reception desk and crossed the short distance to the door to her treatment room and gestured to Ben to go inside. "You know the drill. I'll be in when you're ready."

For a moment he hesitated, as if he was about to say something, but then he simply went into the room and closed the door behind him. Mia pressed a hand to her throat. She could feel her pulse racing beneath her fingertips. Maybe doing this when she wasn't quite up to speed hadn't been such a great idea after all. Just seeing him was enough to upset the rhythm of her breathing, let alone her heart rate.

He'd turned up today in designer jeans and a long-sleeved black polo shirt and the effect was mouthwatering. The fabric clung to the lines of his sculpted body, a body she knew all too well. A body that even in her semi-well state sent all her receptors pinging on full alert. She closed her eyes and drew in a steadying breath. She'd done this before and she could do it again. He was a mass of muscle and tissue and skin and bone. Her job was to massage, relax and provide muscular relief.

Opening her eyes, Mia knocked gently on the door before letting herself in. As usual, the calming scent she had burning in the oil burner hit her immediately, relaxing her and settling her mind into work mode. As she had done the last two times, she straightened the covers over Ben's legs and buttocks before starting her routine.

"How was your day?" she asked conversationally as she pressed her hands against his warm, smooth skin.

"Do you really want to know, or are you merely being polite?" Ben answered from beneath her.

"I'm being polite," she said carefully, determined to keep control of both her temper and her nerves.

He snorted a derisive laugh. "Well, at least you're honest. I suppose if I were to be as honest I'd tell you that I found out some interesting things about you today."

Mia stilled her movements. "You were asking about me? Who? Where?"

He mentioned the Samsons, where they'd met at the New Year's Eve party three and a half years ago.

"Oh," she said quietly, suddenly wishing she'd never embarked upon this conversation in the first place. "I haven't seen them since."

"They said that, too. Seems you haven't made any effort to stay in touch with your old crowd. Why is that, Mia?"

"Like I've said to you before, people change. *I* changed, to be more precise. I couldn't operate on their level anymore and I didn't want to feel as if I had to. Besides, I didn't really know them all that well."

She remembered all too vividly the well-meaning phone

calls, the gently probing questions about how she was managing. Sure, a handful of her old friends had been genuine in their concern but some had simply been digging for gossip, as if the horrible newspaper headlines hadn't been revealing enough. Mia had had enough to focus on with her mother's fragile state and her own pregnancy to have to worry about what her friends and acquaintances thought and who she could trust anymore.

The media had been vicious about her father's financial ruin. Nothing had been sacred. She well remembered the photos plastered in the papers every time she set foot in Queenstown or even further afield—their captions speculating on how much of her daddy's money Mia would be spending on that occasion. Each shot, each conjecture, had been yet another nail in her father's coffin and eventually he hadn't been able to continue any longer.

And then they'd really grown nasty, insinuating how maintaining the lifestyle expected of his women had driven Reuben Parker to take a rope to one of the trees at the back of the property and take his life. It hadn't taken long before Mia had found herself second-guessing every word of condolence, every gesture of comfort, from the people she'd counted among her friends. Eventually it was simply easier to refuse all invitations, issue none herself and retreat into the world her father had left for them. A world she had painstakingly rebuilt piece by piece.

Her bank manager had asked her why she didn't just sell up entirely, settle the outstanding debts and strike out somewhere anew. But Parker's Retreat had been in her father's family for generations. His forebears had hacked out an existence in hostile land to build a dream for generations. She wasn't prepared to let that all go, especially not when she harbored a precious new generation within her own body. And especially not when she felt as if much of it had been her fault.

"You know Jim and Cathy aren't like that. They don't judge people by everyone else's standards."

Mia made a non-committal noise and moved into the next stage of the massage, hoping he'd drop the subject. She should have known better.

"So just how much in debt are you, Mia? Converting this property into a hotel and spa can't have been cheap. Not on top of the other debts I understand you took responsibility for."

"That's between me and my bank manager," she said carefully, hoping her flare of anger didn't color her words. How dare he ask such a personal question?

"I'm guessing with the current economic climate you haven't exactly been running at full capacity, have you?"

"We're doing okay," she insisted.

In all honesty, though, they were barely making ends meet. Yes, they'd done well building up a client base and securing bookings, but she knew that she'd been ambitious with her plans for the hotel and spa. Not wanting to take it in increments by building first the hotel and then the treatment side of the business over time, she'd done it all at once. She'd gone into business in the same manner she'd gone into everything in her life—boots and all. It was all paying off this time—but slowly.

"The contract we signed must have been a godsend, hmmm?"

"I won't deny it was welcome, until I found out exactly who it was with."

He chuckled and beneath her hands she felt his shoulder muscles tense.

"You think you struck a deal with the Devil?"

"You could say that," she said carefully. After all, it was his phrasing, not hers.

"Then you'd do well not to tax my generosity."

Oh boy. Here it came. His demands. She had to concede he definitely had a way about him. Circle slowly, show concern—care, even, if last night was any indicator—and then go straight for the jugular.

"Are you dissatisfied with your stay here?" she asked.

"Not yet, but it's early days."

She focused her energy on a particularly taut section of muscle at the top of his hip and was rewarded by his grunt of discomfort as she did so.

"I shall consider myself warned then," she answered through tight lips and made a silent resolve to ensure her staff was one hundred percent up to speed with the conditions of his occupancy.

There would be no mistakes. None.

The next day, Mia took the morning off. Jasper's doctor had a brief Saturday morning surgery at the clinic, and Mia wanted to take Jasper back into Queenstown to be rechecked. She herself was pleased with his progress, though. Right now he behaved as if he'd never been sick, whereas she was still struggling to recover. It didn't help that her nights were now fractured with dreams of Benedict del Castillo. Dreams which delved into the one day and two nights they'd shared, leaving her aching and irritable when she woke.

Jasper always loved the trips into town and especially loved to watch the gondolas climb the side of the mountain leading up to the Skyline complex. For his third birthday, coming up in just over two and a half months, she planned to take him for a ride to the top and a special birthday meal in the restaurant. She wasn't sure if she was brave enough to take him on the luge ride just yet and hoped he'd be satisfied with watching this year. Right now, though, her little boy was happy to be sitting on Don's lap, pretending to skipper the boat as they drew closer to the public dock.

"Don't worry about waiting for us," she said to Don, "we'll probably head out to the Remarkables Shopping Centre for a bit and after that we'll just get a water taxi home."

"If you're sure," Don said. "I don't mind waiting, you know that."

"Yes, but I think it's more important you be available for Mr. del Castillo should he want the boat for any reason today. Let's not do anything that might ruffle his feathers, hmmm?"

"Anything you say. You're the boss."

Don gave her his trademark smile and ruffled Jasper's hair with one of his work-roughened hands. "So, skipper. Are we ready to dock?"

Jasper nodded enthusiastically and hopped off the older man's lap and made his way to another seat so he wasn't in the way. Mia watched him with pride. So young and yet already so responsible. She'd done a good job so far with him, she told herself. And nothing and no one was going to jeopardize that, no matter how big their threats or how much money they had to wield at their disposal.

The visit to the doctor went smoothly and to Mia's relief, Jas was given the all clear to go back to day care on Monday. As lovely as it had been to have him home, he was rather wearing for her mother on a full-day basis. Something that would only become more obvious as his need for stimulation became more demanding.

Well, she consoled herself, for as long as she kept Parker's Retreat running smoothly, there would be no problem with affording his day care's fees or the fees for the next level of pre-school provided by the facility. Her heart crunched a little on the knowledge that her son was fast growing up. Every day with him was a gift she readily accepted with open arms.

Jasper was excited on the bus ride to the shopping center and jiggled up and down on his seat asking umpteen questions as they passed along the main bus route. The trip to Frankton didn't take long and Mia held his hand firmly as they alighted from the bus. She'd promised him a special treat from the large multipurpose store there, followed by lunch at the café right by the bus stop.

It was as they were moving up and down the toy aisles in the store that Mia suddenly had the sensation she was being watched. She turned her head, catching a glimpse of a young woman staring at her intently before rapidly averting her head and showing a sudden interest in a stand of action figures. Maybe she was just being paranoid, but Mia moved Jasper on to another aisle, distracting him with a junior construction set he'd seen on television and had been nagging at her to get for days now.

The pack was a great deal more expensive than the "treat" she'd planned for him, but the other woman's perusal had left her feeling edgy. For some strange reason it reminded her too much of the way she'd been hounded when her father's scandal had hit the news. Right now she was keen to follow her instincts and get back on the next bus to Queenstown.

At the checkout, she quickly made her purchase and hurried Jasper back to the bus stop.

"I want lunch, Mommy. You said lunch," Jasper complained, and started pulling at her with one hand as he pointed with the other to the café doors.

"I know, honey, but I remembered I have to get back

home. I promise I'll get you something in Queenstown before we get the water taxi back. Okay?"

"No." Jasper's lower lip began to wobble ominously. "I want lunch now."

Juggling her bag and the bulky construction kit, Mia bent to pick Jasper up, but he wasn't having any of it. Simultaneously, she sensed someone beside her. The woman from the store—except now she had someone with her. A man with a camera, its shutter working flat out as he took several photos of her and one very unhappy little boy.

"Ms. Parker, is it true that Benedict del Castillo is staying at your hotel?" the woman asked, her tone smug and more than a little pushy.

"What? I'm sorry, I don't know what you're talking about."

"Come on now, Mia. Benedict del Castillo was seen in Queenstown yesterday and he's news wherever he goes, particularly since his accident. A source tells us you two were lovers some time ago. Is his visit now a reunion?"

Bile rose in Mia's throat and she pulled Jasper up into her arms and turned his head into her shoulder.

"As I said," she answered as calmly as she could, "I have no idea what you're talking about. Now please, you're distressing my son. Stop taking those photos. You're invading my privacy."

She glared at the photographer, who completely ignored her.

"We're in a public area, Mia," the reporter reminded her with a smile that was anything but friendly. "Tell me, how does one of Europe's most sought-after bachelors feel about being a father?"

Eight

Mia clutched Jasper to her so tight he wriggled in protest. She felt a sting of remorse, but right now, having the photographer's camera thrust right in her face hard on the heels of the reporter's last question, she was determined to protect her son's privacy by preventing them from capturing another image of his face. She could only hope against hope that they hadn't already done so.

To her relief, a taxi pulled into the shopping-center car park, disgorging a very obvious pair of foreign tourists. She shot across the roadway and climbed in the open door, pushing Jasper down on the seat beside her.

"I'm sorry, miss," the driver said. "But my current fare is paying me to stay and wait for them."

"Please, I need to get away from those people. I'll pay you double the fare to take me back to the wharf in town. Triple! Just please get us away from here."

"Just a minute, then," he said, and alighted from the car.

Mia watched from behind locked doors as he jogged over to the tourist couple and with a series of gestures indicated he would be back in half an hour. When they nodded Mia groaned with relief.

Beside her, Jasper lay facedown on the car seat, sobbing his little heart out. Mia shrugged out of her coat and covered him with it, her hand stroking his narrow wee shoulders through the material. The driver returned to the cab and got behind the wheel. All the way back to the town center she looked out the back of the cab, noting the red hatchback that followed them every kilometer of the way. For the second time in her life she rued living in what was a relatively small town. There really was no escape. Nothing to even stop them hiring another water taxi and following her out to Parker's Retreat if they really wanted to.

Jasper had finally quieted, she noted with relief, but though the tears had stopped, he still seemed upset and confused. Her heart throbbed for him. He didn't deserve this. Not a bar of it. He was an innocent. A cold chill settled deep inside her. She knew what the media were like. Relentless when they thought they were onto a good story. The prospect of them dragging her innocent child into their gutter press filled her with equal parts of fear and anger.

Of even greater concern was how on earth they'd even found out about Ben's relationship to Jasper, let alone the short-lived affair she and Ben had indulged in. Even her own mother hadn't been privy to the truth.

Just out of Frankton, Mia noticed the red car slow down and pull over to the side of the road. She could see the female reporter with her cell phone to her ear, her free hand gesticulating wildly as she spoke. In the passenger seat the photographer trained his camera on Mia's face and she quickly turned her head away, relieved to see they'd given up the chase for now.

Within fifteen minutes, the cab pulled up at the Queenstown wharf. Her whole body trembling, Mia reached into her purse and pulled out all the money she had in there. She knew it was far more than the fare—even more than triple the fare—but she was so grateful to finally be away from the reporter she didn't even care.

She scooped Jasper from his seat and grabbed the shopping bag with his treat inside—and as she did so, she heard the cab driver's mobile phone chime. He picked it up and answered, his gaze suddenly fixing on hers as she began to get out of the car. Another chill ran down her spine as she watched him end the call and press a few buttons on his phone—which he then aimed directly at her and Jasper. Before she could block his view of them both she heard the telltale click of her picture being taken. Even her knight in shining armor had his price, it seemed.

The reporter must have called the cab company and somehow been patched through to the driver, she surmised as she hustled away toward the water-taxi jetty. She wondered just how much money he'd agreed to, to give her privacy away.

"Come on, Jas, let's get to the boat and get home, hmmm?" she said, trying to keep her voice as upbeat as possible.

"Lunch?" he asked, his voice once again a tear-soaked whimper.

"I'm so sorry, baby. We have to get home."

The construction set bumped against her leg as she half walked, half ran to the jetty. She only hoped that she'd be able to persuade the skipper of the vessel to break his schedule to take her out to Parker's Retreat right now rather than wait for other concession passengers on his regular service.

Thankfully, the skipper was amenable, agreeing to bill the trip—with a premium—to the Parker's Retreat account. As they headed out past the Queenstown Gardens and into the lake Mia finally allowed herself to relax. The rush of adrenaline that had propelled her from the shopping center to here had run its course and right now she felt completely deflated.

Deflated and worried sick about what she was going to do next. She knew she shouldn't be surprised that Ben had been spotted in Queenstown—he'd told her himself that he'd gone out to see friends—but how on earth had they made the connection between him and her? Who amongst her old friends had spilled the beans about their previous affair? Few people had known about it at the time. Jim and Cathy Samson—the couple Ben had seen yesterday—and one of her old girlfriends were the only three that sprang to mind.

She knew for a fact that the Samsons were as fierce about their privacy as anyone could be. But her old girlfriend? Much as it pained her to admit it, Sue had always had a bit of an ax to grind as far as Mia had been concerned. In the shallow social pond in which they'd swum, Mia had always shrugged it off as a touch of misplaced envy, but she'd never believed Sue could be malicious.

She knew Sue worked in the CBD of Queenstown in a building overlooking the wharf. Had she caught a glimpse of Ben when he'd gone into town yesterday? Maybe she'd gone so far as to call the local paper and tell them what little she'd known.

Yes, she was definitely the most likely culprit, though the idea that someone she'd known so well could turn into an enemy so easily really hurt. No matter what the circumstances were, Mia knew she could never do something like that. But the knowledge was cold comfort in the face of what she now had ahead of her.

* * *

Mia saw Ben standing on the dock at Parker's Retreat when the water taxi pulled up behind the Parker's launch. The cream wool Aran-knit sweater that he wore emphasized the width of his shoulders and his stone-washed jeans hugged his hips and thighs in all the right places. He looked strong and confident and put together—all the things that she wasn't, at the moment.

As traumatic as her day had become, she couldn't help but feel a sense of relief that he was here waiting for them. She was going to have to tell him what had happened and she'd rather deal with it sooner than later. First, though, she had some serious making up to do with her little boy.

A little boy who seemed all too happy to be lifted into Benedict's arms rather than be held by his mother a moment longer. Mia didn't blame him for wanting to have nothing to do with her right now. He'd been frightened, had promises broken, and now, without a doubt, he was terribly hungry, as well.

"There have been helicopters overhead all morning," Ben said to her after the water taxi had motored away from the dock.

Mia nodded and swallowed against the lump in her throat.

"Can we talk about it after I've fed Jasper? I promised him lunch back in town, but something happened and we had to leave before he could get anything."

Ben shot her a piercing look. "Something happened?"

"I will tell you the minute he's been fed, I promise."

"Well, then," he said, lifting Jasper high and settling the squealing boy on his shoulders, "we'd better get you some lunch, young man."

Mia was painfully aware of Ben's gaze upon her the whole time she prepared a bowl with nacho chips, tomato ketchup and melted grated cheese for Jasper. Once she'd settled him on the couch with his fuzzy blanket, the bowl of nachos and his favorite DVD on the television, she knew it was time to face the music.

"Tell me, then, why has the place been buzzing with helicopters all morning?" Ben demanded the minute they were more or less alone in the kitchen.

Mia cast a glance at her son, reassuring herself he was happily occupied before answering.

"I think you were spotted during your outing yesterday and that the rumor mill has been well and truly put into action."

"Rumor mill?"

"Jas and I were bailed up outside a shopping center just outside Queenstown late this morning."

She shuddered at the memory—at the sheer and utter helplessness she'd felt with nowhere to turn and no way out.

"And?" Ben prompted.

Mia suddenly wished she'd had more time to think about exactly what she had to say to Ben. More precisely, exactly *how* she was going to say what she had to. One thing she was absolutely positive about. She would not tell him about the questions about Jasper being Benedict's son. It would give him too much power over her—would force her to admit his paternity and with it, his rights to Jas. She wasn't in any way ready to do that.

"Someone has told them about our affair during your last visit," she said bluntly. "They asked me if your being here was a reunion."

"To which you replied?"

"I told them I had no idea what they were talking about, of course. Then I got in a taxi and came back home."

Ben gave her another probing stare. "I have a feeling you're leaving something out."

Mia shook her head. "I've told you what happened. It was horrible the way they harassed us. Jas was so upset."

"They? How many were there?"

"A reporter and a photographer."

"So I imagine we can expect to see some photos of the two of you in the near future."

Mia bristled with anger. "Is that it? Is that all you can say?"

"What else is there to say, Mia? Unless, of course, something else happened that you're holding back from me?"

She tamped down on her fury and dragged in a deep breath. "There's nothing else to say. We had a bad experience that left us both upset. Obviously the helicopters were here taking aerial shots of the retreat and hoping for a glimpse of you. No doubt, no matter what I said, they'll just make up their own stories to suit themselves."

"Exactly," said Ben. "I'll talk to Andre and we'll concentrate on a program that'll keep me away from the public eye. And I'll put any sightseeing trips we'd planned on hold for now. Don't worry, if I know the paparazzi—and I've had some experience with them—they'll disappear as soon as they realize that there's no story here."

Mia nodded, but deep inside she was still very afraid. She, too, had had up close and personal experience with the paparazzi and she knew full well that for as long as they thought they had a lead on something, they'd be more tenacious than a starving dog with a bone. But without giving Ben the full truth about what had happened today, she had no way of telling him how wrong his perception was.

* * *

The following Monday Elsa took Jasper to day care but was quite flustered when she returned back on the boat with Don and, unfortunately, a very teary grandson.

"What happened?" Mia asked her the minute she heard they were both back home.

"It was awful, Mia. A wretched woman came up to me at the wharf and started to follow us, asking all sorts of questions about you and Mr. del Castillo. I didn't even give her the time of day and eventually she disappeared but when we reached day care there were a whole swag of them there. Reporters, photographers. Poor Jasper was terrified and I have to say that the other parents and the staff weren't happy at all."

Mia's heart sunk to the soles of her shoes. Were they not even able to go about their everyday lives now? As much as the money from Benedict's stay was a lifesaver, right now she wished she'd never taken his booking. Her entire world had been turned upside down.

"We'll just have to keep Jasper home until it dies down."

"Dies down? What exactly is 'it,' Mia? Why this sudden interest in our lives again?" her mother pressed.

Mia looked into her worried eyes and realized it was past time for her to tell her mother the truth about Ben and Jasper. To her credit, her mother took the news pretty well.

"So what now? Does he expect to share custody?" Elsa asked.

"I don't know, Mom. To be honest, I haven't even admitted to him that he is Jasper's dad. I'm terrified of what he'll do if he knows for certain."

"He has rights, you know. You can't hide the truth from him forever."

"I know," Mia acknowledged with a weary sigh. "But I'm afraid of just how far he'll try to take those rights. I can't fight someone like him in court. He's from a wealthy family so money is no object if he decided to go for full custody of Jas. You know what will happen. He has enough money for his lawyers to track down every single person I knew before I fell pregnant. If they're put on a stand in the family court, they won't exactly paint a picture of the perfect mother, will they? And then there's our financial position. We're only just making ends meet, here. I can't spare the funds for a protracted legal battle—not after all we've done to hold on to our home."

Her mother put one hand on Mia's shoulder. "Sweetheart, think about what's important here. There's no way to keep the truth a secret forever. If this is going to turn into a battle, you have to face it head-on. You can't hide with your head in the sand. That's exactly what your father did, and look where that left him—where it left us. This," she gestured to the buildings and the land beyond, "it's all just *things*. If you want to keep your son, you're going to have to be prepared to fight for him."

"But Mom, even if we sold another parcel of land, or even the entire complex, we'd have so little to work with. By the time we paid off the business loan…" Her voice trailed off as the helplessness of her situation struck her anew.

"Well, whatever we decide, we'll do it together."

Mia gave her mother a weak smile but deep down there was a deep-seated fear that absolutely nothing she could do at this stage could make things all right again. Even if she could send Ben packing back to Isla Sagrado, she'd have to refund him the money he'd already paid and if that happened, her next mortgage repayment simply wouldn't happen. It would be impossible then to keep the wolves from the door. She felt totally hemmed in. A captive in her own home.

"Would you care to explain the meaning of these?"

Mia looked up from her desk as Benedict came stalking into her office. Her heart gave an all-too-familiar lurch at the sight of him, but that rapidly changed when he slapped not one, but three various issues of New Zealand's weekly women's magazines in front of her. Her hand shook as she reached for the top one.

There, in all their reluctant glory, were Jasper and she at the bus stop at the shopping center. To the right screamed a headline that made her blood turn cold. *Mediterranean Millionaire's Love Child Exposed!*

She dropped the magazine as if it had burned her fingers, and in doing so, saw the cover of the next one with the picture that had obviously been taken by the cab driver. A similar caption burst from the paper. She didn't need to see the next one to know what their feature article was.

"Didn't you say they'd lose interest soon enough?" Mia said in a voice that was not quite steady.

Ben made a raw sound of disgust. "What I can't understand is why you'd admit Jasper is my son to some tabloid gossipmonger but continue to refuse to afford me the same truth."

"I never said anything to them about you or Jasper. In fact, I very clearly told them I had nothing to say and to leave me alone."

"Then where did they get their information?"

Mia shivered. She'd never heard Benedict's voice so cold and controlled. Her emotional defenses rose like a solid wall—the only wall she'd been able to erect during that awful time after her father's death. It had seen her through then and it would hopefully see her through this, too. She gathered her strength to her like some kind of barrier and, imitating his tone, threw out the first words that came to mind.

"For all I know, *you* could have been the one to tip off the media."

She knew the words were a mistake the instant they left her lips.

"If you'll recall, one of the major stipulations in our contract was that you would ensure my privacy. That privacy is well and truly violated now, wouldn't you say? I think we can safely say I had nothing to do with this invasion and I would like to point out that as you have not met this particular term of our agreement, you are in breach. Unless you would like me to rescind our contract, and the second half payment and bonus that would still have been due to you, I suggest you pay attention. I repeat—where did they get their information?"

Mia knew when she was beaten. "I believe one of my old friends may have spilled the beans about our little fling. She was a guest at the party where we met, too—and I had a feeling at the time that she knew who you were, even though she never told me your name. She was…less than pleased that you chose to spend the weekend with me rather than her.

"She moves in the same circles as Jim and Cathy. They could have mentioned to her that you're here, or she may have seen you herself, last Friday, and tipped off the media. She's the type of person who wouldn't hesitate to capitalize on anything that could even remotely show me in a bad light."

"Some friend. I hope she's been paid extremely well, because I intend to see to it that she doesn't make another cent from her knowledge."

"How on earth are you going to do that?" Mia asked, bewildered.

What her friend—her ex-friend, she corrected herself—had done was nasty but it was only hearsay. Which was exactly what these magazines fed on, unfortunately.

"There will be injunctions on everyone involved with this debacle—" He broke off as his cell phone chimed from his pocket.

With a muttered curse he dragged it out and answered.

"*Hola.*"

Mia watched as his face lightened, his expression becoming warm and friendly before rapidly returning to become the hard mask of anger he'd worn a moment ago.

"*Sí.* It is true. I will speak to you as soon as I have confirmation or if there are any further developments."

Ben reverted to rapid Spanish for several minutes, then ended the call and returned his phone to his pocket. She didn't like the look he pinned her with. Somehow she knew she wasn't going to be able to evade him, or the truth, for very much longer.

"It seems the news has reached my home. That was my brother, Alex, demanding to know why I had not yet informed him he was an uncle and that my grandfather is now a great-grandfather."

"Oh, no."

Suddenly it was as if the walls were closing in on her. Her breath caught, trapped in her chest, and her heart began to accelerate. The news had gone global? How on earth could that have happened so very fast? Bile rose in her throat and she reached for the glass of water she constantly kept full on her desk, desperate to ease the sick, burning sensation that spread through her like wildfire.

"Oh, yes." Ben sat down in the visitor's chair opposite

her desk and leaned forward, his elbows resting on the wooden barrier between them. "Now, I want you to tell me everything that happened the other day from the moment you stepped off at the pier until the second I saw you come back."

"It's too late, though, isn't it? There's nothing you can do to undo this."

Mia gestured to the magazines, realizing as she did so that the third one had also printed an old photo of her father's next to that of her and Jasper. Her gut twisted painfully. So they were not even going to leave her father to rest in peace? Hadn't they already done enough when they pilloried him for his financial collapse and drove him to his death?

"I cannot turn back the clock, Mia. Would that I could! But I can make sure that not another scurrilous word is printed about my family. My grandfather is not in the best of health. The last thing he needs right now is something else to add to his troubles." He leaned back in his chair and fixed her with another one of those hard-edged looks he was so painfully good at. "Tell me, and this time, leave nothing out."

By the time Mia had recounted what had happened, Ben was pacing the small confines of her office.

"You mean even the cab driver took a photo of you and Jasper?" His voice boiled with barely restrained fury. "He will regret that action most dearly."

Mia rose from her desk and put a hand on Ben's arm. Beneath her fingers she could feel the heat of his skin through the fine silk of his shirt. She tried to ignore the tingling sensation it aroused in her. There were far more important things to consider here.

"Ben, please, as you said, you can't turn back the clock.

Can we not just focus on making sure they go no further?" she implored him.

"He should pay for what he did to you. What he did to Jasper."

"I know, but don't you see? If you take action against him, even if you take action against Sue, they're only going to make things worse. People like that always do. I don't think I can go through that again. It was bad enough with Dad—it went on for months and months." She prodded her forefinger against the magazine that had included her father's photo on the cover. "It will destroy Mom to have to relive all that. She's only just started grasping her life with both hands again. I can't let her go through that for a second time, too, not to mention how it'll make life impossible for Jasper. I can't do it, Ben. I just can't."

Her voice broke on her final words and to her horror her eyes flooded with tears. And that was when Ben did the last thing she'd imagined he would. He took her in his arms. The solid strength of his body, the firm way he held her, was seductively comforting. His silent support encouraged her to give in, to surrender control. It would be so easy, she thought, and then all thought was suspended as, with the tip of his index finger under her chin, he lifted her face to his and kissed her.

Nine

The taste of him invaded her senses and her body responded like she was starved for physical attention. She kissed him back with all the frustration and tamped down desire she'd suffered from since the moment they'd last touched. Her hands slid over his shoulders, allowing her body to mold against his, to feel the hard core of his strength bolstering her. A sturdy anchor in a sea of fear and concern.

She worked her fingers into his hair, holding him to her, relishing the feel of the silky dark strands threaded through her fingers.

His kiss was consuming and she wanted to be consumed. She wanted everything she'd been too afraid to want for such a very long time. And with that want, she realized what a dangerous path she trod right now—how very much was at stake. Every single reason why she had never let herself dwell on the memory of her time with Benedict flashed through her mind—his touch, his taste, their mutual pleasure. It had been indescribably beautiful and yet over after only thirty-six hours. And then reality had hit—hard.

Mia tore her lips from his and lowered her hands to his shoulders to give him a firm push away from her—though the breaking of contact was almost a physical hurt.

"No, this isn't right," she cried, panting. "It just complicates things."

"*Sí,* it is more than right. We need to do this, Mia. We cannot fight what exists between us. Let me show you how special we can be. Let me be there for you, protect you, make love to you."

Mia gathered all her strength and stepped away from him. Her heart fluttered in her chest like a bird trapped in a net. All in all, that was exactly how she felt. Trapped. When had life become so complicated? She hadn't allowed herself to yearn for the past, for the time when life was more carefree and fun. It was a waste of time in her new world.

She shook her head slowly. "No, Ben. Even if I wanted to, I am not that kind of woman anymore. I have responsibilities to my son and my mother. I have to be there for them one hundred percent. I can't falter."

Ben reached out to take both her hands in his and pressed them flat against his chest.

"Mia, let me share your burden."

If he had read her mind he couldn't have said any words that spoke more directly to her heart.

"I'm afraid."

"Afraid of me?"

Twin lines of concern pulled his brows into a frown.

"Of you? Not exactly. More of what you're capable of doing to me."

"If you let me into your life, I would never hurt you."

"Not physically, no. But you have so much power over me. I'm afraid if I relinquish what control I have left over my life I'll lose everything I've worked so hard for. I don't think you understand how much it means to me."

"I understand. I know what it is like to have the expectations of so many others like a weight on your shoulders. But I also know that no one can do everything on their own."

He bent forward and pressed a kiss to her forehead. The simplicity and sheer undemanding gentleness of the action became her undoing.

"Help me, then. Please?"

He nodded. "First, I think we need to make sure Jasper and Elsa aren't dragged into this any more than they have been already."

Over the next couple of hours they made plans. For Mia it was scarily easy to not only share her responsibilities but to relinquish their control to Ben. After discussions with Don, who suggested Elsa and Jas stay at his daughter's farm just out of Glenorchy, it was merely a matter of waiting for the cover of darkness to let them slip away. Elsa had originally protested, saying she needed to be there for Mia, but Ben had been firm. So too, surprisingly, had Don. When he'd heard what had happened he'd shown an unexpected determination about protecting both Elsa and Jas from any further media intrusion. Eventually Elsa had capitulated. Jas was beside himself at the prospect of being able to go pony riding on the farm and Mia had to fight back tears that he was so happy to leave her.

She rationalized her misery with the relief that Jas would be out of reach to the media until Ben could get the injunctions in place.

Later she watched the boat draw away from the dock

and head down the lake until she saw its navigation lights no longer. The tears that had been all too near the surface all day couldn't be held back a moment longer.

Ben put a comforting arm around her shoulders and guided her back into the hotel.

"I need to go to my apartment," she protested.

"You shouldn't be alone," he said, his voice low and reassuring. "Stay with me tonight."

"Stay with you?"

"I will not force you to do anything you do not want, Mia. I promise you."

She let him take her by her hand. In minutes they were in his suite. His presence was surprisingly soothing and, by increments, Mia felt the tension in her body begin to ease.

"They'll be all right there, won't they?" she asked.

"Don assures me that he will call and let us know when they've arrived and settled in. His daughter's place is quite remote and I'm certain no one followed them. Trust me, Mia. I will do everything in my power to keep Jasper safe, and your mother, too."

"I know," she whispered.

It felt so foreign to have someone else to lean upon, someone to share her worries and concerns. Foreign, and yet distinctly appealing at the same time. The emptiness inside her, opened even wider by Jasper and Elsa's departure, began to fill with something else. Something she was almost too afraid to acknowledge.

Ben still held her hand. His fingers were warm and strong and entangled in her own, securing a link between them that she couldn't ignore any longer. She looked up at him, to the face that had haunted her dreams for the past three and a half years, and knew that she had to be honest with him.

"Jasper is your son," she said, her voice soft and barely audible.

An almost feral glow of possession shone in Ben's eyes before he closed them briefly and tilted his head slightly back. His lips firmed in a straight line and his jaw clenched tight. When he opened his eyes again and looked in hers, she saw a shimmer in their dark brown depths that evidenced the deep and raw emotion there.

The play of emotion on his face was heartrending. Shock, perhaps, that she'd finally stopped stonewalling him, warred with pleasure and then an intensity that she recognized on a gut level. It was the exact same intensity she felt when she looked at Jas—pride, parental ownership and a sense of wonder that this child was her very own. Except now she shared him, with Ben.

"Thank you," he said, and lowered his face to hers, his lips possessing her own in a kiss that was on a different scale to anything they had shared before.

His mouth was almost unbearably gentle as it took hers, supping from her as if she was the sweetest nectar. His hands cupped her face, holding her tenderly and making her feel as though she was the most precious thing in the world to him. Her lonely heart cracked open, as she took everything he offered her. Her arms roped around his waist, her hands splaying across his strongly muscled back as if she was afraid to let go and be cast adrift. To be totally alone again.

Ben carefully drew back from her and rested his forehead against hers.

"What are we going to do now?" Mia asked, almost afraid of the answer he'd give her. "What do you want to do about Jasper?"

"It's been quite a day and we both have had a lot to take in. We can discuss everything later. Besides, right now, I'm sure you need your rest. You take the master suite. I'll go and sleep in the spare room."

Mia shook her head. "No, I can't chase you from your bed. Won't you at least share it with me?"

"Mia, I am only a man. A man who is fiercely attracted to you. I cannot, in all honesty, say I can sleep with you and not want to make love with you."

She placed a finger on his lips and looked him solemnly in the eye.

"Then make love to me, Ben. Please?"

He didn't answer, merely took her by the hand and led her into his bedroom and closed the doors firmly behind them. Tiny shudders rocked Mia's body—part fear, part anticipation. There was no going back now.

He couldn't believe she'd finally opened herself up to him. Even as she stood in front of him now he half expected her to bolt like a frightened doe.

He reached for her jacket, and slowly slid it from her shoulders. Beneath his hands he could feel the tremors that ran through her. Nerves, or desire, he wondered. Perhaps a mix of both. He fought with his own desire to rush this. To push their clothing aside and take her with the passion that had built in him each day he'd been here—the same level of passion that had lain semi-dormant since he'd rolled from their sheets and caught his flight back home to Isla Sagrado all those years ago. She was like a drug in his system. Once taken, forever desired.

But he'd waited this long for their reunion. He could tame his urge to hasten, and shower her with the gentleness and care she seemed to need so badly. It would be no hardship to take his time. Some things were best savored.

He smiled at Mia as he let her jacket fall to the thickly carpeted floor. Her blouse soon followed suit, although her gasp as his knuckles brushed the soft swell of her breast while he undid the buttons almost destroyed the vestiges of control he so stringently held.

Ben closed his eyes a moment, and took a breath, before opening them and feasting his eyes on her translucent skin, bound in delicate white lace.

"You are exquisite," he murmured, trailing his fingertips over one faint blue vein to where it disappeared into the scalloped edge of her bra cup.

He bent his head and traced the line with the tip of his tongue. The scent of her skin invaded his nostrils, urging him to breathe her more deeply. His hands went to the snap at her waist, undoing it and then reaching for her zipper. The rasp as it slid open was a sigh on the air. Her pants fell to her feet and he supported her as she stepped free and kicked off the low-heeled pumps she wore beneath them.

He took a moment to drink in the sight of her, her curves lushly feminine, her secrets innocently hidden behind the white lace of her lingerie. Blood heated in his groin, sending an age-old message to his brain.

His. She was all his.

He reached for the clips that bound her hair in a twist and smiled again as the honey-blond strands fell to caress her neck and shoulders. She'd been stunningly beautiful the first time he'd met her, but there was a luminescence about her now that spoke volumes about the woman she'd become.

She took a tentative step forward, so close now that he could feel her warmth through the thin barrier of his shirt. Then her hands were at his clothes, except they shook so much she could barely undo each button on his shirt. He closed his hands over hers and pulled, sending buttons flying as they popped from the silk fabric. It took only a matter of seconds to toe out of his loafers, undo his belt buckle and drop his trousers.

For the briefest moment his reluctance to let her see his scars, to touch them, froze him, but then she dropped one hand to his boxer briefs and hooked the other around his neck to pull his face to hers and the last vestige of hesitancy fled.

She took his lips in a kiss that almost saw him lose it right there. In fact, when she lightly trailed her fingernails over the hard ridge in his briefs, he couldn't stop himself from groaning into her mouth and thrusting his hands into her hair, holding her to him. Giving her full access to his mouth, his face, his throat. He backed her up against the bed, felt her knees buckle and her body drop onto the wide mattress before following her. Her skin against his was a sensation he'd totally underestimated. Every nerve in his body leaped to full life, doubly sensitized to her every touch.

Ben reached between them and stroked her through her panties. She flexed her hips upward, increasing the pressure of his fingers against her. She was already damp with desire and the knowledge made him feel stronger than he'd ever felt in his lifetime.

"I have dreamed of being with you again, *querida*. Over and over and over again until I began to fear I was a madman, obsessed with you," he said, his voice shaking.

"I have dreamed of you, too. Too many times to count. But this—touching you, feeling you with me—is so much better than a dream and so much better than I remembered."

Ben's fingers slid inside the elastic of her panties and grazed against the nest of curls that protected her inner softness.

"Oh yes," he said, "better, definitely very much better."

He slid one finger along the wet crease of her core—back and forth, back and forth, until she squirmed.

"More, Ben, please more."

He smiled and laid a trail of hot wet kisses down her belly.

"You want more?" he asked.

She nodded, her eyes glittering green pools in her exquisite face. As he watched her, he eased his finger inside her heat, instantly feeling her muscles clamp tight around him.

"Like this?" he asked again.

"More. I want you, Ben. All of you."

"Not yet," he said softly.

He eased another finger inside her, stroking her long and deep. Mia dropped her head back on the bed and closed her eyes, finally giving herself over to the sensations he aroused in her. Knowing her every focus was now on what he was doing to her he pressed his mouth against her mound, tasting her through the fine fabric of her panties and hearing her moan with uninhibited pleasure.

He blew a warm breath through the material then pressed another, firmer kiss against her. She pressed back against him, forcing his fingers deeper inside her, increasing the pressure of his mouth against her. He eased aside the damp fabric and fixed his mouth to the part of her he knew would send her skyward. His tongue flicked the hooded nub nestled in her blond curls and beneath him he felt her shudder, her internal muscles closing on his fingers, holding them tight, tighter. Alternately his tongue swirled then flicked, first slow, then with increasing tempo and he felt her body grow taut as her orgasm built and built but still remained out of reach as he refused to give her what she almost incoherently begged for.

He drew her out for as long as he could bear, relishing

the sounds she made, knowing he had the power to drive her to this edge of sweet madness. It was time to take her over that edge. Ben closed his lips around her rigid bud, suckling it until, with a sharp cry, she tumbled—her body clenching and releasing as the waves crashed over her. He shifted on the bed, quickly yanking off his briefs before more gently easing Mia's down her glorious long legs and then reaching behind her to unclasp her bra. When he took her he wanted there to be nothing between them. Nothing at all.

Her breasts spilled free of the restraining fabric and he could see the faint tracery of silver lines that were her badge of motherhood. If anything the markings only served to make him want her even more. Ben was even more amazed at what she'd achieved on her own.

He eased himself between her legs and positioned himself at her entrance.

"Look at me, Mia," he demanded.

She opened her eyes and he saw the haze of satiation that blurred her vision. Slowly he edged inside her, the thick head of his penis probing bluntly past her inner lips. Her eyes sharpened, awareness flooding back into them. Awareness…and anticipation.

He sank into her welcoming heat, almost coming straight away. Mia wound her legs behind his, holding him close to her. His arms shook as he fought back his climax, as he tried to control the overwhelming urge to lose himself in her, but she began to move beneath him, a smile softly curving her mouth.

Her smile was his undoing. He had been determined to take it slow. To woo her body back to full consciousness before driving her into blissful oblivion again. But he was not strong enough to hold back another second. His hips pistoned against her, and she met his every thrust, until every cell in his body drew tight then released in a rhythmic flood of ecstasy.

She cried out again, and through his pleasure he felt her join him on the wave. Eventually he lowered himself onto her, then rolled slightly to one side and tucked her firmly against his body. He'd been right. Being with Mia again had broken through the barriers that had rendered him useless after the crash. She'd brought him through the darkness and made him feel almost whole again.

Benedict nuzzled against the side of her neck and Mia relished the contact. Her body still fired with aftershocks of pleasure. What they had was amazing—like nothing she'd ever shared with anyone else. Their connection in bed was off the scale and she couldn't help but feel a twinge of sorrow that out of the grip of passion, all they seemed to be able to do was fight.

"You realize this changes things now, don't you?" he said.

"Changes things? Why should it?"

"Now that I know that Jasper is my son, I want to be a part of his life. I'm his father. He has other family who deserve to know him also—*Abuelo,* my brothers. He has a whole other world waiting for him in Isla Sagrado."

A shiver of fear ran across Mia's skin. She snatched up the sheet that had tangled near their feet and wrapped it around her, desperate for some type of shield. She fought her way off the bed and struggled to her feet, clutching the bed linen in a tight fist.

"You're going to take him from me?"

"That would not be the ideal solution."

But it is an option, hung in the air between them.

"Then what is?"

Ben got off the bed and casually walked across the floor to where he'd dropped his pants. He shoved his feet inside the legs and pulled them up. Again Mia's gaze was drawn to the scar tissue that ran in rivers across his lower abdomen. He'd nearly died. Again the realization struck her like a physical blow, and with it the solid truth that her feelings for him had shifted, had somehow irrevocably changed. That now he was far more important to her than she'd ever believed possible. She tried to push the thoughts from her mind, from her heart, but failed miserably.

All the breath sucked out of her body and she lowered herself back down to the edge of the bed. How much worse could this get?

Ben came and sat beside her, the warmth of his body penetrating the cold shell of disbelief that surrounded her. Deep inside she wanted to welcome that warmth—to share the burden of parenthood, to share the burden of rebuilding her family name and building a new business. But she'd done it on her own for so long the prospect of relinquishing control was as terrifying as it was appealing.

"I can make all your troubles go away, Mia. The press, your financial pressures. Everything. But I want you to agree to some things first."

The very idea of allowing him to take charge of the rapidly degenerating situation that was her life was almost as seductive as the sensation of his breath against her neck. But, she reminded herself, a man like Benedict would have a proviso riding on something as far-reaching as "making her troubles go away," and she had a fair idea of what that proviso might be.

She took a second to take stock. In exchange for him solving her problems with the media, etc., he'd have uncontested access to Jasper. A few days ago, she would have refused him outright, but everything had changed since then. Now she realized that she had misjudged Ben before. He *was* capable of being a good father, a man that Jasper could depend on. A man that *she* could depend on, if she would simply allow herself to do so. It sounded like a win-win situation no matter which angle she looked at it. And frankly, she knew when she was beaten. She didn't know if she could fight back one more time.

"Anything. I'll agree to anything."

"First, I want Jasper to undergo a paternity test. It's noninvasive and the results are available promptly."

Mia nodded, "I have no problem with that."

"My second condition hinges on the first. Once we have medical and legal proof that Jasper is my son, we will marry and return to Isla Sagrado. It is my home and it should be Jasper's home, too."

"No!"

The single syllable ripped from her mouth before she could stop it.

Ben narrowed his eyes. "It is not such an impossible thing to ask, is it? You agreed to my conditions just a moment ago, and I'm prepared to be generous with you—to give you my protection, my name and my home. I'm giving you a chance to get away from all the scandal and the unhappy reminders you have here. A chance to watch your son grow to adulthood in a secure and loving environment."

Mia didn't trust herself to speak. Her chin wobbled as she fought back the words she wanted to say—that she was taking everything back; that she'd rather face the media without his help rather than give up her home. Ben could obviously see the battle behind her eyes because he appeared to choose his next words very carefully.

"I would not like to be forced to assert my parental rights

to Jasper by legal means, Mia. If such a thing happened I would seek full custody and I would bring the might of the greatest legal minds in family law, both here and in Isla Sagrado, to fight for what is my right as Jasper's father. And I will win. You can be certain of that."

Ten

Ten

<u></u>

"Why? Why would you do that to him? Why would you be so cruel as to tear him from the only home he has ever known—the only family he's ever had?"

Ben huffed out a breath and pushed himself up off the bed before crossing the room to stand before the window. His shoulders were set in a straight line, his spine equally rigid.

"He has another family, *my* family. We are the last of a dying line, which makes him all the more precious. He's a sign of hope for the future."

"That's a heck of a lot of pressure to put on one little boy, Ben. You told me you have brothers—that hardly seems like a dying line. Aren't you being unrealistic about Jasper's importance?" she asked, stricken by the heavy portent of his words.

"Not according to the curse."

"Curse?"

Ben sighed. "Let me explain it to you fully. Three hundred years ago one of my ancestors took a lover—the governess whom he'd hired to teach his daughters. Over time, she bore him three sons—sons he needed to carry on the family name especially as his wife had borne him three more daughters. He raised the boys as if they were his own legitimate issue. When his wife died, his lover expected him to marry her. After all, he'd already gifted her with *La Verdad del Corazon*—the Heart's Truth—a ruby necklace traditionally given as a betrothal gift to a del Castillo bride-to-be.

"But he chose to marry another and on the wedding day his lover broke into the celebrations and made an accusation before everyone assembled there that he had stolen her sons from her. My ancestor declared her mad and ordered her to be taken away. The stories say that she implored her sons to be true to their real mother, but they stood by their father and told her their real mother was dead. Before the guards could remove her from the banquet hall, the governess flung a curse upon the del Castillo family and swore that if in nine generations we could not learn to live our lives by our family motto of honor, truth and love, every branch of the family would die out.

"The guards took her into custody then, but she broke free and jumped off the cliffs onto the rocks below. Before she fell, she tore the necklace from her neck and threw it into the ocean screaming that only when the curse was broken would it be returned to the family again. Her body was recovered, but the necklace never was."

Mia sat in stunned silence. Surely he didn't believe all that. It was preposterous. A legend of what, three hundred years, having a bearing on her son? She cleared her throat carefully before speaking.

"And you and your brothers, you believe in this curse?"

Ben's shoulders sagged momentarily. "No, we did not. But our grandfather most certainly does and it is for him that we have all agreed to marry and start families so that his final years can be happy ones, surrounded by the great-grandchildren who can prove to him that we are not cursed."

"And here you are, with a ready-made family." Mia could not keep the bitterness from infiltrating her words.

"Mia, this is not something of my own choosing. Each of my brothers and I made a pact, a vow of honor to one another that we are sworn to uphold. It may sound archaic to you, but both Alex and Reynard have taken the first steps to make this right for our grandfather. Now it is up to me."

"But why does it have to be Jasper? Why can't you marry someone else and start a family with them?"

The second the words exited her body she was struck with a fierce shaft of jealousy such as she'd never experienced before. The mere thought of Benedict having children with another woman was poison to her mind.

He turned from the window and faced her before answering with words that suddenly robbed her of breath.

"Because I can no longer father a child."

She didn't even question the veracity of his statement; she could see it in his eyes. He told the truth and it was killing him inside.

"The accident? Your injuries? Is that why?"

He gave her a curt nod.

Suddenly it all made awful sense—why he'd been so adamant that Jasper was his son, why he'd wanted her to admit it and, now, why he'd insisted that she agree to paternity testing so he had irrevocable proof that he had a child of his own.

But she still couldn't help feeling that Jas was being used as a tool in all this. Sure, she could understand that after being injured so severely Ben would feel justified in considering the discovery of his son as a gift. But the whole curse thing and the pact between the brothers? It just didn't sit right with her. He'd said nothing of love, for Jasper even if not for her. How could she agree to her little boy going to a world he didn't know, to have his life mapped out by a man who didn't even love him?

But what else could she do? He literally had her over a financial barrel.

"Do we have to live on Isla Sagrado?" she eventually asked, her voice strained.

"It is my home and the home of my family. My business is there, as is everything else I hold dear."

His words struck at her like pebbles thrown against glass. He couldn't have made it clearer that she and her son were not a part of what he held dear. Not in any way, shape or form. Jasper was a means to fulfill a promise he'd made to his brothers. A promise that was designed to make the final years of an old man happy. And she was merely a step to acquiring that goal—a step that he could and would dispense with, if she persisted in refusing him.

Her father had many failings but one thing Mia never doubted was his love for her and her mother. That very emotion was part of the reason why she was so riddled with guilt for her contribution to what had become more than he could control or eventually bear. How could she agree to let Jasper go with a man who made no mention of offering unconditional love?

"And what of my home, my family, my business? This is where Jasper was born. Parker's Retreat is part of his heritage, too," she argued.

"We can install a manager to run Parker's Retreat for

you and via the Internet and phone I'm sure you can keep a hand in the running of the place. If you wish to continue with your massage therapy I have no doubt that Alex would find your skills a welcome addition to our family's resort facilities on the island.

"As to your remaining family, Elsa is more than welcome to relocate with us. In fact, I'd prefer it because I know it would only cause you concern if you were each on opposite sides of the world."

"How generous of you," Mia responded scornfully.

"It is generous of me, Mia, and you would do well to remember that. You will not suffer for this, I promise you. And on those occasions when we return to New Zealand, you will have the anonymity and privacy that my money can provide for you." His voice hardened. "Bear in mind, I am giving you every incentive to do this the right way but if you don't, I will invoke the clause of our current contract that provides for me to be fully refunded if you have not satisfied the terms as laid out."

He gestured beyond the darkened gardens to where the media's boats would undoubtedly return at daybreak.

"I believe what has been happening here is irrefutable evidence that you are in forfeit, Mia."

Mia swallowed against the solid lump of emotion in her throat. She would not cry. She would not give in to the overwhelming sense of failure that assailed her. Had he no idea how much this place meant to her? It was her life, her identity. It was tangible proof that she could make a success of *something*—be someone her son could not only love, but also admire and aspire to. If she walked away now it was admitting she had bombed in the worst way possible. She not only failed herself, but she'd failed her father's memory as well.

But there was no other option. Through circumstances

over which she'd had no control, she was now forced to adhere to his demands. Mia wound the sheet more tightly around her and stood to face him, her chin up, her eyes clear of the tears she would shed in private.

"Fine, I'll do what you say. But only because you give me no other choice."

Mia was alternately surprised and horrified at the speed with which the paternity testing was completed and the results delivered back to them at Parker's Retreat. The results only bore out what she knew already but Benedict became fired by a new energy when he received the news.

As soon as proof had been delivered, Ben must have taken action against the press because the media had slowly disappeared from the lake near the property. Even a trip to Queenstown didn't bring them back out of the woodwork. Whatever power and money Ben had thrown at the situation, it must have been impressive because Jas and Elsa had been able to return from Glenorchy and Jasper had been able to resume going to his day care. Even Mia was now able to go about her occasional business in town with no more than a random finger pointed from behind a café menu.

And then there was the wedding. Elsa's initial reaction of excitement at the news was tempered with concern, especially when the hollow emptiness in Mia's eyes had made her ask her daughter if she was certain she was doing the right thing.

"I'm doing the only thing, Mom," Mia said as she stared at her reflection in the full-length mirror in her mother's bedroom. "Jasper deserves to know his father, and Ben insisted that it happen on these terms."

The woman staring back was a virtual stranger in the

vintage 1920s wedding gown that had been in her mother's family for generations. It was not quite as impactful as a three-hundred-year-old curse, Mia thought cynically, but it still carried with it the weight of all the dreams and hopes of many brides-to-be—all of whom, if family history was correct—had married for love.

"Well, if you're certain, but it seems to me you are both rushing into this marriage," her mother answered through a mouthful of pins as she marked where the side seams needed to be altered. "I've always been a strong advocate of a couple sharing their child-rearing responsibilities, but usually they've had time to know one another first. You and Ben, well, you can hardly say you know one another all that well, can you?"

Know him? She certainly knew him in the biblical sense, if nothing else. Her inner muscles clenched on the sudden sharp pull of desire that drew through her at the thought of their lovemaking.

"I'm certain, Mom. It's for the best."

"For everyone else, sure, but is it the best thing for you?"

Mia forced a smile. "Why wouldn't it be? He's handsome, he's rich and most importantly, he's Jasper's father."

"But does he love you?"

"He doesn't hate me, so that's a start, right?"

She tried to inject a little humor into the conversation but her mother simply gave her a quelling look. It shouldn't have been so easily done when on her knees and with a mouth looking like she'd consumed a porcupine but she managed. Suddenly Mia realized how far her mother had come from the broken widow of three years ago. It gave her a start to see glimpses of her mother's old strength coming back.

"I just think that this marriage is a little hasty. Couldn't you just take some more time?" Elsa asked.

"Mom, he's due back on Isla Sagrado at the end of the month. It made sense for us to go ahead with the wedding now rather than later. At least we're having it here at home."

"Well, that's another thing. Isn't it strange that he isn't having any of his family here for the wedding? I thought you said they're all very close?"

"We'll have another ceremony there. Did I tell you they have their own chapel in their own castle?" Mia tried to change the subject but not terribly successfully.

Elsa gave her another one of *those* looks before putting her pins away and standing up to cup Mia's face in her hands.

"I love you, darling. I just want you to be happy. You've sacrificed so much at your own emotional expense for too long now. I just wish I didn't feel as if that's what you're still doing in marrying Ben." She pressed a kiss on Mia's forehead then let her go. "Right, then. You'd better get that dress off so I can make those alterations and you'll be all ready for Friday night."

Friday night. It would come soon enough. Mia had been amazed at how quickly the legal side of arranging a marriage here in New Zealand could be taken care of. Despite the rush, Elsa had insisted on everything being done properly and that meant that Mia would be wearing what had originally been Elsa's grandmother's wedding gown.

She and Ben had agreed that they wanted only her mother and Andre as witnesses for the evening ceremony. If anything, as far as Mia was concerned, it would help keep this all from feeling too real.

Mia tried to quell the squadron of butterflies that had taken flight in her stomach as she waited outside the old ballroom, which was now the main dining room of the hotel. Inside, waiting by the deep bay window overlooking the gardens and the lake, was the man she'd lost her heart to. Her heart and her whole life.

She gripped the simple bouquet of dusky pink rosebuds and gypsophila and nodded to the staff member waiting for her signal to open the double doors into the ballroom. While not massive by any standard, the ballroom suddenly appeared to be longer than she remembered. The aisle that had been created between the dining tables was now strewn with flower petals and lined with creamy-colored candles on tall pedestals.

It was a fairytale setting for the kind of wedding she'd always wanted and yet it felt all wrong. Her father should have been walking at her side, and the room should have been filled with friends and colleagues. It should have been a joyful celebration of a mutual love that would endure forever.

Mia closed her eyes briefly on the dreams she'd once had. When she opened them again her gaze found Ben at the end of the aisle. Waiting for her. Somber and dark in a tuxedo, he stood tall and proud—every part of his Spanish-Franco lineage visible in his bearing.

Mia hesitated on the threshold. She loved him enough that a large part of her truly *wanted* to marry him—to go to his side and take vows to become his wife. But by taking that step, she'd be giving up everything else. Her home. Her past. The life she had built for herself. All in exchange for a man who had shown no signs of returning her love. Each particle of her body froze as all her instincts urged her to flee. But where could she go? There were no other choices open to her now. She forced one ballet-slippered foot in front of the other, stepping carefully in time to the music played on the sound system. Elsa stood to the left of the makeshift altar, Jasper's hand held firmly in hers as he stood on a chair and watched the proceedings with eager interest. Mia felt a flicker of surprise to see Don standing close by her mother's other side, looking austerely handsome in a sharply pressed dark suit.

While she knew her mother's eyes were on her, she couldn't look at her. Couldn't stand to see the concern she knew would be mirrored in Elsa's gaze. Instead, Mia kept moving forward, keeping her eyes very firmly on the man she was about to pledge herself to.

As she drew closer to Benedict she grew more and more aware of the flare of satisfaction in his eyes. Her body thrummed to life in answer to the glow. At least that was one side of their marriage she knew would be fulfilling even if their emotional compatibility was unbalanced. But in her heart of hearts she wondered if that would ever be enough. She wanted it all. Could she settle for anything less?

Mia was only a few steps away from the altar when Ben came toward her and took her by the hand, leading her the final distance to where the celebrant waited to conduct the short ceremony that would tie her to Benedict del Castillo forever.

An unexpected thrill shot through her. One of anticipation and laced with threads of hope. She already loved him. Surely it was not impossible to believe that he would come to love her also? A tremulous smile spread across her lips as she looked across to her mother and sent her a silent message that everything would be okay. She knew Elsa understood when her mother gave her a small nod and an answering smile.

The service was simple and without the flowering expectations of a marriage based on mutual love. Still, when Ben promised to honor and keep her all the days of his life a solid feeling of permanence seeped through her, buoying her spirits a little higher. When the celebrant declared them husband and wife, Ben stepped forward to kiss her and as she lost herself in his caress, Mia allowed herself to be imbued by a deep sense of rightness in their being bonded together.

By the time she and Ben stepped forward to sign the marriage certificate and complete the legal undertakings of their marriage Mia had almost convinced herself she felt happy, genuinely happy, for the first time in a very long while.

Her staff had prepared a simple three-course meal for them to share in the restaurant after the service and by the time the last plate had been cleared away, Mia was longing for some alone time with her husband. He'd been attentive throughout their meal, but also gave Jasper the attention he demanded. When Elsa suggested it was time for Jas to be taken to bed and for the newlyweds to be left alone, Mia felt her heart skip a beat.

Ben had barely touched her since they'd made love nearly two weeks ago. Thinking back on it now, it was probably one of the reasons why Elsa was so concerned about whether or not Mia was doing the right thing—their lack of visible connection as a couple. Thankfully, one thing Elsa hadn't had to worry about was the rapport between Jasper and Ben. Already, Mia could see the very positive aspects of Jasper having a father figure in his life.

Their little boy had adapted to Ben's presence already and clamored for Ben's company all the time. Ben treated Jasper with remarkable patience and warmth, stepping into the role of father as if he'd been there all along. Mia was pleased and relieved to see their growing connection, but it only made her more sharply aware of the distance that still remained between her and Ben. But she couldn't afford to think about that now.

Right now there was another aspect of their marriage she was about to focus on. Their wedding night. Tension coiled tight in her gut. She'd thought about this long and hard in the past few days. Been forced to examine her own growing feelings for the man she had agreed to marry. If they were to be married, to provide a strong example to their son, there had to be some communication between them. This marriage had to work. Against all the odds, she wanted to be able to believe that one day her husband could fall in love with her too. Because if he didn't, what on earth was she doing giving up everything she'd worked so hard for?

Eleven

After they'd bid everyone a good-night, they walked arm in arm to Ben's suite. Once inside, Mia suddenly felt awkward. What if he didn't want their marriage to be a normal one? They hadn't exactly discussed what would happen after the ceremony. She swallowed against the sudden dryness in her throat and searched for something to say.

"That went rather well, don't you think?" she eventually managed.

"Of course," Ben replied, shrugging out of his jacket and undoing the gold cufflinks at his wrists. "Did you expect anything less?"

"No, not really. I have good staff. Once they heard we were marrying I didn't have to lift another finger. Between them and my mom they handled it perfectly."

Ben wrenched his tie loose and cast it on an easy chair beside him.

"Actually, I thought you were the perfect one tonight," he said, his voice deep and laced with a very strong note of pride. "You are truly beautiful."

Mia felt a flush of warmth spread through her at his words, all the way to her cheeks, which suddenly felt uncomfortably warm in the face of his praise. She ducked her head slightly, only to feel the heat of his fingertips at her chin as he raised her head to meet his gaze. His very heated and possessive gaze.

Her stomach knotted on a hard pull of desire. One look, one touch, was all it took and she became a melting puddle of need. Her breasts, unfettered by a bra due to the design of her gown, swelled against the chiffon, her nipples drawing into tight, aching beads.

He bent his head to kiss her and Mia met him halfway, a sound of satisfaction sounding deep in her throat as their lips meshed and his arms curved around her, pulling her hard against him, settling her hips to the clear evidence that his desire for her was as palpable as hers for him. He tore his lips from hers, his breathing ragged, his eyes burning with a heat she knew was reflected in her own.

"I would hate to damage that rather delicate gown you're wearing. Let me help you out of it before I lose all control."

His words thrilled her and imbued her with a sense of power. By his own admission, being with her put him at the verge of his control. Knowing the kind of man he was, that was an incredible power, indeed. Surely he had to have some feelings for her? Feelings that went beyond the physical.

She slowly turned around, and pointed over her shoulder to the long trail of pearl beads that tapered down her spine. A smile pulled at her lips when she heard his groan of dismay.

"I suppose it is too much to hope that those are merely for aesthetic appeal and that they hide a zipper instead?"

Mia laughed, a light bubble of joy on the air. "Yes, it is too much to hope for. I don't think zippers even became popular in women's clothing until a good ten years after this was originally made."

"*Dios,* and no one thought to modernize the thing in all this time?" he grumbled teasingly as his fingers began to deftly slide the beads free, exposing her back inch by inch.

Mia laughed again, then gasped as his fingers stroked her uncovered skin, his touch sending tiny fire-bursts through her body.

"Ah, now I understand the principle," Ben murmured and she could hear the smile on his face. "It's to torment you, not me."

Her breath caught again as she felt his lips where his fingers had lingered only seconds before.

"I think I can slip out of it now," she choked, suddenly desperate to disrobe herself of the gown.

"What? And spoil the fun? I don't think so."

It felt as if he moved even slower than before, prolonging the wait for the moment when he could hold apart the gaping edges of the back of her dress and free her from the layers of gossamer-fine silk chiffon and hand embroidery. When his hands finally touched her shoulders and gently pushed the dress off her body, she nearly wept with relief. She stepped free of the dress, eased off her ballet slippers, and stood before him in only a pair of shell pink satin tap pants and a pair of hold up stockings edged in the same shade of shell pink lace.

"*Te desero,*" Ben groaned as he reached for her, palming her naked breasts and lowering his head to place a kiss at the sensitive spot where her shoulder and her neck merged together.

"I want you, too," she whispered, tilting her head to allow him clearer access and relishing the increasing spears of pleasure that rocketed through her as she felt his tongue burn a path along her skin.

This time, it was she who took him by the hand and led him to the bedroom. She who swiftly divested him of his clothing and then stood back in a moment of silent awe as she took in the sight of him—roped muscle and power, smooth skin and silky fine hair, his arousal heavy and engorged—proudly jutting from the dark nest of hair at the apex of his thighs.

She trailed her fingers over his shoulders, down his arms and back up again, before tracing the strength of his chest, the delineation of his ribs and lower toward the scars that evidenced the damage he'd suffered. Ben grabbed her hands and pulled them back up to his chest and kissed her, slowly half walking, half dancing her to the bed.

Ben reached down and pushed his hands inside the waistband of her tap pants and began to ease them off her hips, his fingers brushing over her buttocks and down the back of her thighs. Then he bent to his good knee and slowly rolled down her stockings, pressing soft kisses against the sensitive skin of her inner thighs as he did so.

Mia's legs were trembling and her entire body ached for him. Ben stood up, rubbing his body against her. His erection bumped against her lower belly as he wrapped her in his arms and tumbled with her onto the covers, supporting her weight with his body as they sank into the mattress. Their legs instinctively entwined, their hands skimmed over one another's bodies as their lips fused in a hot wet kiss that she wished would never end.

She loved the feel of him, loved that he was now hers to

take and to touch. She placed her knees on either side of his hips and raised her torso from his so she could better enjoy him with her hands. This was different to when she massaged him. This was personal—both exhilarating and wonderful all at the same time.

Between her legs she could feel the hardness of his arousal, of his desire and need for her. He surged up against her and she fought the urge to give in to his silent demand. First, she wanted to explore him a little more—reacquaint herself with the little things that drove him wild.

She placed her lips very gently around one of his nipples, her tongue spiraling round the flat brown disk from its outer edge to its hardened tip. Her own nipples mirrored his response, in fact it was as if every cell and nerve ending in her body had tautened and honed itself to what thrilled Ben and Ben alone.

Her fingers traced a similar line on his other nipple before she coasted her hand down over his ribs. Beneath her she felt him tense as her fingers neared his scars.

"What is it?" she whispered. "Does that hurt? I thought you were okay with me touching you there."

"Just don't, okay? I don't need the reminder. Not now."

"Ben, your scars are a part of you and they certainly don't scare me or turn me off. Do you want to talk about it? The accident?"

"What, you want to counsel me now? I think I liked it better when we were making love," Ben said and tried to distract her by flipping her over onto her back and pinning her hands at her sides.

His body hovered over hers, his heat all but enveloping her and when he bent to tease her nipples with his tongue, the same way she'd teased him, she nearly lost all sense of reason. But there'd been an edge to Ben's voice that struck at her heart. She pushed back against the fog of desire that threatened to cloud her mind.

"Ben? Why won't you talk about it? Please, I only want to know you better, to understand you. We're married now. As husband and wife we need to be able to talk to one another about anything."

He shoved himself away from her and got up off the bed.

"I thought this was our wedding night, not a therapy session. Now, we can either resume where we left off, or we can sleep apart tonight. It's up to you."

Mia could only stare at him in shock. Why did he refuse to open up to her? In the face of her silence he gave his head a brief shake and turned and stalked out of the bedroom.

"Ben!" she called, suddenly gaining her voice back and getting up to run after him, but as she reached the door to the main bedroom she heard the telltale snick of the lock being turned on the second bedroom, the one that was to be Jasper's, on the other side of the suite.

Stunned, she stared at the door. Barely daring to believe that her husband had walked out on her on their wedding night and over something so trivial. Was this how it was to be between them? Her wanting to give Ben everything she had and Ben holding everything back?

Ben threw himself onto the narrow bed and stared up at the luminous star-studded ceiling, his body taut with unrelieved tension. Why did she have to try and force the issue? They'd been married less than a few hours and already she wanted to delve inside his head. Even *he* didn't want to go there. Didn't want to face the mortality that had so terrified him while he'd been locked in the metal cage that had almost become his coffin. Didn't want to face the failure he'd become. Didn't want his wife to see that side of him.

Ben knew that Mia needed him to be strong, to be able to take care of her and Jasper. Without his strength—without his power and wealth and authority to shield her from the press, to protect her family and reputation—she'd never have succumbed to his need to make her and Jasper *his*. She had resisted him for far too long, but he had her now—her and Jasper. They were the family he'd despaired of ever being able to create, and he wasn't going to do anything to risk losing them. If his wife needed him to be strong, he'd be strong. And he would allow no sign of weakness. Not even at her request.

Instead, he would focus on what he had, rather than what he'd lost. He had a wife and a son and that was all that mattered. That and ensuring Jasper and Mia had all the best of everything that life had to offer—including his unwavering protection to keep them both safe all his days.

He had fulfilled his obligations to the rest of his family, as well. The curse, such as it was, had to be broken now. *Abuelo* could rest easy. Hell, they could all rest easy.

But as he pulled the covers over his naked body he had to force himself to shut out the sense that somewhere he had still failed. As a man. As a husband. And as a father.

After a fitful night spent tossing and turning alone in her bed, Mia woke to hear rain driving against the windows. She lay in the bed and tried again to make sense of what had happened last night. Ben had shut down completely—emotionally and physically—when she'd pressed him to talk about his accident. That it had been harrowing she had no doubt, but to refuse to talk about it altogether? It just wasn't healthy. Why didn't he trust her to help him?

A sound at the bedroom door made her stiffen in the sheets. She turned to watch the door swing slowly open. Ben stood framed in the doorway, a towel wrapped around his waist.

"Did I wake you?" he asked.

"No, I was already awake."

In the gloom of early morning it was hard to make out his expression. Ben lifted a hand to rub at his eyes, the action showing her an unexpected vulnerability. He took a step into the room, hesitated, then took another until he was beside the bed.

"I'm sorry about last night. I spoke too harshly."

Mia merely watched him, her eyes searching his face to see if he really meant the words or if he was merely paying lip service. Even in the semi-dark of the room she could see anguish behind Ben's eyes. The honest emotion struck her to her core and without realizing what she was doing she reached for him, tugging him down onto the bed beside her.

Ben's arms enfolded her body and as her sheet slid away she felt the heat of his skin sear hers. Their coming together was not as intense as their first coupling had been, nor was it as loaded with heat and anticipation as last night's abortive lovemaking. Instead, it was as if there was a flow of give and take. A mingling of minds and bodies.

When her climax wrung her body, the sensation was so bittersweet that Mia felt tears spring to her eyes. As Ben reached his own pinnacle she couldn't help feeling that even though, in this moment, they were as together as a couple could be, there still lay an unbreachable gulf between them.

They drifted off to sleep in the aftermath, their bodies touching, Ben's fingers entwined in her own, and yet somehow she still felt unspeakably alone.

When she woke again, the sun was full in the sky and the rain had stopped. Outside the window, she could see the freshness of the rain-washed gardens—their brilliant greens a symbol of all that was fresh and new. She hoped that it was equally symbolic of the beginning of her marriage to Benedict del Castillo but she couldn't quite nudge away the sense that the path ahead of them would not be smooth.

Ben had already woken and she could hear him in the bathroom. If they'd been any other normal married couple, she would be in there with him by now, perhaps even sharing the shower stall, lathering up one another's bodies before indulging again in sating one another's appetites. But they weren't a normal couple, and they wouldn't be a normal family either, she realized. Not as long as there was this imbalance between them. Benedict would always have the financial upper hand. He'd always have Jasper to use as leverage over her. And once they moved to Isla Sagrado—a place she'd never even seen—the advantage would be even stronger on his side. As much as she loved her son's father, she wished their reunion could have been so very much different.

The bathroom door opened and Ben came through, dressed in his usual workout gear. Before the wedding, they'd agreed to continue with their daily routines as normal, suggesting they'd enjoy a honeymoon together once they were on Isla Sagrado. Everyone had accepted their choice without much demur but right now it just made Mia feel even more as if she was simply the means to an end in Ben's world.

"What time is Elsa bringing Jasper today?" Ben asked, confirming her belief.

"After lunch."

"I'll get him earlier, after my session today. I really want us to spend as much time together as possible before we head home."

But this is our home. Mia bit back the words that begged to be spoken and took a deep breath.

"Sure," she said.

She slid from the bed, crossed to the sliding doors of the closet and grabbed a robe. The empty hanger jangled on the rod. She sensed Ben's gaze on her body as if it was a physical caress and she wrapped the robe around her—her choice of armor flimsy, but effective.

"You cannot blame me for being eager to spend time with my son."

"No, you're right, I can't." And she was pleased that he seemed so committed to spending time with Jasper. She just wished he showed more interest in spending time with *her*—outside of bed, that is. "Would you like me to pull him from day care next week also? After all, we'll be leaving at the end of the week anyway."

Ben shook his head. "No, let's keep him in his routine for now. But I'll adjust my schedule with Andre so I can take him to day care and collect him myself."

Mia nodded her understanding.

"I'll still see you alone for my massage this afternoon, *sí?*" he asked as he bent to tie the laces on his trainers. "Your mother will still take care of Jasper in the afternoon as usual?"

She shot him a look of surprise. "Of course she will, but do you still want to go through with those?"

"They are a part of my rehabilitation and our original contract, are they not?"

Ben moved swiftly to close the distance between them. His hands slipped inside her robe to cup her breasts. The instant he touched her, her nipples beaded into tight buds against the palms of his hands and a flame of desire licked through her, warming her nether regions with a heat that shamed her. She still wanted him with every breath, with every thought, with every touch. She was hopelessly trapped in a snare of her own making.

"Yes, they are indeed," she said through suddenly dry lips.

"Then I look forward to it, and you, later."

He bent and kissed each aching tip before fastening his lips on hers in a kiss that left her in some doubt as to whether his massage this afternoon would be conducted within the realms of her professional employment—but no doubt at all that her fears had been confirmed. He wanted her physically, but that was the extent of their relationship for him.

As she watched him leave she tried to find some satisfaction in knowing that he would probably be in greater physical discomfort than she was for most of the day. Even so, it was little consolation.

When Elsa came to collect Jasper before Ben's massage she asked Mia if she could speak with her for a moment in her office. After giving Jas a packet of crayons and a coloring book to scribble in, Mia gave her mother her full attention.

"Mom, what gives? This feels like an appointment or something, rather than a mother-daughter chat," Mia said as they settled in two chairs.

"Well, this isn't exactly a social visit."

A trickle of unease ran down Mia's spine. "What do you mean, Mom? You're okay, aren't you? I thought the cardiologist was really pleased with your management and heart health the last time you saw him."

Elsa waved a graceful hand in the air. "Oh, no, don't

worry, darling. It's nothing to do with me physically. More to do with me personally, actually."

Mia stared at her mother. She looked different today. As if she was bursting with news but was working hard to keep it suppressed.

"I'd like to apply for the manager's position here at Parker's Retreat."

"What? Why?"

"Now, I know that I'm probably underqualified for the role and that it's been some time since I was in the paid workforce, but I've realized, with your marriage to Ben, that it's past time I picked myself up and dusted myself off and got on with my life. I've relied on you far too long and it's time you could rely on me again now."

Mia couldn't believe her mother's words and grasped at the only straws she could to try to sway her from this sudden and very unwelcome suggestion.

"Mom, it's a huge undertaking, and what about us? Don't you want to come to Isla Sagrado? Ben has it all arranged. I thought you were happy about that?"

"I'm sure Jasper will settle in quite nicely without me. Besides, the three of you need time to get used to one another as a family, especially if you want to make this marriage of yours work. And *you* do, don't you?"

Elsa gave her daughter a look that told Mia she had already gleaned the truth of her daughter's feelings.

"Mom—" Mia started, ready to protest.

"Look, the last thing you need is your mother hanging around and clogging up your marriage. And please don't try telling me I have no experience in running this place. I have probably more knowledge than you had when you started, plus I have the advantage of being able to pick your brain when I need help. Honestly, you've set things up so well here all it needs is a gentle hand at the tiller and it'll be smooth sailing all the way. We have a great staff, and if the forward bookings are anything to go by, I'll be far too busy to miss you all."

"You don't have to miss us—you should be coming with us, too."

Elsa shook her head. "No, darling, my mind is made up. Even if you don't let me take on the management role here at the hotel I've already decided to stay here—in Queenstown if I can't stay at Parker's Retreat. I…"

To Mia's surprise a faint blush stained her mother's cheeks, but that surprise was nothing compared to the bolt that came from the blue with her mother's next words.

"I may as well come straight out with it. Don and I have become close in the past few months and I would really like to give our friendship a chance to develop. It may come to something, or it may not. And yes, I know he's younger than me but there's something about that man that makes me feel younger, too. I gave up on so much when Reuben died, I'm not going to give up on anything else ever again."

Mia rose from her seat and rounded her desk to give her mother a huge hug, words spilling from her lips automatically, without her being truly aware of what she was saying. She knew she'd said all the right things when the smile broke out on her mother's face, but as Elsa left her office and closed the door behind her Mia felt completely cast adrift. How had she been so oblivious to the changes in her mother's life? Had she been so wrapped up in her work that she'd missed all the signs that her mother was ready to risk a new relationship and reach for happiness again?

As for what Elsa had said about taking over as manager at Parker's Retreat, Mia couldn't tell her mother "no," could she? Not when for the first time in a long time she could see that Elsa was actually looking forward to the future and had a purpose—had someone to support and nurture her. But without Elsa in Mia's corner when they moved to the other side of the world, who would be there for her?

Twelve

"Why doesn't Mommy sleep in her own bed?"

The clear tones of his son's voice roused Ben from a deep slumber. A slumber he'd earned after yet another spectacular night in his wife's arms. It didn't matter how aloof she kept herself during each day, the nights were most definitely their own. The mornings, however, were another matter.

Ben opened his eyes and fixed them on the dark-headed miniature of himself standing at the foot of their bed. Mia was doing a wonderful job of feigning sleep, her fists clenched in the sheets and holding them firmly against her naked body.

"You're awake early, *mi hijo.*"

"What's a ee-kho?" Jasper scrunched up his little face in concentration as he twisted his tongue around the unfamiliar word.

"It's the word for you, my son."

"And you're my daddy!" Jasper said with great exuberance as he climbed up on the bed and settled in between his parents.

"Yes, and I'm your daddy."

Ben gathered Jas in a big hug. He knew he'd never get over the incredible sense of pride that swelled within his chest every time he saw his little boy. The knowledge that the accident that had robbed him of the choice of fatherhood had not been the final death knell on his dreams and his promise to his family was at times overwhelming. Ben couldn't wait until *Abuelo* saw Jasper in the flesh.

They'd called the old man on Skype last night. Ben had installed the necessary hardware and software on Elsa's computer, so she and Mia could stay in touch more closely when they left. Of course they'd had to try the system out and *Abuelo* had been surprised beyond belief that he could finally meet his first great-grandchild through the Internet. While *Abuelo*'s bluster over having to learn to master modern technology had been voluble, there was no mistaking the silver track of tears on the old man's face when he'd laid eyes on Jasper for the first time. Alex and Rey had hardly been able to get a look-in, let alone say "hi" to their nephew after that.

Mia had had a brief chance to talk with her friend Rina Woodville, who was engaged to Ben's brother, Rey, and who'd set up Ben's visit to Parker's Retreat, but despite Rina's huge excitement over the fact he and Mia had married and were coming to settle on Isla Sagrado, Ben sensed a deep unhappiness behind Mia's facade.

The knowledge he was personally responsible for that unhappiness had settled like a burr under his skin. He was willing to accept that he'd been hasty in his demands, forcing Mia to accept a marriage and relocation at practically a moment's notice. He'd concentrated for so long on what he would not be able to do that when the proof he'd already succeeded had come into his life, it was all he'd been able to think of.

But his choices and decisions had been far-reaching and he'd failed to fully take Mia's wishes into consideration when he'd made them. Hell, if he was honest with himself, he hadn't even tried to take Mia's wishes into consideration. The truth was a painful thing to face. He owed her everything—from the warm, living, breathing proof of his longevity currently squirming in his arms to the return of his sense of honor and integrity toward his family.

But what of his honor and integrity with respect to Mia? The knowledge that he'd failed her was a bitter truth to swallow and one he needed to face squarely. Face and make amends for.

"Come on, Jas," he whispered to his son, "let's give Mommy a lie-in and we'll go and get dressed and find out what's for breakfast today."

"I'm very hungry," Jasper informed him solemnly.

As Ben rolled from the bed and grabbed some clothes before going through to Jasper's room to help him get dressed, he resolved to find a way to make this up to Mia. She had agreed—granted, under duress—to do as he'd asked. There had to be a way to give her back that sense of identity and pride he sensed she'd felt she'd lost along the way.

An idea occurred to him as he and Jasper entered the dining room of the hotel twenty minutes later. His lips curled in satisfaction and he reached for his mobile phone so he could start to put in action the necessary moves.

In the end, the process of acquiring his surprise for Mia took a couple of days to engineer to completion. Still, Ben was well pleased when things were concluded to his satisfaction. He was even more pleased when he discussed his plans with Elsa and she agreed to take Jasper for the night so he could surprise Mia with a quiet romantic dinner for just the two of them.

After his massage that afternoon, one that actually stuck to massage and not into the activity he usually enticed her into, Ben let her into his plans. Some of them, at least. He swung himself upright on the massage table and pulled Mia in between his legs.

"Wear something special for dinner tonight, okay?"

"Special? What kind of special?" Mia asked with her head cocked to one side.

"The kind of special you can wear in public."

"Oh, I see—that kind of special. Do we have plans for tonight, then?"

"We do." He nodded. "It occurred to me that we've never actually been on a date, so I'm going to do my best to remedy that situation."

"A date? That's a little late now, isn't it?"

"It's never too late, especially when your date is as beautiful and sexy as you."

Ben punctuated his sentence with kisses along Mia's throat and collarbone.

"Are we eating here?" she asked.

"No, I thought we could give the chef the night off and head into Queenstown. Something lakeside. Your mom said she'll have Jas for the night. What do you think?"

Mia smiled and her green eyes lit with genuine joy that matched the smile on her lips.

"That sounds really nice. What time do you want me?"

"Ah, *querida*," his voice deepened and he rocked her pelvis against his, letting her feel the incontrovertible proof that was there, "I always want you."

Her breathing hitched and her eyes glazed, the pupils growing large and dark. It was another thing they shared. She, too, was as addicted to their lovemaking as he was, and enjoyed it with an abandon she never exhibited in her day-to-day actions. He shifted his hands and gripped her hips, gently easing her away from him.

"Go, while I can still let you go. Have a relaxing soak in the tub and take your time getting ready. It's going to take me a while to be acceptable in polite company myself."

"I could always do something about that for you," she teased, her hands resting on the tops of his thighs, her fingers only inches from his aching flesh.

"Don't tempt me. I'm saving myself for later."

"It promises to be a special night, then." She smiled and for a split second Ben regretted his decision to put her off for now.

"A very special night," he concurred.

He looked at her and knew he'd made the right determination with his surprise. Beneath the generous lover he could see the signs of strain that told of the number of times she slipped from their bed at night to go over figures at the small desk in the main sitting room of their suite. He'd seen her often enough to know that despite the money he'd paid to her for his exclusive use of Parker's Retreat, the hotel and spa were still very much in their earliest stages and as such were financially vulnerable.

Yes, he was absolutely certain about his gift, surprise, whatever you wanted to call it. It was all she'd ever dreamed of and more. The anticipation of being the man to give it to her was so sweet he could almost taste it on his tongue. And he couldn't wait to see her reaction.

Queenstown's lights glittered their reflection on the lake as they approached the main center. They alighted at the wharf and Ben drew Mia's arm through his as they walked toward the restaurant he'd booked for the evening. It was only a short distance but the wind blew a freezing chill straight off the surrounding snowcapped mountains. For a moment Ben felt a deep sense of longing to be home again on Isla Sagrado's sun-baked rock, but he consoled himself that it was only a matter of days now before he had his new family back where they belonged.

The wind whipped Mia's hair across his cheek and he caught a whiff of the scented shampoo she used. The fragrance was so typical of the woman on his arm. Subtle and sweet and yet with a hint of musk that revealed the earthy lover who fulfilled him so completely. Yes, she had given him everything and tonight, in return, he would do the same.

The restaurant he'd booked was up a set of stairs and overlooked the lake with floor-to-ceiling windows. They were shown to a table with a clear view of Marine Parade and the bustling activities there. A resort town, Queenstown was a mecca to skiers and snowboarders alike at this time of year, not to mention those who came simply to drink in the wondrous natural beauty of the area or who preferred to seek their thrills in more extreme sports.

It suddenly shocked Ben to realize that he no longer classified himself in that category. Even immediately after his accident he'd been determined to regain his physical prowess so he could prove to himself he was just as good as before, if not better. He'd already ordered a new model of the car he'd crashed—beating his coast road time being in the forefront of his mind at the time.

But now he knew he'd never attempt that record again, nor would he willingly risk his life in the pursuit of yet another adrenaline rush. He had begun to understand what it must have been like for *Abuelo* to lose his only son and daughter-in-law in the avalanche that had claimed their lives, and how difficult it must have been to continue to raise Ben and his brothers with their penchant for fast cars and even faster women.

He had so much to look forward to with Jasper. He wanted to be there for all the key moments in his son's life—and not run the risk of missing anything chasing some meaningless thrill. And he wanted to be a good example to Jasper. The prospect of his son taking the wheel of an overpowered metal monster and driving it full tilt along any kind of road set his heart in ice.

What an idiot he'd been, tempting fate and railing against the strictures of family. Even more so when he'd turned his back on the very dictates that made the del Castillos who they were. Honor. Truth. Love. He'd never understood them until now. But he had time to make things right. Starting with tonight. With his gift to Mia he could honestly feel as though he'd met all his obligations as a husband and father. It would give them all a fresh, clean start.

Mia loved this restaurant. From the location, the staff, the menu, the wine list—it was everything she enjoyed about dining out. Sure it wasn't the highest of the high class but there was a welcoming sense of comfort in coming here and the massive square fireplace in the centre of the dining floor almost gave it the feel of being in someone's home, rather than in one of Queenstown's many eateries.

Ben was particularly solicitous tonight and she lapped up the attention. In fact, she almost started to believe they were a real couple. One with shared hopes and dreams for the future—right up until the moment he pulled a folded packet of papers from his pocket and laid them on the table between them.

"What's that?" she asked, and wished the words unsaid

the minute she'd uttered them. Some instinct warned her that what would come next was not what she really wanted to know.

"It's my gift to you. I may have gone about our marriage the wrong way by forcing you to agree to my conditions, but I hope this can make it up to you and to Jasper. I want you to know that I will always be there to look after you both and to make your life easier."

Easier? She didn't want him to make her life easier. She wanted him to learn to love her. Why was it that whenever they talked about their marriage or their life together, love was never even mentioned? They were already immensely compatible in the bedroom and they certainly appeared to be on the same wavelength with regard to parenting. She knew they could make a decent go of things if he'd just let down his barriers and let himself love them both as much as they already loved him.

"Don't gifts usually come in wrapping paper with bows?" she asked, trying and failing to inject a note of humor into her voice.

"Not this one, although I could order some champagne if that would make you feel more festive."

Mia shook her head. "No, no more wine for me tonight."

Ben pushed the packet across the table so it sat directly in front of her. "Then perhaps you should open this."

Mia slowly picked up the packet and squeezed the sides, tipping the contents onto the placemat. A sheaf of papers, folded lengthwise, spilled onto the mat. She picked it up and opened them, instantly recognizing the letterhead of the leading law firm in town. She quickly scanned the letter, then, with disbelief, checked the papers behind it.

Like an automaton she folded them again and put them back into the packet.

"Well?" Ben asked, his eyes alight with pleasure.

"It's the bank papers confirming my outstanding loan has been repaid in full," she said woodenly, "and a copy of the deed to Parker's Retreat showing the mortgage has been discharged. Why?"

"Why? I thought you'd be pleased. I told you I'd take care of you and Jasper, and I have. Parker's is yours free and clear now. Isn't that what you wanted?"

Mia swallowed against the solid lump of disappointment that lodged in her throat. What she wanted? Of course it was what she wanted—in time. And on her own terms. She'd been prepared to work for that. She didn't want things handed to her on a platter anymore. She'd finally learned, the hard way, the value of hard work and the sense of accomplishment that accompanied it.

What was it he'd said earlier—that he'd wanted to make her life easier? Didn't he realize that she didn't want an easy life? She'd had an easy life before—a life of extravagance without a thought to the real cost. She thought Ben had noticed that she wasn't that girl anymore. She didn't want "easy." She wanted difficult and challenging and worthwhile, so that at the end of the day, she'd know that she'd *earned* everything she had. Instead, this made her feel as if she'd been bought. Was this just another way for him to keep her under his control?

This wasn't the action of a man who was even contemplating love. It was a stamp of ownership, pure and simple.

Mia laid the packet down on the table and looked up to meet his eyes. She saw confusion reflected there, but nothing else. No hope of pleasing her. No expression of tenderness. And inside, her own hopes suffocated and died.

Ben's brows drew into a straight line, a sure sign of

his displeasure. What had he thought she'd do, she wondered—leap into his arms and thank him effusively for his generosity?

"You aren't pleased," he stated across the table, the rift between them far wider than a couple of feet of polished wood.

"That I'm now indebted to you? No."

He made a sweeping movement with one hand, slicing the air as if he could negate her denial as easily. "You are not indebted to me. This is a gift. My gift to you. I owed you this, if not more."

"You *owed* me? Funny. That'll explain why it doesn't feel like a gift. Ben, did you really think you could buy me and Jasper by buying out my loans?"

"Buy you?"

"Yes, buy me."

"Rest assured I do not consider you *bought*. I had no obligation to give you anything, Mia, but I understand how important your financial security is to you. I thought it would bring you pleasure to know you don't have to struggle anymore. To know that nothing and no one can ever threaten what you've built up." He shrugged. "It seems I was wrong. Either way, what has been done cannot be undone. The place is yours. Do with it what you will."

His dismissive tone brought tears to her eyes. All right, so he hadn't intended his surprise to be another tie of obligation, but it was clear it hadn't truly been meant as a gift. He'd chosen to throw money at the problem rather than making the effort to truly understand how much making a success of Parker's had meant to her. His "gift" showed no understanding of her—or even how much she'd consented to walk away from when she'd agreed to marry him and accompany him to his home. As far as Ben was concerned he'd done his part and that was all she'd ever get from him.

And she'd learned the hard way, money didn't buy you everything. Least of all the one thing she really wanted.

Her husband's love.

Their journey back to the hotel was completed in strained silence.

In their suite Mia missed Jasper's presence with a physical ache, but she would have to put up with waiting to see him in the morning. She went through the motions of getting ready for bed in a state of numbed shock. All of this was really hers. Lock, stock and two smoking barrels. Yet it would never feel hers again. Ben had taken the pride of making it on her own away from her, without even stopping to consider what he'd done. All he'd seen was a way to salve his own conscience.

She slid into the cool sheets on their bed as he went through to the bathroom. He'd dimmed the bedroom lights while she'd readied for bed—setting the scene for seduction, for the coupling that had become their only common ground since their wedding. But tonight she wanted none of it.

She realized that she and she alone was to blame for the situation she was in. She'd allowed Benedict to believe that she was prepared to settle for this and only this in their marriage. It was time she put things straight.

When Ben slipped into the bed behind her and reached to pull her into the curve of his body, she resisted.

"No," she said quietly.

"No?" Ben questioned, his hand sliding over her hip and up to cup her breast.

"I don't want to make love with you."

"Your body makes a liar of you, *querida,*" he said, and she could hear the smile on his face.

She put her hand over his and deliberately moved it off her body before rolling over to face him.

"My physical response is one thing, Ben. But my emotional one is something else. You showed me tonight that you don't really know me at all, and when I tried to explain that to you, you simply pushed my feelings aside because they weren't what you wanted to hear. I'm sorry for you, Ben. For me, making love is not something purely for physical release—not anymore. It's supposed to be something special. Something shared by two people in love."

"Our lovemaking is always something special," he insisted.

"It's still just sex, Ben, and it's not enough for me. For some reason you think that if you throw enough money and charm at a situation it'll be okay. But there's more to life than that. *We* could have more than that.

"I'm not going to let you close yourself off from me in every way that truly matters and then compensate for whatever it is that you're putting yourself through by trading off with solving my financial situation and making me climax every night."

"I haven't heard you complain about the climaxes," he said, his voice lethally even, his dark eyes glittering in the semi-light of their room.

"No, I haven't. But they're not enough, Ben."

She rolled over in the bed and presented Ben with her back.

"Good night," she said, her voice muffled in the pillow into which she burrowed her face.

She couldn't let him see the tears that had begun to streak her cheeks, couldn't let him know that even as disappointed as he'd made her feel tonight, she still wanted

him with every breath in her body. But she was worth more
than that. She was worth his love, and she wasn't going to
give up until she had it.

Thirteen

Ben lay still in the darkness. It had been a couple of hours since Mia's breathing had settled in the deep, slow rhythm of sleep. She'd been crying—he knew it and he couldn't do a darn thing about it. Didn't know where to begin.

Her rejection of his gift, of him, had cut far deeper than he'd wanted to admit and certainly deeper than he'd wanted to examine. But since sleep had proven completely elusive, he was forced to think about it and try to work out what exactly had gone wrong.

The evening had started so well. The dinner had been superb, the setting idyllic if a little busy for his tastes. But everything had fallen apart the moment he'd given her the papers. She'd accused him of not knowing her at all—with the implication that he did not care enough to learn about her, as if he was treating her like an expendable commodity. The very thought that she could come to that conclusion was as puzzling as it was infuriating.

He *did* care about her. That was why he had done what he had. To please her. To take care of her problems, the way he had promised himself he would. He had the advantage of money and being able to solve her financial difficulties. Why, as her husband, should he not do so? Her problems were sorted, allowing her to do with Parker's Retreat every single thing she'd ever wanted to do. Wasn't that what she wanted?

She'd given him so much—all he'd wanted was to give her something in return. Maybe she'd simply been taken by surprise. He had no doubt that when Mia had taken some time to consider the ramifications of his gift fully, she'd appreciate it better. Maybe all she needed was some space. Some time to consider what he'd done and why.

Yet as he finally drifted off into slumber a small voice at the back of his mind asked him why he still felt as if something was missing. Something vital and important. Something that lay just outside his grasp.

The morning didn't bring any fresh answers with it except a desire to return home and get his life back on its even keel as soon as possible. He left Mia sleeping, and made the necessary calls. The charter company assured him a plane would be at his disposal at Queenstown Airport in two days' time.

Two days. The thought that he'd be back home, back to normal in such a short period was invigorating. He loved the area here, but he also loved his mountains and valley. The vineyards he'd nursed to full production, the winery where he and his head winemaker explored methods to bring out the best in their grapes to produce award-winning wines year after year. Those were the challenges he looked forward to embracing once more.

Isla Sagrado meant family and tradition to him, but also, it was a place that was his. He'd made it and it was home. Most importantly, he was ready to be back there with Mia and Jasper. No more hiding away. No more facing the future alone.

A sound from the bedroom door stirred him from his reveries. Mia was awake. She came through to the sitting room, tying her robe about her waist and moving with an unconscious grace that sent a surge of longing straight to his groin. No matter what passed between them, their physical connection only grew stronger. It was more than most marriages had.

He decided to take the bull by the horns and let her know of their changed travel plans.

"I've confirmed our departure for Isla Sagrado. We'll be leaving in two days."

"Two days?"

All the color in her cheeks faded, throwing her green eyes into relief against the dark hollows that shadowed them.

"Yes. I was booked here for four weeks. That time is up and I have accomplished so much more than I'd imagined in that time. There's nothing to keep us here any longer, and the sooner you and Jasper settle into your new home the better."

"But I still have so much to do here."

"Mia, I know you were expecting another week with Elsa to complete her training, but there's nothing you can't deal with from Isla Sagrado just a easily. Let her take over now. She's itching to do so, and your being here is holding her back."

Mia flinched as if he'd physically hurt her. Twin spots of color appeared in her cheeks.

"I've made her manager. I'm letting her take over everything. How could I possibly be holding her back?"

He stood up and caught her upper arms before she could wheel away from him.

"*Querida,* I handled things last night clumsily, as I have handled almost everything between us since my arrival. I'm sorry for that, but can you blame me for wanting to take you and Jasper home and show you off to my family?"

"And can you blame me for wanting to make sure my business and my mother are taken care of first? *You're* the one going home, Ben. I'm the one *leaving* the only home I've ever known—and now you're saying I'll be leaving it sooner even than we'd planned."

Benedict sighed, but he refused to be drawn into an argument even though Mia was very obviously spoiling for one. "You are my wife, Jasper is my son. I want you both to become a part of my life, in my home country. Is that so hard to understand?"

Mia shook her head and her eyes emptied of all their fire. "No, it's not hard to understand. It just doesn't make it any easier to bear, that's all."

Mia went through the motions all day, showing her mother the online booking system, referring her to the manuals she'd had set up when the system went live if Elsa had a question—because goodness only knew Mia wouldn't be available to answer them at the drop of a hat once they were gone. It was all well and good for Ben to say she could run her business via the Internet and phone calls, but Isla Sagrado was a good twelve hours behind New Zealand, which made scheduling meetings through Skype or other contact methods problematic.

Jasper had been over the moon when she'd picked him up this morning and told him that they'd be going to Isla Sagrado in only two more sleeps. Of course, he had no concept that going there would mean leaving all this behind, maybe for good.

She wished she had that innocent expectation about the life facing them in Isla Sagrado…but even more than that, she wished she had the simple assurance that Jasper had of being loved by Ben. But it was as if Ben had encased his emotions in ice—determined not to allow himself to feel anything for her except desire. He was holding back from her, and until he could crack apart that glacier that held his heart hostage, their marriage could never truly be happy.

She'd noted a difference in him when he'd first arrived, a difference that had become more marked in the time he'd been here. It was as if he was skimming the surface of everything. Cautious about feeling too much. The only time she believed he was totally up front and honest was when they were in bed together. When, with his body, he didn't hold back on anything.

Maybe that's what she needed to do, she realized. Hoping the words she'd uttered last night could chip away at the barriers shielding his heart was futile. She needed to take positive action to make him face what she was certain was the truth.

She wasn't a quitter and she wasn't going to be a spineless bystander in her marriage either. She loved Benedict del Castillo, and one way or another she would make sure he knew it.

Ben had left a message with her earlier in the day to say that he wouldn't be at the spa for his usual massage, as he was taking Andre into town for a farewell meal and a few drinks. Andre had decided to stay on in New Zealand a little longer and see a bit of the country while he could, so he wouldn't be joining them on their trip to Isla Sagrado. Ben's plans played into her hands nicely. By the time he returned to Parker's Retreat he'd hopefully be feeling mellow and ready for what she had in store for him.

Making her preparations took a little time, but she knew it was worth it when she saw their bedroom transformed with numerous scented candles and the bed prepared for the very special massage she had planned for her husband. Jasper, tired from his second-to-last day at day care, had settled to bed early and she had no doubt he'd sleep the whole night through. All she had to do now was ready herself before Ben returned.

Mia had just finished smoothing her favorite scented body lotion into her legs when she heard the main door to their suite open. She stood up, letting the sheer rose-colored nightgown that was all she'd chosen to wear slide over her body. She put the lotion back on the dresser, her hands trembling with anticipation. Ben entered the room and fixed her with a questioning gaze, his dark brows rising ever so slightly.

"What's this?" he asked, his voice wary.

"You missed your massage today," Mia said, moving forward to take his coat from him before throwing it over the squat Queen Anne chair in the corner. "I thought with the travel we have coming up that you'd be more comfortable if we stuck with your program. But first, a spa bath."

She reached for the buttons on his shirt, undoing each one with painstaking care before pulling his shirttails from his trousers and casting the shirt to the floor. She leaned into him, inhaling softly. The scent of wood smoke—the smell most predominant in the air in town—clung to him and blended with the freshness of his cologne to make an almost unbearably sexy combination.

Taking him by the hand, Mia led him to their bathroom. More candles lit the tiled room, their reflection in the large mirrors on the walls adding to the glow of warmth and intimacy. Her hands made short work of his belt and trousers before guiding him to the bath. Scented bubbles danced on the water's surface. Mia flipped the switch for the jets, and indicated to Ben that he should occupy the body-form-shaped seat so he could gain the most benefit from their therapeutic pulsation.

"Aren't you joining me?" he asked.

Mia shook her head. "I have other plans. Tell me about your evening. Where did you go?"

While Ben told her about the pub meal he and Andre had shared, she poured a glass of red wine and sipped from it before holding the glass to his lips so he could drink from it also—his lips partaking of the ruby liquid from exactly the same spot her own lips had rested upon. He watched her like a hawk, a flush spreading across his cheeks as she licked a tiny droplet of wine from the edge of the glass before offering it back to him.

"What's this about Mia?" he growled. "Last night you didn't want a bar of me."

Mia considered her words carefully. "I was overemotional. I'm sorry. If it's any consolation, refusing you last night punished me as much as you."

"It's no consolation at all. I still cannot understand why you were so upset. So angry."

And that was the problem, she thought. He couldn't conceive of the fact that making her own way here was so important, so vital to her identity and for her own need to make amends for the strain she'd caused her father. But had she been unfair, expecting him to automatically understand? He didn't know what she had been through—and as much as she accused him of being closed off emotionally, she hadn't fully shared herself, either. That would change right now.

"I think, for you to understand that, you'd really have

to walk in my shoes over the past three and a half years. I went from having everything, and working for none of it—taking it all for granted—to having nothing and having to claw it all back."

"Wouldn't most people welcome the prospect of having all their worries solved for them?"

"Most people, yes," she conceded.

"But not you."

"No, not me, because for the first time in my life I actually appreciated how hard I had to work for things and I deeply regret how complacent I'd become over it all. Sure, it wasn't easy, but it redefined me. Made me realize how shallow my life had been before. Having you hand everything back to me on a platter again, well, it just made me feel as if you still saw me as that girl you met the first time. Not the woman I am now."

The woman who loves you. The words echoed in her heart, but she was too afraid to say them aloud.

There was a pause while Ben considered this before he replied. "I think I can understand to a degree. It's probably why my brothers and I have chosen very different paths to expand in our family's business portfolios. We complement one another, but we're each our own master—we do things our own way. That way, we're each able to make our own mark and know that our achievements are uniquely ours."

Ben fell silent and Mia wondered whether she'd said too much, or even too little. She passed Ben the wine goblet and watched as he took another sip before taking it back, then she hit the button that stopped the jets in the spa bath.

"I think that's enough for now," she said and stood to get a large fluffy white towel for him.

Ben stood and she watched the rivulets of water run off his body and into the tub. Once he was out of the bath she moved closer and began to dry him off, taking her time, stroking the thick toweling in firm sweeps across his back and down over his buttocks before drying the backs of his legs. Then she gave her attention to his chest, his abdomen, his groin.

He was fully aroused by the time she was finished, but when he reached for her she gently shook her head.

"Not yet. As I said, I have plans for you. Come over by the bed," she whispered with a smile before pulling away.

She guided him facedown onto the bed and then straddled his legs and reached for the lotion she'd prepared earlier, one infused with heady, exotic scents. She stroked the lotion into his skin in long, flowing movements that started at the base of his spine and worked up his back.

As her hands smoothed over his shoulders, she felt the tension knotted there and doubled her efforts, working into the tissue before lightly skimming away, replacing her hands with butterfly light kisses before returning again with her fingers. Once she was satisfied he was completely relaxed she shifted to the foot of the bed and gave his legs the same attention. As she bent to kiss behind his knees she finally allowed herself to acknowledge the slow, steady burn uncoiling from deep inside her.

With each forward motion her breasts swung against her night gown—fuller, heavier. The sheer silk caressed her nipples with the softness of a lover's touch, but it wasn't enough. She wanted more. She wanted Ben. She forced herself to calm down, to focus on what she wanted for the long term, rather than what she wanted right now.

She rose up onto her knees, shifting her weight fully off him for the moment.

"Roll over, Ben," she instructed, surprised to hear the strain in her voice.

Slowly he turned over, baring his body to her, all of his body. She kept her eyes very firmly on his, knowing how he felt about the scars that crisscrossed his abdomen, understanding on an unspoken level that, more than anything, it was their constant reminder of his mistake that made him hate them so.

Ben's eyes were dark, the blackness of his pupils consuming his irises, the flicker of candlelight reflected in their bottomless depths.

Again Mia straddled his thighs, teasingly avoiding his arousal. She leaned forward to massage his chest, her hands still soft with lotion, and felt his erection buck against her as her nightgown stroked his sensitive skin.

Still she maintained eye contact, although it became more and more of a challenge to her with every movement she made. Avoiding his abdomen completely, she shifted her hands to the top of Ben's thighs, trickling her fingers higher until they coasted along the shape of his hips then behind to his buttocks and back again.

Without letting her gaze waver she lowered herself until her breath shimmered over his swollen shaft. He'd never allowed her this intimacy before. Every time they'd been together he'd been all about her pleasure before taking his own. With his hands and his tongue, he'd wrought the ultimate pleasure upon her. Now she wanted to do the same for him.

Fully expecting a protest, she kissed the tip of him. A bead of moisture appeared and she instinctively darted her tongue out to taste him. Ben groaned at the head of the bed, indistinguishable words spilling from his mouth, his hands fisted in the sheets.

An overwhelming sense of power and control suffused her, together with the knowledge that she was only doing this with the gift of his permission. That he wanted her to be with him, to do this to him, as much as she did herself.

Mia let her lips skim the smoothly swollen head, each time following up with the barest of touches with her tongue. He writhed beneath her, and she took his stretch of control as her signal. She closed her mouth over him, swirling her tongue around him and tasting his essence. She changed her position slightly so she could take him more deeply, driving him nearly wild with the alternate swirling and sucking of her tongue and mouth.

She felt his shaft thicken even more and became aware of her answering moisture pooling between her legs. She ached for him, ached to take him inside her and drive them both to completion. Mia let go of him and arched herself upward, pulling off her nightgown as she did so.

Ben's eyes flew open as she positioned herself above him, felt the hard nub of him at her entrance. She eased her hips forward and back across his sensitive flesh, coating him with her moisture, driving herself mad at the same time.

His hands unfurled in the covers and gripped her hips, halting her teasing. She placed her own hands over his and slowly lowered her body, taking him inside her in a slow, steady glide. She gasped as her body stretched and filled. This was more than sex, more than making love. It was a total unity of body and spirit.

Could he feel it, too? Did his heart swell and contract in time with the movement of their bodies the way hers did?

She braced her hands on his shoulders, felt his hands reach up and cup her breasts, his thumbs abrading their taut peaks, his finger gently kneading the full soft flesh.

Her orgasm took her by surprise, convulsing through her in a streak of lightning, making her body tremble, her inner muscles repeatedly clench and release. Beneath her, Ben thrust his hips upward, a harsh groan rippling from his throat as his body reached its zenith and triggered off yet another burst of pleasure to pulse through her body.

She collapsed, boneless, onto his prone form, her heart thudding in her chest. As aftershocks continued to pulse through her she found the courage to say the words her heart had held hostage.

"I love you, Ben."

Underneath her, she felt his body tense; his hands stilled their gentle stroking. She waited for his response. For the words that would answer her declaration. But only silence hung in the air surrounding them.

Regret pierced her like a frozen arrow. It didn't matter what she did, or said, he would never let her past the barriers he'd built between himself and the world. Mia rolled off him and moved to the edge of the bed, pulling the covers up over her. Ben shifted to lie behind her, his body spooning hers. But the physical warmth that emanated from him couldn't touch the cold, lonely place in her chest where her heart had beaten for him.

Fourteen

Her words were still in his head in the morning as he eased himself from the bed and went into the bathroom to shower.

I love you, Ben.

It had shocked him to realize how much her words had meant to him, and he knew she'd expected something in return. She'd deserved far more than the silence he'd given her. But love? He didn't even think he was capable of love anymore. He certainly didn't deserve it. Not from her. She deserved so much better—deserved a man undamaged by life who could give her every gift of his love.

He'd thought it would be enough to make her world right again, ensure that she and Jasper were provided for. But now he understood why she'd been so offended by his gift earlier. That wasn't what she wanted from him—she wasn't interested in gifts that money could buy. What she wanted was his love. And he wasn't sure he could give it.

I love you, Ben.

The words cascaded over him like the hot water of the shower jets. He let his head rest on the shower wall, allowing the water to flow down his back. Since his crash he'd existed in a state of alternating anger and frustration, both directed very firmly at himself. He'd taken unnecessary risks, and he'd paid the price. But now, it seemed, everyone around him had to pay the price, too, even Mia.

She was a great mother to Jasper and she deserved the chance to have more children if she wanted to. With him she didn't even have that choice. She might say she loved him now, but what of the future? It wasn't as easy as he'd thought it would be all along—simply transplanting her into his world, his life. Now that he understood what drove and motivated her, he wondered how she could continue to love him if he ripped her away from everything she held dear—everything she'd worked so hard for.

She had a purpose here, one he finally understood. He'd scoffed when she'd said she'd changed from the girl he'd first met. But he'd been an arrogant fool. She'd changed far more than she realized. Become a woman worthy of the kind of love and support a proper husband should give her. But he didn't have it in him to be that man, which meant only one thing. He had to let her go. He had to return to Isla Sagrado without her, without Jasper. It was the only way he could live with himself.

And if the curse proved to be true after all—if he was punished for his failure to treat her with the honor, honesty and love that she deserved—well, he could only hope that his respect for his family and his determination to have their wishes honored, even if he'd failed, would be enough to satisfy the governess. He'd finally admitted the truth to himself about his failings, and while he didn't deserve

Mia's love, perhaps the fact she thought him worthy of it would be enough.

But despite all his rationalizations, Ben knew he would be breaking her heart when he left, and that knowledge cut him deep. Still, he was certain she'd be better off without him. And that was the only thing that gave him the strength to make this choice.

He snapped off the shower faucets and stepped out of the stall, drying himself swiftly. The condensation cleared rapidly on the heated bathroom mirrors and he was faced with his own reflection, his eyes riveted on the external evidence of the damage wrought on his body by his own stupidity. He'd robbed himself of the future he'd always believed would be his. He couldn't do the same to Mia.

Ben went silently into the bedroom, quickly dressed and let himself out of the room. He'd tell her of his decision later today, when Jasper was at day care. The preschool was having a farewell party for Jas, but he couldn't stop that. Suffice that Jas would be back there on Monday again, after the weekend. He hoped that it wouldn't confuse the little boy too much, and he reminded himself that children were resilient and adapted to change far more easily than most adults.

As he closed the bedroom door behind him he cast a lingering look over the woman who had given him so very much—pleasure of unspeakable heights, her love, his son—and he knew he was doing the right thing for them all.

Mia stared at Ben in total shock. Her skin felt too tight for her body, her face frozen, her hands clenched into fists.

"You what?"

"You heard me, Mia. I'll be leaving for Isla Sagrado on my own tomorrow. It's for the best."

"For the best? What on earth are you talking about? We're married, husband and wife, we're supposed to be together, aren't we? And what about Jasper? Do you honestly mean to say that after everything you've done to prove he's your son, and in marrying me, that you're going to just walk away from us?"

She heard her pitch rise higher and higher, heard the wobble in her voice that foretold of the tears burning at the back of her eyes, but she could control none of it. All she knew right at this moment was that the man she loved, the father of her son, had told her he was leaving without them.

In that moment all her scruples about leaving New Zealand vanished. What had she been thinking, living her life as if all that mattered was redeeming the past? The past was over and done with, and nothing she did could change that. The only thing that mattered now was finding a life that could make her happy and seizing on to it with everything she had. For her, happiness meant spending the rest of her life with the man she loved. Was the chance of that now gone forever? What had happened to make him change his mind so abruptly?

She'd slept late this morning and so had Jasper, and it'd been a mad dash to get him ready on time for his last day at day care. Once she'd waved him off on the boat with Elsa she'd gone to her office to finalize some paperwork, and that's where Ben had found her half an hour later.

Her life had seemed so normal a few moments ago—now it was spiraling crazily out of control. She stared in disbelief at the man she'd married. The man who'd turned into a total stranger before her very eyes.

"I've made my decision. I'm not changing it, Mia. You should be happy."

"*You've* made *your* decision?" She shook her head in disbelief. "We're married, Ben. You can't just walk away from that."

"We can remain married, until you meet someone else."

His face remained impassive, but she saw a swiftly veiled hint of pain reflected in the depths of his eyes.

"Until I meet someone else," she repeated, her voice flat. "I told you last night that I love you, Ben. I don't want anyone else, and nor does Jasper. He loves his daddy, too. You can't do this to us."

"It's for the best. In time, I'm sure you'll see that."

Ben remained adamant, his arms crossed over his torso, his feet firmly planted shoulder-width apart—holding his metaphorical ground against her, if not his physical one.

"Why? Why are you doing this to us?"

Her voice finally broke and the dam holding back her tears did so, also. They slid, unchecked, down her pale cheeks. Ben's face twisted, and he looked away and took a deep breath. When he spoke his voice was painstakingly controlled.

"I was wrong to treat you as I did—with no consideration for you or your dreams and hopes for the future. I shouldn't have tried to take those opportunities away from you. I have no place in that future. You deserve to achieve everything you set out to do. At least now that can happen."

But you're doing the same thing now! Mia wanted to shout at him, but she knew the words would fall upon deaf ears. He had made up his mind and now he was leaving. If he'd offered her the same opportunity a couple of weeks ago she would have grabbed at it with both hands—but right now she felt as if her life was being torn in two.

"What about your grandfather? What about the curse you told me about?"

"I will explain it all to *Abuelo*. My—" he hesitated a moment and swallowed before continuing "—infertility, everything. He has a great-grandson, I hope that is enough for him to understand that his obsession with the curse was just that, an obsession and not the truth. If not, well, he's an old man and can be forgiven for some irrationality from time to time."

"So that's it, then?" Mia couldn't believe his words. Not after everything they'd gone through to get to this point.

"*Sí*. I will stay in a hotel in Queenstown tonight and be at the airport early tomorrow for my flight. Don is waiting with the boat for me now. My luggage is already on board and I've taken the liberty of having your and Jasper's things moved back into your apartment. I'm sure the sooner you both settle back into your old routine the better for everyone."

Her head whirled. He'd planned that far ahead already? Only yesterday they were going to undertake this journey together, and now he was leaving without them? She struggled for something to say, anything that would hold him here for a moment longer—anything that might give her a chance to make him change his mind.

"Will you at least say goodbye to Jasper before you leave?"

"I think it's best if I don't. He might be upset and he'll adjust faster the sooner I'm not here, I'm sure. There's one favor I would ask of you, though. I will understand if you don't wish to grant it but I beg of you, please bring Jasper to Isla Sagrado for his third birthday. My family has missed his birth and two birthdays already. I will arrange everything for you from my end and I would be grateful if we could all be together for the occasion."

"You could have us there permanently, Ben. We could be leaving with you tomorrow."

"No, I can't do that to you, Mia. I've been a selfish fool. At least allow me this—let me give you your life back, the life you deserve."

Mia's throat closed on the lump of emotion that swelled there, and as Ben turned to go she reached out and grabbed him by the arm.

"So, this is it? Won't you even kiss me goodbye?"

He shook his head and gently uncurled her fingers from his arm.

"Mia, I know how much this is hurting you. I have no wish to prolong your pain for any longer than absolutely necessary. I will let you know when I arrive back on Isla Sagrado. Perhaps you'll let Jasper talk to me online from time to time, so he doesn't forget me completely?"

Mia pushed her fist to her lips, afraid that if she opened her mouth something that sounded completely inhuman would come out. Incapable of words, she nodded, then watched helplessly as Ben walked away. Taking her broken heart with him.

"What do you mean he's gone?" Elsa asked, her voice confused.

"Just that, Mom. He's going back without us. He doesn't want us anymore."

"I'm sure that's not true," her mother said. "He might not know it or even want to admit it, but I'm sure he loves you. Can't you follow him?"

"And what? Face his rejection again? Even I can only take so much, and it's not as if I only have myself to consider."

Mia looked across the room to where Jasper played with

his toys, totally and happily absorbed in his imaginary world.

"Have you told him yet?"

"No, I can't bring myself to, not when I still feel so raw myself. Maybe tomorrow. He'll probably start asking questions by then."

Elsa rose from her seat at the dining table where she and Mia had both merely chased their dinner around their plates. She bent to give her daughter a hug.

"What am I going to do, Mom?" Mia asked, her voice fracturing on the words.

"Take each day as it comes, my darling. It's the only thing you can do."

With her mother's words ringing in her ears, Mia readied Jasper for bed, going through the motions without really paying attention. By the time she slid into the sheets of her own bed, in her own room, she knew that sleep would be the last thing to happen tonight. Her mind replayed that final scene with Ben, over and over, and tears slid unheeded from her eyes, soaking into her pillow.

Morning brought no ease to her sorrow and Mia found herself watching the skies for a glimpse of the private jet that would be taking off any time now and taking Ben back to Isla Sagrado. After giving Jas his breakfast she decided to take him with her over to the hotel, so she could finalize arrangements for a group booking of writers from Australia due to arrive early next week on a retreat. She'd have her full complement of staff back on deck come Monday, and she wanted to be sure everything would be spot on for the group when they arrived.

She was intercepted by Elsa and Don, who suggested they take Jasper to the Queenstown Gardens and lunch in town. While she would have preferred the distraction of his company, Mia agreed. At least it would mean it would be that much longer before he started asking questions about Ben. The prospect of being alone with her thoughts was a daunting one, but in her office she threw herself into the itinerary, complete with spa sessions, for the incoming group.

She'd been working for about an hour when a sound outside her office distracted her. She paid it no mind, knowing that the cleaners were due to give the admin area a bit of a spruce-up this weekend before the hotel resumed its usual operations, and she didn't even lift her head when she heard the knock at her office door.

"Come in," she said absently.

Briefly she wondered who on earth would be bothering her today—her office had already been vacuumed and dusted and her plants watered. She wasn't even supposed to be here, let alone working. She was supposed to be on her way to Isla Sagrado, she reminded herself with a sharp pang of regret.

"Back to work, already?"

Ben's deep voice resonated on the air, making her stop in her work and lift her head in a sharp movement. She couldn't believe her eyes. He stood in front of her—large as life and, despite the hollows under his eyes, twice as gorgeous. She forced herself to take a breath, and then another one, while her hands gripped the edges of her desk. She hardly dared to move in case he'd disappear like an apparition.

"Mia, are you okay?" Ben moved swiftly around the desk and pulled her to her feet. "I'm sorry. I didn't mean to shock you."

"You're back," she stated blankly.

"*Querida,* I couldn't leave."

Words still failed her, but the warmth of his hands holding hers was unbelievably real.

"I've been a complete fool. I thought I could walk away from you, let you have your life back. But I'm so much more selfish than that. I don't want to let you go. I want you and Jasper in my life every day, not just for visits every so often throughout a year, and I'll be damned if I let anyone else have you either."

Mia finally found her voice. "Why did you go? I told you I love you, Ben. How could you leave me, us, like that?"

He closed his eyes for a moment and when he opened them she could see the deep remorse reflected in them.

"I never wanted to cause you more pain. In my arrogance I thought it would be best for us to break cleanly, before you learned to hate me all over again."

"Ben, I've never hated you. I could never—"

"I know that—I understand now. Love isn't like that, is it?" He gave her a rueful smile. "I was afraid to love you. Afraid that one day you'd regret marrying me and wish for more than I offered you. More children, raising them here at Parker's Retreat, your work. I thought it would be an easy thing to walk away and leave you to your world, but I am a weak man, Mia. I want it all. I want you, I want Jasper—I want us to have a life together.

"I didn't want to love you, to open myself up to being vulnerable to you." He shook his head. "How could I have been such an idiot? I thought I was undeserving of your love, that I wasn't strong enough—man enough. But from the moment I left here yesterday I hurt—a pain far worse than I endured after my accident—and it is the kind of hurt that I know I will bear for the rest of my life, unless you can forgive me for being such an idiot, for hurting you so badly."

Mia gripped Ben's hands tightly, afraid to let him go in case they'd somehow lose this precious connection between them. A connection she wanted with all her heart. "Ben, there's nothing to forgive. I love you. I will always love you. I don't care if we can't have any more children. Okay, to be totally honest, and you deserve my total honesty, I am sorry that we can't give Jasper a brother or sister but I can accept that if I have *you*. We have a beautiful, strong and healthy son. He's a gift for us both, all the more precious because he will always be our only child. I don't know if I'll ever fully understand what drove you away from us—I'm just glad you're back."

She reached up and pressed her lips to his, kissing him with both the pent-up love inside her and relief that he had returned. When Ben broke their kiss and leaned his forehead against hers they were both breathing unevenly.

"I've learned a powerful lesson, Mia. I always thought a man's strength was tied into his masculinity. In his prowess as a male of the species and all that it entailed. It's part of what drove me to test myself more every time I tried something—physically, mentally, emotionally. And each time I'd succeed, I'd convince myself I was that much stronger, that much better as a man. Until my accident. It made me accept that when all is said and done, I'm *only* a man. A man with failings—even more so now as a result of that crash.

"We have a creed in our family—'Honor, Truth, Love.' They're the very words the governess cursed us to learn to uphold three hundred years ago and I'm ashamed that not even nearly losing my life made me grasp just how important that ethos, and living it, is. It took nearly losing you to make me appreciate just how important those words are to me, to my life—to *our* life together.

"I love you, Mia. With all that I am, failings and all, I love you. And I promise you, I will honor you all my life, with the truth always between us and with my undying love for you and Jasper."

Mia's heart swelled as she heard the words she'd waited so long to hear from his lips. A tremulous smile spread across her face.

"Does this mean we'll be leaving for Isla Sagrado together now?" she asked, mentally repacking all those things that had been unpacked back in her apartment only yesterday.

"No."

She reeled back from him, stunned at his monosyllabic reply.

"No? What do you mean, no? How can you say you love me in one breath and then say we can't come with you to Isla Sagrado in the next? You can't do that to me, Ben. You can't."

He reached for her and dragged her stiff and unwilling body back into the cradle of his arms.

"I mean that if you'll let me, I want to stay here. With you and Jasper. I can do what I do anywhere in the world, Mia. Goodness knows my vineyard and winery have managed quite nicely without me since my accident and they will continue to do so. But what I can't have anywhere in the world is the knowledge that you're fulfilling the dreams and goals you've set for yourself here. So here is where we belong until you say otherwise.

"I love you and Jasper more than anything in the world. I could no more walk away from you than I could stop breathing. I nearly lost my life once before, Mia, and I didn't believe I could ever feel that scared or that vulnerable again. But I am now. You and Jasper are my life now. Without you both I am nothing, no one. I'm not prepared to risk it all again. I've been forced to face some hard lessons in my life recently and at least I can say I have learned from them. I know now that my strength, such as it is, is not tied up in my achievements or my fertility or how fast I can drive a car. My strength is tied to my love for you and for our son. Will you let me stay with you?"

Mia raised her hands and her fingers traced the defined planes of Ben's features. Features of the man she knew she would love for every day of the rest of her life.

"I will never let you go again, Benedict del Castillo. You're my husband, the father of my son, and the only man I will ever love. I don't care where we live—home will be any place that I share with you."

Joy filled her, replacing the remnants of sorrow, overwhelming the disappointments and the fears she'd borne in the past. And she knew, without a shadow of a doubt, that her future—*their* future—was one they could step toward with a full heart and without hesitation.

Epilogue

Their commitment ceremony in the chapel at the castillo last night had been beautiful—it was a moment Ben knew he'd treasure for the rest of his life. Insisting they were already married, Mia hadn't wanted the pomp involved in a second full wedding here on Isla Sagrado, where they'd brought Jasper and his new family face-to-face for the first time, but she'd acceded to his wish to reaffirm his promises to her with his family as witness.

Seeing the delight on *Abuelo*'s face had made the struggle of the previous months worthwhile. Knowing he'd done his part and finally brought joy to his grandfather's heart, and peace to his soul, was priceless. Having done so was more precious than any gift on earth, and had been more enriching than he'd imagined.

In the chapel, Ben had felt the weight of expectation of nine generations of del Castillos upon him as he'd exchanged vows with Mia in front of their family, in the private ceremony that had held more meaning for them both than the wedding he'd forced upon them both only weeks ago.

And now, walking with Mia and Jasper, together with his brothers and their chosen life partners, on the beach below the castillo, Ben finally felt at peace with his world.

"Rey, I think we should can the big wedding and just have something small in the chapel," Rina said to her fiancé, breaking in to Ben's thoughts.

"Are you sure you want that? You already have everything planned ahead," Reynard responded, bringing her hand to his lips and kissing her knuckles.

"I know, I know. Old habits die hard, but since last night I've been thinking that it would mean more to me if we married at the castillo. Kept it small and intimate and made it sooner. Ben and Mia's ceremony was so beautiful, so *theirs,* you know? I want that for us, too."

"Alex and I had our own private ceremony in the chapel, just the two of us," Loren, Alex's wife, admitted in her gentle voice. "It was very special and uniquely ours. I think you're making a good decision. When all is said and done, it's between the two of you. That's what's most important, yes?"

Out the corner of his eye Ben saw Alex squeeze Loren to his side, silently affirming her words.

Reynard gave his fiancée a loving look that told her she could do whatever she wanted as long as he remained at her side.

"You do what you need to." He smiled. "All I want is this engagement to be over so we can be husband and wife. I can't believe my little brother beat us to the punch."

Ben laughed. "I always was faster than you, Rey. About time you admitted it."

"Never!" Rey teased in return. "But hey, I'm really

happy for you, Ben. A wife *and* a son? I think we can safely say the curse is well and truly lifted, don't you?"

As he and Alex concurred, Ben's heart swelled. He really had it all now.

"Where is Jas?" Mia asked, her voice suddenly strained with a note of anxiety.

Ben cast his eyes up the beach. They were nearing the headland upon which the castillo perched and the beach curved away from them, its rough shores obscured from their view. He couldn't see Jasper anywhere.

"He wouldn't have gone near the water's edge, would he?" Loren asked, a corresponding thread of concern creeping into her words.

"No, he knows better than that. He's grown up around water, but he's not used to waves such as you have here. If a rogue wave has washed up..." Mia's voice trailed off.

In unspoken agreement the three brothers broke into a run, the women close behind, all of them pounding along the sand until they reached the headland.

"There he is," shouted Alex. "He's all right."

Ben didn't halt until he reached Jasper, swooping his precious boy into his arms and holding him close, silently vowing he would never let him out of his sight again.

"You gave me a scare, *mi hijo*. Stay where I can see you next time, okay?"

"Okay, Daddy," Jasper said with a smile that rocketed straight to Ben's heart.

As he settled his son back on the sand and the women caught up, he noticed that Jasper clutched something in one hand.

"What's that you have there?" he asked, holding out his hand.

Jasper uncurled his pudgy fingers, revealing a tangle of heavy gold chain with something large and solid nestled amongst it. Ben's blood ran cold. *Dios!* It was *La Verdad del Corazon*. The Heart's Truth. The necklace the governess had cast from the cliffs so very long ago. He reached out and took the necklace from Jasper's hand, letting it swing in the air in front of him, the massive heart-shaped ruby surprisingly clean and glowing brilliantly in the sunlight.

Both Alex's and Rey's faces were white with shock.

"Is that what I think it is?" Rey asked, his voice little more than a whisper.

"*Sí,*" Alex replied, lost for more words.

Mia knelt in the sand next to Jas.

"Where did you find that, darling?"

"The smiling lady gave it to me," he answered, looking fretfully from one adult to the other, his little face beginning to crumble as he picked up the vibes that strained between them.

Ben squatted next to Mia.

"It's okay, Jas. We're just surprised, that's all. Tell me about the lady. Where did she come from?"

Jasper pointed to the waves crashing on the rocks on the water's edge. "Over there, from the water. Daddy, where's she gone now?"

Ben smiled and hugged Jas to him. "I can't see her, my boy. Maybe she's gone home now, to be at rest."

He slowly straightened and exchanged a look with his brothers. While none of them said a word, each held his woman a little closer. The irrefutable proof that the curse was finally broken lifted an unseen weight from their shoulders, enriching them with the promise of a happy future for them all, forevermore.

On the cliff top high above the beach a woman watched the family below. Finally, a true family in every sense of the word. She lifted both hands to her lips, then threw her arms wide to encompass them in her imaginary embrace before fading away, her face serene and smiling, her soul at peace at last.

* * * * *

BREAKING
BAILEY'S RULES

BRENDA JACKSON

To the man who will always and forever be the
love of my life, Gerald Jackson, Sr.

Pleasant words are a honeycomb.
Sweet to the soul and healing to the bones.
—*Proverbs 16:24*

Prologue

Hugh Coker closed his folder and looked up at the five pairs of eyes staring at him.

"So there you have it. I met with this private investigator, Rico Claiborne, and he's convinced that you are descendants of someone named Raphel Westmoreland. I read through his report and although his claims sound pretty far-fetched, I can't discount the photographs I've seen. Bart, every one of your sons could be a twin to one of those Westmorelands. The resemblance is that strong. I have the photographs here for you to look at."

"I don't want to see any photographs, Hugh," Bart Outlaw said gruffly, getting out of his chair. "Just because this family might look like us doesn't mean they are related to us. We are Outlaws, not Westmorelands. And I'm not buying that story about a train wreck over sixty years ago where some dying woman gave her baby to my grandmother. That's the craziest thing I've ever heard."

He turned to his four sons. "Outlaw Freight Lines is

a multimillion-dollar company and people will claim a connection to us just to get what we've worked so hard to achieve."

Garth Outlaw leaned back in his chair. "Forgive me if I missed something, Dad, but didn't Hugh say the Westmorelands are pretty darn wealthy in their own right? I think all of us have heard of Blue Ridge Land Management. They are a Fortune 500 company. I don't know about the rest of you, but Thorn Westmoreland can claim me as a cousin anytime."

Bart frowned. "So what if they run a successful company and one of them is a celebrity?" he said in a cutting tone. "We don't have to go looking for any new relatives."

Maverick, the youngest of Bart's sons, chuckled. "I believe they came looking for us, Dad."

Bart's frown deepened. "Doesn't matter." He glanced at Hugh. "Send a nice letter letting them know we aren't buying their story and don't want to be bothered again. That should take care of it." Expecting his orders to be obeyed, Bart walked out of the conference room, closing the door behind him.

Sloan Outlaw stared at the closed door. "Are we going to do what he says?"

"Do we ever?" his brother Cash asked, grinning while watching Hugh put the papers back in his briefcase.

"Leave that folder, Hugh," Garth said, rubbing the back of his neck. "I think the old man forgot he's no longer running things. He retired a few months ago, or did I imagine it?"

Sloan stood. "No, you didn't imagine it. He retired but only after the board threatened to oust him. What's he's doing here anyway? Who invited him?"

"No one. It's Wednesday. He takes Charm to lunch on Wednesdays" was Maverick's response.

Garth's brow bunched. "And where is Charm? Why didn't she attend this meeting?"

"Said she had something more important to do," Sloan said of their sister.

"What?"

"Go shopping."

Cash chuckled. "Doesn't surprise me. So what are we going to do Garth? The decision is yours, not the old man's."

Garth threw a couple of paperclips on the table. "I never mentioned it, but I was mistaken for one of those Westmorelands once."

Maverick leaned across the table. "You were? When?"

"Last year, while I was in Rome. A young woman, a very beautiful young woman, called out to me. She thought I was someone named Riley Westmoreland."

"I can see why she thought that," Hugh said. "Take a look at this." He opened the folder he'd placed on the conference room table earlier and flipped through until he came to one photograph in particular. He pulled it out and placed it in the center of the table. "This is Riley Westmoreland."

"Damn," chorused around the table, before a shocked silence ensued.

"Take a look at the others. Pretty strong genes. Like I told Bart, all of you have a twin somewhere in that family," Hugh said. "It's—"

"Weird," Cash said, shaking his head.

"Pretty damn uncanny," Sloan added. "Makes the Westmorelands' claims believable."

"So what if we are related to these Westmorelands? What's the big deal?" Maverick asked.

"None that I can see," Sloan said.

"Then, why does the old man have a problem with it?"

"Dad's just distrustful by nature," Cash answered Maverick, as he continued to stare at the photographs.

"He fathered five sons and a daughter from six different women. If you ask me, he was too damn trusting."

"Maybe he learned his lesson, considering that some of our mothers—not calling any names—turned out to be gold diggers," Sloan said, chuckling.

Hugh shook his head. It always amazed him how well Bart's offspring got along, considering they all had different mothers. Bart had managed to get full custody of each of them before their second birthdays and he'd raised them together.

Except for Charm. She hadn't shown up until the age of fifteen. Her mother was the one woman Bart hadn't married, but the only one he had truly loved.

"As your lawyer, what do you want me to do?" Hugh asked. "Send that letter like Bart suggested?"

Garth met Hugh's gaze. "No. I believe in using more diplomacy than that. I think what has Dad so suspicious is the timing, especially with Jess running for senator," he said of their brother. "And you all know how much Dad wants that to happen. His dream has been for one of us to enter politics. What if this is some sort of scheme to ruin that?"

Garth stood and stretched out the kinks from his body. "Just to be on the safe side, I'll send Walker to check out these Westmorelands. We can trust him, and he's a good judge of character."

"But will he go?" Sloan asked. "Other than visiting us here in Fairbanks, I doubt if Walker's been off his ranch in close to ten years."

Garth drew in a deep breath and said, "He'll go if I ask him."

One

Two weeks later

"**W**hy are they sending their representative instead of meeting with us themselves?"

Dillon Westmoreland glanced across the room at his cousin Bailey. He'd figured she would be the one with questions. He had called a family meeting of his six brothers and eight cousins to apprise them of the phone call he'd received yesterday. The only person missing from this meeting was his youngest brother, Bane, who was on a special assignment somewhere with the navy SEALs. "I presume the reason they are sending someone outside their family is to play it safe, Bailey. In a way, I understand them doing so. They have no proof that what we're claiming is the truth."

"But why would we claim them as relatives if they aren't?" Bailey persisted. "When our cousin James contacted you a few years ago about our relationship with them, I don't recall you questioning him."

Dillon chuckled. "Only because James didn't give me a chance to question anything. He showed up one day at our Blue Ridge office with his sons and nephews in tow and said that we were kin. I couldn't deny a thing when looking into Dare's face, which looked just like mine."

"Um, maybe we should have tried that approach." Bailey tapped a finger to her chin. "Just showed up and surprised them."

"Rico didn't think that was a good idea. From his research, it seems the Outlaws are a pretty close-knit family who don't invite outsiders into their fold," Megan Westmoreland Claiborne said. Rico, her husband, was the private investigator hired by the Westmorelands to find members of their extended family.

"And I agreed with Rico," Dillon said. "Claiming kinship is something some people don't do easily. We're dealing with relatives whose last name is Outlaw. They had no inkling of a Westmoreland connection until Rico dropped the bomb on them. If the shoe was on the other foot and someone showed up claiming they were related to me, I would be cautious, as well."

"Well, I don't like it," Bailey said, meeting the gazes of her siblings and cousins.

"We've picked up on that, Bay," Ramsey Westmoreland, her eldest brother said, pulling her ear. He then switched his gaze to Dillon. "So when is their representative coming?"

"His name is Walker Rafferty and he's arriving tomorrow. I thought that would be perfect since everyone is home for Aidan and Jillian's wedding this weekend. The Atlanta Westmorelands will be here as well, so he'll get to meet them, too."

"What does he intend to find out about us?" Bailey wanted to know.

"That you, Bane, Adrian and Aidan are no longer hellions," Stern Westmoreland said, grinning.

"Go to—" Bailey stopped and glanced at everyone staring at her. "Go wash your face, Stern."

"Stop trying to provoke her, Stern," Dillon said, shaking his head. "Rafferty probably wants to get to know us so he can report back to them that we're an okay group of people. Don't take things personally. Like I said, it's just a precaution on their part." He paused as if an idea had come to him. "And, Bailey?"

"Yes?"

"Since you're the most apprehensive about Mr. Rafferty's visit, I want you to pick him up from the airport."

"Me?"

"Yes, you. And I expect you to make a good impression. Remember, you'll be representing the entire family."

"Bailey representing the entire family? The thought of that doesn't bother you, Dil?" Canyon Westmoreland said, laughing. "We don't want to scare him off. Hell, she might go ballistic on him if he rubs her the wrong way."

"Cut it out, Canyon. Bailey knows how to handle herself and she will make a good impression," Dillon said, ignoring his family's skeptical looks. "She'll do fine."

"Thanks for the vote of confidence, Dillon."

"You got it, Bailey."

Bailey knows how to handle herself and she will make a good impression.

Dillon's words rang through Bailey's head as she rushed into the airport fifteen minutes late. And she couldn't blame her delay on traffic.

That morning she had been called into her boss's office to be told she'd been promoted to features editor. That

called for a celebration and she'd rushed back to her desk
to call her best friend, Josette Carter. Of course Josette
had insisted they meet for lunch. And now Bailey was late
doing the one thing Dillon had trusted her to do.

But she refused to accept that she was off to a bad
start…even if she was. If Mr. Rafferty's plane was late
it would not hurt her feelings one iota. In fact today she
would consider it a blessing.

She headed toward baggage claim and paused to look
at an overhead monitor. Mr. Rafferty's plane had been on
time. Just her luck.

Upon reaching the luggage carousel for his plane, she
glanced around. She had no idea what the man looked like.
She had tried looking him up online last night and couldn't
find him. Josette had suggested Bailey make a sign with
his name, but Bailey had rolled her eyes at the idea. Now,
considering how crowded the airport was, she acknowledged that might have been a good idea.

Bailey checked out the people retrieving their luggage.
She figured the man was probably in his late forties or
early fifties. The potbellied, fiftysomething-year-old man
who kept glancing at his watch with an anxious expression
must be her guy. She was moving in his direction when a
deep husky rumble stopped her in her tracks.

"I believe you're looking for me, Miss Westmoreland."

Bailey turned and her gaze connected with a man who
filled her vision. He was tall, but that wasn't the reason
her brain cells had suddenly turned to mush; she was used
to tall men. Her brothers and cousins were tall. It was the
man's features. Too handsome for words. She quickly surmised it had to be his eyes that had made her speechless.
They were so dark they appeared a midnight blue. Just
staring into them made her pulse quicken to a degree that
ignited shivers in her stomach.

And then there was his skin tone—a smooth mahogany. He had a firm jaw and a pair of luscious-looking lips. His hair was cut low and gave him a rugged, sexy look.

Gathering her wits, she said, "And you are?"

He held his hand out to her. "Walker Rafferty."

She accepted his handshake. It was firm, filled with authority. Those things she expected. What she didn't expect was the feeling of warmth combined with a jolt of energy that surged through her body. She quickly released his hand.

"Welcome to Denver, Mr. Rafferty."

"Thanks. Walker will do."

She tried to keep her pulse from being affected by the throaty sound of his voice. "All right, Walker. And I'm—"

"Bailey Westmoreland. I know. I recognized you from Facebook."

"Really? I looked you up but didn't find a page for you."

"You wouldn't. I'm probably one of the few who don't indulge."

She couldn't help wondering what else he didn't—or did—indulge in, but decided to keep her curiosity to herself. "If you have all your bags, we can go. I'm parked right outside the terminal."

"Just lead the way."

She did and he moved into step beside her. He was certainly not what she'd expected. And her attraction to him wasn't expected, either. She usually preferred men who were clean shaven, but there was something about Walker Rafferty's neatly trimmed beard that appealed to her.

"So you're friends with the Outlaws?" she asked as they continued walking.

"Yes. Garth Outlaw and I have been best friends for as long as I can remember. I'm told by my parents our friendship goes back to the time we were both in diapers."

"Really? And how long ago was that?"

"Close to thirty-five years ago."

She nodded. That meant he was eight years older than she was. Or seven, since she had a birthday coming up in a few months.

"You look just like your picture."

She glanced at him. "What picture?"

"The one on Facebook."

She changed it often enough to keep it current. "It's supposed to work that way," she said, leading him through the exit doors. And because she couldn't hold back her thoughts she said, "So you're here to spy on us."

He stopped walking, causing her to stop, as well. "No. I'm here to get to know you."

"Same thing."

He shook his head. "No, I don't think it is."

She frowned. "Either way, you plan to report back to the Outlaws about us? Isn't that right?"

"Yes, that's right."

Her frown deepened. "They certainly sound like a suspicious bunch."

"They are. But seeing you in person makes a believer out of me."

She lifted a brow. "Why?"

"You favor Charm, Garth's sister."

Bailey nodded. "How old is Charm?"

"Twenty-three."

"Then, you're mistaken. I'm three years older so that means she favors me." Bailey then resumed walking.

Walker Rafferty kept a tight grip on the handle of his luggage while following Bailey Westmoreland to the parking lot. She was a very attractive woman. He'd known Bailey was a beauty because of her picture. But he hadn't expected that beauty to affect him with such mind-boggling intensity. It had been a while—years—since he'd been so aware of a woman. And her scent didn't help. It had such an alluring effect.

"So do you live in Fairbanks?"

He looked at her as they continued walking. Her cocoa-colored face was perfect—all of her features, including a full pair of lips, were holding his attention. The long brown hair that hung around her shoulders made her eyes appear a dark chocolate. "No, I live on Kodiak Island. It's an hour away from Fairbanks by air."

She bunched her forehead. "Kodiak Island? Never heard of the place."

He smiled. "Most people haven't, although it's the second largest island in the United States. Anchorage and Fairbanks immediately come to mind when one thinks of Alaska. But Kodiak Island is way prettier than the two of them put together. Only thing is, we have more bears living there than people."

He could tell by her expression that she thought he was teasing. "Trust me, I'm serious," he added.

She nodded, but he had a feeling she didn't believe him. "How do people get off the island?"

"The majority of them use the ferry, but air is most convenient for me. I have a small plane."

She lifted a brow. "You do?"

"Yes." There was no need to tell her that he'd learned to fly in the marines. Or that Garth had learned right along with him. What he'd told her earlier was true. He and Garth Outlaw had been friends since their diaper days and had not only gone to school together but had also attended the University of Alaska before doing a stint in the marines. The one thing Garth hadn't done with Walker was remain with him in California after they left the military. And Garth had tried his hardest to talk Walker out of staying. Too bad he hadn't listened.

He'd been back in Alaska close to ten years now and he

swore he would never leave again. Only Garth could get
him off the island this close to November, his son's birthday month. Had his son lived he would be celebrating his
eleventh birthday. Thinking of Connor sent a sharp pain
through Walker, one he always endured this time of year.

He kept walking beside Bailey, tossing looks her way.
Not only did she have striking features but she had a nice
body, as well. She looked pretty damn good in her jeans,
boots and short suede jacket.

Deciding to remove his focus from her, he switched
it to the weather. Compared to Alaska this time of year,
Denver was nice. Too damn nice. He hoped the week here
didn't spoil him.

"Does it snow here often?" he asked, to keep the conversation going. It had gotten quiet. Too quiet. And he was
afraid his mind would dwell on just how pretty she was.

"Yes, usually a lot this time of year but our worst days
are in February. That's when practically everything shuts
down. But I bet it doesn't snow here as much as in Alaska."

He chuckled. "You'd bet right. We have long, extremely
cold days. You get used to being snowed in more so than
not. If you're smart, you'll prepare for it because an abun-
dance of snow is something you can count on."

"So what do you do on Kodiak Island?" she asked.

They had reached her truck. The vehicle suited her. Although she was definitely feminine, she didn't come across
as the prissy type. He had a feeling Bailey Westmoreland
could handle just about anything, including this powerful-
looking full-size pickup. He was of the mind that there was
something innately sensuous about a woman who drove a
truck. Especially a woman who was strikingly sexy when
she got out of it.

Knowing she was waiting for an answer to his question,
he said, "I own a livestock ranch there. Hemlock Row."

"A cattle ranch?"

"No, I raise bison. They can hold their own against a bear."

"I've eaten buffalo a few times. It's good."

"Any bison from Hemlock Row is the best," he said, and didn't care if it sounded as if he was bragging. He had every right to. His family had been in the cattle business for years, but killer bears had almost made them lose everything they had. After his parents' deaths he'd refused to sell and allow Hemlock Row to become a hunting lodge or a commercial fishing farm.

"Well, you'll just have to send me some to try."

"Maybe you'll get to visit the area one day."

"Doubt it. I seldom leave Denver," she said, releasing the lock on the truck door for him.

"Why?"

"Everything I need is right here. I've visited relatives in North Carolina, Montana and Atlanta on occasion, and I've traveled to the Middle East to visit my cousin Delaney once."

"She's the one who's married to a sheikh, right?" he asked, opening the truck door.

"Jamal *was* a sheikh. Now he's king of Tehran. Evidently you've done research on the Westmorelands, so why the need to visit us?"

He held her gaze over the top of the truck. "You have a problem with me being here, Bailey?"

"Would it matter if I did?"

"Probably not, but I still want to know how you feel about it."

He watched her nibble her bottom lip as if considering what he'd said. He couldn't help studying the shape of her mouth and thinking she definitely had a luscious pair of lips.

"I guess it bothers me that the Outlaws think we'd claim

them as relatives if they weren't," she said, her words breaking into his thoughts.

"You have to understand their position. To them, the story of some woman giving up her child before dying after a train wreck sounds pretty far out there."

"As far-out as it might sound, that's what happened. Besides, all it would take is a DNA test to prove whether or not we're related. That should be easy enough."

"Personally, I don't think that's the issue. I've seen photographs of your brothers and cousins and so have the Outlaws. The resemblance can't be denied. The Westmorelands and the Outlaws favor too much for you not to be kin."

"Then, what is the issue and why are you here? If the Outlaws want to acknowledge we're related but prefer not to have anything to do with us, that's fine."

Walker liked her knack for speaking what she thought. "Not all of them feel that way, Bailey. Only Bart."

"Who's Bart?" she asked, breaking eye contact with him to get into the truck.

"Bart's their father," he answered, getting into the truck, as well. "Bart's father would have been the baby that was supposedly given to his grandmother, Amelia Outlaw."

"And Amelia never told any of them the truth about what happened?" Bailey asked, snapping her seat belt around her waist. A waist he couldn't help notice was pretty small. He could probably wrap his arms around it twice.

He snapped his seat belt on, thinking the truck smelled like her. "Evidently she didn't tell anyone."

"I wonder why?"

"She wouldn't be the first person to keep an adoption a secret, if that's what actually happened. From what Rico Claiborne said, Clarice knew she was dying and gave her baby to Amelia, who had lost her husband in that same wreck. She probably wanted to put all that behind her and start fresh with her adopted son."

After she maneuvered out of the parking lot, he decided to change the subject. "So what do you do?"

She glanced over at him. "Don't you know?"

"It wasn't on Facebook."

She chuckled. "I don't put everything online. And to answer your question, I work for my sister-in-law's magazine, *Simply Irresistible*. Ever heard of it?"

"Can't say that I have. What kind of magazine is it?"

"One for today's up-and-coming woman. We have articles on health, beauty, fashion and, of course, men."

He held her gaze when the truck came to a stop. "Why 'of course' on men?"

"Because men are so interesting."

"Are we?"

"Not really. But since some women think so, we have numerous articles about your gender."

He figured she wanted him to ask what some of those articles were, but he didn't intend to get caught in that trap. Instead, he asked, "What do you do at the magazine?"

"As of today I'm a features editor. I got promoted."

"Congratulations."

"Thanks." An easy smile touched her lips, lips that were nice to look at and would probably taste just as nice.

"I find that odd," he said, deciding to stay focused on their conversation and not her lips.

The vehicle slowed due to traffic and she looked at him. "What do you find odd?"

"That your family owns a billion-dollar company yet you don't work there."

Bailey broke eye contact with Walker. Was he in probing mode? Were her answers going to be scrutinized and reported back to the Outlaws?

Walker's questions confirmed what she'd told Dillon. Those Outlaws were too paranoid for her taste. As far as she was concerned, kin or no kin, they had crossed the line by sending Walker Rafferty here.

But for now she would do as Dillon had asked and tolerate the man's presence…and his questions. "There's really nothing odd about it. There's no law that says I have to work at my family's corporation. Besides, I have rules."

"Rules?"

"Yes," she said, bringing the truck to a stop for a school bus. She looked over at him. "I'm the youngest in the family and while growing up, my brothers and cousins felt it was their God-given right to stick their noses in my business. A little too much to suit me. They only got worse the older I got. I put up with it at home and couldn't imagine being around them at the office, too."

"So you're not working at your family's company because you need space?"

"That's not the only reason," she informed him before he got any ideas about her and her family not getting along. "I'm not working at Blue Ridge Land Management because I chose a career that had nothing to do with real estate. Although I have my MBA, I also have a degree in journalism, so I work at *Simply Irresistible*."

She was getting a little annoyed that she felt the need to explain anything to him. "I'm sure you have a lot of questions about my family and I'm certain Dillon will be happy to answer them. We have nothing to hide."

"You're assuming that I think you do."

"I'm not assuming anything, Walker."

He didn't say anything while she resumed driving. Out of the corner of her eye, she saw he'd settled comfortably in the seat and was gazing out the window. "First time in Denver?" she asked.

"Yes. Nice-looking city."

"I think so." She wished he didn't smell so good. The scent of his aftershave was way too nice.

"Earlier you mentioned rules, Bailey."

"What about them?" She figured most people had some sort of rules they lived by. However, she would be the first to admit that others were probably not as strict about abiding by theirs as she was about abiding by hers. "I've discovered it's best to have rules about what I will do and not do. One of my rules is not to answer a lot of questions, no matter who's asking. I put that rule in place because of my brother Zane. He's always been too nosy when it came to me and he has the tendency to take being overprotective to another level."

"Sounds like a typical big brother."

"There's nothing typical about Zane, trust me. He just likes being a pain. Because of him, I had to adopt that rule."

"Name another rule."

"Never get serious about anyone who doesn't love Westmoreland Country as much as I do."

"Westmoreland Country?"

"It's the name the locals gave the area where my family lives. It's beautiful and I don't plan to leave. Ever."

"So in other words, the man you marry has to want to live there, too. In Westmoreland Country?"

"Yes, if such a man exists, which I doubt." Deciding to move the conversation off herself and back onto the Outlaws, she asked, "So how many Outlaws are there?"

"Their father is Bart and he was an only child. He has five sons—Garth, Jess, Cash, Sloan and Maverick—and one daughter, Charm."

"I understand they own a freight company."

"They do."

"All of them work there?"

"Yes. Bart wouldn't have it any other way. He retired last year and Garth is running things now."

"Well, you're in luck with my brother Aidan getting married this weekend. You'll see more Westmorelands than you probably counted on."

"I'm looking forward to it."

Bailey was tempted to look at him but she kept her eyes on the road. She had to add *sexy* to his list of attributes, no matter how much she preferred not to. Josette would be the first to say it was only fair to give a deserving man his just rewards. However, Bailey hated that she found him so attractive. But what woman wouldn't? Manly, handsome and sexy was a hot combination that could play havoc on any woman's brain.

"So were you born in Alaska or are you a transplant?" she asked him out of curiosity.

"I was born in Alaska on the same property I own. My grandfather arrived in Fairbanks as a military man in the late 1940s. When his time in the military ended he stayed and purchased over a hundred thousand acres for his bride, a woman who could trace her family back to Alaska when it was owned by Russia. What about your family?"

A smile touched Bailey's lips. "I know for certain I can't trace my grandmother's family back to when Alaska was owned by Russia, if that's what you're asking."

It wasn't and she knew it, but couldn't resist teasing him. It evidently amused him if the deep chuckle that rumbled from his throat was anything to go by. The sound made her nipples tingle and a shiver race through her stomach. If the sound of his chuckle could do this to her, what would his touch do?

She shook her head, forcing such thoughts from her mind. She had just met the man. Why was she feeling such a strong attraction to him? This wasn't usually how it worked with her and men. Most of the time she thought of them as a nuisance, not an attraction.

"You okay?"

The truck had slowed down for traffic again and she took a quick look over at him. She wished she hadn't when she met those gorgeous dark eyes. "Yes, why would you think I'm not?"

"You shivered just now."

He had to have been watching her mighty close to have known that. "Just a little chill."

"Then, maybe I should turn up the heat."

Turn up the heat? She immediately jumped to conclusions until he reached out toward her console and turned the knob. *Oh, he meant that heat.* Within seconds, a blast of warmth flowed through the truck's vents.

"Better?"

"Yes. Thanks," she said, barely able to think. She needed to get a grip. Deciding to go back to their conversation by answering his earlier question, she said, "As far as my family goes, we're still trying to find out everything we can about my great-grandfather Raphel. We didn't even know he had a twin brother until the Atlanta Westmorelands showed up to claim us. Then Dillon began digging into Raphel's past, which led him to Wyoming. Over the years we've put most of the puzzle pieces together, which is how we found out about the Outlaws."

Bailey was glad when she finally saw the huge marker ahead. She brought the truck to a stop and looked over at him. "Welcome to Westmoreland Country, Walker Rafferty."

Two

An hour later Walker stood at the windows in the guest bedroom he'd been given in Dillon Westmoreland's home. As far as Walker could see, there was land, land and more land. Then there were the mountains, a very large valley and a huge lake that ran through most of the property. From what he'd seen so far, Westmoreland Country was beautiful. Almost as beautiful as his spread in Kodiak. Almost, but not quite. As far as he was concerned, there was no place as breathtaking as Hemlock Row, his family home.

He'd heard the love and pride in Bailey's voice when she talked about her home. He fully understood because he felt the same way about his home. Thirteen years ago a woman had come between him and his love for Hemlock Row, but never again. Now he worked twice as hard every day on his ranch to make up for the years he'd lost. Years when he should have been there, working alongside his father instead of thinking he could fit into a world he had no business in.

But then no matter how much he wished it, he couldn't change the past. Wishing he'd never met Kalyn wouldn't do because if he hadn't met her, there never would have been Connor. And regardless of everything, especially all the lies and deceit, his son had been the one person who'd made Walker's life complete.

Bringing his thoughts back to the present, Walker moved away from the window to unpack. Earlier, he'd met Dillon and Ramsey, along with their wives, siblings and cousins. From his own research, Walker knew the Denver Westmorelands' story. It was heartbreaking yet heartwarming. They had experienced sorrows and successes. Both Dillon's and Ramsey's parents had been killed in a plane crash close to twenty years ago, leaving Dillon, who was the eldest, and Ramsey, the second eldest, to care for their thirteen siblings and cousins.

Dillon's parents had had seven sons—Dillon, Micah, Jason, Riley, Canyon, Stern and Brisbane. Ramsey's parents had eight children, of which there were five sons—Ramsey, Zane, Derringer and the twins, Aidan and Adrian—and three daughters—Megan, Gemma and Bailey. The satisfying ending to the story was that Dillon and Ramsey had somehow managed to keep all their siblings and cousins together and raise them to be respectable and law-abiding adults. Of course, that didn't mean there hadn't been any hiccups along the way. Walker's research had unveiled several. It seemed the twins—Adrian and Aidan—along with Bailey and Bane, the youngest of the bunch, had been a handful while growing up. But they'd all made something of themselves.

There were definitely a lot of Westmorelands here in Denver, with more on the way to attend a wedding this weekend. The ones he'd met so far were friendly enough. The ease with which they'd welcomed him into their group was pretty amazing, considering they were well aware of the reason he was here. The only one who seemed bothered by his visit was Bailey.

Bailey.

Okay, he could admit he'd been attracted to her from the first. He'd seen her when she'd entered the baggage claim area, walking fast, that mass of curly brown hair slinging around her shoulders with every step she took. She'd had a determined look on her face, which had made her appear adorable. And the way the overhead lights hit her features had only highlighted what a gorgeous young woman she was.

He rubbed his hand down his face. The key word was *young*. But in this case, age didn't matter because Kalyn had taught him a lesson he would never forget when it came to women, of any age. So why had he suddenly begun feeling restless and edgy? And why was he remembering how long it had been since he'd been with a woman?

Trying to dismiss that question from his mind, Walker refocused on the reason he was here…as a favor to Garth. He would find out what his best friend needed to know and return to Kodiak. Already he'd concluded that the Westmorelands were more friendly and outgoing than their Alaskan cousins. The Outlaws tended to be on the reserved side, although Walker would be the first to say they had loosened up since Bart retired.

Walker knew Garth better than anyone else did, and although Garth wasn't as suspicious as Bart, Garth had an empire to protect. An empire that Garth's grandfather had worked hard to build and that the Outlaws had come close to losing last year because Bart had made a bad business decision.

Still, Walker had known the Outlaws long enough to know they didn't take anything at face value, which was why he was here. And so far the one thing he knew for certain was that the Westmorelands and the Outlaws were

related. The physical resemblance was too astounding for
them not to be. Whether or not the Westmorelands had an
ulterior motive to claiming the Outlaws as relatives was
yet to be seen.

Personally, he doubted it, especially after talking to
Megan Westmoreland Claiborne. He'd heard the deep emotion in her voice when she'd told him of her family's quest
to find as many family members as they could once they'd
known Raphel Westmoreland hadn't been an only child
as they'd assumed. She was certain there were even more
Westmoreland relatives out there, other than the Outlaws,
since they had recently discovered that Raphel and Regi-
nald had an older brother by a different mother.

In Walker's estimation, the search initiated by the Westmorelands to find relatives had been a sincere and heartfelt
effort to locate family. It had nothing to do with elbowing
in on the Outlaws' wealth or sabotaging Jess's chances of
becoming an Alaskan senator, as Bart assumed.

Walker moved away from the window the exact moment his cell phone rang. He frowned when he saw the
caller was none other than Bart Outlaw. Why would the
old man be calling him?

"Yes, Bart?"

"So what have you found out, son?"

Walker almost laughed out loud. *Son?* He shook his
head. The only time Bart was extranice was when someone had something he wanted. And Walker knew Bart
wanted information. Unfortunately, Bart wouldn't like
what Walker had to say, since Bart hated being wrong.

"Found out about what, Bart?" Walker asked, deciding
to be elusive. He definitely wouldn't tell Bart anything before talking to Garth.

He heard the grumble in Bart's voice when he said,
"You know what, Walker. I'm well aware of the reason

Garth sent you to Denver. I hope you've found out something to discredit them."

Walker lifted a brow. "Discredit them?"

"Yes. The last thing the Outlaws need are people popping up claiming to be relatives and accusing us of being who we aren't."

"By that you mean saying you're Westmorelands instead of Outlaws?"

"Yes. We *are* Outlaws. My grandfather was Noah Outlaw. It's his blood that's running through my veins and no other man's. I want you to remember that, Walker, and I want you to do whatever you have to do to make sure I'm right."

Walker shook his head at the absurdity of what Bart was saying. "How am I to do that, Bart?"

"Find a way and keep this between us. There's no reason to mention anything to Garth." Then he hung up.

Frowning, Walker held the cell phone in his hand for a minute. That was just like Bart. He gave an order and expected it to be followed. No questions asked. Shaking his head, Walker placed a call to Garth, who picked up on the second ring.

"Yes, Walker? How are things going?"

"Your father just called. We might have a problem."

"I heard Walker Rafferty is a looker."

Bailey lifted the coffee cup to her lips as Josette slid into the seat across from her. Sharing breakfast was something they did at least two to three times a week, their schedules permitting. Josette was a freelance auditor whose major client was the hospital where Bailey's sister Megan worked as a doctor of anesthesiology.

"I take it you saw Megan this morning," Bailey said, wishing she could refute what Josette had heard. Unfortunately, she couldn't because it was true. Walker was a looker. Sinfully so.

"Yes, I had an early appointment at the hospital this morning and ran into your sister. She was excited that the Outlaws had reached out to your family."

Bailey rolled her eyes. "Sending someone instead of coming yourself is not what I consider reaching out. One of the Outlaws should have come themselves. Sending someone else is so tacky."

"Yes, but they could have ignored the situation altogether. Some people get touchy when others claim them as family. You never know the reason behind it."

Since Bailey and Josette were pretty much regulars at McKays, the waitress slid a cup of coffee in front of Josette, who smiled up at the woman. "Thanks, Amanda." After taking a sip, Josette turned her attention back to Bailey. "So tell me about him."

"Not much to tell. He looks okay. Seems nice enough."

"That's all you know about him, that he looks okay and seems nice enough?"

"Is there something else I should know?"

"Yes. Is he single? Married? Divorced? Have any children? What does he do for a living? Does he still live with his mother?"

Bailey smiled. "I didn't ask his marital status but can only assume he's single because he wasn't wearing a ring. As far as what he does for a living, he's a rancher. I do know that much. He raises bison."

"I take it he wasn't too talkative."

Bailey took another sip of coffee as she thought of the time she'd spent with Walker yesterday. "He was okay. We had a polite conversation."

"Polite?" Josette asked with a chuckle. "You?"

Bailey grinned. She could see why Josette found that amusing. Bailey wasn't known for being polite. "I prom-

ised Dillon I'd be on my best behavior even if it killed me."
She glanced at her watch. "I've got to run. I'm meeting
with the reporter taking my old job at nine."

"Okay, see you later."

After Bailey walked out of the restaurant, she couldn't
help but think about Josette's questions. There was a lot
Bailey didn't know about Walker.

She'd remedy that when she saw him later.

Walker was standing in front of Dillon's barn when
Bailey's truck pulled up. Moments later he watched as
she got out of the vehicle. Although he tried to ignore it,
he felt a deep flutter in the pit of his stomach at seeing her
again. Today, like yesterday, he was very much aware of
how sensuous she looked. Being attracted to her shouldn't
be anything he couldn't handle. So why was he having a
hard time doing so?

Why had he awakened that morning looking for her at
the breakfast table, assuming she lived with Dillon and
his wife, since she didn't have her own place? Later, he'd
found out from her brother Ramsey that Bailey floated,
living with whichever of her brothers, sisters or cousins
best fit her current situation. But now that most of her relatives had married, she stayed in her sister Gemma's house
since Gemma and her husband, Callum, had their primary
home in Australia.

He continued to watch her, somewhat surprised by his
own actions. He wasn't usually the type to waste his time
ogling a woman. But with Bailey it couldn't be helped.
There was something about her that demanded a man's attention regardless of whether he wanted to give it or not.
Her brothers and cousins would probably skin him alive if
they knew just where his thoughts were going right now.

The cold weather didn't seem to bother her as she moved
away from the truck without putting on her coat. Dressed

in a long-sleeved shirt, a long pencil skirt that complimented her curves and a pair of black leather boots, she
looked ready to walk the runway.

Squinting in the sun, he watched as she walked around
the truck, checking out each tire. She flipped her hair away
from her shoulders, and he imagined running his fingers
through every strand before urging her body closer to his.
There was no doubt in his mind he would love to sample
the feel of their bodies pressed together. Then he would
go for her mouth and—

"Walker? What are you doing here?"

Glad she had interrupted his thoughts, he replied, "I'm
an invited guest, remember?"

She frowned as she approached him. "Invited? Not the
way I remember it. But what I'm asking is why are you out
here at the barn by yourself? In the cold? Where is everyone? And why didn't you say something when I got out of
the truck to let me know you were over here?"

He leaned back against the barn's door. "Evening, Bailey. You sure do ask a lot of questions."

She glared at him. "Do I?"

"Yes, especially for someone who just told me yesterday
that one of her rules is not answering a lot of questions,
no matter who's asking. What if I told you that I happen
to have that same rule?"

She lifted an angry chin. Was it his imagination or was
she even prettier when she was mad? "I have a right to ask
you anything I want," she said.

He shook his head. "I beg to differ. However, out of
courtesy and since nothing you've asked has crossed any
lines, I'll answer. The reason I'm outside by the barn is because I just returned from riding with Ramsey and Zane.
They both left for home and I wasn't ready to go in just
yet."

"Zane and Ramsey actually left you out here alone?"

"Yes, you sound surprised that they would. It seems there are some members of your family who trust me. I guess your brothers figure their horses and sheep are safe with me," he said, holding her gaze.

"I didn't insinuate—"

"Excuse me, but I didn't finish answering *all* your questions," he interrupted her, and had to keep from grinning when she shut her mouth tightly. That same mouth he'd envisioned kissing earlier. "The reason I didn't say anything when you got out of the truck just now was because you seemed preoccupied with checking out your tires. Is there a problem?"

"One needs air. But when I looked up from my tires you were staring at me. Why?"

She had to know he was attracted to her. What man in his right mind wouldn't be? She was beautiful, desirable—alluring. And he didn't think the attraction was one-sided. A man knew when a woman was interested.

But he didn't want her interest, nor did he want to be interested in her. He refused to tell her that the reason he hadn't said anything was because he'd been too mesmerized to do so.

"I was thinking again about how much you and Charm favor one another. You'll see for yourself when you meet her."

"*If* I meet her."

"Don't sound so doubtful. I'm sure the two of you will eventually meet."

"Don't sound so sure of that, Walker."

He liked the sound of his name from her lips. Refusing to go tit for tat with her, he changed the subject. "So how was your day at work, Bailey?"

Stubbornly, Bailey told herself he really didn't give a damn how her day went. So why was he asking? Why did she find him as annoying as he was handsome? And why, when she'd looked up to see him staring at her, had she felt something she'd never felt before?

There was something so startling about his eyes that her reaction had been physical. For a second, she'd imagined the stroke of his fingers in her hair, the whisper of his heated breath across her lips, the feel of his body pressed hard against hers.

Why was her imagination running wild? She barely knew this man. Her family barely knew him. Yet they had welcomed him to Westmoreland Country without thinking things through. At least, that was her opinion. Was her family so desperate to find more relatives that they had let their guard down? She recalled days when a stranger on their land meant an alarm went out to everyone. Back then, they'd never known when someone from social services would show up for one of their surprise visits.

Knowing Walker was waiting for her to answer, she finally said, "It went well. It was my first day as a features editor and I think I handled things okay. You might even say I did an outstanding job today."

He chuckled. "No lack of confidence on your part, I see."

"None whatsoever." It was dusk and being outside with him, standing by the barn in the shadows, seemed way too intimate for her peace of mind. But there was something she needed to know, something that had been on her mind ever since Josette had brought it up that morning.

Not being one to beat around the bush when it came to things she really wanted to know, she asked, "Are you married, Walker?"

Walker stared at her, trying to fight the feel of air being sucked from his lungs. Where the hell had that question come from? Regardless, the answer should have been easy enough to give, especially since he hadn't been truly married even when he'd thought he had been. How could there be a real marriage when one of the parties took betrayal to a whole new level?

Silence reigned. Bailey had to be wondering why he hadn't answered. He shook off the unpleasant memories. "No. I'm not married." And then he decided to add, "Nor do I have a girlfriend. Any reason you want to know?"

She shrugged those beautiful shoulders that should be wearing a coat. "No. Just curious. You aren't wearing a wedding ring."

"No, I'm not."

"But that doesn't mean anything these days."

"You're right. Wearing a wedding ring doesn't mean anything."

He could tell by her frown that she hadn't expected him to agree with her. "So you're one of those types."

"And what type is that?"

"A man who has no respect for marriage or what it stands for."

Walker couldn't force back the wave of anger that suddenly overtook him. If only she knew how wrong she was. "You don't know me. And since you don't, I suggest you keep your damn assumptions to yourself."

Then, with clenched teeth, he walked off.

Three

The next morning Bailey sat behind the huge desk in her new office and sipped a cup of her favorite coffee. Yesterday had been her move-in day and she had pretty much stayed out of the way while the maintenance crew had shifted all the electronic equipment from her old office into this one. Now everything was in order, including her new desk, on top of which sat a beautiful plant from Ramsey and Chloe.

She couldn't help thinking, *You've come a long way, baby*. And only she and her family truly knew just how far she'd come.

She'd had some rebellious years and she would be the first to admit a little revolutionary spirit still lived within her. She was better at containing it these days. But she still liked rousing her family every once in a while.

Growing up as the youngest Westmoreland had had its perks as well as its downfalls. Over the past few years, most of her family members had shifted their attention away from her and focused on their spouses and children. She adored the women and men her cousins, brothers and sisters had married. And when she was around her family she felt loved.

She thought of her cousin Riley's new baby, who had been born last year. And there were still more babies on the way. A whole new generation of Denver Westmorelands. That realization had hit her like a ton of bricks when she'd held Ramsey and Chloe's daughter in her arms. Her first niece, Susan, named after Bailey's mother.

Bailey had looked down at Susan and prayed that her niece never suffered the pain of losing both parents like Bailey had. The agony and grief were something no one should have to go through. Bailey hadn't handled the pain well. None of the Westmorelands had, but it had affected her, the twins—Adrian and Aidan—and Bane the worst because they'd been so young.

Bailey cringed when she thought of some of the things she'd done, all the filthy words that had come out of her mouth. She appreciated her family, especially Dillon and Ramsey, for not giving up on her. Dillon had even taken on the State of Colorado when social services had wanted to take her, Bane and the twins away and put them in foster care.

He had hired an attorney to fight to keep them even with all the trouble the four of them were causing around town. Because somehow he'd understood. Somehow he'd known their despicable behavior was driven by the pain of losing their parents and that deep down they weren't bad kids.

"Little hell-raisers" was what the good people of Denver used to call them. She knew it was a reputation the four of them were now trying to live down, although it wasn't always easy. Take last night, for instance.

Walker Rafferty had almost pushed her into reacting

like her old self. She hated men who messed around after marriage. As far as she was concerned, the ones who messed around before marriage weren't any better but at least they didn't have a wedding ring on their finger.

Pushing away from her desk, she moved to the window. Downtown Denver was beautiful, especially today, seeing it from her new office. The buildings were tall, massive. As far as she was concerned, no other city had more magnificent skyscrapers. But even the breathtaking view couldn't make her forget Walker's callous remark.

Just like Bailey would never forget the pain and torment Josette had suffered while being married to Myles. Against their parents' wishes the two had married right out of high school, thinking love would conquer all as long as they were together. Within a year, Josette found out Myles was involved with another woman. To add insult to injury, he'd blamed Josette for his deceit, saying that it was because she'd decided to take night classes to get a college degree that she'd come home one night to find him in their bed with another woman. A woman who happened to be living in the apartment across the hall.

That was why Bailey had been so mad about Walker's insinuations that wearing a wedding ring meant nothing to a man. She'd been so angry that she'd only hung around Dillon's place long enough to hug his sons, Denver and Dade, before leaving.

It was obvious that Walker was just as mad at her as she was with him, but she didn't have a clue as to why. Yes, maybe her reaction had been a bit too strong, but seriously, she didn't give a royal damn. She called things the way she saw them. If he hadn't meant what he said, he should not have said it.

The beeping of the phone on her desk got her attention and she quickly crossed the room to answer it. It was an interoffice call from Lucia. Ramsey's wife, Chloe, was the magazine's founder and CEO but it was Chloe's best friend Lucia who ran things as editor in chief. Lucia was married to Bailey's brother Derringer. Although it was nice having her sisters-in-law as first and second in command at the magazine, it also put a lot of pressure on Bailey to prove that whatever accolades and achievements she received were earned and well deserved and not the result of favoritism. Just because Chloe and Lucia were Westmorelands, that didn't mean Bailey deserved preferential treatment of any kind. And she wouldn't have it any other way.

"Yes, Lucia?"

"Hi, Bailey. Chloe stopped by and wants to see you."

Bailey raised an arched brow. What could have brought Chloe out of Westmoreland Country so early today? It wasn't even nine in the morning yet. After marrying Ramsey, Chloe had pretty much decided to be a sheep rancher's wife and rarely came into the office these days.

Bailey slid into her jacket. "Okay. I'll be right there."

Deciding to take the longest route back to Dillon's place, Walker rode the horse and enjoyed the beauty of the countryside. There was a lot about Westmoreland Country that reminded him of Kodiak Island, minus the extremely cold weather, of course. Although the weather here was cold, it was nothing compared to the harsh winters he endured. It was the middle of October and back home the amount of snowfall was quadruple what they had here.

But the differences in the weather weren't what was bothering him today. What bothered him today had everything to do with the dreams he'd had last night. Dreams of Bailey. And that talk they'd had by the barn.

Even now the memory of their conversation made him angry. She'd had no right to assume anything about him. No right at all. She didn't know him. Had no idea the hell he'd been through or the pain he'd suffered, and was still suffering, after almost ten years. Nor did she have any idea what he'd lost.

By the lake, he slowed the horse and took a deep breath. The mountain air was cleansing; he wished it could cleanse his soul, as well. After bringing the horse to a stop he dismounted and stared at the valley below. *Awesome* was the only word he could use to describe what he saw.

And even though he was mad as hell with Bailey, a part of him thought she was pretty awesome, as well. What other way was there to describe a woman who could rile his anger and still star in his erotic dreams? He had awakened several times during the night with an erection. It had been years since that had happened. Not since he'd returned to Kodiak from California.

He had basically thrown himself into working the ranch, first out of guilt for not being there when his father had needed him, and then as a therapeutic way to deal with the loss of Connor. There were some days he'd worked from sunup to sundown. And on those nights when his body had needed a woman it had been for pleasure and nothing else. Passionate but emotionless sex had become his way of life when it came to relationships, but even that had been years ago.

Walker no longer yearned for the type of marriage his parents and grandparents had shared. He was convinced those kinds of unions didn't exist anymore. If they did, they were the exception and not the norm. He would, however, admit to noticing the ease with which the Westmoreland men openly adored their wives, wearing their hearts on their sleeves as if they were a band of honor. So, okay, Walker would include the Westmorelands in the exceptions.

He remounted the horse to head back. Thoughts of Bailey hadn't ended with his dreams. Even with the light of day, she'd invaded his thoughts. That wasn't good.

He had told Dillon he would leave the Monday after this weekend's wedding, but now he figured it would be best if he returned to Kodiak right after the wedding. The farther, and the sooner, he got away from Bailey, the better.

He'd learned enough about the Westmorelands and would tell Garth what he thought, regardless of Bart's feelings on the matter. If Bart thought he could pressure Walker to do otherwise, then he was mistaken.

Walker had nothing to lose since he'd lost it all already.

Bailey walked into Lucia's office to find her sisters-in-law chatting and enjoying cups of coffee. Not for the first time Bailey thought her brothers Ramsey and Derringer had truly lucked out when they'd married these two. Besides being beautiful, both were classy women who could be admired for their accomplishments. Real role models. The two had met at a college in Florida and had remained best friends since. The idea that they'd married brothers was remarkable, especially since the brothers were as different as day and night. Ramsey was older and had always been the responsible type. Derringer had earned a reputation as a womanizer of the third degree. Personally, Bailey had figured he would never settle down and marry. Now not only was he happily married but he was also the father of a precious little boy named Ringo. He had stepped into the role of family man as if he'd been made for it.

Chloe glanced up, saw Bailey standing in the doorway, smiled and crossed the room to give her a hug. "Bay, how are you? You rushed in and out of Dillon's place last night. We barely spoke, let alone held a conversation. How's day two in your new position?"

Bailey returned her sister-in-law's smile. "Great. I'm

ready to roll my sleeves up and bring in those feature stories that will grow our readership."

Chloe beamed. "That's good to hear. I wanted to congratulate you on your promotion and let you know how proud I am of you."

"Thanks, Chloe." Bailey couldn't help but be touched by Chloe's words. She had begun working for the company as a part-timer in between her classes at the university. She had liked it so much that she'd changed her major to journalism and hadn't regretted doing so. It was Chloe, a proponent of higher education, who had encouraged her to also get her MBA.

"So what brings you out of Westmoreland Country so early?"

"I'm meeting Pam in a little while. She wants me to sit in on several interviews she's hosting today. She's hiring a director for her school."

Bailey nodded. Dillon's wife, Pam, was a former actress and had opened an acting school in her hometown of Gamble, Wyoming, a few years ago. The success of that school had led her to open a second one in Denver.

Taking her by the arm, Chloe said, "Come sit with us a minute. Share a cup of coffee and tell me how you like your office."

"I love it! Thanks to the both of you. The view is simply stunning."

"It is, isn't it?" Lucia said, smiling. "That used to be my office and I regretted giving it up. But I have to admit I have a fantastic view in here, as well."

"Yes, you certainly do," Bailey said, agreeing, glancing around the room that was double the size of her office. When her gaze landed on Lucia's computer screen, Bailey went still.

"Recognize him?" Lucia asked, adjusting the image of a face until it took up the full screen.

Bailey sucked in a deep breath as she felt the rapid thud of her pulse. Even if the clean-shaven face had thrown her for a quick second, the gorgeous eyes staring at her were a dead giveaway, not to mention that smile.

"It's Walker Rafferty," she said. He looked years younger, yet his features, sharp and sculpted, were just as handsome.

Chloe nodded, coming to stand beside her. "Yes, that's him. At the time these photos were taken most people knew him as Ty Reklaw, an up-and-coming heartthrob in Hollywood."

Shocked, Bailey looked back at the computer screen. Walker used to be an actor? No way. The man barely said anything and seemed to keep to himself, although she knew he'd formed a pretty solid friendship with her brothers and male cousins.

What had Chloe just said? He'd been an up-and-coming heartthrob in Hollywood? Bailey studied his image. Yes, she could definitely believe that. His grin was irresistibly devastating, to the point where she felt goose bumps form on her arms.

She glanced back at Chloe and Lucia. "He's an actor?"

"He used to be, around ten years ago and he had quite a following. But then Ty Reklaw left Hollywood and never looked back," Chloe said, sitting back down in her chair.

A frown bunched Bailey's forehead. "Reklaw? As in Reklaw, Texas?"

Lucia chuckled as she poured Bailey a cup of coffee. "I doubt it. Probably Reklaw as in the name Walker spelled backward. You know how movie stars are when they don't want to use their real names."

Bailey's gaze narrowed as an idea popped into her head. "Are you sure Walker Rafferty is his real name?"

"Yes. I asked Dillon."

Bailey's brow raised. "Dillon knew who he was?"

"Only after Pam told him. She remembered Walker

from the time she was in Hollywood but she doubted he remembered her since their paths never crossed."

Bailey nodded. Yes, she could imagine any woman remembering Walker. "So he used to be an actor with a promising future. Why did he leave?"

Lucia took a sip of her coffee. "Pam said everyone assumed it was because of the death of his wife and son. They were killed in a car accident."

"Oh, my God," Bailey said. "How awful."

"Yes, and according to Pam it was quite obvious whenever he and his wife were seen together that he loved and adored her. His son had celebrated his first birthday just days before the accident occurred," Lucia said. "The loss was probably too great and he never recovered from it."

"I can understand that." Having lost both her parents in a tragic death a part of her could feel his pain. She reflected on their conversation last night when she'd asked if he was married. He'd said no and hadn't told her he was a widower.

She then remembered the rest of their conversation, the one that had left them both angry. From his comment one might have thought the sanctity of marriage didn't mean anything to him. Or had she only assumed that was what he'd meant? She shuddered at the thought.

"Bailey? Are you okay?"

She looked up at the two women staring at her. "Not sure. I might have offended Walker big-time last night."

"Why? What happened?" Lucia asked with a look that said she wished she didn't have to ask.

Bailey shrugged. "I might have jumped to conclusions about him and his attitude about marriage and said something based on my assumptions. How was I to know he'd lost his wife? I guess he said what he did because the thought of marrying again is painful for him."

"Probably since, according to Pam, he was a dedicated husband and father, even with his rising fame."

Bailey drew in a deep breath, feeling completely awful. When would she learn to stop jumping to conclusions about everything? Dillon and Ramsey had definitely warned her enough about doing that. For some reason she was quick to automatically assume the worst about people.

"Is that why you rushed in and out of Dillon and Pam's place last night? Because you and Walker had words?" Chloe asked.

"Yes. At the time I was equally mad with him. You know how I feel about men who mess around. Before marriage or after marriage."

Chloe nodded. "Yes, Bailey. I think we all know. You gave your poor brothers and cousins hell about the number of girlfriends they had."

"Well, I'm just glad they came to their senses and settled down and married." Bailey began pacing and nervously nibbled her bottom lip. Moments later she stopped and looked at the two women. "I need to apologize to him."

"Yes, you do," both Lucia and Chloe agreed simultaneously.

Bailey took a sip of her coffee as a question came to mind. "If Walker was so hot in Hollywood, then why don't I remember him?"

Lucia smiled. "If I recall, ten years ago you were too busy hanging with Bane and getting into all kinds of trouble. So I'm not surprised you don't know who was hot and who was not. I admit that although I remember him, he looks different now. Still handsome but more mature and definitely a lot more rugged. The beard he wears now makes him nearly unrecognizable. I would not have recalled who he was if Pam hadn't mentioned it. Of course when she did I couldn't wait to look him up this morning."

"Was he in several movies?" Bailey asked. She intended to find any movies he'd appeared in as soon as she left work.

"No, just two. One was a Matthew Birmingham flick, where Walker played opposite actress Carmen Atkins, as her brother. That was his very first. He was hot and his acting was great," Chloe said, smiling. "According to Pam, although he didn't get an award nomination, there are those who thought he should have. But what he did get was a lot of attention from women and other directors in Hollywood. It didn't take him long to land another role in a movie directed by Clint Eastwood. A Western. He'd just finished filming when his wife and son were killed. I don't think he hung around for the premiere. He left for Alaska and never returned."

Bailey didn't say anything. She was thinking about how to get back in Walker's good graces. "I'll apologize when I see him tonight."

"Good luck," Chloe said, chuckling. "When I left this morning, Thorn and his brothers and cousins had arrived for the wedding and you know what that means."

Yes, she knew. There would be a card game tonight. Men only. And she had a feeling Walker would be invited. Then she had an idea. For the past ten years Walker had lived on his ranch on that remote island. He'd indicated last night that he wasn't married and didn't have a steady girlfriend, which meant he was a loner. That made him just the type of man she needed to interview for one of the magazine's spring issues. She could see him being the feature story. She'd wait and share her idea with Chloe and Lucia until she had all the details worked out.

Bailey then recalled that Walker would be returning to Alaska on Monday after the wedding. That didn't give her much time. She looked back down at Walker's photo.

Getting an exclusive interview with him would definitely mean big sales for the magazine.

She took another sip of her coffee. Now, if she could only get Walker to agree.

Four

Walker threw out a card before glancing at the closed door. How many times had he done that tonight? And why was he expecting Bailey to show up at a men-only card game? The main reason was because it was Bailey, and from what he'd heard from her brothers and cousins, Bailey did whatever Bailey wanted to do. But he'd heard more fondness than annoyance in their voices and figured they wouldn't want it any other way.

So here he was, at what had to be close to midnight, in what was known as Dillon's man cave, playing cards with a bunch of Westmorelands. He would admit that over the past three days he'd gotten to know the Denver Westmorelands pretty well, and today he'd met their cousins from Atlanta, which included those living in Montana.

Walker couldn't help but chuckle at Bart's accusation that the Westmorelands had targeted the Outlaws for monetary gain. Walker knew for a fact that wasn't true. Even if their land development company wasn't making them

millions, from the talk around the table, the horse training business a few of the cousins owned was also doing
extremely well.

"I hear you chuckling over there, Walker. Does that
mean you have a good hand?"

He glanced over at Zane and smiled. "If I did you'd be
the last person to know until it counted."

That got a laugh from the others. In a way, he was surprised at the ease he felt being around them, even those
Westmorelands he'd only met that day. When he'd returned
to Kodiak from his stint in Hollywood, he'd shut himself
off from everyone except the Outlaws and those members
of the community he'd considered family. As an only child,
he wasn't used to a huge family, but he was being educated
about how one operated, Westmoreland-style.

Thorn was telling everyone about the bike he'd just built
for a celebrity. Walker just continued to study his hand. He
could have added to the conversation, since he happened
to know the man personally. But he stayed silent. That was
a life he'd rather not remember.

Walker heard the knock on the door and all it took was
the tingle that moved up his arm to let him know it was
Bailey. The mere thought that he could want her with such
intensity should have frozen him cold, especially after
what she'd accused him of last night. Instead, the opposite
was happening. He had dreamed of her, allowed her to invade his mind all day, and now his body was responding
in a way it did whenever a man wanted a woman.

"Come in," Dillon yelled out. "And whoever you are,
you better be a male."

Bailey stuck her head in the door. "Sorry to disappoint
you, Dil. I decided to check and make sure all of you are
still alive and in one piece. I can just imagine how much
money has been lost about now," she said with a grin as
she stepped into the room.

Walker was the only one who bothered to look up at her. She was gorgeous. Her hair hung like soft waves across her shoulders and her outfit, a pair of jeans and a blue pullover sweater, emphasized her curves, making her look feminine and sexy as hell.

All he could do was stare at her, and then she met his eyes. Bam! The moment their gazes connected he felt something slam into him. He was sure it had the same effect on her. It was as if they were the only two people in the room, and he was glad her family was more interested in studying their cards than studying them.

One of the things he noticed was the absence of that spark of anger in her eyes. It had definitely been there last night. Instead, he saw something else, something that had heat drumming through every inch of his body. Had frissons of fire racing up his spine. Was he imagining it?

"Go away, Bay. You'll bring me bad luck," wailed her cousin Durango, who'd flown in from Montana. He held his gaze steady on the cards in his hand.

"You're probably losing big-time anyway," she said, chuckling, breaking eye contact with Walker to look at Durango. "Another reason I'm here is to rescue Walker." Her gaze returned to Walker. "He's probably tired of your company about now, but is too nice to say so. So I'm here to rescue him."

Walker saw twelve pairs of eyes shift from their cards to him, but instead of seeing even a speck of curiosity, he saw pity as if they were thinking, *We're glad it's you and not us*. Their gazes then returned to their cards.

"We're not stupid, Bay," Zane Westmoreland said, grinning and throwing a card out. "You think you can pump Walker for information about our plans for Aidan's bachelor party. But we've told Walker the rules. What we say in this room stays in this room."

"Whatever," she said, rolling her eyes. "Well, Walker, do you want to be rescued?"

He didn't have to think twice about it, although he was wondering about her motive. "Why not," he said, sliding back his chair. "But it's not because I haven't enjoyed the company," he said, standing and placing his cards down. "It's because I refuse to lose any more money to you guys. All of you are professional gamblers whether you admit it or not."

Dillon chuckled. "Ian is the only true gambler in the family. We're just wannabes. If he was here you wouldn't be walking out with your shirt on, trust me."

Walker smiled. "Can't wait to meet him." He moved across the room toward the door where Bailey stood. "I'll see you guys in the morning."

"Not too early, though," Zane cautioned, throwing out a card. "This game will probably be an all-nighter, so chances are we'll all sleep late."

Walker nodded. "I'll remember that."

"Any reason you felt the need to rescue me?"

Bailey glanced over at Walker as they headed toward the stairs. "I thought you might want to go riding."

"Horseback riding? This time of night? In this weather?"

She chuckled. "Not horseback riding. Truck riding. And yes, this time of night or, rather, this time of morning since it's after midnight. And it's a nice night. At least nicer than most. Besides, there's something I need to say to you."

He stopped walking and held her gaze. "Didn't get all your accusations off your chest last night?"

She knew she deserved that. "I was out of line and jumped to conclusions."

He crossed his arms over his chest. "Did you?"

"Yes, and if it's okay with you I'd like to talk to you

about it. But not here. So if you're up to riding, I know the perfect place where we can have a private conversation."

From his expression she could tell he was wondering what this private conversation would be about. However, instead of asking he merely nodded and said, "Okay, lead the way."

Bailey nodded, too, and then moved forward. Once they made it downstairs she grabbed her coat and waited while he got his. The house was quiet. Everyone with a lick of sense had gone to bed, which didn't say a lot for herself, Walker, her cousins and brothers. But she had been determined to hang around and talk to Walker.

When they stepped outside she saw the temperature had dropped. It was colder than she'd thought. She glanced over at him. "It won't take long for Kent to warm up."

"Kent?"

She nodded, shoving her hands into the pockets of her coat. "Yes. My truck."

He chuckled. "You gave your truck a name?"

"Yes. He and I go a long way back, so we're best buds. I take care of him and he takes care of me." She smiled. "Let me rephrase that. JoJo helps me take care of him."

"JoJo is Stern's wife, right? The mechanic?"

"Yes," Bailey said, reaching her truck. "The best in Denver. Probably the country. The wor—"

"Okay, I get the picture."

She threw her head back and laughed as she opened her truck door. She climbed inside, buckled up and waited until he did the same. "So where are we headed?" he asked.

She looked over at him. "Bailey's Bay."

Walker had heard about Bailey's Bay and had even covered parts of it yesterday while out horseback riding with Ramsey and Zane. He'd been told by Dillon that Westmoreland Country sat on over eighteen hundred acres.

Since Dillon was the eldest, he had inherited the main house along with the three hundred acres it sat on. Everyone else, upon reaching the age of twenty-five, received one hundred acres to call their own. Bailey had decided to name each person's homestead and had come up with names such as Ramsey's Web, Stern's Stronghold, Zane's Hideout, Derringer's Dungeon and Megan's Meadows. She had named hers Bailey's Bay.

"I understand you haven't built on your property yet," he said, looking out the window. Because of the darkness, there wasn't much to see.

"That's right. There's no need. I have too many cousins and siblings with guest rooms at their homes. And then there's Gemma's house that sits empty most of the time since she's living in Australia."

He didn't say anything but figured shifting from guest room to guest room and from house to house would get old. "You do plan to build one day though, right?"

"Yes, eventually. Right now Ramsey uses a lot of my land for sheep grazing, but that won't stop me when I'm ready. I know exactly where I intend to sit my home, and it's far away from the grazing land."

"I bet your place will be a beauty whenever you decide to build." He had seen all the other homes. Each one was breathtaking and said a lot about the owners' personalities. He wondered what design Bailey would choose. Single story that spread out with several wings? Or a two-story mansion erected like a magnificent piece of art? Either one would be a lot of house for one person. But then didn't the same hold true for the house he lived in? All that land and all that house.

"Yes. I plan to make it a masterpiece."

He didn't doubt that and could even visualize the home she would probably build for herself.

"Bailey's Bay was chosen for me and sits next to Zane's

and between Ramsey and Dillon's properties." She chuckled. "That was a deliberate move on my brothers' and cousins' parts since they figured Zane would stay in my business, and Dillon and Ramsey were the only two people I would listen to."

"Are they?"

"Pretty much, but sometimes I won't listen to anyone."

He couldn't help but smile. Bailey was definitely a rebel. That was probably some of her appeal. That, along with her sensuality. He doubted she knew just how sensual she was. It would be any man's downfall when she did realize it.

They didn't say anything for a while, until she brought the truck to a stop. "Here we are."

Thanks to the full moon and the stars overhead he could make out the lake. It stretched wide and endless and the waters were calm. From riding out here with Zane and Ramsey he knew the lake ran through most of the Westmoreland land. "Gemma Lake, right?"

"Yes. Raphel named it after my great-grandmother. I never knew them, or my grandparents for that matter. They died before I was born. But I heard they were great people and they left a wonderful legacy for us to be proud of."

Walker thought about the legacy his own parents, grandparents and great-grandparents had left and how he'd almost turned his back on that legacy to go after what hadn't been his dream but had been Kalyn's dream. Never again would he allow any woman to have that much power over him.

So why was he here? He had been in a card game and Bailey had showed up, suggesting they leave, and he had. Why? Was he once again allowing a woman to make decisions for him?

Walker glanced over at her. She stared straight ahead and he wondered what she was thinking. He looked back at the lake. It was peaceful. He liked being here with Bailey, parked, sharing this moment with her.

He was well aware they were attracted to each other, although neither of them had acted on it. But the desire was there nonetheless. Whenever they were alone there was always some sort of sexual aura surrounding them. Like now.

Even when there were others around he was aware of her. Like that first night when everyone had shown up at Dillon's for dinner. Walker had kept looking across the table at her, liking the sexy sound of her laugh. He had to be honest with himself—he had deliberately waited for her last night, outside by the barn, knowing she would eventually drop by Dillon's house since Zane had mentioned she did it every day.

The effect she was having on him bothered him, which was why he'd changed his plans so he could leave Saturday evening after the wedding instead of on Monday. The last thing he needed was to get involved with Bailey Westmoreland. He would never marry again, and all he could ever offer her was an affair that led nowhere. That wouldn't be good for her and could affect the friendships he'd made with her family.

He glanced over at her. "You said you wanted to talk," he prompted. The sooner they finished the sooner they could leave. Being out here alone with her could lead to trouble.

She looked over at him. He could barely see her features in the moonlight but he didn't need a bright light to know she was beautiful. She had rolled down the window a little and the cold air coming in enhanced her scent. It was filling his nostrils with the most luscious aroma.

But her looks and her scent weren't the issue; nor should they be. He had to remember he deserved better than a woman who could be another Kalyn.

"About last night."

That got his attention. "What about it?"

"I owe you an apology."

"Do you?"

"Yes. I made accusations that I should not have."

Yes, she had, but he couldn't help wondering what had made her realize that fact. "What makes you so sure?"

She frowned. "Are you saying that I was right?"

"No, that's not what I'm saying. You need to do something about being quick to jump to conclusions."

She waited a second, tapping her fingers on the steering wheel before saying, "I know. My family warns me about it all the time."

He touched her shoulder for emphasis. "Then, maybe you should listen to them."

He suddenly realized touching her had been a mistake. With her layered clothing he was far from coming into contact with bare skin, but he could still feel sensuous heat swelling his fingertips.

"I try to listen."

The catch in her voice sent a ripple of desire through him. He shifted in his seat when a thrumming dose of heat ripped through his gut. "Maybe you should try harder, Bailey."

What made Walker so different from any other man? His touch on her shoulder affected her in a way no man's touch had ever affected her before. How did he have the ability to reach her inner being and remind her that she was a woman?

Personal relationships weren't her forte. Most of the guys in these parts were too afraid of her brothers and cousins to even think of crossing the line, so she'd only had one lover. For her it had been one and done, and executed more out of curiosity than anything else. She certainly hadn't been driven by the kind of sexual desire she was feeling with Walker.

There was a spike of heat that always rolled in her stomach whenever she was around him, not to mention the warmth that settled in the area between her legs. Even now, just being in the same vehicle with him was making her breasts tingle. Had his face inched a little closer to hers?

Suggesting they go for a late-night ride might not have been a good idea after all. "I'm not perfect," she finally said softly.

"No one is perfect," he responded huskily.

Bailey drew in a sharp breath when he rubbed a finger across her cheek. She fought back the slow moan that threatened to slip past her lips. His hand on her shoulder had caused internal havoc; his fingers on her face were stirring something to life inside her that she'd never felt before.

She needed to bring an end to this madness. The last thing she wanted was for him to misunderstand the reason she'd brought him here. "I didn't bring you out here for this, Walker," she said. "I don't want you getting the wrong idea."

"Okay, what's the right idea?" he asked, leaning in even closer. "Why did you bring me out here?"

Nervously, she licked her lips. He was still rubbing a finger across her cheek. "To apologize."

"Apology accepted." Then he lowered his head and took possession of her mouth.

Five

Walker deepened the kiss, even while trying to convince himself that he should not be kissing Bailey. No way should his tongue be tangling with hers or hers with his.

But she tasted so damn good. And he didn't want to stop. Truth be told, he'd been anxiously waiting for this minute. He would even admit he'd waited ever since that day at the airport when he'd first thought her lips were a luscious pair. A pair he wanted to taste. Now he was getting his chance.

Her tongue was driving him insane. Her taste was hot, simply addictive. She created a wildness within him, unleashing a sexual beast that wanted to consume every bone-melting inch of her. When had he kissed any woman so thoroughly, with such unapologetic rawness?

He tangled his fingers in her hair, holding her mouth captive as his mouth and tongue sucked, licked and teased every delicious inch of her mouth. This kiss was so incredibly pleasurable his testicles ached. If he didn't end things now, this kiss could very well penetrate his very soul.

He reluctantly broke off the kiss, but made sure his mouth didn't stray far. He could feel the sweet, moist heat of her breath on his lips and he liked it. He liked it so much that he gave in to temptation and used his tongue to trace a path along her lips. Moments later that same tongue tracked a line down her neck and collarbone before returning to her mouth.

She slowly opened her eyes and looked at him. He knew he shouldn't be thinking it, but at that moment he wished the truck had a backseat. All the things he would do to her filled his mind.

"That was some acceptance," she whispered hotly against his lips.

He leaned forward and nibbled around her chin. "Acceptance of what?"

"My apology. Maybe I should apologize more often."

He chuckled lightly, leaning back to meet her gaze. "Do you often do or say things that require an apology?"

"So I'm told. I'm known to put my foot in my mouth more often than not. But do you know what?"

"What?"

"I definitely like your tongue in my mouth a lot better, Walker."

Walker drew in a ragged breath. He was learning there was no telling what would come out of that luscious mouth of hers. "No problem. That can be arranged."

He leaned in and kissed her again; this time was more intense than the last. He figured he needed the memory of this kiss to take back to Kodiak for those long cold nights, when he would sit in front of the fireplace alone and nurse a bottle of beer.

She was shivering in his arms and he knew it had nothing to do with the temperature. She was returning his kiss in a way that ignited every cell in his body, and tasted just as incredibly sexy as she looked. Never had he sampled a woman whose flavor fired his blood to a degree where he actually felt heat rushing through his veins.

He could do a number on her mouth forever, and would have attempted to do so if he hadn't felt her fingers fumbling with the buttons on his shirt. He needed to end this now or else he would be a goner. There was only so much he could take when it came to Bailey.

Walker broke off the kiss, resting his forehead against hers. The needs filtering through him were as raw as raw could get. Primitive. It had been years since a woman had filled him with such need. He was like a starving man who was only hungry for her.

"I didn't bring you out here for this, Walker."

Her words had come out choppy but he understood them. "You said that already." He kept his forehead plastered to hers. There was something so alluring about having his mouth this close to hers. At any time he could use his tongue to swipe a taste of her.

"I'm saying it again. I only wanted to park and talk."

He chuckled against her lips. "That's all?"

Now it was her turn to chuckle. "You are so typically male. Ready to get laid, any time or any place."

"Um, not really. I have very discriminating taste. And speaking of taste," he said, leaning back slightly so he could look into her eyes, "I definitely like yours."

Bailey nervously licked her lips. What was a woman supposed to say to a line like that? In all honestly, there was nothing she could say, especially while gazing into the depths of Walker's dark eyes. He held her gaze hostage and there was nothing she could do about it. Mainly because there was nothing she wanted to do about it. His eyes had her mesmerized, drawing her under his spell.

The same thing had happened earlier when she'd watched his two movies back-to-back. What Chloe had said was true. His performances in both roles had been award-worthy material. Sitting there, watching him on her television screen, was like watching a totally different person. She could see how he'd become a heartthrob in a short period of time. His sexiness had been evident in his clothes, his voice and the roles he'd chosen. And those lovemaking scenes had blazed off the charts. They'd left her wishing she had been the woman in those scenes with him. And tonight, as unbelievable as it seemed, she had lived her own memorable scene with him.

She had to remember the reason she had brought him here. Apologizing for last night was only part of it. "There's something else I need to talk to you about, Walker."

He tipped his head back. "Is there?"

"Yes."

"Can I kiss you again first?" he asked, rubbing his thumb over her bottom lip.

Bailey knew she should say no. Another kiss from him was the last thing she needed. She feared it would detonate her brain. But her brain was halfway gone already, just from the sensuality she heard in his voice. His thumb gently stroking her lip stirred a need that primed her for something she couldn't define but wanted anyway.

He was staring at her, waiting for an answer. She could feel the effects of his spellbinding gaze all over her body. Suddenly she felt bold, empowered, filled with a burning need. Instead of answering him, she pushed in the center console, converting the truck from bucket seats to bench seats. Easing closer to him, she wrapped her arms around his neck and tilted her mouth up to his. "Yes, Walker. You can kiss me again."

And as if that was all he needed to hear, he swooped down and sucked her tongue into his mouth. Bailey couldn't help but moan. He was consuming her. She sensed a degree of hunger within him she hadn't recognized in the other kisses. It was as if he was laying claim to her mouth, branding it in a way no other man had or ever would, and all while his knuckles softly stroked her jaw.

She kissed him back with the same greediness. No matter what costar she'd watched him with earlier, he was with her now. This was real, no acting involved. The only director they were following was their own desire, which seemed to be overtaking them.

Walker's hand reached under her sweater to caress her stomach, and she moaned at the contact. The feel of his fingers on her bare flesh made her shiver, and when he continued to softly rub her skin she closed her eyes as awareness spiked fully into her blood.

The moment he released her mouth, she leaned closer and used her tongue to lick the corners of his lips. His hand inched upward, stroking her ribs, tracing the contours of her bones until he reached her breasts. She drew in a deep breath when his fingertips drew circles on the lace bra covering her nipples. The twin buds hardened and sent a signal to the juncture of her thighs. When he pushed her sweater out of the way, her body automatically arched toward him.

As if he knew what she wanted, what she needed, he undid the front clasp of her bra. As soon as her breasts sprang free, he lowered his mouth to them. Her nipples were hard and ready for him and he devoured them with a greediness that had her moaning deep in her throat.

When she felt the truck's leather touch her back, she realized he had lowered her onto her back. She ran her hands over his shirt and began undoing the buttons, needing to touch his bare skin like he was touching hers. Moments later, her fingers speared into the hair covering his chest. She heard him growl her name seconds before he captured her wrists, holding her captive while his tongue swirled languorously over her stomach. Her skin sizzled everywhere his mouth touched. And when his mouth reached her navel, he laved it with his tongue. Her stomach muscles flexed beneath his mouth.

Walker was convinced Bailey's body was calling out to him. He was determined to answer the call. She tasted wonderful and when she rocked her body beneath his mouth he couldn't help but groan. His control was eroding. He'd thought all he wanted was a kiss to remember, but he discovered he wanted something more. He wanted her. All of her. He wanted to explode in the heat she was generating. But first, he wanted to fill her with the rapturous satisfaction she needed.

Raising his head, he met her gaze. The fire in her eyes almost burned him. "Lift up your hips, Bailey," he whispered.

When she did as he requested, he unsnapped her jeans and worked the denim down past her thighs. He then grazed his fingers against the scrap of lace covering her femininity. He inhaled deeply, drawing her luscious scent through his nostrils. His heart pounded hard in his chest and every cell in his body needed to please her. To give her a reason to remember him. Why that was important, he wasn't sure. All he knew was that it was.

His erection jerked greedily in anticipation of her feminine taste. When he lowered his head and eased his tongue inside her, he forced himself not to climax just from the delicious flavor of her. She pushed against his shoulders and then, seconds later, gripped him hard, holding his mouth right there as she moaned his name. He delved deep inside, stroking her, lapping up her taste with every inch of his tongue.

She lifted her hips to his mouth and he gripped her thighs tightly, devouring her in a way he'd dreamed of doing every night since he'd met her. Her scent and her taste filled him with emotions and sensations he hadn't felt in years.

He felt her body jerk beneath his mouth in an explosive orgasm. She screamed his name, but he kept his mouth crushed to her, sucking harder and hoping this was one intimate kiss she would never, ever forget.

Moments later, after he felt her body go still, except for the shuddering of her breath, he slowly withdrew his tongue—but not before brushing his lips over her womanly mound. Marking. Branding. Imprinting.

"Walker…"

"Yes, baby. I'm here." He eased over her body and kissed her.

Bailey's breath caught in her throat. When Walker finally released her mouth, she could only lie there enmeshed in a web of sensations that had left her weak but totally fulfilled. Never in her life had she experienced anything like what Walker had done. How he had made her feel. The pleasure had been so sharp she might never recover. He had taken her to rapturous heights she hadn't known existed between a man and a woman.

"I think we better go," Walker said softly as he rezipped her jeans, placing a kiss on her stomach. When she felt the tip of his tongue around her belly button, she whispered his name.

He took his time refastening her bra, cupping her breasts and licking her nipples before doing so. Then he pulled her sweater down before helping her into a sitting position. She was tempted to resist. She wanted to lie there while memories washed over her.

"Your breasts are beautiful, you know, Bailey."

She shook her head. No, she didn't know. No other man had ever complimented her breasts. But then, no other man would have had a reason to do so. She drew in a deep breath, rested her head against the seat and closed her eyes. Had she actually experienced an orgasm from a man going down on her? In a parked truck?

"The lake is beautiful tonight."

How could he talk about how beautiful the lake was after driving her into a sexual frenzy and blowing her mind? And just think, he hadn't even made love to her. What he'd given her was an appetizer. She could only imagine what the full course meal would be like.

She slowly opened her eyes and followed his gaze through the windshield to the lake. She knew he was giving her time to pull herself together, clear her head, finish straightening up her clothes. She took another deep breath. In her mind she could still feel his mouth on her breasts and between her thighs. It took her a while to respond to what he'd said. "Yes, it's beautiful. I love coming here. Day or night. Whenever I need to think."

"I can see this being a good thinking spot."

She decided not to add that he'd just proved it was a good making-out spot, as well. She glanced over at him and saw the buttons of his shirt were still undone, reminding her of when her tongue had licked his skin. Her blood seared at the memory.

"What we did tonight was wrong, Bailey. But I don't regret it."

She didn't regret it, either. The only thing she regretted was not taking things further. They were adults, not kids. Consenting adults. And if they had enjoyed it, then what was the problem? "And why was it wrong?"

"Because you deserve more than a meaningless affair and that's all I can offer you."

She didn't recall asking for more. "What makes you think I want any more than that, Walker? I'm not into serious relationships, either. They can get messy."

He lifted a brow. "How so?"

"Men have a tendency to get possessive, territorial. Act crazy sometimes. Trust me, I know. I grew up with twelve of them. That's why I have my rules."

"Bailey's Rules, right?"

"Yep. Those are the ones."

"So if you don't do affairs, what do you do? I assume you date."

"When it suits me." No need to tell him she'd never had a steady boyfriend. "I assume you date, too."

"Yes, when it suits me," he said, repeating her words.

"So we understand each other," she said, wondering if they really did.

"Yes, I guess you can say that," he said, buttoning his shirt. "And now is as good a time as any to mention that I've decided to return to Kodiak right after the wedding on Saturday instead of on Monday as planned."

Her jaw dropped in surprise. "You're leaving Saturday?"

"Yes."

"Why?"

He looked over at her. "There's no need to stay here any longer than that. What I have to tell the Outlaws won't change. Your family is good people, and it will be Garth and his brothers' loss if they listen to Bart and decide not to meet all of you."

She didn't say anything while she considered her plans for him to be interviewed by one of her writers. "I need you to stay until Monday…at least."

He glanced over at her with keen, probing eyes. "Why do you need me to stay until Monday?"

Something cautioned her to choose her words carefully. "Remember earlier, I told you there was something else I needed to discuss with you?"

He nodded. "Yes, I remember."

"Well, it was about a favor I need to ask."

"What kind of favor?"

She nervously nibbled at her bottom lip. "Today I found out that you used to be an actor. Ty Reklaw."

He didn't say anything for a minute. "So what of it? And what does that have to do with me staying until Monday?"

She heard a tinge of annoyance in his voice and had a feeling he didn't like being reminded of his past. "I understand you were at the peak of your acting career when you left Hollywood to return to Alaska. I was sorry to hear about you losing your family. Must have been a difficult time for you."

She paused and when he didn't say anything, she pressed on. "It's been almost ten years and you're still alone, living on your island. It just so happens that *Simply Irresistible* will be doing an article about men who are loners and I would love to make you our feature story."

He still didn't say anything. He merely stared at her. She swallowed deeply, hesitating only a second before asking, "So will you do it? Will you let me schedule an interview for you with one of my writers to be our feature story?"

It was then, there in the moonlight, that she saw the stiffening of his jaw and the rage smoldering in his gaze. "No. And you have a lot of damn nerve. Is that what this little truck ride was about, Bailey? How far did you intend to go to get me to say yes?"

Her gaze narrowed. "What are you asking? Are you insinuating I used my body to get my way?"

"Why not? I've been approached in the past by reporters who will do just about anything for a story."

"Well, I'm not one of them. The main reason I asked you here was to apologize for my behavior last night. Then I wanted to ask a favor of you."

"And why do you think I would want to be interviewed?

I left Hollywood for a reason and I've never looked back. Why would I want to relive those years?"

"You have it all wrong. The article we plan to publish will have nothing to do with your time in Hollywood. You're a loner and we want to find out why some men prefer that kind of life."

"Have you ever considered the fact that not everyone needs to constantly be around people? It's not as if I'm some damn recluse. I have friends. Real friends. Friends who know how to respect my privacy when I need them to. And they are the ones whose company I seek."

"Yes, however—"

"But you wouldn't understand that. You're dependent on your family for your livelihood, your happiness and your very reason for breathing. That's probably why you've made it one of your rules never to stray too far away from them."

His words fired her up. "And is there anything wrong with that?"

"Not if that's how you choose to live. Which is nobody's business. Just like how I choose to live is nobody's business, either. What makes you think I want to broadcast how I chose to live after losing two of the most important people in my life?"

He wasn't letting her get a word in. "If you just let me finish, I can explain wh—"

"There's nothing to explain. You just got this promotion to features editor and you need a story. Sorry, I refuse to accommodate you. Go find your story someplace else."

An hour or so later, Walker was back in his guest room and still finding it hard to accept the ease with which Bailey had asked that favor of him. Did she not realize the magnitude of the favor she'd asked or did she not care? Was she so into her family that she had no understanding or concept that some people preferred solitude? That not everyone wanted a crowd?

He could only shake his head, since he doubted he could get any angrier than he was at that minute. And he had just warned himself not to let her or any woman who'd shown the same persuasive powers Kalyn had possessed to get close to him. Yet he'd fallen under Bailey's spell after that first kiss. After the second, he'd been a goner.

Even now, memories of those kisses were embedded into the core of his soul. The mere idea of another woman getting that much under his skin stopped him cold with a helplessness he felt in every bone of his body.

He let out a slow, controlled breath. In less than a week he'd allowed Bailey to penetrate an area of his mind he'd thought dead forever. And earlier tonight when he'd reached across the seat and dragged her body against his, it hadn't mattered that they were both fully clothed. Just the idea of her being in his arms had brought out his primitive animal instincts. He'd wanted to mate with her. How he'd found the strength to deny what they'd both wanted was beyond his ability to comprehend, but he had. And for that he was grateful. There was no telling how far she would have gone to get her story. She might have had him eating out of her hands while he spilled his guts.

A part of him wanted to think she was just a woman, easy to forget. But he knew she wasn't just any woman. She wasn't the only person with rules, and somehow Bailey had breached all the rules he'd put in place. At the top of his list was not letting another woman get to him.

Whether it was her making him smile or her making him frown, or her filling him with the degree of anger like he was feeling now—she made him feel too much.

He heard the sound of doors opening and closing downstairs and figured the card game had run its course. Pretty much like he'd run his.

It would be to his advantage to remain true to what he knew. Bailey called it being a loner, but he saw it as surviving.

Bailey glanced at her watch as she got out of her truck once she'd reached Ramsey's Web. Most of her day had been filled with meetings, getting to know her new staff as they got to know her management style. It was important for them to know they were a team.

However, no matter how busy she'd stayed today, thoughts of Walker had filled her mind. He was furious with her, angrier than he'd been two nights ago. Was his anger justified? Had she crossed the line in asking him to do that piece for the magazine?

She was still upset about his insinuation that she would go as far as to use her body to get what she wanted. She didn't play those kinds of games, and for him to assume she did didn't sit well with her. So the way she saw it, they'd both been out of line. They'd both said things they probably regretted today. But she had to remember that Walker was a guest of her family, and the last thing she wanted to be was guilty of offending him. Dillon had placed a lot of confidence in her, and her family would never forgive her if she had offended Walker.

She needed to talk to someone about it before she saw Walker today, and the two people she could always go to for advice were Dillon and Ramsey. There was a chance she would run into Walker at Dillon's place, so she thought it best to seek out Ramsey and ask how she could fix things with Walker before the situation got too out of hand.

She found her eldest brother in his six-car garage with his head stuck under the hood of his Jeep. She loved Ramsey's Web and during her brother's before-Chloe days, she'd spent time here getting deliberately underfoot, knowing he wouldn't have it any other way. The two years when Ramsey had lived in Australia had been hard for her.

The sound of her footsteps must have alerted him to her presence. He lifted his head and smiled at her. "Bay? How are things going?"

"Fine. I would give you a hug but I don't want grease all over me. Why are you changing your oil instead of letting JoJo do it?"

Ramsey chuckled as he wiped his hands. "Because there are some things I'd rather do myself, especially to this baby here. She's been with me since the beginning."

Bailey nodded. She knew the Jeep had been Ramsey's first car and the last gift he'd gotten from their parents. It had been a birthday gift while he'd been in college. "You still keep it looking good."

"Always." He leaned back against the Jeep and studied her curiously. "So what's going on with you, Bailey Joleen Westmoreland?"

This was her eldest brother and he'd always had the ability to read her when others couldn't. "It's Walker."

He lifted a brow. "What about Walker?"

She glanced down at her pointed-toe boots a second before meeting Ramsey's gaze. "I think I might have offended him."

Ramsey crossed his arms over his chest, and she could tell from his expression that he didn't like the sound of that. "How?"

"It's a long story."

"Start from the beginning. I have time."

So she did, not rushing through most of the story and deliberately leaving out some parts. Such as how she'd found Walker utterly attractive from the first, how they'd both tried to ignore the sexual chemistry between them and how they'd made out in her truck last night.

"Well, there you have it, Ram. I apologized to him last

night about my wrong assumptions about his feelings on marriage, but I made him mad again when I asked him to do the interview."

Ramsey shook his head. "Let me get this straight. You found out he used to be a movie star who left Hollywood after the deaths of his wife and child, yet you wanted to interview him about being a loner since that time?"

Ramsey sounded as if he couldn't believe she'd done such a thing. "But that wasn't going to be the angle to the story," she argued. "*Simply Irresistible* isn't a tabloid. I'm not looking for details of his life in Hollywood. Women are curious about men who hang back from the crowd. Not everyone is interested in a life-of-the-party type of male. Women see loners as mysterious and want to know more about them. I thought Walker would be perfect since he's lived by himself for ten years on that ranch in Alaska. I figured he could shed some light on what it's like to be a loner."

"Think about what you were asking him to do, Bay. You were asking to invade his space, pry into his life and make public what he probably prefers to keep private. I bet if you had run your idea by Chloe or Lucia, they would have talked you out of it. Your plan was kind of insensitive, don't you think?"

With Ramsey presenting it that way she guessed it was. She honestly hadn't thought about it that way. She had seen an opportunity and jumped without thinking. "But I would have made the Hollywood part of his life off-limits. It was the loner aspect I wanted to concentrate on. I tried to explain that to him."

"And how were you planning to separate the two? Our pasts shape us into the people we are today. Look at you. Like him, you suffered a double loss. A quadruple one, to be exact. And look how you reacted. Would you want someone to show up and ask to interview you about that?

How can you define the Bailey you are today without remembering the old you, and what it took to make you grow from one into the other?"

His question had her thinking.

"And I think you missed the mark on something," he added.

She lifted a brow. "What?"

"Assuming being a loner means being antisocial. You can be a loner and still be close to others. Everybody needs some *me* time. Some people need it more so than others. Case in point, I was a loner before Chloe. Even when I had all of you here with me in Westmoreland Country, I kept to myself. At night, when I came here alone, I didn't need anyone invading my space."

She nodded, realizing something. "But I often invaded it, Ram."

"Yes, you did."

Bailey wondered, for the first time, if he had minded. As if reading her thoughts, he said, "No, Bay. Your impromptu visits never bothered me. All I want you to see is that not everyone needs a crowd. Some people can be their own company, and it's okay."

That was practically what Walker had said. In fact, he had gone even further by saying she was dependent on a crowd. Namely, her large family.

"Looks as if I need to apologize to Walker again. If I keep it up, he's going to think 'I'm sorry' is my middle name. Guess I'll go find him."

"That's going to be pretty difficult."

Her brow furrowed. "Why?"

"Because Walker isn't here. He's left."

"Left?"

"Yes, left. He's on his way back to Alaska. Zane took him to the airport around noon."

"B-but he had planned to stay for the wedding. He

hadn't met everyone since some of the cousins won't be coming in until tomorrow."

"Couldn't be helped. He claimed something came up on his ranch that he had to take care of."

What Ramsey didn't say, but what she figured he was thinking, was that Walker's departure had nothing to do with his ranch and everything to do with her. "Fine. He left. But I'm going to apologize to him anyway."

"Um, I probably wouldn't ask Dillon for Walker's phone number if I were you, especially not if you tell him the same story you just told me."

Bailey nibbled her bottom lip. How was she going to get out of the mess she'd gotten herself into?

Six

"So tell me again why you cut the trip short."

Walker glared across the kitchen at his best friend, who had made himself at home, sitting at Walker's table and greedily devouring a bowl of cereal.

"Why? I've told you once already. The Westmorelands are legit. I didn't have to prolong the visit. Like I said, no matter what Bart believes, I think you and your brothers should take them seriously. They're good people."

Walker turned to the sink with the pretense of rinsing out his coffee cup. What he'd told Garth about the Westmorelands being good people was true—up to a point. As far as he was concerned, the jury was still out on Bailey.

Bailey.

There was no way Walker could have hung around another day and breathed the same air that she did. He clenched his jaw at the thought that he had allowed her to get under his skin. She was just the type who could get embedded in a man's soul if he was weak enough to let it happen.

On top of everything else, she was as gutsy as the day was long. She'd definitely had a lot of nerve asking him to do that interview. She was used to getting what she wanted, but he wasn't one of her brothers or cousins. He had no reason to give in to her every wish.

"You actually played cards with Thorn Westmoreland?" Garth asked with what sounded like awe.

"Yes," Walker said over his shoulder. "He told us about the bike he's building for some celebrity."

"Really? Did you mention that you used to be an actor and that you know a lot of those folks in Hollywood?"

"No."

"Why not?"

Walker turned around. "I was there to get to know them, not the other way around, Garth. They didn't need to know anything about me other than that I was a friend to the Outlaws who came in good faith to get to know them."

But that hadn't stopped them from finding out about his past anyway. He wasn't sure who all knew, since the only person who'd mentioned anything about his days in Hollywood was Bailey. If the others knew, they'd been considerate enough to respect his privacy. That had been too much to expect of Bailey. All she'd seen was an opportunity to sell magazines.

"I think I'll take your advice and suggest to the others that we pay those Westmorelands a visit. In fact, I'm looking forward to it."

"You won't be disappointed," Walker said, opening the dishwasher to place his cup inside. "How are you going to handle Bart? Do you have any idea why he's so dead set against any of you establishing relationships with your new cousins?"

"No, but it doesn't matter. He'll have to get over it."

Garth glanced at his watch. "I hate to run but I have a meeting back in Fairbanks in three hours. That will give Regan just enough time to fly me out of here and get me back to the office."

Regan Fairchild had been Garth's personal pilot for the past two years. She'd taken her father's place as the corporate pilot for the Outlaws after he retired. "I'll see you out."

When they passed through the living room, Garth glanced over at Walker. "When you want to tell me the real reason you left Denver early, let me know. Don't forget I can read you like a book, Walker."

Walker didn't want to hear that. "Don't waste your time. Go read someone else."

They had almost made it across the room when Walker's doorbell sounded. "That's probably Macon. He's supposed to stop by today and check out that tractor he wants to buy from me."

They had reached the door and, without checking to see who was on the other side, Walker opened it. Shocked, his mouth dropped open as his gaze raked over the woman standing there.

"Hello, Walker."

He recovered, although not as quickly as he would have liked. "Bailey! What the hell are you doing here?"

Instead of answering, her gaze shifted to the man standing by his side. "Hey, you look like Riley," she said, as her face broke into a smile.

It was a smile that Garth returned. "And you look like Charm."

She chuckled. "No, Charm looks like me. I understand I'm older."

"Excuse me for breaking up this little chitchat, but what are you doing here, Bailey?" Walker asked in an annoyed tone.

"Evidently she came here to see you, and on that note,

I am out of here. I need to make that meeting," Garth said, slipping out the door. He looked over his shoulder at Walker with an expression that clearly said, *You have a lot of explaining to do.*

To Bailey, Garth said, "Welcome to Hemlock Row. I'll let the family know you're here. Hopefully Walker will fly you into Fairbanks."

"Don't hold your breath for that to happen," Walker said. He doubted Garth heard as he quickly darted to his parked car. His best friend had a lot of damn nerve. How dare he welcome anyone to Walker's home?

Walker turned his attention back to Bailey, trying to ignore the flutter in his stomach at seeing just how beautiful she looked. Nor did he want to concentrate on her scent, which had filled his nostrils the moment he'd opened the door.

Walker crossed his arms over his chest. "I've asked you twice already and you've yet to answer," he said in a harsh tone. "What are you doing here?"

Bailey blew out a chilled breath, wrapped her arms around herself and tried not to shiver. "Could you invite me inside first? It's cold out here."

He hesitated, as if he were actually considering doing just the opposite, and then he stepped back. She hurriedly came inside and closed the door behind her. She had dressed in layers, double the amount she would have used in Denver, yet she still felt chilled to the bone.

"You might as well come and stand in front of the fireplace to warm up."

"Thanks," she said, surprised he'd made the offer. After sliding the carry-on bag from her shoulders, she peeled off her coat, then her jacket and gloves.

Instead of renting a car, she had opted for a cab service, even though the ride from the airstrip had cost her a pretty penny. But she hadn't cared. She'd been cold, exhausted and determined to get to Walker's place before nightfall.

The cabbie had been chatty, explaining that Walker seldom got visitors and trying to coax her into telling him why she was there. She'd let him talk, and when he'd figured out she wasn't providing any information, he'd finally lapsed into silence. But only for a little while. Then he'd pointed out a number of evergreen trees and told her they were mountain hemlocks, a tree common to Alaska. He'd told her about the snowstorm headed their way and said she'd made it to the island just in time or she would have been caught in it. Sounded to her as if she would get caught in it anyway since her return flight was forty-eight hours from now. The man had been born and raised on the island and had a lot of history to share.

When the cabbie had driven up to the marker for Hemlock Row, the beautiful two-story ranch house that sat on Walker's property made her breath catch. It was like looking at a gigantic postcard. It had massive windows, multiple stone chimneys and a wraparound porch. It sat on the Shelikof Strait, which served as a backdrop that was simply beautiful, even if it was out in the middle of nowhere and surrounded by snow. The only other house they'd passed had to be at least ten to fifteen miles away.

Walker's home was not as large as Dillon's, but like Dillon's, it had a rustic feel, as if it belonged just where it sat.

"Drink this," Walker said, handing her a mug filled with hot liquid. She hadn't realized he'd left her alone. She'd been busy looking around at the furniture, which seemed warm and welcoming.

"Thanks." She took a sip of what tasted like a mixture of coffee, hot chocolate and a drop of tea. It tasted delicious. As delicious as Walker looked standing directly in front of her, barefoot, with an open-collar sweater and jeans riding low on his hips. What man looked this mouthwatering so early in the day? Had it really been a week since she'd seen him last? A week when she'd thought about him every day, determined to make this trip to Kodiak Island, Alaska, to personally deliver the apology she needed to make.

"Okay, now that you've warmed up, how about telling me what you're doing here."

She lowered the cup and met his gaze. After telling Lucia and Chloe what she'd done and what she planned to do, they had warned her that Walker probably wouldn't be happy to see her. She could tell from the look on his face that they'd been right. "I came to see you. I owe you an apology for what I said. What I suggested doing with that piece for the magazine."

He frowned. "Why are you apologizing? Doing something so inconsiderate and uncaring seems to be so like you."

His words hurt but she couldn't get mad. That was unfortunately the way she'd presented herself since meeting him. "That goes to show how wrong you are about me and how wrong I was for giving you reason to think that way."

"Whatever. You shouldn't have bothered. I don't think there's anything you can do or say to change my opinion of you."

That angered her. "I never realized you were so judgmental."

"I'm as judgmental as you are."

She wondered if all this bitterness and anger were necessary. Possibly, but at the moment she was too exhausted to deal with it. What should have been a fifteen-hour flight had become a twenty-two-hour flight when the delay of one connection had caused her to miss another. On top of everything else, due to the flight chaos, her luggage was heaven knew where. The airline assured her it would be found and delivered to her within twenty-four hours. She hoped that was true because she planned to fly out again in two days.

"Look, Walker. My intentions were good, and regardless of what you think of me I did come here to personally apologize."

"Fine. You've apologized. Now you can leave.'

"Leave? I just got here! Where am I to go?"

He frowned. "How did you get here?"

"I caught a taxi from the airport."

A dark brow lowered beneath a bunched forehead. "Then, call them to come pick you up."

He couldn't be serious. "And go where? My return flight back to Denver isn't for forty-eight hours."

His frown deepened. "Then, I suggest you stay with your cousins in Fairbanks. You've met Garth. He will introduce you to the others."

Her spine stiffened. "Why can't I wait it out here?"

He glared at her. "Because you aren't welcome here, Bailey."

Walker flinched at the harshness of his own words. He regretted saying them the moment they left his lips. He could tell by the look on her face that they'd hurt her. He then remembered how kind her family had been to him, a virtual stranger, and he knew that no matter how he felt about her, she didn't deserve what he'd just said. But then, what had given her the right to come here uninvited?

He watched as she placed the cup on the table and slid back into her jacket. Then she reached for her coat.

"What the hell do you think you're doing?" he asked, noticing how the loud sound of his voice seemed to blast off the walls.

She lifted her chin as she buttoned up her coat. "What does it look like I'm doing? Leaving. You've made it clear you don't want me here, and one thing I don't do is stay where I'm not wanted."

He wanted to chuckle at that. Hadn't her cousins and brothers told him, jokingly, how she used to impose herself on them? Sometimes she'd even done so purposely, to rattle any of their girlfriends she hadn't liked. "Forget what I said. I was mad."

When her coat was buttoned practically to her neck, she glared at him. "And you're still mad. I didn't come all the way here for verbal abuse, Walker. I came to apologize."

"Apology accepted." The memory of what had followed the last time he'd said those words slammed into his mind. He'd kissed her, feasting on her mouth like a hungry man who'd been denied food for years.

He could tell from the look in her eyes that she was remembering, as well. He figured that was the reason she broke eye contact with him to look at the flames blazing in the fireplace. Too late—the wood burning wasn't the only thing crackling in the room. He could feel that stirring of sensual magnetism that always seemed to surround them. It was radiating more heat than the fireplace.

"Now that I think about it, staying here probably isn't a good idea," she said, glancing back at him.

He released a deep breath and leaned back on his heels. She was right. It wasn't a good idea, but it was too late to think about that now. "A storm's headed this way so it doesn't matter if you don't think it's a good idea."

"It matters to me if you don't want me here," she snapped.

He rubbed his hand down his face. "Look, Bailey. I think we can tolerate each other for the next forty-eight hours. Besides, this place is so big I doubt if I'll even see you during that time." To be on the safe side, he would put her in one of the guest rooms on the south wing. That part of the house hadn't been occupied in over fifteen years.

"Where's your luggage?" he asked. The quicker he could get her settled in, the quicker he could ignore her presence.

"The airline lost it, although they say it has just been misplaced. They assured me they will deliver it here within twenty-four hours."

That probably wasn't going to happen, he thought, but figured there was no reason to tell her that. "Just in case they're delayed, I have a couple of T-shirts you can borrow to sleep in."

"Thanks."

"If you're hungry I can fix you something. I hadn't planned on preparing dinner till later, but there are some leftovers I can warm up."

"No, thanks. I'm not hungry. But I would appreciate if I could wash up and lie down for a bit. The flight from Anchorage was sort of choppy."

"Usually it is, unfortunately. I'll show you up to the room you'll be using. Just follow me."

Seven

The sound of a door slamming somewhere in the house jarred Bailey awake and had her scrambling to sit up in bed and try to remember where she was. It all came tumbling back to her. Kodiak Island, Alaska. Walker's ranch.

She settled back down in bed, remembering the decision she had made to come here. She could finally admit it had been a bad one. Hadn't Walker said she wasn't welcome? But she had been determined to come after deciding a phone-call apology wouldn't do. She needed to tell him in person that she was sorry.

And she would even admit that a part of her had wanted to see him face-to-face. Everyone in the family had been surprised he'd left early, and although no one questioned her about it, she knew they suspected she was to blame. And she had been. So no one had seemed surprised when she announced her plans to travel to Kodiak. However, Dillon had pulled her aside to ask if that was something she really wanted to do. She'd assured him that it was, and told him she owed Walker an apology and wanted to deliver it to him personally.

So here she was, in an area as untamed and rugged as the most remote areas of Westmoreland Country. But there were views she had passed in the cab that had been so beautiful they had almost taken her breath away. Part of her couldn't wait to see the rest of it.

Bailey heard the sound of a door slamming again and glanced over at the clock on the nightstand. Had she slept for four hours?

She suddenly sniffed the air. Something smelled good, downright delicious. Walker had been cooking. She hoped he hadn't gone to any trouble just for her. When her stomach growled she knew she needed to get out of bed and go downstairs.

She recalled Walker leading her up to this room and the two flights of stairs they'd taken to get here. The moment she'd followed him inside she'd felt something she hadn't felt in years. Comfort. Somehow this guest room was just as warm and welcoming as the living room had been.

It might have been the sturdy-looking furniture made of dark oak. Or the huge bed that had felt as good as it looked. She couldn't wait to sleep in it tonight. Really sleep in it. Beneath the covers and not on top like she'd done for her nap. Getting out of bed, she headed for the bathroom, glad she at least had her carry-on containing her makeup and toiletries.

A few minutes later, feeling refreshed and less exhausted, she left the guest room to head downstairs. She hoped Walker was in a better mood than he'd been in earlier.

Walker checked the timer on the stove before lifting the lid to stir the stew. He'd cooked more than the usual amount since he had a houseguest. Bailey had been asleep for at least four hours and even so, her presence was disrupting his normal routine. He would have driven around his land by now, checking on the herds and making sure everything was ready for the impending snowstorm. He'd talked to Willie, his ranch foreman, who had assured him everything had been taken care of.

That brought his thoughts back to Bailey, and he uttered an expletive under his breath. He'd figured out the real reason, the only one that made sense, as to why she was here, using an apology as an excuse. She probably thought she could make him change his mind about doing the interview, but she didn't know how wrong she was.

As far as he was concerned, she'd wasted her time coming here. Although he had to admit it had been one hell of a gutsy move. As gutsy as it was crazy. He'd warned her the first day they'd met that winters in Alaska were a lot worse than the coldest day in Denver. Evidently she hadn't believed him and now would find out the truth for herself. She had arrived nearly frozen.

But nearly frozen or not, that didn't stop the male in him from remembering how good she'd looked standing on his porch. Or how she'd looked standing by his fireplace after she'd removed layer after layer of clothing.

He had awakened this morning pretty much prepared for anything. He figured it was only a matter of time before Garth showed up. And a snowstorm blowing in was the norm. What he hadn't counted on was Bailey showing up out of Alaska's cold blue sky. When he'd left Denver, he had assumed their paths wouldn't cross again. There was no reason why they should. Even if the Outlaws kindled a relationship with the Westmorelands, that wouldn't necessarily mean anything to *him*, because he lived here on the island and seldom flew to Fairbanks.

"Sorry I overslept."

He turned around and then wished he hadn't. She was

still wearing the clothes she'd had on earlier, since she didn't have any others, but his gaze moved beyond that. From what he could tell, she wasn't wearing any makeup and she had changed her hairstyle. It no longer hung around her shoulders but was pulled back in a ponytail. The style made her features look younger, delicate and sexy enough to make his lower body throb.

"No problem," he said, turning his attention back to the stove.

He'd seen enough of her. Too much for his well-being. Having her standing in the middle of his kitchen, a place he'd never figured she would be, was sending crazy thoughts through his head. Like how good she looked in that particular spot. A spot where Kalyn had never stood. In fact, his wife had refused to come to Kodiak. She hadn't wanted to visit the place where he was born. Had referred to it as untamed wilderness that lacked civilization. She hadn't wanted to visit such a remote area, much less live there. She was a California girl through and through. She'd lived for the beaches, the orange groves and Hollywood. Anything else just didn't compute with her.

"What are you cooking? Smells good."

He inwardly smiled, although he didn't want to. Was that her way of letting him know she was hungry? "Bison stew. My grandmother's recipe," he said over his shoulder.

"No wonder it smells good, then."

Now, aren't you full of compliments, he thought sarcastically, knowing she was probably trying to be nice for a reason. But he wasn't buying it, because he knew her motives. "By the time you wash up I'll have dinner on the table."

"I've washed up and I can help. Thanks to Chloe I'm pretty good in the kitchen. Tell me what you need me to do."

"Why Chloe?"

"In addition to all her other talents, she is a wonderful

cook and often prepares breakfast for Ramsey and his men. Remind me to tell you one day how she and Ramsey met."

He came close to saying that he wouldn't be reminding her of anything, and he didn't need her to do anything, unless she could find her way back to the airport. But he reined in his temper and said, "You can set the table. Everything you need is in that drawer over there." He never ate at a set table but figured it would give her something to do so she wouldn't get underfoot. Not that trying to put distance between them really mattered. Her scent had already downplayed the aroma of the stew.

The ringing of his cell phone on the kitchen counter jarred him out of his thoughts. He moved from the stove to pick it up, recognizing his foreman's ringtone.

"Yes, Willie? What is it?"

"It's Marcus, boss," Willie said in a frantic tone. "A big brown's got him pinned in a shack and nothing we can do will scare him off. We've been firing shots, but we haven't managed a hit."

"Damn. I'm on my way."

Walker turned and quickly moved toward the closet where his parkas hung and his boots were stored. "Got to go," he said quickly. "That was Willie Hines, my foreman. A brown bear has one of my men holed up in a shack and I need to get there fast."

"May I go?"

He glanced over his shoulder to tell her no. Then he changed his mind. It probably had something to do with that pleading look on her face. "Yes, but stay out of the way. Grab your coat, hat and scarf. And be quick. My men are waiting."

She moved swiftly and by the time he'd put on his boots she was back. He grabbed one of the rifles off the rack. When she reached up and grabbed a rifle off the rack as well, he stared at her. "What do you think you're doing?"

"I'm not a bad shot. Maybe I can help."

He doubted she could and just hoped she stayed out of the way, but he didn't have time to argue. "Fine, let's go."

"I thought bears normally hibernated in the winter," Bailey said, hanging on in the Jeep. Walker was driving like a madman and the seat belt was barely holding her in place. On top of that, her thick wool coat was nothing against the bone-chilling wind and the icy slivers of snow that had begun to fall.

"It's not officially winter yet. Besides, this particular brown is probably the same one who's been causing problems for the past year. Nothing he does is normal. There's been a bounty on his head for a while now."

Bailey nodded. Although bears were known to reside in the Rockies, they were seldom seen. She'd known of only one incident of a bear in Westmoreland Country. Dillon had called the authorities, who had captured the bear and set him free elsewhere. She then remembered what Walker had told her the first day they'd met. There were more bears than people living on Kodiak Island.

The Jeep came to a sudden stop in front of three men she figured worked for Walker. He was out of the truck in a flash and before she could unbuckle her seat belt, he snapped out an order. "Stay put, Bailey."

She grudgingly did as she was told and watched him race toward the men. They pointed at the scene taking place a hundred or so feet ahead of them. The creature wasn't what she'd expected of a brown bear. He was a huge grizzly tearing away at a small, dilapidated shack, pawing through timber, lumber and planks trying to get to the man trapped inside. Unless someone did something, it wouldn't take long for the bear to succeed. And if anyone tried shooting the bear now, they would place the man inside the shack at risk.

She didn't have to hear what Walker and his men were saying to know they were devising a plan to pull the bear's attention away from the shack. And it didn't take long to figure out that Walker had volunteered to be the bait. Putting his own life at risk.

She watched, horrified, as Walker raced forward to get the bear's attention, coming to a stop at what seemed to be just a few feet from the animal. At first it seemed as if nothing could dissuade the bear. A few more loose timbers and he would get his prey. She could hear the man inside screaming in fright, begging for help before it was too late.

Walker then picked up a tree limb and hit the bear. That got the animal's attention. Bailey held her breath when the bear turned and went charging after Walker. The plan was for Walker to lure the bear away from the shack so his men could get a good shot. It seemed the ploy was working until Walker lost his balance and fell to the ground.

Bailey was out of the Jeep in a flash, her rifle in her hand. She stood beside the men and raised her gun to take a shot.

"There's no way you can hit that bear from here, lady," one of the men said.

She ignored his words, knowing Walker would be mauled to death unless she did something. She pulled the trigger mere seconds before the bear reached Walker. The huge animal fell and it seemed the earth shook under the weight.

"Did you see that?"

"She got that grizzly and her rifle doesn't even have a scope on it."

"How can she shoot like that? Where did she come from?"

Ignoring what the three men were saying, she raced over to Walker. "Are you okay?"

"I'm fine. I just banged my leg against that damn rock when I tripped."

Placing her rifle aside, she leaned down to check him

over and saw the red bloodstain on the leg of his jeans. He wasn't fine.

She turned to his men, who were looking at her strangely. "He's injured. I need two of you to lift him and take him to the Jeep. The other one, I need to check on the man in the shack. I think he passed out."

"I said I'm fine, Bailey, and I can walk," Walker insisted.

"Not on that leg." She turned to the men. "Lift him and take him to the truck," she ordered again.

"Don't anyone dare lift me. I said I can walk," Walker snapped at the two men who moved toward him.

"No, you can't walk," she snapped back at him. She then glared at his men, who stood staring, unsure whose orders to follow. "Do it!" she demanded, letting them know she expected her order to be followed regardless of what Walker said.

As if they figured any woman who could shoot that well was a woman whose order should be obeyed, they quickly moved to lift Walker. He spewed expletives, which they all ignored.

"I'll call Doc Witherspoon to come quick," one of the men said after they placed Walker in the Jeep. "And we'll be right behind you to help get him out once you reach the ranch house."

She quickly got in on the driver's side. "Thanks."

She glanced over at Walker, who was now unconscious, and fought to keep her panic at bay. Of all the things she figured she'd have to deal with upon reaching Alaska, killing a grizzly bear hadn't been one of them.

Eight

Walker came awake, then reclosed his eyes when pain shot up his leg. It took him a while before he reopened them. When he did, he noted that he was in his bed and flat on his back. It didn't take him long to recall why. The grizzly.

"Bailey?" he called out softly when he heard a sound from somewhere in the room.

"She's not here, Walker," a deep masculine voice said.

He didn't have to wonder who that voice belonged to. "Doc Witherspoon?"

"Who else? I only get to see you these days when you get banged up."

Walker shook his head, disagreeing. "I never get banged up."

"You did this time. Story has it that bear would have eaten you alive if that little lady hadn't saved you."

The doctor's words suddenly made Walker remember what he'd said earlier. "Bailey's not here? Where is she?"

"She left for the airport."

Airport? Bailey was returning to Denver already? "How long have I been out, Doc?" he asked. A lot of stuff seemed fuzzy in his mind.

"Off and on close to forty-eight hours. Mainly because I gave you enough pain pills to down an elephant. Bailey thought it was best. You needed your rest. On top of all that, you were an unruly patient."

Who cared what Bailey thought when she wasn't there? He then replayed in his mind every detail of that day with the bear. "How's Marcus?"

"I treated him for shock but he's fine now. And since he's a ladies' man, he's had plenty of women parading in and out of his place pretending to be nurses."

Walker nodded, trying to dismiss the miserable feelings flooding through when he thought about Bailey being gone. She'd told him she was returning to Denver within forty-eight hours, so what had he expected? Besides, hadn't he wanted her gone? Hadn't he told her she wasn't welcome? So why was he suddenly feeling so disheartened? Must be the medication messing with his mind.

"You have a nasty cut to the leg, Walker. Went real deep. You lost a lot of blood and I had to put in stitches. You've got several bruised ribs but nothing's broken. If you stay off that leg as much as possible and follow my orders, you'll be as good as new in another week or so. I'll be back to check on you again in a few days."

"Whatever." Walker knew Doc Witherspoon would ignore his surly attitude; after all, he was the same man who'd brought Walker into the world.

Walker closed his eyes. He wasn't sure how long he slept, but when he opened his eyes some time later, it was a feminine scent that awakened him. Being careful not to move his leg, he shifted his head and saw Bailey sitting in the chair by the bed reading a book. He blinked to make sure he wasn't dreaming. It wouldn't be the first time he'd dreamed of her since leaving Denver. But never had he dreamed of her sitting by the bed. In all his dreams she had been in the bed with him.

He blinked again and when she still sat there, he figured it was the real thing. "Doc said you left for the airport."

She glanced over at him and their gazes held. Ripples of awareness flooded through him. Why was her very presence in his room filling every inch of space within it? And why did he want her out of that chair and closer to the bed? Closer to him?

She broke eye contact to brush off a piece of lint from her shirt. "I did leave for the airport. Their twenty-four hours were up and I hadn't gotten my luggage."

"You went to the airport to get your luggage?"

"Yes."

He couldn't explain the relief that raced through him. At the moment he didn't want to explain it. He felt exhausted and was in too much pain to think clearly. "I thought you were on your way back to Denver."

"Sorry to disappoint you."

He drew in a deep breath. She'd misunderstood and was assuming things again. Instead of telling her how wrong she was, he asked, "Well, did you get your luggage?"

"Yes. They'd found it, but were taking their time bringing it here. I guess I wasn't at the top of their priority list."

He bet they wished they hadn't made that mistake. She'd probably given them hell.

"You want something to eat?" she asked him. "There's plenty of bison stew left."

Walker was glad because he was hungry and remembered he'd been cooking the stew when he'd gotten the call about Marcus. "Yes. Thanks."

"I'll be right back."

He watched Bailey get out of the chair and place the

book aside before heading for the door. He couldn't help but appreciate the shape of her backside in sweats. At least his attention to physical details hadn't lessened any. He brought his hand to his jaw and realized he needed to trim his beard.

When Bailey pulled the door shut behind her, Walker closed his eyes and again remembered in full detail everything that had happened down by the shack. The one thing that stuck out in his mind above everything else was the fact that Bailey Westmoreland had saved his life.

"Yes, Walker is fine just bruised and he had to get stiches in his leg," she said to Ramsey on the phone. "I hated killing that bear but it was him or Walker. He was big and a mean one."

"You did what you had to do, Bay. I'm sure Walker appreciated you being there."

"Maybe. Doesn't matter now, though. He's confined to bed and needs help. The doctor wants him to stay off his leg as much as possible. That means I need to tell Chloe and Lucia that I'll need a few more days off. Possibly another week."

"Well, you're in luck because Lucia is here, so I'll let you speak to both her and Chloe. You take care of yourself."

"Thanks, I will. I miss everyone."

"And we miss you. But it's nice to have you gone for a while," he teased.

"Whatever," she said, grinning, knowing he was joking. She was certain every member of her family missed her as much as she missed them.

A short while later she hung up. Chloe and Lucia had understood the situation and told her to take all the time she needed to care for Walker. She appreciated that.

Drawing in a deep breath, she glanced around the kitchen.

Over the past three days she had become pretty familiar with it. She knew where all the cooking equipment was located and had found a recipe book that had once belonged to Walker's grandmother. There was a family photo album located in one of the cabinets. She'd smiled at the pictures of Walker's family, people she figured were his parents and grandparents. But nowhere in the album did she find any of his wedding pictures or photographs of his wife and child.

She looked out the window. It was snowing hard outside and had been for the past two days. She had met all the men who worked on Walker's ranch. They had dropped by and introduced themselves and told her they would take care of everything for their boss. News of her encounter with the bear had spread and a lot of the men stared at her in amazement. She found them to be a nice group of guys. A number of them had worked on the ranch when Walker's father was alive. She could tell from the way they'd inquired about Walker's well-being that they were very fond of him and deeply loyal.

She snorted at the thought of that. They evidently knew a different Walker from the one she'd gotten to know. Due to all the medication the doctor had given him, he slept most of the time, which was good. And he refused to let her assist him to the bathroom or in taking his baths. Doctor Witherspoon had warned him about getting the stitches wet and about staying off his leg as much as possible, so at least he was taking that advice. One of his men had dropped off crutches for him to use, and he was using them, as well.

Snow was coming down even worse now and everything was covered with a white blanket. The men had made sure there was plenty of wood for the fireplace and she had checked and found the freezer and pantry well stocked, so there was nothing for her to do but take things one day at a time while waiting for Walker to get better.

Garth had called for Walker and she'd told him what had happened. He'd left his number and told her to call if she needed anything or if Walker continued to give her trouble. Like she'd told Garth, Walker had pretty much slept for the past three days. When he was awake, other than delivering his meals and making sure he took his medication, she mostly left him alone.

But not today. His bedroom was dark and dreary and although the outside was barely any better, she intended to go into his room and open the curtains. And she intended for him to get out of bed and sit in a chair long enough for her to change the linens.

According to Garth, Walker had a housekeeper, an older woman by the name of Lola Albright, who came in each week, no matter how ugly the weather got outside. She had located Ms. Albright's phone number in the kitchen drawer and called to advise her that she need not come this week. Somehow, but not surprisingly, the woman had already heard what happened. After complimenting Bailey for her skill with a gun, she had thanked Bailey for calling and told her if she needed anything to let her know. Ms. Albright and her husband were Walker's closest neighbors and lived on a farm about ten miles away.

Grabbing the tray with the bowl of chicken noodle soup that she'd cooked earlier, Bailey moved up the stairs to Walker's bedroom. She opened the door and stopped, surprised to see him already out of bed and sitting in the chair.

The first thing she noticed was that he'd shaved. She couldn't stop her gaze from roaming over his face while thinking about just how sexy he looked. He was as gorgeous without facial hair as he was with it. He had changed clothes and was looking like his former self. A part of her was grateful he was sitting up, but then another part of her was annoyed that he hadn't asked for her assistance.

"Lunchtime," she said, moving into the room and putting the tray on a table beside his chair. She wanted to believe he said thanks, although it sounded more like a grunt. She moved across the room to open the curtains.

"What do you think you're doing?"

Without turning around, she continued opening the curtains. "I thought you might want to look outside."

"I want the curtains closed."

"Sorry, but now they're open." She turned back around and couldn't help but shiver when she met his stare. His *glare* was more like it, but his bad mood didn't bother her. After five brothers and a slew of male cousins she knew how to deal with a man who couldn't have his way.

"Glad you're up. I need to change the linens," she said, moving toward the bed.

"Lola's my housekeeper. She's coming tomorrow and can do it then."

"I talked to Lola this morning and told her there was no need for her to come out in this weather. I can handle things while I'm here."

He didn't say anything but she could tell by his scowl that he hadn't liked that move. And speaking of moves, she felt his eyes on her with every move she made while changing the sheets. She could actually feel his gaze raking across her. When she finished and turned to look at him, his mouth was set in a hard, tight line.

"You know, if you keep looking all mean and cranky, Walker, you might grow old looking that way."

His frown deepened. "No matter what you do, I won't be changing my mind about the interview. So you're wasting your time."

Drawing in a deep, angry breath, she moved across the room to stand in front of him. She leaned down a little to make sure her eyes were level with his. "You ungrateful bastard!"

That was followed by a few more obscenities she hadn't

said since the last time Dillon had washed out her mouth with soap years ago. But Walker's accusations had set her off. "Do you think that's why I'm here? That I only killed that bear, hung around, put up with your crappy attitude just because I want an interview? Well, I've got news for you. I don't want an interview from you. You're no longer a viable candidate. Women are interested in men who are loners but decent, not loners who are angry and couldn't recognize a kind deed if it bit them on the—"

She hadn't expected him to tug on a lock of her hair and capture her mouth. She hadn't expected him to kiss her with a hunger that sent desire raging through her, flooding her with memories of the night they'd parked in her truck at Bailey's Bay.

Convincing herself she was only letting him have his way with her mouth because she didn't want to move and hurt his leg, she found herself returning the kiss, moaning when his tongue began doing all kinds of delicious things to hers.

They were things she had dreamed about, and craved—but only with him. She could admit that at night, in the guest room, in that lonely bed, she had thought of him, although she hadn't wanted to do so. And since all she had were memories, she had recalled how he had licked a slow, wet trail from her mouth to her breasts and then lower.

Her thoughts were snatched back to the present when she felt Walker ease up her skirt and softly skim her inner thighs. His fingers slipped beneath the elastic of her panties before sliding inside her.

She shuddered and his finger moved deeper, pushing her over the edge. She wanted to pull back but couldn't. Instead, she followed his lead and intensified the kiss while his fingers did scandalous things.

Then he released her mouth to whisper against her wet lips, "Come for me again, Bailey."

As if his request was a sensual command her body had to obey, ragged heat rolled in her stomach as her pulse throbbed and her blood roared through her veins. Her body exploded, every nerve ending igniting with an intensity that terrified her. This time was more powerful than the last, and she had no willpower to stop the moan released from her lips. No willpower to stop spreading her thighs wider and arching her mouth closer to once again be taken.

That was when Walker placed his mouth over Bailey's again, kissing her with no restraint. He deepened the kiss, pushing his fingers even farther inside her. He loved the sounds she made when she climaxed; he loved knowing he was the one to make it happen. And he intended to make it happen all over again. Moments later, when she shuddered and groaned into his mouth, he knew he had succeeded.

She grabbed his shoulders, and he didn't flinch when she dug her fingers into his skin. Nor did he flinch when she placed pressure on his tongue. He merely retaliated by sucking harder on hers.

He had been hungry for her taste for days. Each time she had entered his bedroom, he had hated lying flat on his back, not being able to do the one thing he'd wanted to do—kiss her in a way that was as raw as he felt.

Most of the time he'd feigned sleep, but through heavy-lidded eyes he had watched her, studied her and longed for her. He'd known each and every time she had walked around his room, cursing under her breath about his foul mood, using profanity he'd never heard before. He had laid there as his ears burned, pretending to sleep as she called him every nasty name in the book for being so difficult and pigheaded.

He'd also known when she'd calmed down enough to sit quietly in the chair by his bed to read, or softly hum while flipping through one of his wildlife magazines. And he would never forget the day she had worn a sweater and a pair of leggings. She had stretched up to put something away on one of the top shelves in his room and caused his entire body to harden in desire watching her graceful movements. And the outlines of her curves covered by those leggings... His need for her had flowed through him like a potent drug, more intoxicating than the medication Doc Witherspoon had him taking. Knowing she was off-limits, because he had decided it had to be so, had only sharpened his less-than-desirable attitude.

But today had been different. He had awakened with his raging hormones totally out of control. He'd felt better and had wanted to clean himself up, move around and wait for her. He hadn't anticipated kissing her but he was glad he had.

There were multiple layers to Bailey Westmoreland, layers he wanted to unpeel one at a time. The anticipation was almost killing him.

Growling low in his throat, he slowly pulled his mouth away and pulled his fingers from inside her. Then, as she watched, he brought those same fingers to his lips and licked them in slow, greedy movements.

He held her gaze, tempted to take possession of her mouth again. Instead, he whispered, "Thank you for saving my life, Bailey."

He could tell his words of thanks had surprised her. Little did she know she would be in for a few more surprises before she left his ranch to return to Denver.

"And thank you for letting me savor you," he whispered. "To have such a filthy mouth, you have a very delicious taste."

And he meant it. He loved the taste of her on his fingers. Bailey was a woman any man would want to possess. The good. The bad. And the ugly. And for some reason that he didn't understand or could explain, he wanted that man to be him.

With that thought planted firmly in his mind, he leaned close, captured her mouth with his and kissed her once again.

Nine

"What have you gotten yourself into, Bailey?" she asked herself a few days later while standing outside on Walker's front porch.

This was the first time the weather had improved enough for her to be outside. As far as she could see, snow covered everything. It had seemed to her that it hadn't been snowflakes falling for the past several days but ice chips. The force of them had hit the roof, the windowpanes and blanketed the grounds.

Yesterday, Josette told her a bad snowstorm had hit Denver and threatened to close the airport. Bailey had endured Denver's snowstorms all her life, but what she'd experienced over the past few days here in Alaska was far worse. Even though parts of this place reminded her of Denver, looking out at the Strait from her bedroom window meant she saw huge glaciers instead of mountains. And one of the ponds on Walker's property had been a solid block of ice since she'd arrived.

Wrapping her hands around the mug of coffee she held in her hand, she took a sip. Would her question to herself ever be answered? Was there even an answer? All she knew was that she had to leave this place and return home before…

Before what?

Already Walker had turned her normally structured mind topsy-turvy. It had started the day he'd kissed her in his bedroom. Oh, he'd done more than kiss her. He had inserted his fingers inside her and made her come. Just like before. But this time he had tasted her on his fingers, letting her watch. And then he'd kissed her again, letting her taste herself on his lips.

At least when that kiss had ended she'd had the good sense to get out of the room. And she had stayed out until it was time to deliver his dinner. Luckily when she'd entered the room later that day, he had been asleep, so she had left the covered tray of food by his bed. Then Willie had dropped by that evening to visit with Walker and had returned the tray to the kitchen. That had meant she didn't have to go up to his room to get it.

She had checked on him before retiring for the night and he'd been sitting up again, in that same chair. After asking him if there was anything he needed before she went to bed, she had quickly left the room.

That had been three days ago and she'd avoided going into his room since then. She'd only been in to deliver his food. Each time she found him dressed and sitting in that same chair. It was obvious he was improving, so why hadn't she made plans to leave Kodiak Island?

She kept telling herself she wanted to wait until Dr. Witherspoon assured her that Walker could manage on his own. Hopefully, today would be that day. The doctor had arrived an hour ago and was up there with Walker now. It shouldn't be long before Bailey could work her way out of whatever she'd gotten herself into with Walker.

Knowing that if she stayed outside any longer she was liable to turn into a block of ice, she went back inside. She was closing the door behind her as Dr. Witherspoon came down the stairs.

"So how is our patient, Doctor?" she asked the tall, muscular man who reminded her of a lumberjack more than a doctor.

"Walker's fine. The stiches are out and he should be able to maneuver the stairs in a day or so. I'm encouraging him to do so in order to work the stiffness out of his legs."

Bailey nodded as she sat her coffee mug on a side table. "So he's ready to start handling things on his own now?"

"Pretty much, but I still don't want him to overdo it. As you know, Walker has a hard head. I'm glad you're here to make sure he doesn't overexert himself."

Bailey nibbled her bottom lip before saying, "But I can't stay here forever. I have a job back in Denver. Do you have any idea when it will be okay for me to leave?"

"If you have pressing business to attend to back home then you should go now. I'm sure Lola won't mind moving in for a few days until Walker's fully recovered."

Dr. Witherspoon was giving her an out, so why wasn't she taking it? Why was she making herself believe she was needed here?

"Just let me know when you plan to leave so I'll know what to do," the doctor added. "I'm sure you know Walker would prefer to be by himself after you leave, but that's not wise. Personally, I think he needs you."

The doctor didn't know just how wrong he was. Sure, Walker liked kissing her, but that didn't mean he needed her. "I doubt that very seriously. He'll probably be glad to have me gone."

"Um, I don't think so. I've known Walker all his life. I

delivered him into the world and looked forward to delivering his son, but his wife wouldn't hear of it. She wanted their son born in California. She wasn't too fond of this place."

Dr. Witherspoon paused, and a strange look appeared on his face, as if he'd said too much. "Anyway, if you decide to leave before the end of the week, let me know so I can notify Lola."

"I will."

Before reaching the door, the doctor turned. "Oh, yes, I almost forgot. Walker wants to see you."

Bailey lifted a brow. "He does?"

"Yes." The doctor then opened the door and left.

Bailey wondered why Walker would ask to see her. He'd seen her earlier when she'd taken him breakfast. She hadn't been able to decipher his mood, mainly because she hadn't hung around long enough. She'd placed the tray on the table and left. But she had seen that he'd opened the curtains and was sitting in what was evidently his favorite chair.

After taking a deep breath, she moved toward the stairs. She might as well go see what Walker wanted. All things considered, he might be summoning her to ask her to leave.

"Dr. Witherspoon said you wanted to see me."

Walker turned around at the sound of Bailey's voice. She stood in the doorway as if ready to sprint away at a moment's notice. Had his mood been as bad as Doc Witherspoon claimed? If so, she had put up with it when any other woman would not have. "Come in, Bailey, I won't bite."

He wouldn't bite, but he wouldn't mind tasting her mouth again.

She hesitated before entering, looking all around his bedroom before looking back at him. That gave him just enough time to check her out, to appreciate how she looked in her sweats, sweater and jacket. She wore her hair pinned back from her face, which showed off her beautiful bone structure. Although he hadn't stuck around to meet her sister Gemma, he had met Megan. There was a slight resemblance between the two but he thought Bailey had a look all her own. Both were beautiful women but there was a radiance about Bailey that gave him pause whenever he saw her.

"Okay, I'm in," she said, coming to stand in front of him. However, he noted she wasn't all in his face like last time. She was keeping what she figured was a safe distance.

"You're standing up," she observed.

"Is there a reason for me not to be?"

She shrugged. "No. But normally you're sitting down in that chair over there."

He followed her gaze to the chair. "Yes. That chair has special meaning for me."

"It does? Why?"

"It once belonged to my mother. I'm told she used to sit in it and rock me to sleep. I don't recall that, but I do remember coming in here at night and sitting right there on the floor while she sat in that chair and read me a story."

"I heard you tell Dillon you're an only child. Your parents didn't want any more children?"

"They wanted plenty, which is why they built such a huge house. But Mom had difficulties with my birth and Doc Witherspoon advised her not to try again."

"Oh."

A moment of silence settled between them before Bailey said, "You didn't say why you wanted to see me."

No, he hadn't. He stared at her, wishing he wasn't so fascinated with her mouth. "I need to apologize. I haven't been the nicest person the past several days." No need to tell her Doc Witherspoon hadn't spared any punches in telling Walker just what an ass he'd been.

"No, you haven't. You have been somewhat of a grouch, but I've dealt with worse. I have five brothers and a slew of male cousins. I've discovered men can be more difficult than sick babies when they are in pain."

"Regardless, that was no reason to take out my mood on you and I apologize."

She shrugged. "Apology acc—" As if remembering another time those words had set off a kiss between them, she quickly modified her words. "Thank you for apologizing." She turned to leave.

"Wait!"

Bailey turned back around. "Yes?"

"Lunch."

She raised a brow. "What about it?"

"I thought we could eat lunch together."

Bailey eyed Walker speculatively before asking, "Why would you want us to eat lunch together?"

He countered with a question of his own. "Any reason we can't? Although I appreciate you being here, helping out and everything, you're still a guest in my home. Besides, I'm doing better and Doc suggested I try the stairs. I figured we could sit and eat in the kitchen. Frankly, I'm tired of looking at these four walls."

She could see why he would be. "Okay, I'll serve you lunch in the kitchen."

"And you will join me?"

Bailey nibbled her lips. How could she explain that just breathing the same air as him was playing havoc on her nervous system?

Even now, just standing this close to him was messing with her mind. Making her remember things she shouldn't. Like what had happened the last time she'd stayed this long in this bedroom. And he wanted them to share lunch? What would they talk about? One thing was for certain— she would let him lead the conversation. She would not give him any reason to think she was interviewing him undercover. He'd already accused her of having under-handed motives.

When she'd walked into this room, she hadn't counted on him standing in the middle of it. She'd been fully aware of his presence the moment she'd opened the door. He was dressed in a pair of well-worn jeans and a flannel shirt that showed what an impressive body he had. If he'd lost any weight she couldn't tell. He still had a solid chest, broad shoulders and taut thighs. She'd been too taken with all that masculine power to do anything but stand and stare.

Without the beard his jaw looked stronger and his mouth—which should be outlawed—was way too sexy to be real.

Bailey couldn't stop herself from wondering why he wanted to share lunch with her. But then, she didn't want to spend time analyzing his reason. So she convinced her-self it was because she would be leaving soon, return-ing to Denver. Then there would be no reason for their paths to cross again. If things worked out between the Westmorelands and the Outlaws, she could see Walker hanging out with her brothers and cousins every now and then, but she doubted she would be invited to attend any of those gatherings.

Knowing he was waiting for an answer, she said, "Yes, I'll share lunch with you."

Ten

"So, Bailey, who taught you how to shoot?"

She bit into her sandwich and held up her finger to let him know it would be a minute before she could answer because she had food in her mouth. Walker didn't mind watching her anyway.

"The question you should probably ask is who *didn't* teach me to shoot. My brothers and cousins were quick to give me lessons, especially Bane. He's so good that he's a master sniper with the navy SEALs. Bane taught me how to hit a target. I don't want to sound as if I'm bragging, but I'm an excellent shot because of him."

"You're not bragging, just stating a fact. I'm living proof, and note I said *living* proof. There's no doubt in my mind that grizzly would have done me in if you hadn't taken it down."

"Well, I'm glad I was there."

He was glad she'd been there, too. At the sight of a huge grizzly any other woman would have gone into shock. But not Bailey. She had showed true grit by bringing down that bear. She'd made that shot from a distance he doubted even he could have made. His three men had admitted they could not have made it without running the risk of shooting him.

"My men are in awe of you," he added. "You impressed them."

She frowned. "I didn't do it to impress anyone, Walker. I did what I felt I had to do. I wasn't going after accolades."

That, he thought, was what made her different. Most of the women he knew would use anything to score brownie points. Hadn't making a good impression meant everything to Kalyn?

"I think you're the real hero, Walker. You risked your life getting that bear away from the shack before it got to Marcus."

He shrugged. "Like you said, I did what I felt I had to do. I wasn't going after accolades." He blinked over at her and smiled. He was rewarded when she smiled back.

Just what was he doing flirting with her? He was pretty rusty at it. There hadn't been a woman he'd really been attracted to since Kalyn. He'd had meaningless affairs solely for the purpose of quenching raging hormones, but he hadn't been interested in a woman beyond sex...until now.

He bit into his sandwich. "This is good. I hope I didn't get underfoot while you prepared lunch, but I couldn't stay in my bedroom a minute longer."

"Thanks, and no, you didn't get underfoot."

But he had made her nervous, he was sure of it. She'd been leaning over looking into the refrigerator when he'd walked into the kitchen. The sight of her sweats stretched over a curvy bottom had definitely increased his testosterone level. He had been happy just to stand there, leaning against the kitchen counter with an erection, and stare. After closing the refrigerator she'd nearly dropped the jars of mayo and mustard when she'd turned around to find him there. Of course she'd scolded him for coming down the stairs without her assistance, but he'd ignored all that. He wasn't used to a woman fussing over him.

She'd made him sit down at the table and had given him a magazine that had been delivered by the mailman earlier. Instead of flipping through the pages, he'd preferred watching her move around the kitchen. More than once she'd caught him staring and he'd quickly glanced back down at the magazine.

Walker would be the first to admit he'd picked up on a difference in the atmosphere of his home. It now held the scent of a woman. Although the guest room she was using was on the opposite side of the house, the moment he'd walked out of his bedroom, the scent of jasmine had flowed through his nostrils. At first he'd been taken off guard by it but then he decided he preferred it to the woodsy smell he was used to. It was then that he realized someone other than himself occupied the house for the first time since his parents' deaths. His privacy had been invaded, but, surprisingly, he didn't have a problem with it. Bailey had a way of growing on a person.

"Will you be returning to your room after you finish lunch?" she asked.

He glanced over at her. "No. There're a few things I need to do."

"Like what?"

He lifted a brow. Did she think whatever he did was any of her business?

As if she read his mind, she said, "I hope you're not planning to do anything that might cause a setback, Walker."

He heard the concern in her voice and clearly saw it in her eyes. It reminded him of what had been missing in his life for almost ten years. A woman who cared.

A woman he desired.

Although they had never made love, they had come close. It didn't take much to remember a pair of perfectly shaped breasts or the wetness of her femininity. Going down on a woman wasn't part of his regular lovemaking routine, but Bailey's scent had made him want to do it for her, and after that first time he'd found her flavor addictive.

So yes, he desired her. With a passion. Whenever he saw her, his mind filled with all the things he'd love to do to her. It had been a long time since he'd slept with a woman, but that wasn't the issue. He desired Bailey simply because she was a woman worthy of desiring. There had been this attraction between them from the start, and they both knew it. The attraction was still alive and kicking, and they both knew that, as well.

How long were they planning to play the "try to ignore it" game?

"No setbacks for me. I intend to follow Dr. Witherspoon's orders."

"Good."

Did Bailey realize she liked getting in the last word? "I need to go over my books, replenish my stock and order more branding equipment. I'll be fine."

She nodded before getting up from the table. She reached for his plate and he placed his hand on hers. He immediately felt a sizzle race up his spine and he fought to ignore it. "I can take care of my own plate. I appreciate you being here but I don't want you to feel as if you have to wait on me. I'm doing better."

What he didn't add was that he was doing well enough for her to go back home to Westmoreland Country. However, for reasons he wasn't ready to question, her leaving was not what he wanted.

"Fine," she said, moving away from the table.

He tried concentrating on his cup of coffee, but couldn't.

He watched her move around the room, putting stuff away. He enjoyed watching how her body looked in sweats. Whenever she moved, so did his sex as it tingled with need.

"Any reason you're staring?" she asked, turning to meet his gaze.

She looked younger today. Softer. It could be the way the daylight was coming in through the window. "You got eyes in the back of your head, Bailey?"

"No, but I could feel you staring."

In that case there was no need to lie. "Yes, I was staring. You look good in that outfit."

She looked down at herself. "In sweats? You've got to be kidding me. You must have taken an extra pill or two this morning."

He smiled as his gaze raked over her. "No, I didn't take an extra pill or two. Just stating the facts."

He sensed she didn't believe him. She brushed her fingers through her hair as if his comment had given her reason to wonder if she looked just the opposite. Possibly disheveled and unkempt. He found that interesting. How could she not know she looked good no matter what she wore? And she probably had no idea that her hot, lush scent filled the kitchen instead of the scent of what she'd prepared for lunch.

As if dismissing what he'd said, she turned back to the sink. "Are you going to sit there and stare or are you going to work in your office?" she asked over her shoulder a few moments later.

"I think I'll just sit here and stare for a while."

"It's not nice to stare."

"So I've heard."

She swung around and frowned at him. "Then, stare at something else, Walker."

A smile touched the corner of his lips. "There's noth-

ing else in this kitchen I would rather stare at than you."
And he meant it.

"Sounds as if you've got a case of cabin fever."

"Possibly, but I doubt it."

She placed the dish towel on the counter. "So what do
you think it is?"

He placed his coffee cup down, thinking that was easy
enough to answer. "Lust. I'm lusting after you, Bailey."

A drugging urgency slammed into Bailey's chest, making her nipples pucker and fire race through her veins.
Now, more than before, she felt the weight of Walker's
gaze. She didn't usually feel feminine in sweats, but he
had a way of making her feel sexy even when she didn't
have a right to feel that way.

And while he sat there, watching her every move, she
was fully aware of what was going through his mind. Because she was pretty certain it was the same thing going
through hers. This seductive heat was beginning to affect
her everywhere—in her breasts, deep in the juncture of
her thighs and in the middle of her stomach. The memories of those two kisses they'd previously shared only
intensified the hot, aching sensations overwhelming her
common sense.

She heard him slide the chair back and watched as he
slowly stood. "You can come here or I'm coming over
there," he said matter-of-factly in a deep voice.

She swallowed, knowing he was serious. As serious as
she was hot for him. But was she ready for this? A meaningless affair with Walker? Hadn't he told her that night
in the truck at Bailey's Bay that all he could offer was a
meaningless affair? At the time, she'd responded by saying that kind of relationship didn't bother her. Her future
was tied to Westmoreland Country and not to any man.
There wasn't that much love in the world.

But there was that much passion. That much desire. To a degree she'd never encountered before. She couldn't understand it, but there was no denying the way her body responded to him. It responded in a way it had never reacted to another man. A part of her believed this was no accident. What was taking place between them was meant to be. Not only was that thought a discovery, it was also an acceptance.

It was that acceptance that pushed her to say, "Meet me halfway."

He nodded and moved toward her. She moved toward him. Bailey drew in a deep breath with every step, keeping her gaze fixed on his face. That strong, square chin, those gorgeous dark eyes, his delicious mouth. He was such a striking figure of a man whose looks alone could make a woman shiver. Toss in her nightly naughty dreams and it made her bold enough to turn those dreams into reality.

When they met in the center of the kitchen, he wrapped his arms around her with a possessiveness that took her breath away.

"Be careful of your leg," she warned softly after managing to breathe again. She liked the feel of his body pressed hard against hers.

"My leg isn't what's aching," he said with a huskiness she heard. "Something else is."

She knew what that something else was. She could feel his erection pressed against the juncture of her thighs. Even while recovering from his injury, his strength amazed her. Although he annoyed her at times by not asking for help, his willpower and independence were admirable. And the thought that this was one particular area where this strong, sexy specimen of a man *did* need her sent her mind and body soaring.

He pulled back slightly to look down at her and she almost melted from the heat in his eyes. The feel of him cupping her bottom to keep their middles connected wasn't helping matters. "Our first time making love should be in a bed, Bailey. But I'm not sure I can make it that far. I need you now," he said in a voice filled with need.

"I'm okay with that, Walker. I need you now, too." She was being honest with him. When it came to sex, she felt honesty was the best policy. She detested the lies and games some couples played.

He pulled her back into his arms when he said, "There's something I need to warn you about."

Now she was the one to pull back slightly to look up at him. "What?"

"It's been a long time since I've been with a woman. A few years. About five."

The information, which he hadn't had to give her, tugged at something deep inside her. "It's been a long time since I've been with a man, as well. More than five years."

He smiled and she knew why. She'd been around the males in her family long enough to know they had no problems with double standards. They could sleep around but didn't want to know their women had done the same.

She wrapped her arms around his neck. "What about your leg? How do you plan for this to work? Got any ideas?"

"I've got plenty and I plan to try out every last one of them."

His words made her heart pound hard against her chest. "Bring it on, Walker Rafferty."

"Baby, I intend to do just that." And then he lowered his mouth down to hers.

Eleven

Sensation ripped through Walker the moment their mouths connected. He eased his tongue into her mouth and kissed her with a hunger that had her groaning. In response his erection pressed even harder against his zipper.

He captured her tongue with his and did the kinds of erotic things he'd dreamed of doing. He sucked as if the need to taste her was as essential to him as breathing. He deepened the kiss and tightened his arms around her. She tasted of heat and a wildness that he found delectable.

But then he found everything about her delectable— the way she fit in his arms, the way their bodies melded together like that was the way they were supposed to be.

Walker slowly eased away from her mouth and drew in a deep satisfying breath, missing the feel of her already. "Take off your clothes," he whispered against her lips.

She raised a brow. "In here?"

He smiled. "Yes. I want to make love to you here. We'll try out all the other rooms later."

She chuckled. "Horny, aren't we?"

He leaned in and licked her lips. "Like I said, it's been five years."

"In that case…"

Moving out of his arms, she took a few steps back and began removing her clothes. He watched her every move, getting more turned on with each stitch she discarded. When she had stripped down to nothing but her panties and bra, he finally released the breath he'd been holding.

He was weak in the knees from looking at her and he leaned against the breakfast bar for support. He needed it when she removed her bra and then slowly peeled her panties down her thighs. He couldn't help growling in pleasure.

It was only then he remembered something very important.

"Damn."

She lifted a concerned brow. "What's wrong?"

"Condoms. I don't have any down here. They're upstairs in my nightstand."

She shook her head. "No need, unless you're concerned about it for health reasons. I'm on the pill to regulate my periods."

He nodded. The thought of spilling inside her sent all kinds of luscious sensations through him. "No concerns. I'm okay with it, if you are."

"I'm okay with it."

He couldn't help but rake his gaze over her naked body. "You are beautiful, Bailey. From the top of your head to your pretty little feet, you are absolutely beautiful."

Bailey had never allowed any man's compliments to go to her head…until now. Walker sounded so serious and the look on his face was so sincere that her heart pounded in appreciation. She wasn't sure why his opinion of how she looked mattered, but it did. And she immediately thought of a way to thank him. Reclaiming the distance separating them, she leaned up on her toes and brushed her lips across his. Then she licked a line from one corner of his mouth to the other in a slow and provocative way.

She smiled in pleasure when she heard his quick intake of breath, glad to know she was getting to him as much as he was getting to her. "Now for your clothes, Walker, and I intend to help you." She intended to do more than that but he would find that out soon enough. He braced against the breakfast bar as she bent down to remove his shoes and socks.

Now for his shirt. She leaned forward and undid the buttons while occasionally leaning up to nip and lick his mouth. The more he moaned the bolder she got as she assisted him out of his shirt and then his T-shirt.

Wow, what a chest. She ran her fingers through the coarse hair covering it. She loved the feel of it beneath her hands. She trailed kisses from his lips, past his jawline to his chest and then used her teeth to nibble on his nipples before devouring them with her tongue and lips.

"Bailey." He breathed out her name in a forced whisper. "I need you."

She needed him, too, but first…

She reached down and unsnapped his jeans before easing down his zipper. Then she inserted her hand into the opening to cup him. She smiled at how thick he felt in her hand. "Um, I think we should get rid of your jeans and briefs, don't you?"

Instead of giving him a chance to answer, she kissed him again, using her tongue to further stir the passion between them. She heard him moan, which was followed by a deep growl when she sucked on his lower lip.

"Don't think I can handle this much longer," he said through clenched teeth.

"Oh, I think you can handle more than you think you can, Walker. Let's see."

She helped him remove his jeans and briefs and then stood back and raked her gaze over him before meeting his eyes. "You are so buff. So gorgeously handsome. So—"

Before she could finish he pulled her to him, capturing her lips in an openmouthed kiss as raw as it was possessive. And when she felt his hand between her legs, she broke off the kiss to ease out of his arms.

"Not so fast. I'm a guest in your home, so today I get to have my way," she whispered.

With that, her fingers gripped his hardness and gently squeezed, loving the feel of his bare flesh in her hands.

"Don't torture me, baby."

Torture? He hadn't endured any torture yet, she thought, as she continued to fondle his thick width, texture and length, loving every minute of it. He was huge, and she intended to sample every single inch.

In a move she knew he was not expecting, she dropped down on her knees and took him into the warmth of her mouth.

"Bailey!"

Walker grabbed her head but instead of pulling her mouth away, he wrapped his fingers in the locks of her hair. He lost all control while watching her head bob up and down. Every muscle in his body trembled and his insides shivered with the impact of her mouth on him. She was pushing him deliciously over the edge. He felt ready to explode.

It was then that he tugged on her hair, using enough force to pull her mouth from him. She looked up at him and smiled, licking her lips. "I need to get inside you now," he said in a guttural growl. He had reached his limit.

In a surprise move, he pulled her up and lifted her to sit on the kitchen table, spreading her legs wide in the process.

Thanks to her, his control was shot to hell. He trailed his fingers through the curls surrounding her feminine folds. She wasn't the only one who wanted a taste. He lowered his head to her wetness.

"Walker!"

He ignored her screaming his name as his tongue devoured her as she'd done to him. And when she wrapped her legs around his neck and bucked her hips against his mouth he knew he was giving her a taste of her own medicine.

When he'd pushed her far enough, he spread her legs farther, positioned his body between them and thrust until he was fully embedded within her. Then he held tight to her hips as he went deeper with every plunge.

Something inside him snapped, and his body moved with the speed of a jackhammer. When she wrapped her legs around his waist he threw his head back and filled his nostrils with her scent.

They came together, him holding tight to her hips. Why this felt so right, he wasn't sure. All he knew was that it did. He needed this. He needed her. And from the sounds of her moans, she needed him.

They were both getting what they needed.

Bailey came awake and shifted in Walker's arms, recalling how they'd made it out of the kitchen to the sofa in his living room. She eased up and tried to move off him when she remembered his leg.

His arms held tight around her like a band of steel. "Where do you think you're going?"

She looked down at him and remembered why he was down there and she was on top. Upon his encouragement, she had shown him that she wasn't only a good shot. She was a pretty damn good rider, as well.

She glanced at the clock. It was close to eight. They had slept almost through dinner. Okay, she would admit they hadn't slept the entire time. They had slept in between their many rounds of lovemaking.

"Your leg," she reminded him, holding his gaze.

He had a sexy, sluggish look in his eyes.

"My leg is fine."

"It's after eight and you didn't take your medicine at five."

A smile curved his lips. "I had another kind of medicine that I happen to like better."

She shook her head. "Tell that to your leg when it starts hurting later."

"Trust me, I will. Making love to you is better than any medicine Doc Witherspoon could have prescribed for me." And then he pulled her mouth down to his and kissed her in a slow, unhurried fashion that clouded her mind. She was grateful for the ringing of her cell phone until she recognized the ringtone.

She broke off the kiss and quickly scooted off Walker to grab her phone off the coffee table, being careful not to bump his leg. "Dillon! What's going on?"

"Hey, Bay. I was calling to check to see how Walker is doing."

She glanced over at Walker who was stretched out naked on the sofa. She licked her lips and then said to Dillon, "Walker is doing fine. Improving every day. The doctor is pleased with his progress."

"That's good to hear. And how are you doing? Is it cold enough there for you?"

"Yes, I'm doing good," she said, glancing down at her own naked body. It was a good thing Dillon had no idea just how good she was doing. "There was a bad snow-storm here."

"I heard about that. You took plenty of heavy clothing didn't you?"

"Yes, I'm good."

"You most certainly are," Walker whispered.

She gave Walker a scolding glance, hoping Dillon hadn't heard what Walker had said.

"Do you have any idea when you'll be coming back home?" Dillon asked.

She swallowed hard and switched her gaze from Walker to the window when she said, "No, I don't know when I'll be back. I don't want to leave Walker too soon. But when the doctor says Walker can handle things on his own, I'll be back."

"All right. Give Walker my regards and tell him the entire family is wishing him a speedy recovery."

"Okay. I'll tell him. Goodbye, Dillon."

"Goodbye, Bay."

She clicked off the phone and held it in her hand a second before placing it back on the table.

"What did Dillon want you to tell me?"

"That the family is wishing you a speedy recovery."

He nodded and pulled up into a sitting position. "That's nice of them."

She smiled and returned to the sofa to sit beside him. "I have a nice family."

"I'll have to agree with you there. You didn't say how the wedding went."

Her smile widened. "It was wonderful and Jill made a beautiful bride. I don't know who cried the most, Jill, Pam or their other two sisters." She paused and then added, "Ian, Reggie and Quade hated they didn't get the chance to meet you."

"And I hate I didn't get the chance to meet them."

She couldn't help but remember he'd left because of her. She looked at him. "Do you think you'll ever return to Denver to visit?"

Walker captured the back of her neck with his hand and brought her mouth closer to his. He nibbled around her lips before placing an openmouthed kiss on her neck. "Um, will you make it worth my while if I do?"

She closed her eyes, loving the way Walker ravished her with his mouth and tongue. Desire coiled in her stomach. "I can't make any promises, but I'll see what I can do."

He pulled back slightly and she opened her eyes and met his gaze. She saw a serious glint in the dark depths as he said, "Dillon asked when you were coming home."

He'd presented it as a statement and not a question. "Yes. I told him when you got better."

He nodded, holding fast to her gaze. "I'm better."

Bailey drew in a deep breath, wondering if he was telling her that because he was ready for her to leave. "Have I worn out my welcome?"

He gently gripped her wrist and brought it to his lips, placing a light kiss on her skin. "I don't think that's possible."

She decided not to remind him he was a loner. A man who preferred solitude to company. "In that case, I'll stay another week."

He flashed a sexy smile. "Or two?"

She tried not to blink in surprise that he was actually suggesting she hang around for two weeks instead of one. She glided her hand across the firmness of his jaw. "Yes. Or two."

As if he was satisfied with her answer, he leaned in and opened his mouth against hers.

Twelve

Walker left his bathroom and glanced across the room at his bed and the woman in it. This was the third night she'd spent with him and it was hard to remember a time when she hadn't. A part of him didn't want to remember it.

He rubbed a hand down his face. Bailey in his bed was something he shouldn't get used to. It was countdown time, and in a little less than two weeks she'd be gone and his life would return to normal.

Normal meant living for himself and nobody else. Garth often teased him about living a miserable life. Misery didn't need company. *He* didn't need company, but Bailey had made him realize that five years had been too long to go without a woman. He was enjoying her in his bed a little too damn much. And that unfortunately wasn't the crux of his problem. The real kicker was that he was enjoying her…even without the sex.

He hadn't gotten around to working until yesterday, and she had found what she claimed was the perfect spot in his office to sit and work on the laptop she had brought with her. That way she was still connected to her job in Denver.

They had worked in amicable silence, although he'd been fully aware of her the entire time. Her presence had made him realize what true loneliness was because he didn't want to think of a time when she wouldn't be there.

Forcing that thought to the back of his mind, he moved across the room to rekindle the flames in the fireplace. While jabbing at the wood with the poker, he glanced back over his shoulder when he heard Bailey shift around. She looked small in his huge bed. She looked good. As if she belonged.

He quickly turned back to the fire, forcing his thoughts off her and onto something else. Like Morris James's visit yesterday. The rancher had wanted to meet Bailey after hearing all about her. Word of how she'd downed that bear had spread quickly, far and wide. Morris wanted to present Bailey with the ten-thousand-dollar bounty she'd earned from killing the animal.

Bailey had refused to take it and instead told Morris she wanted to donate the money to charity, especially if there was one in town that dealt with kids. The surprised look on Morris's face had been priceless. What person in her right mind gives up ten thousand dollars? But both Walker and Morris had watched her sign the paperwork to do just that.

As he continued to jab the poker in the fire another Bailey moment came to mind. He recalled the day he'd stepped out onto his front porch for the first time in a week. While sipping a cup of coffee he'd watched in fascination as Bailey had built a snowman. And when she'd invited him to help her, he had. He hadn't done something like that since he was a kid and he had to admit he'd enjoyed it.

For a man who didn't like having his privacy invaded, not only had she invaded that privacy, but for the time being she was making privacy nonexistent. Like when he'd come downstairs for breakfast this morning to find all four of his men sitting at his table. Somehow she'd discovered it was Willie's birthday and she'd wanted to do something special. At first Walker had been a little annoyed that she'd done such a thing without confiding in him, but then he realized that was Bailey's way—to do as she pleased. He couldn't help but smile at that.

But then he frowned upon realizing it was also Bailey's way to be surrounded by people. Although he was used to loneliness, she was not. She had a big family and was used to having people around all the time. He figured the loneliness of Alaska would eventually drive her crazy. What if she decided to leave before the two weeks?

Why should he give a damn if she did?

He returned the poker to the stand, not wanting to think about that. He was expecting another visit from Doc Witherspoon tomorrow. Hopefully it would be his last for a while. He couldn't wait to take out his plane and fly over his land. And he didn't want to question why he wanted Bailey with him to share in the experience.

"Walker?"

He glanced across the room. Bailey was sitting up in his bed. Her hair was mussed up and she had a soft, sleepy and sexy look on her face. Although she held the covers up to her chest, she looked tempting. Maybe because he knew that beneath all those bedcovers she was naked. "Yes?"

"I'm cold."

"I just finished stoking the fire."

"Not good enough, Alaskan. I'm sure you can do better than that."

Oh, yes, he definitely could. He removed his robe and headed for the bed, feeling a deep ache in his groin. The moment he slid in bed and felt her thigh brush against his, the ache intensified. He pulled her into his arms, needing to hold her. He knew there would come a time when he wouldn't be able to do that. The thought had him drawing in a deep, ragged breath.

She pulled back and ran her gaze over his face. "You okay?"

"Yes."

"Your leg?"

"Is fine. Back to the way it used to be. Only lasting reminder is that little scar."

"Trust me, Walker, no woman will care about that scar when you've got this to back things up," she said, reaching her hand beneath the covers to cup him, then stroke him. Walker drew in another ragged breath. Bailey definitely knew how to get to the heart of the matter. And when he saw the way she licked her lips and how the darkness of her eyes shone with desire, his erection expanded in her hand.

She leaned close to his ear and whispered, "Okay, Walker, what's it going to be? You ride me or I ride you? Take your pick."

He couldn't stop the smile that curved his lips. It was hard—damn difficult, outright impossible—not to tap into all his sexual fantasies when she was around and being so damn accommodating. And she would be around for eleven more days. He intended to make the most of what he considered the best time of his life.

"Um," he said, pulling her back into his arms. "How about if we do both?"

Over the next several days Walker and Bailey settled into a gratifying and pleasurable routine. Now that Walker was back at 100 percent, he would get up every morning around five o'clock to work alongside his men. Then at nine, instead of hanging around and eating Willie's cooking like he normally did, he hightailed it back to the ranch house, where Bailey would have breakfast waiting on him. No matter how often he told her that she didn't have to go out of her way, she would wave her hand and brush off his words. After placing the most delectable-looking meal in front of him, she would go on and on about what a beautiful kitchen he had. It was one that would entice someone to cook whether they wanted to or not, she claimed.

He began to see his kitchen through her eyes and finally understood. In all the years he had lived here, he'd never thought of his kitchen, or any kitchen, as beautiful. It was a place to cook meals and eat. But she brought his attention to the space, its rustic look. But what she said she liked most was sitting at the table and looking out at the strait. On a clear day the waters looked breathtaking. Just as breathtaking as Gemma Lake, she'd told him. It was during those conversations that he knew she missed her home. Hadn't one of her rules been to never venture far from Westmoreland Country for too long?

Garth had dropped by twice to check on Walker, and because his best friend had been calling every day to see how he was doing, Garth wasn't surprised to find Bailey still there. Garth didn't seem surprised at how comfortable she'd made herself in Walker's home, either. And Walker had caught Garth staring at them with a silly-looking grin on his face more than once.

Garth had mentioned to Bailey that he'd gotten in touch with her family and had spoken to Dillon and Ramsey, and that he and his brothers would be flying to Denver in a few weeks. Bailey mentioned that she would be back home by then and that she and her family would anxiously await Garth's visit. Her comment only made Walker realize that he didn't have a lot of time left with her.

Lola was back on her regular housekeeping schedule and told him more than once how much she liked Bailey. He figured it was because Bailey was chattier with her than he'd ever been. And he figured since Lola had only one bed in the house to make up, the older woman had pretty much figured out that he and Bailey were sharing it. That had suited Lola since she'd hinted more than once that he needed a woman in his life and that being alone on the ranch wasn't good for him.

Walker took a sip of his coffee while looking out at the strait. He remembered the day Bailey had gone into town with him to pick up supplies. News of her and the bear had spread further than Walker had imagined it would, and she'd become something of a legend. And if that wasn't enough, Morris had spread the word about what she'd done with the bounty money. Her generous contribution had gone to Kodiak Way, the local orphanage. Walker hadn't visited the place in years, not since he'd gone there on a field trip with his high school. But he'd decided on that particular day to stop by with Bailey, so she could see where her money had gone.

It had amazed him how taken she'd been with all the children, but he really should not have been surprised. He recalled how much she adored her nieces, nephews and little cousins back in Denver and just how much they'd adored her. He and Bailey had spent longer at the orphanage than he had planned because Bailey couldn't miss the opportunity to take a group of kids outside to build a snowman.

He then recalled the day he'd taken her up in his single-engine plane, giving her a tour of his land. She had been in awe and had told him how beautiful his property was. When she'd asked him how he'd learned to fly, he'd opened up and told her of his and Garth's time together in the marines. She'd seemed fascinated by everything he told her and he'd gotten caught up in her interest.

It had been a beautiful day for flying. The sky had

been blue and the clouds a winter white. From the air he had pointed out his favorite areas—the lakes, small coves, hidden caves and mountaintops. And he'd heard himself promising to one day cover the land with her in his Jeep.

And then there had been the day when she'd pulled him into his office, shoved him down into the chair at his desk and proceeded to sit in his lap so she could show him what she'd downloaded on his desktop computer. Jillian and Aidan had returned from their three-week honeymoon to France, Italy and Spain, and had uploaded their wedding video. Bailey thought that since he'd missed the wedding, he could watch the video.

As far as weddings went, it had been a nice one. Bailey had pointed out several cousins he hadn't met and their wives and children. He agreed that Jillian had been a beautiful bride and he'd seen the love in Aidan's eyes when she'd walked down the aisle on Dillon's arm.

Watching the video made Walker recall his own wedding. Only thing, his wedding had been nothing more than a circus. His parents and Garth had tried to warn him with no luck. A few nights ago he'd dreamed about Kalyn and Connor. A dream that had turned into a nightmare, with Bailey waking him up.

The next day, even though he'd seen the probing curiosity in her eyes, she hadn't asked him about it and he hadn't felt the need to tell her.

Walker took another sip of his coffee and glanced down at his watch. Bailey should be coming down for breakfast any minute. He had finished his chores with the men earlier than usual and had rushed back to the ranch house. More than once he'd been tempted to go upstairs and wake her but he knew if he did they might end up staying in bed the rest of the day. He then thought about the phone call he'd received an hour ago from Charm. It seemed Charm couldn't wait to meet her look-alike and asked that he fly Bailey to Fairbanks this weekend. He hadn't made any promises, but he'd told her he would talk to Bailey about it.

Moments later, he heard her upstairs and felt his sex stir in anticipation. Only Bailey could put him in such a state, arousing him so easily and completely. And he would admit that her mere presence in his home brought him a kind of joy he hadn't thought he would ever feel again.

But then he also knew it was the kind of joy he couldn't allow himself to get attached to. Just as sure as he knew that when he got up every morning the strait would be filled with water, he knew that when Bailey's days were up, she would be leaving.

Already he'd detected a longing in her and figured she'd become homesick. It was during those times that he was reminded of the first day they'd met. She'd told him about her rules and her love for Westmoreland Country. She'd said she never intended to leave it. And since he never intended to leave Kodiak, that meant any wishful thinking about them spending their lives together was a waste of his time.

Walker's grip on the cup tightened. And hadn't she told him about men getting possessive, becoming territorial and acting crazy sometimes? Sadly, he could now see himself doing all three where she was concerned.

It was nobody's fault but his own that he was now in this state. He'd known her rules and had allowed her to get under his skin anyway. But he could handle it. He had no choice. He would store up memories of the good times, and those memories would get him through the lonely nights after she left.

He heard her moving around upstairs again and sat his coffee cup down. Temptation was ruling his senses now.

Desire unlike anything he'd ever felt before took control of him, had him sliding back from the table and standing. Walker left the kitchen and moved quickly toward the stairs, seeking the object of his craving.

Thirteen

"What am I going to do, Josette? Of all the stupid, idiotic, crazy things I could have done, why did I fall in love with Walker Rafferty?" Bailey asked. She held her mobile phone to her ear and paced Walker's bedroom. Talk about doing something dumb.

She had woken up that morning and glanced out the window on her way to the bathroom. She'd seen Walker and his men in the distance, knee deep in snow, loading some type of farm equipment onto a truck. She had stared at him, admiring how good he looked even dressed in a heavy coat and boots with a hat on his head. All she could think about was the night before, how he had made love to her, how he'd made her scream a number of times. And how this morning before leaving the bed he had brushed a good-morning kiss across her lips.

Suddenly, while standing at the window and ogling him, it had hit her—hard—that all those emotions she'd been feeling lately weren't lust. They were love.

She had fallen head over heels in love with Walker.

"Damn it, Josette. I should have known better."

"Calm down, Bailey. There's nothing stupid, idiotic or crazy about falling in love."

"It is if the man you love has no intention of ever loving you back. Walker told me all he could ever offer is a meaningless affair. I knew that and fell in love with him anyway."

"What makes you think he hasn't changed his mind? Now that the two of you have spent time together at his ranch, he might have."

"I have no reason to think he won't be ready for me to leave when my two weeks are up. Especially after that stunt I pulled the other day. Inviting his men for breakfast without his permission. Although he didn't say anything, I could tell he didn't like it."

"Are you going to tell him how you feel?"

"Of course not! Do you want me to feel even more stupid?"

"So what are you going to do?"

Bailey paused, not knowing how she intended to answer that. And also knowing there was really only one way to answer it. "Nothing. Just enjoy the time I have with him now and leave with no regrets. I believe the reason he refuses to love anyone else is because he's still carrying a torch for his late wife. There's nothing I can do about that and I don't intend to try."

Moments later, after ending her phone call with Josette, Bailey walked back over to the window. Today the weather appeared clearer than it had been the past couple of days. She missed home, but not as much as she'd figured she would. Skype had helped. She communicated regularly with her nieces and nephews and little cousins and, according to Ramsey, although several wives were expecting new babies in the family, none had been born.

Everyone was expecting her home for Thanksgiving and was looking forward to her return.

She had worked out a system with Lucia where she could work remotely from Alaska. Doing so helped fill the long days when Walker was gone. In the evenings she looked forward to his return. Although they had established an amicable routine, she knew it was just temporary. Like she'd told Josette, there was no doubt in her mind Walker would expect her to leave next week. Granted, she knew he enjoyed her as his bedmate, but she also knew that, for men, sex was nothing more than sex. She had found that out while watching her then-single Westmoreland brothers and cousins. For her and Walker, there could never be anything between them other than the physical.

Even so, she could sense there was something bothering Walker. More than once she'd awakened in the night to find him standing at the window or poking the fire. And then there had been the night he'd woken up screaming the words, "No, Kalyn! Don't! Connor! Connor!"

She had snuggled closer and wrapped her arms around him, and pretty soon he had calmed down, holding her as tightly as she held him. The next day over breakfast she had expected him to bring up the incident, but he hadn't. She could only assume he didn't remember it or didn't want to talk about it. But she had been curious enough to check online and she'd found out Kalyn had been his wife and Connor his son.

Bailey turned when she heard the bedroom door opening, and there Walker stood, looking more handsome than any man had a right to look. As she stood there staring, too mesmerized by the heat in his eyes to even speak, he closed the door and removed his jacket, then tossed it across the chair.

She'd seen that look in his eyes before, usually in the evenings after he'd spent the entire day on the range. It wasn't quite nine in the morning. She swallowed. Now he was unbuttoning his shirt. "Good morning, Walker."

"Good morning, Bailey." He pulled the belt from his jeans before sitting in the chair to remove his boots and socks. His eyes never left hers.

"You've finished your chores for the day already?"

"No."

"No?"

"Yes, no. The guys took my tractor over to the Mayeses' place for Conley to look at it. He's the area mechanic. Nothing much to do until they get back, which won't be for hours."

She nodded. "I see."

"I came in for coffee and had a cup before hearing you move around up here, letting me know you were awake." Now he was unzipping his pants.

"And?" she asked, as if she really didn't know.

He slid his pants down muscular thighs. "And—" he crooked his finger "—come here a minute."

He stood there stark naked. She couldn't help licking her lips as her gaze moved from his eyes downward, past his chest to the thatch of dark hair covering his erection. "Before or after I take off my clothes?" she asked.

"Before. I want to undress you."

At that moment she didn't care that she'd just finished putting on her clothes. From the look in his eyes, he was interested in more than just taking off her clothes.

Drawing in a deep breath and trying to ignore the throb between her legs, she crossed the room on wobbly knees. Was she imagining things or was his erection expanding with each step she took? When she stopped in front of him, he placed both hands on her shoulders. She felt the heat of his touch through her blouse.

"You look good in this outfit," he said, holding fast to her shoulders as his gaze raked over her.

"Thanks." It was just a skirt and blouse. Nothing spectacular.

"You're welcome." Then he captured her lips with his. Her last coherent thought was *But this kiss is spectacular.*

Walker was convinced, and had been for some time, that Bailey was what fantasies were made of. What he'd told her was the truth. She looked good in that outfit. Truth be told, she looked good in any outfit...especially in his shirts. Those were the times he felt most possessive, territorial, crazy with lust...and love. All the things that she'd once stated were total turnoffs for her.

He continued kissing her, moving his mouth over her lips with a hunger he felt all the way to his toes. He had wanted this kiss to arouse her, get her ready for what was to come. He figured she knew his motives because of the way she was responding. Their tongues tangled madly, greedily, as hot and intense as it could get.

His hands left her shoulders and cupped her backside, pressing her body against his. There was no way she didn't feel his erection pressing against the juncture of her thighs.

He'd watched her crossing the room and noticed her gaze shifting from his face to his groin, checking him out. He really didn't know why. Nothing about that part of his body had changed. She had cupped it, taken it into her mouth and fondled it. So what had she found so fascinating about it today?

As if she'd guessed his thoughts, she glanced up to meet his eyes just seconds before reaching him. The tint that darkened her cheeks had been priceless, and instead of stripping her clothes off like he'd intended, he kissed her. He'd overplayed his hand with Bailey. This young woman had done what no other could have done. She was on the verge of making him whole. Making him want to believe in love all over again. Restoring his soul to what it had been before Kalyn had destroyed it.

He slowly broke off the kiss. His hands returned to her shoulders only long enough to remove her blouse and unhook her bra. And then he tugged her skirt and panties down past her hips and legs to pool at her feet. He looked his fill. Now he understood her earlier fascination with him because he was experiencing the same fascination now.

Yes, he'd seen it all before. Had tasted and touched every single inch. But still, looking at her naked body almost took his breath away. She was beautiful. His body ached for her in a way it had never ached for another woman…including Kalyn.

That realization had him lifting her into his arms, carrying her to the bed. He placed her on it and joined her there. He had intended to go slow, to savor each moment as long as he could. But she had other ideas.

When they stretched out together on the huge bed, her mouth went for his and kissed him hungrily. The same way he'd kissed her moments ago. The only difference was that her hands were everywhere, touching, exploring and stroking. He joined in with his own hands, frenzied with the need to touch her and let his mouth follow. She squirmed against him, biting his shoulders a few times and licking his chest, trying to work her mouth downward. But he beat her to the punch. She released a gasp when he tightened his hold on her hips and lowered his head between her legs.

He'd only intended to lick her a few times, but her taste made that impossible. He wanted more, needed more, and he was determined to get everything he wanted.

He heard her moans, felt her nails dig deep into his shoulders. He knew the moment her pleasure came, when she was consumed in an orgasm that had her writhing beneath his mouth.

Lust ripped through him, triggered by her moans. He

had to be inside her now. Easing his body over hers, their gazes held as he slowly entered her. It took all his strength not to explode right when she arched her back and lifted her hips to receive every last inch of him. She entwined her arms around his neck and then, in a surprise move, she leaned up slightly and traced his lips with the tip of her tongue.

Something snapped inside him and he began thrusting in and out of her, going deeper with every downward plunge. Over and over, he fine-tuned the rhythm, whipping up sensation after exquisite sensation.

"Walker!"

When she screamed his name, the same earthshaking orgasm that overtook her did the same to him. A fierce growl escaped his lips when he felt her inner muscles clench him, trying to hold him inside.

This was how it was supposed to be. Giving instead of taking. Sharing instead of just being a recipient.

When their bodies had gone limp, he found the strength to ease off her and pull her into his arms, needing to hold her close to his heart. A part of him wished they could remain like that forever, but he knew they couldn't. Time was not on their side.

He knew her rules, especially the one about staying in Westmoreland Country. And he knew the promise he'd made to his father, about never taking Hemlock Row for granted again. That meant that even if Bailey agreed to a long-term affair, there would be no compromise on either of their parts.

Even so, he was determined to stock up on all the memories he could.

"Charm called."

Bailey's body felt weak as water but somehow she managed to open her eyes and meet Walker's gaze. She was convinced the man had more stamina than a bull. And wasn't she seven years younger? He should be flat on his back barely able to move...like her.

She found the strength to draw in a slow breath. Evidently he was telling her this for a reason and there was only one way to find out what it was. "And?"

"And she asked me to bring you to Fairbanks this weekend. Let me rephrase that. She kind of ordered me to."

Bailey couldn't help but chuckle. "Ordered. I didn't think anyone had the nerve to order you to do anything."

"Charm thinks she can. She considers me one of her brothers and she thinks she can wrap all of us around her finger. Like you do with your brothers and cousins."

That got another chuckle from her. "I don't know about that anymore." When he eased down beside her, she snuggled against him. "So are you going to do it? Are you going to take me to Fairbanks?"

He looked over at her. "I thought you didn't want to have anything to do with the Outlaws."

"I never said that. I just didn't like how they handled their business by sending you to Denver instead of coming themselves." Reaching up, she entwined her arms around his neck. "But I'm over that now. If they hadn't sent you, then we would not have met."

She grimaced at the thought of that, and for the first time since meeting Walker she decided the Outlaws had definitely done her a favor. Even if he didn't love her, she now knew how it felt to fall in love with someone. To give that person your whole heart and soul. To be willing to do things you never thought you would do.

Now she understood her sisters. She'd always thought Megan and Gemma were plumb loco to consider living anywhere other than Westmoreland Country. Megan not so much, since she stayed in Westmoreland Country six months out of the year and spent the other six months in

Rico's hometown of Philly. But Gemma had made Australia her permanent home and only returned to Denver to visit on occasion. Megan and Gemma had chosen love over everything else. They knew home was where the heart was. Now Bailey did, too.

"You've gotten quiet on me."

She glanced over at Walker and smiled. "Only because you haven't answered my question. So are you going to take me to Fairbanks?" She knew that was a big request to make, because he'd mentioned once that he rarely left his ranch.

She could tell he was considering it and then he said, "Only if you go somewhere with me tomorrow."

She lifted a brow. "Where?"

He pulled her closer. "You'll know when we get there."

She stared at him silently, mulling over his request. She was curious, but she knew she would follow him to the ends of the earth if he asked her to. "Yes, I will go with you tomorrow."

Fourteen

The next morning Walker woke up with a heavy heart, pretty much like he'd done for the past ten years. It was Connor's birthday. In the past he'd spent the day alone. Even Garth knew not to bother him on that anniversary. Yet Bailey was here, and of all things he had asked her to go to Connor's grave with him, although she had no idea where they were headed.

"You're still not going to give me a hint?" Bailey asked when he placed his Stetson on his head and then led her outside. Bundled up in her coat, boots, scarf and a Denver Broncos knitted cap, she smiled over at him. Snow covered the ground but wasn't as deep as yesterday.

He shook his head. "Don't waste your smile. You'll know when we get there." She had tried to get him to tell her last night and again this morning, but he wouldn't share. He had thoroughly enjoyed her seductive efforts, though.

"I didn't know you were so mean, Walker."

"And I've always known you were persistent, Bailey. Come on," he said, taking her gloved hand to lead her toward one of his detached garages. When he raised the door she got a peek of what was inside and almost knocked him down rushing past him.

"Wow! These babies are beauties," she said, checking out the two sleek, black-and-silver snowmobiles parked beside one of his tractors. "Are they yours?"

He nodded, leaning against the tractor. "Yes, mine and Garth's. He likes to keep his here to use whenever he comes to visit. But today, this will be our transportation to get where we're going."

"Really?" she gasped excitedly, nearly jumping up and down.

Walker couldn't ignore the contentment he felt knowing he was the one responsible for her enthusiasm. "Yes. You get to use Garth's. I asked his permission for you to do so. He figures any woman who can shoot a grizzly from one hundred feet away should certainly know how to operate one of these."

Bailey laughed. "It wasn't exactly a hundred feet away and yes, I can operate one of these. Riley has one. He loves going skiing and takes it with him when he does. None of us can understand it, but he loves cold weather. The colder the better."

Walker opened a wooden box and pulled out two visored helmets and handed her one. "Where we're going isn't far from here."

She looked up at him as she placed her helmet on her head. "And you still won't give me a hint?"

"No, not even a little one."

Of all the places Bailey figured they might end up, a cemetery wasn't even on her list. When they had brought the snowmobiles to a stop by a wooden gate she had to blink to make sure she wasn't imagining things.

Instead of asking Walker why they were there, she followed his lead and got off the machine. She watched as he opened a box connected to his snowmobile and pulled out a small broom. He then took her gloved hand in his. "This way."

Walking through snow, he led her through the opening of the small cemetery containing several headstones. They stopped in front of the first pair. "My grandparents," he said softly, releasing her hand to lean down and brush away the snow that covered the names. *Walker and Lora Rafferty.*

She glanced up at him. "You were named after your grandfather?"

He nodded. "Yes. And my father."

"So you're the third?"

He nodded again. "Yes, I'm the third. My grandfather was in the military, stationed in Fairbanks, and was sent here to the island one summer with other troops to work on a government project for a year. He fell in love with the island. He also fell in love with a young island girl he met here."

"The woman who could trace her family back to Alaska when it was owned by Russia?" Bailey asked, letting him know she remembered what he'd told her about his grandparents that first day they'd met.

A smile touched one corner of his mouth. "Yes, she's the one. They married and he bought over a thousand acres through the government land grant. He and Lora settled here and named their property Hemlock Row, after the rows of trees that are abundant on the island. They only had one child. My father."

They then moved to the second pair of headstones and she guessed this was where his parents were buried. *Walker and Darlene Rafferty.* And the one thing she noticed was that they had died within six months of each other.

She didn't want to ask but had to. "How did they die?"

At first she wasn't sure he would answer, but then his voice caught in the icy wind when he said, "Mom got sick. By the time the doctors found out it was cancer there was nothing that could be done. She loved Hemlock Row and wanted to take her last breath here. So we checked her out of the hospital and brought her home. She died less than a week later."

Bailey studied the date on the headstone. "You were here when she died?"

"Yes."

She did quick calculations in her head. Walker had lost his wife and son three months before he'd lost his mother and subsequently his father. He had fled Hollywood to come here to find peace from his grief only to face even more heartache when he'd arrived home. No wonder he'd shut himself off from the world and become a loner. He had lost the four people he'd loved the most within a year's time.

She noticed his hold on her hand tightened when he said, "Dad basically died of a broken heart. He missed Mom that much. Six months. I'm surprised he lasted without her that long. She was his heart, and I guess he figured that without her he didn't need one."

Bailey swallowed. She remembered Ramsey telling her that at least their parents had died together. He couldn't imagine one living without the other. Like Walker's, her parents had had a very close marriage.

"My father was a good one," Walker said, breaking into her thoughts. "The best. He loved Hemlock Row, and when I was a teenager he made me promise to always take care of it and keep it in the family and never sell it. I made him a promise to honor his wishes."

She nodded and recalled hearing her father and uncle had made their father and grandfathers the same such promises. That was why her family considered Westmoreland Country their home. It had been land passed to them from generation to generation. Land their great-grandfather Raphel had worked hard to own and even harder to maintain.

Walker shifted and they moved toward the next headstone. She knew before he brushed the snow off the marker who it belonged to. His son. *Connor Andrew Rafferty.*

From the dates on the headstone, he'd died four days after his first birthday, which would have been…today. She quickly glanced over at the man standing beside her, still holding her hand as he stood staring at the headstone with a solemn look on his face. Today was his son's birthday. Connor would have been eleven today.

There were no words Bailey could say because at that moment she could actually feel Walker's pain. His grief was still raw and she could tell it hadn't yet healed. So she did the only thing she could do. She leaned into him. Instead of rejecting her gesture, he placed his arms around her waist and gently drew her against his side.

They stood there together, silently gazing at the headstone. She was certain his mind was filled with memories of the son he'd lost. Long minutes passed before Walker finally spoke. "He was a good kid. Learned to walk at ten months. And he loved playing hide-and-seek."

Bailey forced a smile through the tears she tried to hold back. She bet he was a good daddy who played hide-and-seek often with his son. "Was he ever hard to find?"

Walker chuckled. "All the time. But his little giggle would always give him away."

Walker got quiet again, and then he turned her in his arms to face him. He touched her chin with his thumb. "Thanks for coming here with me today."

"Thanks for bringing me. I know today has to be painful for you."

He dropped his hand and broke eye contact to look up at the snow-covered mountains behind her. "Yes, it is every year. There are some things you just can't get over."

Bailey nodded. She then glanced around, expecting to see another headstone, and when she didn't, she gazed at Walker and asked, "Your wife?"

He looked back down at her and took her hand. "What about her?"

"Is she not buried here?"

He hesitated a moment and then said, "No." And then he tightened his hold on her hand. "Come on. Let's head back."

Later that night as Walker lay in bed holding Bailey in his arms while she slept, he thought about their time together at the cemetery. Today had been the first time he'd allowed anyone in on his emotions, his pain, the first time he'd shared his grief. And in turn, he had shared some of his family's history with her. It was history he hadn't shared with any other woman but Kalyn. The difference in how the two women had received the information had been as different as day and night.

Kalyn hadn't wanted to hear about it. Said he should forget the past and move on. She was adamant about never leaving Hollywood to return here to live. She never even visited during the three years they'd been married. How she had hated a place she'd never seen went beyond him. And she had told him that if his parents died and he inherited the place, he should sell it. She'd listed all the things they could buy with the money.

On the other hand, Bailey had listened to his family's history today and seemed to understand and appreciate everything he'd told her. She had even thanked him for sharing it with her.

He hadn't been able to verbalize his own appreciation so he'd expressed it another way. As soon as they returned to his ranch, he had whisked her into his arms, carried her up the stairs and made love to her in a way he'd never made love to any other woman.

Walker released his hold on Bailey now to ease out of bed and cross the room. He stared into the fire as if the heat actually flickered in his soul. Today, while making love to Bailey, he kept telling himself that it was only lust that made him want her so much. That it was appreciation that drove him. He refused to consider anything else. Anything more. And yet now he was fighting to maintain his resolve where she was concerned.

He didn't want or need anyone else in his life. And although he enjoyed her company now, he preferred solitude. Once she was gone, everything in his life would get back to normal. And she *would* leave, he didn't doubt that. She loved Westmoreland Country as much as he loved Hemlock Row.

He inhaled deeply, wanting to take in the smell of wood and smoke. Instead, he was filled with Bailey's scent. "Damn it, I don't want this," he uttered softly with a growl. "And I don't need her. I don't need anyone."

He released a deep breath, wondering whom he was trying to convince.

He knew the answer to that. He had to convince himself or else he'd end up making the mistake of the century, and one mistake with a woman was enough.

When Bailey had noticed Kalyn wasn't buried there, for a second he'd been tempted to confide in her. To tell her the whole sordid story about his wife and her betrayal. But he couldn't. The only living person who knew the whole story was Garth, and that was the way Walker would keep it. He could never open himself up to someone else—definitely not another woman.

He heard Bailey stirring in bed and his body responded, as usual. He wondered how long this erotic craving for her would last. He had a feeling he would have an addiction long after she was gone. But while she was here he would enjoy her and store up the memories.

"Walker?"

He turned and looked toward the bed. "I'm over here."

"I want you here."

His thoughts were pensive. He wanted to be where she was, as well. He crossed the room and eased back into bed, drawing her into his arms. They only had a few more days together and then she would be gone. She would return to Westmoreland Country without looking back. In the meantime, he would make sure the days they had together were days he could cherish forever.

Fifteen

"I don't believe it," Charm Outlaw said, caught up in a moment of awe as she stared at Bailey. "We do favor. I didn't believe Garth and Walker, but now I do." She gave Bailey a hug. "Welcome to Fairbanks, cousin."

Bailey couldn't help but smile, deciding she liked Charm right away. Everyone had been right—they did look alike. Charm's five brothers also favored their Westmoreland cousins. "Thanks for the invite. I hadn't expected all of this."

"All of this" was the dinner party Charm had planned. Walker had flown them to Fairbanks and Garth had sent a limo to pick them up from the airport. The limo had taken a route through the city's downtown. Even though a thick blanket of snow covered the grounds, Bailey thought downtown Fairbanks was almost as captivating as downtown Denver.

Walker had given her a bit of Fairbanks's history, telling her that it was a diverse city thanks to the army base there. A lot of ex-military personnel decided they liked the area and remained after their tour of duty ended. He also told her Alaska had the highest ratio of men to women than anywhere else in the United States. Online dating was popular here and a lot of the men actually solicited mail-order brides.

After resting up at the hotel for a couple of hours, another limo had arrived to deliver them to the Outlaw Estates. Bailey couldn't help but chuckle when she remembered the marker at the entrance of the huge gated residence. It said, "Unless you're an outlaw, stay out. Josey Wales welcomed." Walker had told her the sign had been Maverick Westmoreland's idea. He was a huge fan of Clint Eastwood. The Outlaw mansion sat on over fifty acres of land.

Already Bailey had met Charm and Garth's brothers— Jess, Sloan, Cash and Maverick. In addition to their resemblance to the Westmorelands, they carried themselves like Westmorelands, as well. All five were single and, according to Charm, the thought of getting married made her brothers break out in hives. Jess, an attorney, seemed like the least rowdy of the four, and she wasn't surprised that he had announced his candidacy for senator of Alaska. He indicated he knew of Senator Reggie Westmoreland and although they hadn't met yet, Jess had been surprised to discover they were related. He looked forward to meeting Reggie personally. He'd been following Reggie's political career for a number of years and admired how he carried himself in Washington. He also knew of Chloe's father, Senator Jamison Burton, and hoped as many others did that he would consider running for president one day.

"Every Outlaw is here and accounted for except Dad. He's not dealing with all this very well and decided to make himself scarce tonight."

Garth cleared his throat, making it apparent that he felt

Charm had said too much. Bailey hadn't been bothered by Charm's words since on the flight over Walker had prepared her for the fact that Bart Outlaw still hadn't come around. For the life of her she couldn't understand what the big deal was. Why did Bart Outlaw refuse to acknowledge or accept that his father had been adopted?

Walker had also shared that Garth, his brothers and Charm all had different mothers but the brothers had been adopted by Bart before their second birthdays. Charm hadn't joined the group until she was in her teens. Her mother had sent her to Bart after Charm became too unruly. It sounded as if Bailey and Charm had a lot in common, although Dillon never entertained the thought of sending her anywhere.

One thing Bailey noted was that Walker never left her side. Not that it bothered her, but his solicitous manner made it obvious the two of them were more than friends. Every so often he would ask if she was okay. He'd told her before they'd arrived that if the Outlaws got too overbearing at any time, she and Walker would return to the hotel.

She saw a different Walker around the Outlaws. She knew he and Garth were best friends but it was obvious he had a close relationship with the others, as well. This Walker was more outgoing and not as reserved. But then he'd acted the same way around her brothers and cousins once he'd gotten to know them.

"How long are you staying in Fairbanks, Bailey?" Charm asked her. "I'm hoping you'll be here for a few days so we can get some shopping in."

Before she could answer, Walker spoke up. "Sorry to disappoint you, Charm, but Bailey's returning to Denver on Monday."

"Oh," Charm said, clearly disappointed.

Bailey didn't say anything, merely took a sip of her wine. It sounded as if Walker was counting the days.

"Well, I guess I'll have to make sure I'm included in that trip to Denver with my brothers later this month."

"Then, you'll be in luck because the women who married into the family, as well as me and my sister Megan, all love to shop," Bailey said, trying to put Walker's words to the back of her mind.

Charm's face broke into an elated grin.

Garth shook his head. "Shopping should be Charm's middle name." He checked his watch. "I hate to break up this conversation, but I think dinner is ready to be served."

Charm hooked Bailey's arm in hers as they headed toward the dining room and whispered, "So tell me, Bailey. Are there any real cute single guys in Denver?"

Walker sat with a tight jaw while he listened to Garth give his father hell. Deservedly so. Although Bart had finally shown up for dinner, he'd practically ignored Bailey. It had been obvious from his expression when he'd walked into the dining room and saw Bailey sitting beside Charm that he'd done a double take. He'd definitely noticed the resemblance between the two women. Yet that seemed to spike his resentment. So, like Garth and his brothers, Walker couldn't help wondering why Bart was so dead set against claiming the Westmorelands as kin. It seemed Garth was determined to find out.

After dinner, even before dessert could be served, Garth had encouraged Charm to show Bailey around while he and his brothers had quickly ushered their father upstairs. Garth had invited Walker to sit in on the proceedings.

"You were outright rude to Bailey, Dad."

Bart frowned. "I didn't invite her here."

"No, we did. And with good reason. She's our cousin."

"No, she's not. We are Outlaws, not Westmorelands."

"You're not blind, Dad. You saw the resemblance between Charm and Bailey with your own eyes. Bailey even remarked on how much you favor her father and uncle."

"That means nothing to me," Bart said stubbornly.

Garth drew in a deep breath, and Walker knew his best friend well enough to know he was getting fed up with his father's refusal to accept the obvious. "Why? Why are you so hostile to the idea that your father was adopted? That does not mean he wasn't an Outlaw. All it means is that he had other family—his biological family—that we can get to know. Why do you want to deprive us of that?"

A brooding Bart was silent as he glanced around the room at his sons and at Walker. It was Walker who received the most intense glare. "You were to take care of this, Walker. Things should not have gotten this far. You were to find a way to discredit them."

"That's enough, Dad! How could you even ask something like that of Walker?" Garth asked angrily.

Instead of answering, Bart jerked to his feet and stormed out of the room.

His sons watched his departure with a mixture of anger and confusion on their faces.

"What the hell is wrong with him?" Jess asked the others.

Garth shook his head sadly. "I honestly don't know. You weren't there that day Hugh first told us about the Westmorelands. Dad was adamant that we not claim them as relatives no matter what. When he found out I sent Walker anyway, he was furious."

Sloan shook his head. "There has to be a reason he is handling things this way."

"I agree," Maverick said, standing. "Something isn't right here."

"I agree with Maverick," Walker said. There was something about Bart's refusal to accept that his father was adopted that didn't make sense. "There has to be a reason

Bart is in denial. He might have his ways, but I've never figured him to be an irrational man."

"I agree," Cash said, shaking his head. "And he actually told you to find a way to discredit the Westmorelands?"

Walker nodded slowly. "You heard him for yourself."

"Damn," Sloan said, refilling his glass with his favorite after dinner drink. "I agree with Maverick and Walker. Something isn't right. Since Dad won't level with us and tell us what's going on, I suggest we hire someone to find out."

Cash glanced over at his brother, frowning. "Find out what?"

"Hell, I don't know" was Sloan's frustrated reply.

The room got quiet until Walker said, "Have any of you considered the possibility that there's something that went on years ago within the Outlaw family that you don't know about? Something that makes Bart feel he has to maintain that his father was the blood son of an Outlaw?"

Garth sat down with his drink. "I have to admit that thought has occurred to me."

"In that case," Jess said, "we need to find out what."

"You worried it might cause a scandal that will affect your campaign?" Sloan asked his brother.

"I have no idea," Jess said soberly. "But if there's something I need to worry about, then I want to find out before the media does."

Garth nodded. "Then, we're all in agreement. We look into things further."

Everyone in the room nodded.

"I'm sorry about my father's behavior at dinner, Bailey. I honestly don't know what has gotten into him," Charm said apologetically as she led Bailey back to the center of the house.

"No apology needed," Bailey said. "I was anticipating

such an attitude. Walker prepared me on the flight here from Kodiak. He said Bart might not be friendly to me."

"Um," Charm said, smiling. "Speaking of Walker. The two of you look good together. I'm glad he's finally gotten over his wife."

Bailey drew in a deep breath, not sure that was the case. It was quite obvious to her that he was still grieving the loss of his wife and son. And because of the magnitude of that grief, he refused to open up his heart to anyone else. "Looks can be deceiving, Charm."

She raised a brow. "Does that mean you're actually leaving to return to Denver on Monday?"

"No reason for me to stay. Like I said, looks can be deceiving."

Charm lifted her chin. "In this case, I think not. I've noticed the way Walker looks at you. He looks at you—"

Probably like a horny man, Bailey thought silently. There was no need to explain to Charm that the only thing between her and Walker was their enjoyment of sex with each other.

At that moment, Bailey's cell phone went off. At any other time she would have ignored it, wishing she'd remembered to turn off the ringer, but not this time. This particular ringtone indicated the call was from her cousin Bane.

"Forgive my rudeness," Bailey said to Charm as she quickly got the phone out of her purse, clicked it on and said to the caller, "Hold on a minute."

She then looked at Charm. "Sorry, but I need to take this call. It's my cousin Bane. He's a navy SEAL somewhere on assignment, and there's no telling when he'll have a chance to call me again."

"I understand. And if you need to talk privately you can use any of the rooms off the hall here. I'll be waiting for you downstairs in the main room."

Bailey gave Charm an appreciative smile. "Thanks." She quickly stepped inside one of the rooms and turned on the lights. "Bane? What's going on? Where are you?"

"Can't say. And I can't talk long. But I'm going to need your help."

"My help? For what?"

"I need to find Crystal."

Bailey frowned thoughtfully. "Bane, you know what Dillon asked you to do."

"Yes, Bay. Dil asked that I grow up and accept responsibility for my actions, to make something of myself before thinking about reclaiming Crystal. I promised him that I would and I have. Enough time has passed and I don't intend to wait any longer. In a couple of weeks I'll be on an extended military leave."

"An extended leave? Bane, are you okay?"

"I'll be better after I find Crystal, and I need your help, Bay."

Everyone had left the family room to return to the dining room for dessert except for Garth and Walker. Garth refilled Walker's glass with Scotch before proceeding to fill his own.

"So," Garth said, after taking a sip. "Do you think there's something Dad's not telling us?"

Walker, with his legs stretched out in front of him, sat back on the sofa and looked at Garth before taking a sip of his own drink. "Don't you?"

"Yes, and I'm going to hire a private detective. I don't want Hugh involved. He and Dad go way back, and there might be some loyalty there that I don't want to deal with."

"I agree. What about Regan? Isn't some member of her family a PI?"

Garth nodded, studying the drink in his glass. "Yes, her sister's husband. I met him once. He's an okay guy.

I understand he's good at what he does. I might call him tomorrow."

"I think that's a good idea."

They were silent for a spell and then Garth asked, "So what's going on with you and Bailey?"

Walker took another sip of his drink. "What makes you think something is going on?"

Garth rolled his eyes. "I can see, Walker."

Walker met his best friend's stare. "All you see is me interested in a woman who's hot. That's nice to have on those cold nights, especially for a man who's been without a female in his bed for a while. You heard her. She's leaving on Monday. Good riddance."

Bailey paused outside the closed door, not wanting to believe what Walker had just said. She'd been making her way back downstairs when she'd heard voices from one of the rooms. The voices belonged to Garth and Walker and when she'd heard her name she'd stopped.

Backing away from the door now, tears filled her eyes. She quickly turned and bumped right into Charm.

"Bailey, I was downstairs wondering if you'd gotten lost or something and—"

Charm stopped talking when she saw the tears in Bailey's eyes. "Bailey? What's wrong? Are you all right?"

Bailey swiped at her tears. "Yes, I'm fine."

Charm frowned. "No, you're not." She then glanced beyond Bailey to the closed door and the voices she heard. "What's going on? What did you hear? Did someone say something to upset you? Is Dad in that room with Garth and Walker? Did you overhear something Dad said?"

When Bailey didn't say anything, an angry Charm moved past her toward the door, ready to confront whoever was in the room about upsetting Bailey.

Bailey grabbed her hand. "No, please. Don't. It's okay."

She swiped again at her eyes. "Thanks for your family's hospitality, Charm, but I need to leave." Bailey wanted to put as much distance between her and Walker as she could. "Will you call me a cab? I need a ride to the airport."

Charm frowned. "The airport? What about Walker? What am I supposed to tell him?"

To go to hell, Bailey thought. But instead she said, "You can tell him I got a call…from a family member…and I need to get back to Denver immediately."

Charm's frown deepened. "Do you really want me to tell him that?"

"Yes."

Charm didn't say anything for a minute, then nodded. "Okay, but I won't call you a cab. I'll take you to the airport myself."

Garth stared hard at Walker. "What you just said is nothing more than bull and you know it."

Walker took another sip of his drink before quirking a brow. "Is it?"

"Yes. You've fallen in love with Bailey, Walker. Admit it."

Walker didn't say anything for a long minute. Garth knew him well. "Doesn't matter if you think it's bull or not."

"It does matter. When are you going to let go of the past, Walker? When are you going to consider that perhaps Bailey is your future?"

Walker shook his head. "No, she's not my future. She has these rules, you see. And one of them is that she will never leave Westmoreland Country. And I, on the other hand, made a deathbed promise to my father never to leave Hemlock Row again."

"But you will admit that you love her?" Garth asked.

Walker closed his eyes as if in pain. "Yes, I love her.

I love her so damn much. God knows I tried to fight it, but I couldn't. These past three weeks have been the best I've ever had. I thought I could live my life as a bitter and lonely man, but she's made me want more, Garth. She's made my house a real home. And she likes Hemlock Row."

"Then, what's the problem?"

He met Garth's inquisitive stare. "The problem is that I can't compete with her family. She needs them more than she could ever need me."

"Are you sure of that?"

"Yes. She's been homesick. I honestly didn't expect her to stay in Alaska this long. Already she's broken one of her rules."

"Maybe she had a reason to do so, Walker. Maybe you're that reason."

"I doubt it."

Garth was about to say something else when there was a knock on the door. "Come in."

Sloan entered. "Charm just left with Bailey."

Walker raised a brow. "Left? Where did they go? Don't tell me Charm talked Bailey into hitting some shopping mall tonight."

Sloan shook his head. "No. It seems Bailey got a call from some family member and had to leave. I don't know all the details but Charm is taking her to the airport. Bailey is booking a flight back to Denver. Tonight."

Sixteen

"Ma'am, please buckle your seat belt. The plane will be taking off in a minute."

Bailey nodded and did what the flight attendant instructed. She'd arrived at the Fairbanks airport with no luggage, just the clothes on her back. Charm had promised to go to the hotel and pack up her things and ship them to her. She would do the same for the clothes Bailey had left behind at Hemlock Row.

Luckily Bailey could change her ticket for a fee. And she didn't care that she had two connecting flights before she reached Denver, one in Seattle and the other in Salt Lake City. All she cared about was that in twelve hours she would be back in Westmoreland Country. She hadn't even called her family to let them know her change in plans. She would get a rental car at the airport and go straight to Gemma's house. She needed to be alone for a while before dealing with her family and their questions.

She drew in a deep breath, not wanting to think about

Walker. But all she could remember were the words he'd told Garth. So he would be glad when she was gone, would he? Well, he was getting his wish. She had been a fool to think he was worthy of her love. All he'd thought was that she was a hot body to sleep with.

But then, hadn't he told her up front all he wanted from her was a meaningless affair? Well, tonight he'd proved that what they'd shared had been as meaningless as it could get. Knowing it would take at least two hours before the plane landed in Seattle, she closed her eyes to soothe her tattered mind. At that moment she hoped she never saw Walker again.

"Damn her," Walker growled, taking his clothes out of the drawers and slinging them into the luggage that was opened on his bed. He intended to fly back to Kodiak Island tonight. There was no need to hang around. Bailey was why he'd left Hemlock Row to come here in the first place. And then what did she do? She hauled ass the first time she got a call from home.

However, now he knew that even that was a lie. Thinking she'd had a real family emergency, he'd placed a call to Dillon, who didn't know what he was talking about. As far as Dillon knew, nobody had called Bailey.

So now, on top of everything else, she had lied to him. She couldn't wait until Monday to leave? She had to leave tonight? Hell, she hadn't even taken the time to pack her clothes. What the hell was he supposed to do with them?

But what hurt more than anything was that she hadn't even had the decency to tell him goodbye. He felt like throwing something. Why did falling in love always end in heartache for him?

He continued to throw everything in his luggage when he heard a knock on the door. He hoped it wasn't Garth, trying to talk him out of leaving. There was no way he could stay. He wanted to go home to Hemlock Row, where loneliness was expected. Where he could drown his sorrows in a good stiff drink.

When the knocking continued, he moved to the door and snatched it open. Both Garth and Charm stood there. "I'm leaving tonight, Garth, and there's nothing you can say to stop me."

Garth and Charm walked past him to enter the hotel room. "I agree you should leave tonight, but not for Hemlock Row."

Walker looked at Garth. What he'd said didn't make any sense. "Then, where the hell am I supposed to go?"

"To head off Bailey. Stop her from making it to Denver."

That statement came from Charm. He glared at her. "And why on earth would I do that?"

Charm placed her hand on her hip and glared back at him. "Because you and Garth are the reason she left. I don't know what the two of you said about her while huddled in that room together tonight, but whatever you said, she overheard it and it had her in tears. I thought Dad was in there with you and figured he'd said something rude and gave him hell about it. But he said what Bailey overheard must have been a conversation between the two of you," she said, shifting her furious gaze between him and Garth.

Walker frowned. "For your information, I didn't say a damn thing that would have…"

He stopped speaking, swallowed hard and then glanced over at Garth. "Surely you don't think she heard—"

"All that crap you said?" Garth interrupted to ask, shaking his head. "I hope not. But what if she did?"

Walker rubbed a hand down his face. *Yes, what if she did?* "Damn it, I didn't mean it. In fact, later on in the conversation I admitted to falling in love with her."

"You love her?" Charm asked, smiling.

"Yes."

"Well, I doubt she heard that part. In fact, I'm one hundred percent certain she didn't. She was crying as if her heart was broken."

Walker checked his watch. "I've got to go after her."

"Yes, you do," Garth agreed. He then looked at Charm. "Do you have her flight information? I'm sure she has a connecting flight somewhere."

"She has two," Charm answered. "The first is in Seattle and then another in Salt Lake City."

Garth checked his watch. "I'll contact Regan and have her get the jet ready. If we act fast, you can get to Seattle the same time Bailey does. Maybe a few minutes before. And in case you've forgotten, Ollie is director of Seattle's Transportation Security Administration. Knowing the top dog of the TSA might prove to be helpful."

Walker nodded. He, Garth and Oliver Linton had served in the marines together and the three had remained good friends. "You're right." Walker was already moving, grabbing his coat and hat. Like Bailey, he was about to fly with just the clothes on his back.

Bailey took a sip of her coffee. She hated layovers, especially lengthy ones. She had another hour before she could board her connecting flight to Salt Lake City. And then she would have to wait two more hours before finally boarding the plane that would take her home to Denver.

Home.

Why didn't she have that excited flutter in her stomach that she usually had whenever she went on a trip and was on her way back to Denver? Why did she feel only hurt and pain? "That's easy enough to answer," she muttered to herself. "The man you love doesn't love you back. Get over it."

She drew in a deep breath, wondering if she ever would get over it. If it had been Monday and she'd been leaving because her time in Kodiak was over, it probably would have been different. But hearing the words Walker had spoken to Garth had cut deep. Not just into her heart but also into her soul. Evidently, her time at Hemlock Row had meant more to her than it had to him. All she'd been to him was a piece of ass during the cold nights. He'd practically said as much to Garth.

After finishing off her coffee, she tightened her coat around herself. For some reason she was still feeling the harsh Alaskan temperatures. She hated admitting it, but she missed Hemlock Row already, although she refused to miss Walker. She wished she could think of his ranch without thinking of him. She would miss Willie, Marcus and the guys, as well as Ms. Albright. She would miss standing at Walker's bedroom window every morning to stare out at Shelikof Strait. And she would definitely miss cooking in his kitchen. When she finally got around to designing her own home on Bailey's Bay, she might steal a few of his kitchen ideas. It would serve him right if she did.

"Excuse me, miss."

She glanced up into the face of an older gentleman wearing a TSA uniform. "Yes?"

"Are you Bailey Westmoreland?"

"Yes, I'm Bailey Westmoreland." She hoped nothing was wrong with her connecting flight. She didn't want the man to tell her it was canceled or delayed. She was ready to put as much distance between herself and Alaska as she could.

He nodded. "Ms. Westmoreland, could you please come with me?"

She stood. "Yes, but why? Is something wrong? What's going on?" She didn't have any luggage so there was no way they could have found anything in it. And her ticket was legit. She had made the proper changes in Fairbanks. As far as she was concerned she was all set.

"I'm unable to answer that. I was advised by my director to bring you to his office."

"Your director?" She swallowed. This sounded serious. She hoped she and some terrorist didn't have the same name or something. *Oh, crap.* "Look, sir," she said, following the man. "There must be some mistake."

She was about to say she'd never had done a bad thing in her life and then snapped her mouth shut. What about all those horrific things she, Bane and the twins had done while growing up? But that had been years ago. The sheriff of Denver, who was a good friend of Dillon's, had assured him that since the four of them had been juveniles their records would be wiped clean, as long as they didn't get into any trouble as adults. She couldn't speak for the twins, and Lord knew she couldn't vouch for Bane, but she could certainly speak for herself.

So she did. "Like I said, there must be a mistake. I am a law-abiding citizen. I work for a well-known magazine. I do own a gun. Several. But I don't have any of them with me."

The man stopped walking and looked over at her with a keen eye. She swallowed, wishing she hadn't said that. "I hunt," she quickly added, not wanting him to get the wrong idea. "I have all the proper permits and licenses."

He merely nodded. He then opened a door. "You can wait in here. It won't be long."

She frowned, about to tell him she didn't want to wait in there, that she was an American with rights. But she was too tired to argue. Too hurt and broken. She would wait for the director and see why she was being detained. If she needed an attorney there were a number of them in the Westmoreland family.

"Fine. I'll wait," she said, entering the room and glancing around. It was definitely warmer in here than it had been at the terminal gate. It was obvious this was some kind of meeting room, she thought, shrugging out of her coat and tossing it across the back of a chair. There were no windows, just a desk, several chairs and a garbage can. A map of Washington State was on one wall and a map of the United States on the other. There was a coffeepot on the table in the corner, and although she'd had enough coffee tonight to last her a lifetime, she crossed to the pot, hoping it was fresh.

That was when she heard the door behind her open. Good, the director had arrived and they could get down to business. The last thing she needed was to miss her connecting flight. She turned to ask the man or woman why she was here and her mouth dropped open.

The man who walked into the room was not the TSA director. It was the last person she figured she would see tonight or ever again.

"Walker!"

Seventeen

Walker entered the room and closed the door behind him. And then he locked it. Across the room stood the woman he loved more than life itself. She'd overheard things straight from his lips that had all been lies, and now he had to convince her he hadn't meant any of what he'd said.

"Hello, Bailey."

She backed up, shock written all over her face. "Walker, what are you doing here? How did you get here? *Why* are you here?"

He shoved his hands into his pockets. He heard the anger in her voice. He also heard the hurt and regretted more than ever what he'd said. "I thought we had a conversation once about you asking a lot of questions. But since I owe you answers to each and every one of them, here goes. I came here to talk to you. I got here with Garth's company jet. And I'm here because I owe you an apology."

She stiffened her spine. "You should not have bothered.

I don't think there's anything you can do or say to make me accept your apology."

He recalled when he'd said something similar to her the day she'd shown up at Hemlock Row. "But I did bother, because I know you heard what I said to Garth."

She crossed her arms over her chest. "Yes, I heard you. Pretty loud and clear. And I understood just what I was to you while I was at Hemlock Row and how you couldn't wait for me to leave."

"I didn't mean what I said."

"Sure you did. If nothing else, I've discovered you're a man who says exactly what he means."

He leaned against the wall, tilted his hat back and inhaled deeply, wishing her scent didn't get to him. And he wished she didn't look so desirable. She was still wearing the outfit she'd worn at the Outlaws'—black slacks and a bronze-colored pullover knit sweater with matching jewelry. She looked good then and she looked good now, four hours and over two thousand miles later.

But he liked Bailey best when she wasn't wearing anything at all. When she lay in his bed naked, with her breasts full and perky, the nipples wet from his tongue, and her feminine mound, hot, moist and ready for—

He sucked in a sharp breath and abruptly put an end to those thoughts. "Can we sit and talk?"

She frowned. "I honestly don't want to hear anything you have to say."

"Please. Both times when you apologized to me, I accepted your apologies."

"Good for you, but I have no intention of accepting yours."

She was being difficult, he knew that. He also knew there was only one way to handle Bailey. And that was by not letting her think she had the upper hand. "We are going to talk whether you want to listen to what I say or not. I locked that door," he said, removing his hat to place on a rack and then crossing the room to sit in one of the chairs. "And I don't intend for it to be opened until I say so. I forgot to mention that the director of the TSA here is an old marine friend of mine."

She glared at him. "You can't hold me here like some kind of hostage. I will sue you both."

"Go ahead and do that, if you desire. In the meantime you and I are staying in here until you agree to listen to what I have to say."

"I won't listen."

"I have the time to wait for you to change your mind," he said, leaning back in the chair so the front legs lifted off the floor. He closed his eyes. He heard her cross the room to the door and try it. It was locked. He didn't reopen his eyes when he heard her banging on it, nor when he heard her kick it a few times.

He knew the exact moment when a frustrated and angry Bailey crossed the room to stand in front of him. "Wake up, you bastard. Wake up and let me out of here."

He ignored her, but it wasn't easy. Especially when she began using profanity the likes of which he'd never heard before. He'd heard from one of her cousins that she used to curse like a sailor—worse than a sailor—as a teen, and Walker had even heard her utter a few choice words that day in his bedroom when he'd pissed her off. But now, to-night, she was definitely on a roll.

He would let her have her say—no matter how vulgar it was—and then he would have his. He would tell her ev-erything. Including the fact that he loved her. He didn't ex-pect her to love him back. It was too late for that, although he doubted it would have happened anyway. Bailey loved Westmoreland Country. She was married to it.

It seemed her filthy mouth wouldn't run out of steam anytime soon, so he decided to put an end to it. He'd gotten the picture, heard loud and clear what she thought of him. He slowly opened his eyes and stared at her. "If you recall, Bailey, I once told you that you had too delicious a mouth to fill it with nasty words. Do I need to test it to make sure it's still as delicious as the last time I tasted it?"

She threw her hair over her shoulder, fiery mad. "I'd like to see you try."

"Okay." He grabbed her around the waist and tumbled her into his lap. And then he kissed her.

She tried pushing him away, but just for a minute. Then, as if she had no control of her own tongue, it began tangling with his, sucking as hard as he was. And then suddenly, as if she realized what she was doing, she snatched her mouth away, but she didn't try getting off his lap.

"I hate you, Walker."

He nodded. "And I love you, Bailey."

She'd opened her mouth, probably to spew more filthy words, but what he'd said had her mouth snapping closed. She stared at him, not saying anything, and then she frowned. "I heard what you told Garth."

"Yes, but if you had hung around, you would have heard him say that I was talking bull because he knew how I felt about you. He's been my friend long enough to know. And then I admitted to having fallen in love with you."

She stared at him, studying his face. How long would it be before she said something? Finally she did. "You can't love me."

He shifted her in his lap, both to keep her there but also to bring some relief to the erection pressing painfully against his zipper. "And why can't I love you?"

"Because you're still in love with your wife. You've been grieving for her for ten years and you want me to believe I came along and changed that in less than a month?"

He knew he had to tell her the truth. All of it. He had to tell her what only he and Garth knew. Doing so would bring back memories. Painful memories. But he loved her. And he owed her the truth.

"Yes, I guess that would be hard to believe if I had been grieving for Kalyn for ten years. But I stopped loving my wife months before she died. I stopped loving her when I found out she was having an affair with another man."

Bailey swallowed. Of all the things she'd expected him to say, that wasn't it. "Your wife was unfaithful?" she asked, making sure she'd heard him correctly.

"Yes, among a number of other things."

She lifted a brow. "What other things?"

Walker drew in a deep breath before lifting her from his lap to place her in the chair beside him. He paced the room a few times before finally leaning against the wall.

"I need to start at the beginning," he said in a low, husky tone. But she'd been around Walker enough to detect the deep pain in his voice. "I was in the marines, stationed at Camp Pendleton. A few of the guys and I took a holiday to LA, preferring to tour the countryside. We came across a film crew making a movie. Intrigued, we stopped and, believe it or not, they asked us to be extras."

He paused before continuing, "One of the women who had a small role caught my eye and I caught hers."

"Kalyn?"

He looked over at Bailey. "Yes. That night she and I met at a restaurant and she told me her dream was to become an actress, that she was born in Los Angeles and loved the area. We slept together that night and a few times after that. I was smitten, but I thought that would be the end of it. It was only a few months before my time in the marines ended and I was looking forward to heading home. Both Garth and I were."

He paused. "Dad had written and I knew the ranch was

becoming a handful. He couldn't wait for me to come home to help. I told him I would. Practically promised."

He moved away from the wall to sit in the chair beside her. "I basically broke that promise. A few days before I was supposed to leave I got a call. Someone had viewed a clip of me as an extra and liked what they saw. They didn't know whether I could act or not but thought I had what they termed 'Hollywood looks.' They called me to try out for a part in some movie. I didn't get the part but they asked me to hang around for a week or two, certain they could find me work."

He leaned back in the chair as he continued. "Kalyn said she was happy for me. She also told me she thought she was pregnant. I never questioned her about it, although Garth suggested I should. I didn't listen to him. Nor did I listen when he tried to get me to leave California and return home, reminding me that my dad needed me. All I could think about was that Kalyn might be pregnant and I should do the honorable thing and marry her. So I did."

"Was she pregnant?" Bailey asked curiously.

"No. She said it was a false alarm, but I was determined to make my marriage work regardless. I loved her. I suggested we leave LA and move to Kodiak Island, but she wouldn't hear of it. She would cry every time I brought up the subject. She told me she hated a place she'd never seen and she never wanted to go there."

Bailey couldn't imagine anyone not liking Hemlock Row, especially before they'd seen it.

"I talked to my dad and he told me to stay with my wife and make my marriage work and that he would hire a couple more men to help out around the ranch," Walker continued. "Although he didn't say it, I knew he was disappointed that I wasn't coming home with my wife.

"A few months later I got the chance at a big role and my career took off from there. Kalyn was happy. She loved being in the spotlight as my wife. But I missed home and when I told her I'd made up my mind to leave and return to Alaska, she told me she was pregnant."

Bailey lifted a brow. "Was she really pregnant this time?" she asked in a skeptical voice. It sounded to her as though Kalyn's claim that first time had been a trick just to get Walker to marry her.

"Yes, she was this time. I went with her to the doctor to confirm it. Things got better between us. I fell in love with Connor the moment I heard his heartbeat. And months later, when I felt him move in Kalyn's stomach, I think my son and I connected in an unbreakable bond. I couldn't wait for him to be born. When he finally arrived I thought he was perfect. I couldn't wait to take him home for my parents to meet their grandson."

"You took him home to Hemlock Row?"

"Yes, but not until he was almost a year old. Kalyn refused to let me take him any sooner than that. Connor loved it there with his grandparents. I took him everywhere and showed him everything. Kalyn didn't go with us and told me I could only be gone with Connor for a week. I was upset about it but was grateful that my parents got to meet Connor and he got to meet them. A few months after I returned to LA I learned my mom was sick and the doctors couldn't figure out why. I went home a few times and each time I did, Kalyn gave me hell."

Bailey frowned. "She didn't want you to go home to check on your sick mother?" she asked, appalled.

"No, she didn't. Things got pretty bad between us, although we worked hard to pretend otherwise. In public we were the perfect, happily married Hollywood couple, but behind closed doors it was a different story."

He stood again to pace and when he came to a stop in front of where she sat, her heart almost stopped. The look on his face was full of hurt and anguish. "Then one day

I came home and she dropped a bombshell. She told me that for the past year and a half she'd been having an affair with a married man and he'd finally decided to leave his wife for her."

He drew in a deep breath and closed his eyes. When he reopened them, he said, "And she also wanted me to know that Connor was not my son."

"No!"

The pain of his words hit Bailey like a ton of bricks, so she could imagine how Kalyn's words must have hit him. The son he'd fallen in love with was not his biological son. She couldn't imagine the pain that must have caused him.

"I told her I didn't care if Connor was my biological son or not. He was the son of my heart and that's all that mattered. I loved him. She only laughed and called me a fool for loving a child that wasn't mine."

There were a lot of words Bailey could think of to describe Walker's deceased wife, and none of them were nice. "What happened after that? Did she move out?"

"No. Her lover must have changed his mind about leaving his wife. When I came home one evening after picking up Connor from day care, she ignored both of us and stayed in her room. I knew something was wrong, I just didn't know what.

"A few days later, on the set, I got a call letting me know there'd been an accident. It seemed Kalyn lost control of the car in the rain. She was killed immediately but Connor fought for his life. I rushed to the hospital in time to give my son blood. He'd lost a lot of it."

"So he *was* your biological son!"

"Yes, Connor was my biological son. She had intentionally lied to me, or she might have been sleeping with both me and her lover and honestly didn't know which one of us was Connor's father. Connor lasted another day and then I lost him. I lost my son."

A tear slipped from Bailey's eye, and when more tears began to fall, she swiped at them. He hadn't deserved what his wife put him through. No man would have deserved that.

"But that wasn't the worst of it," she heard him say as she continued swiping at her tears.

"It wasn't?" She couldn't imagine anything worse than that.

"No. After the funeral, I came home and found a letter Kalyn had written to me. She left it in a place where she figured I would find it."

Bailey's brows bunched. "A letter."

He nodded. "Yes. She wanted me to know the car wreck wasn't an accident. It was intentional."

Bailey's heart stopped. "Are you saying that…" She couldn't finish the question.

"Yes," he said softly with even deeper pain in his voice. "Kalyn committed suicide. Being rejected by her lover was too much for her and she couldn't live another day. She wanted to take her lover's son with her."

She saw the tears misting his eyes. No wonder his son was buried in his family's cemetery but his son's mother was not. The awful things she'd done, and the fact that she'd hated Hemlock Row sight unseen.

"Nobody knows about that letter but Garth. He was with me when I found it. We decided turning it over to the authorities would serve no purpose. It would be better to let everyone continue to believe what happened had been an accident."

Bailey nodded. "Did you ever find out the identity of Kalyn's lover?"

"No, although I had my suspicions. I never knew for certain." He paused. "I told myself that I would never love or trust another woman. And I hadn't. Until you. I didn't want to fall in love with you, Bailey. God knows I fought it tooth and nail. But I couldn't stop what was meant to be. Yes, I said what I said to Garth, but I was in denial, refusing to accept what I knew in my heart was true. I'm sorry for the words I said. But the truth is that I do love you. I love you more than I've ever loved any other woman."

She eased out of the chair and went to him, pulled him to her and held him. He had been through so much. He had lost so much. He had experienced the worst betrayal a man could suffer. Not only had Kalyn intentionally taken her life, she had taken the life of an innocent child.

Walker pulled back and looked at her. "I know there can never be anything between us. You don't love me and I understand that. You're in love with your land, and I accept that, too, because I'm in love with mine. I made Dad another promise, this one I intend to keep. I'll never leave Hemlock Row again."

She stared deep into the dark eyes that had always mesmerized her. "You just said you loved me, yet you're willing to let me go back to Westmoreland Country?"

"Yes, because that's your real love. I know your rules, Bailey."

A smile touched her lips. "And I'm breaking the one I thought I would never break."

He looked at her questionably. "What are you saying?"

She wrapped her arms around his neck. "I'm saying that I love you, too. I realized I loved you weeks ago. I think that's why I came to Kodiak to personally apologize. I missed you, although I would never have admitted that to myself or to you. I do love you, Walker, and more than anything I want to make a home with you at Hemlock Row."

"B-but what about Westmoreland Country?"

She chuckled. "I love my home, but Gemma and Megan were right. Home is where the heart is, and my heart is with you."

He studied her features intently. "Are you sure?"

She chuckled again. "I am positive. I'm officially breaking Bailey's Rules."

And then she slanted her mouth over his, knowing their
lives together were just beginning.

A few days later, Walker eased out of the bed. Bailey
grabbed his thigh. "And where do you think you're going?"

He smiled. "To stoke the fire. I'll be back."

"Holding you to it, Alaskan."

Walker chuckled. He couldn't believe how great his life
was going. Everyone was happy that he'd gotten everything
straightened out with Bailey and she had decided to stay.
Next week was Thanksgiving and they would leave Kodiak Island to spend the holiday with her family in Westmoreland Country.

After stoking the fire and before he returned to bed, he
went to the drawer and retrieved the package he'd put there
earlier that day. Grabbing the box, he went back to the bed.

"Bailey?" She opened her eyes to look at him. "Yes?"

"Will you marry me?"

When she saw the box he held she almost knocked him
over struggling to sit up. "You're proposing to me?"

He smiled. "Yes."

"B-but I'm in bed, naked and—"

"Just made love to me. I can't think of any other way to
complete things. I want you to know it's never been just
sex with us…although I think the sex is off the charts."

She grinned. "So do I."

He opened the box and she gasped at the ring shining
back at her in the firelight. "It's beautiful, Walker."

"As beautiful as my future wife," he said, sliding the
ring on her finger. Halfway there, he stopped and eyed her
expectantly. "You didn't say yes."

"Yes!"

He slid the ring the rest of the way and then pulled her

into his arms. "My parents would have loved you," he whispered against her ear.

"And I would have loved them, too. And I would have loved Connor."

He pulled back. "He would have loved you." Walker held her hand up and looked at it. "I thought the timing was right since I'll be taking you home next week. I don't want your family to think I'm taking advantage of you. When they see that ring they will know. I love you and intend to make you my wife. Just set the date. But don't make me wait too long."

"I won't."

He brushed his thumb across her cheek. "Thanks for believing I was worthy of breaking your rules, Bailey."

"And thanks for believing I am worthy of your love and trust, Walker."

Their mouths touched, and she knew tonight was the beginning of how things would be for the rest of their lives.

Epilogue

Thanksgiving Day

Bailey looked around the huge table. This was the first time that every one of her brothers, sisters and cousins— the Denver Westmorelands—had managed to come home for Thanksgiving. Even Bane was here. The family had definitely multiplied with the addition of wives, husbands and children. She and Walker would tie the knot here in Westmoreland Country on Valentine's Day.

Everyone was glad to see Bane. It had been years since he'd been home for Thanksgiving. In fact, they hadn't seen him since that time he'd shown up unannounced at Blue Ridge Land Management, surprising Stern and Adrian.

Bailey wondered if she was the only one who noticed he seemed pensive and preoccupied. And not for the first time she wondered if something had happened on his last covert operation that he wasn't sharing with them.

"You okay, baby?" Walker leaned over to ask her.

She smiled at him. "Yes, I'm fine. You love me and I love you, so I couldn't be better."

The announcement that she was marrying and leaving Westmoreland Country had everyone shocked. But all they had to do was look at her and Walker to see how happy they were together.

Thanks to Lucia and Chloe, Bailey would still work for *Simply Irresistible*, working remotely from Kodiak Island. She'd been doing it for a while now and so far things were working out fine.

The Outlaws, all six of them, had come to visit, and just like Bailey had known, everyone had gotten along beautifully. They were invited to the Denver Westmorelands' annual foundation banquet and said they would return in December to attend. That way they would get to meet their Westmoreland cousins from Atlanta, Montana, North Carolina and Texas. Word was that Bart still hadn't come around. According to Walker, Garth intended to find out why his father was being so difficult.

Since Gemma, Callum and their kids were in town, Bailey and Walker were staying at the bed-and-breakfast inn Jason's wife, Bella, owned. It was perfect, and she and Walker had the entire place to themselves.

Bailey figured she would eventually get around to building her own place so she and Walker could have somewhere private whenever they came to visit, but she wasn't in any hurry.

After clinking on his glass to get everyone's attention, Dillon stood. "It's been years since we've had everyone together on Thanksgiving, and I'm thankful that this year Gemma and Bane were able to come home to join us. And I'm grateful for all the additions to our family, especially one in particular," he said, looking over at Walker and smiling.

"I think Mom, Dad, Uncle Thomas and Aunt Susan

would be proud of what we've become and that we're still a family."

Bailey wiped a tear from her eye. Yes, they were still a family and always would be. She reached under the table for Walker's hand. She had everything she could possibly want and more.

"You wanted to see me, Dil?" Bane asked, walking into Dillon's home office. Out the window was a beautiful view of Gemma Lake.

Dillon glanced up as his brother entered. Bane appeared taller, looked harder, more mature than he'd seemed the last time he'd been home. "Yes, come on in, Bane."

Dinner had ended a few hours ago and after a game of snow volleyball the ladies had gathered in the sitting room to watch a holiday movie with the kids, and the men had gathered upstairs for a card game. "I want to know how you're doing," Dillon said, studying his baby brother.

"Fine, although my last assignment took a toll on me. I lost a good friend."

Dillon shook his head sadly. "I'm sorry to hear that."

"Me, too. Laramie Tucker was a good guy. The best. We went through the academy together."

Dillon knew not to ask what happened. Bane had explained a while back that all his assignments were confidential. "Is that why you're taking a military leave?"

Bane eased down in the chair across from Dillon's desk. "No. It's time I find Crystal. If nothing else, Tuck's death taught me how fragile life is. You can be here today and gone tomorrow."

Dillon came around and sat on the edge of his desk to face his brother. "Not sure if you knew it, but Carl Newsome passed away a few years ago."

Bane shook his head. "No, I didn't know."

"So you haven't seen Crystal since the Newsomes sent her away?"

"No. You were right. I didn't have anything to offer her at the time. I was a hothead and Trouble was my middle name. She deserved better, and I was willing to make something of myself to give her better."

Dillon nodded. "It's been years, Bane. The last time I talked to Emily Newsome was when I heard Carl had died. I called to offer my condolences. I asked about Crystal and Emily said Crystal was doing fine. She was working on her master's degree at Harvard with plans to get a doctorate."

Bane didn't say anything as he listened to what Dillon was saying. "That doesn't surprise me. Crystal was always smart in school."

Dillon stared at his brother, wondering how Bane had figured that out when most of the time he and Crystal were playing hooky. "I don't want to upset you, Bane. But you don't know what Crystal's feelings are for you. The two of you were teens back then. First love doesn't always mean last love. Although you might still love her, for all you know, she might have moved on. Have you ever considered the possibility that she might be involved with someone else?"

Bane leaned back in his chair. "I don't believe that. Crystal and I had an understanding. We have an unbreakable bond."

"But that was years ago. You just said you haven't seen her since that day Carl sent her away. For all you know, she could be married by now."

Bane shook his head. "Crystal wouldn't marry anyone else."

Dillon lifted a brow. "And how can you be so sure of that?"

Bane held his brother's stare. "Because she's already married, Dil. Crystal is married to me, and I think it's time to go claim my wife."

* * * * *

LET'S TALK
Romance

For exclusive extracts, competitions
and special offers, find us online:

f facebook.com/millsandboon

⬛ @millsandboonuk

🐦 @millsandboon

Or get in touch on 0844 844 1351*

For all the latest titles coming soon, visit
millsandboon.co.uk/nextmonth